An End To Potential

Emily Swiers

First paperback edition January 2026

Book Cover design by Sukutangan
ISBN (paperback): 979-8-9896404-2-3
ISBN (ebook): 979-8-9896404-3-0

Chapter One

The interview was over the moment the conversation veered off to the left and past the guardrails and plunged to certain doom. It began innocuously, with questions related to the rumored project her film production company was tackling and the undercurrent of backlash for speaking with the now-canceled actor.

Kana was short in her response. "Why would I care about rumors? I know the truth." She wanted to be immune to rumors, repeatedly telling herself that men twice her age were foraging through the cities, sniffing for a crumb of gossip to sell and exploit to the highest buyer, and wasting her mental energy on them was beneath her. And while rumors were cruel, they were necessary to fan the flames in a specific direction, drop tidbits here, a hint to a private follow-up rendezvous there, but sometimes the change of wind sent the licking flames into her face.

In the privacy of the dressing room, with Kana's reflection the only witness to her reddened face and neck, her nails sliced into the palms of her hands as the interviewer's follow-up question repeated in her mind.

"Your mother has developed a world-changing drug, and

normally, a militaristically purposed drug isn't in the spotlight—people care more about the newest weight loss pill. What is it like to be the daughter of Josephine Ambrose?"

Wasn't that strange, the power in a name? Even before Kana was born, she was associated with Josephine Ambrose: Josephine's daughter, Josephine's protégé, Josephine's heir. The titles stitched patterns through her skin like needlework, over her bones and blood, over her mind and heart that made her different from Josephine, but the world only saw those etchings across her flesh. Josephine's history was hers, and some days she lay under the crushing weight; on the good days, she shouldered it, and the compression of her lungs lessened enough that she could breathe.

Today, despite the failed interview fiasco, she was in decent spirits. It had been nearly three years since the last attack. Kana wiggled out of the long skirt and kicked the fabric to the side. The artificially chilled air pumped through the ducts above, sending a cold front against her flesh. With her nomadic lifestyle, hopping from five-star hotels around the world, to sailing on yachts, she was easing into a seemingly normal life.

Her phone vibrated on the glass coffee table where she had left the annoying device. An image of a cartoon chipmunk flashed on the screen. Her shoulders lowered from her ears. A well-timed distraction was just what she needed.

"You only call for two reasons," she answered as she snatched her bra hanging on the bare clothing rack. "Whatever the tabloid said isn't true. And there's no way I'm returning to Oshiya."

Bexley laughed. The sound was a cooling balm, easing the heat accumulating in Kana's chest. There was a rustling noise of fabric moving. It had to be close to three in the morning. Bexley usually rose with the sun; if she was still awake, something must have kept her up. "There was a rather amusing picture of you and Davenport's uncle."

Kana's reflection mirrored her snide smile. Without a doubt, there was a rather comical picture of her exiting through the not-so-secret side door from the earlier week's soiree. The sniveling man, known for collecting the grime and gunk of people's lives like a kitchen sponge, was captured stumbling down three steps, hands outstretched to grab onto Kana, as if she would break his fall.

"He's lucky I only threatened to expose his after-office activities. If your call isn't about the trashy articles, we can end this now." There was no way Kana was returning to Oshiya.

An exaggerated sigh emanated from the phone. Kana expected hot air to blow out from her screen. "What did she bribe you with?" She didn't try to hide the venom at the thought of Josephine. Bexley and Josephine rarely interacted, but after the pink lemonade fiasco, Kana's trust in Bexley grew a microfracture for the first time.

Kana leaned into her reflection, closing her left eye. The colors were altered, the blue and green logos across the makeup brands and the brush handles were a muted teal. The candy apple red liner sliced over her black lashes. As she reopened her eye, the colors returned. A parting gift from an unfortunate incident, when she lost the ability to see blue and yellow in her left eye.

"It's not her," Bexley said. Kana could picture Bexley's small head shaking. "*Igotapostcard.*" Bexley's voice slurred the sentence into one long word.

Kana stopped mid-stroke, the severe red line cutting half of her right eyelid. "Not possible."

Bexley didn't respond, but her breathing pattern hitched, and a shaky swallow spoke volumes.

"Bexley, it's not possible. I killed him," Kana said in a flat line tone. She opened her right eye; both eyes were slashed red. Her cheekbones had become more prominent as she shed her baby fat, but her face had remained unchanged since she was thirteen. From the edge of her upper lip, curving to her left ear, should be a deep and ugly scar. A second line of puckered scar tissue should be along her neck. If the blade had dug a millimeter deeper, it would have nicked her carotid, but it didn't, and no one would be the wiser. Her skin was unblemished. The scarred flesh was lasered away with the best treatment technology offered.

When she was still a young teen, she despised Josephine for removing the scars and scrubbing away the evidence she wanted to show the world. A reminder: *look at me; I survived*. Kana knew it was for selfish reasons; having a mutilated daughter in the limelight wasn't the Ambrose image. But, even worse, she knew Josephine had made the right call. Kana would have loathed herself even more, fixating on the mountainous stitched skin every time she saw herself in the mirror or on a magazine cover.

The tip of her tongue ran across the fleshy inside of her cheek stroking the raised scar, the only physical mark left on her body from the attack. "Whoever sent the postcard wanted to scare you. I'll have Oliver look into it."

"Kana," Bexley whispered her name. The breathy tone sent Kana a decade into the past. Kana gripped the edge of the vanity, her knuckles bulging through the thin skin. "This isn't just about me. You need to be safe."

"Don't worry about me. It's nothing but a hysterical true crime lover who knows the anniversary date and thought it would be a funny joke. Leave Oliver with the postcard, close your eyes, and pick someplace to visit for a week, a month, whatever you need, book a flight and hotel, and send me the bill." She hung up. The phone clattered with a heavy thunk on the thick glass. Her head of black hair hung like a final curtain call between her tight shoulders.

He was dead. They were all dead.

She inhaled deeply and thrust her head back in the air to finish painting her face. The urge to visit a beach was strong. Crete was beautiful at this time, or Aruba. She sent a text.

As she zipped up her boots, the air felt damp, as if she passed under a mist machine.

With a fluid sweep of her hand, her hair moved over her

shoulder just in time to catch the far-left wall crunching as if it were made from paper, the paint cracking in long wrinkles until a polished capped-toe Oxford emerged.

"Go to Bexley," Kana said as Oliver's body stepped out of the ripped portal of space and into the dressing room. He looked immaculate, but she noted that his typical three-piece suit was missing. He'd opted for a brushed cashmere sweater and single-pleated wool pants.

"A fan left a postcard," she continued as she smoothed the hem of the skirt, still in only her bra. Her sharp gaze met Oliver's in the full-length mirror. His hooded eyes didn't drift anywhere along her body, intent on her face in the reflection.

"Whoever sent the calling card has balls," she said as she tucked the silk blouse into her mini skirt. "And I'll be ready with a pair of garden shears." She smiled, the tips of her canines winking. Oliver didn't blink. As usual, his impassive expression remained, knowing she didn't back down from a promise.

"Tell the magazine I won't be returning," Kana said.

Oliver exhaled through his nose. "Kana." Her name was a huff of irritation.

"And that interviewer, she's done. Is it so difficult to stick to the questions at hand? No, it isn't."

"You are not having a temper tantrum and sacking everyone."

"No," Kana snapped, "only the woman who couldn't do her job."

Oliver's right index finger twitched at his side. She imagined he was stopping the urge to stroke his jaw in annoyance.

"I want a flight to Aruba." She moved on from the interviewer. Her fate was sealed.

Oliver's trimmed salt-and-pepper beard moved as he spoke. "A conference between Ambrose Inc. and Zion.K. is being held there."

Kana's lips puckered. She would steer clear of that situation. World War III might begin between those companies.

"Portugal."

"The VP is visiting the embassy this week," Oliver replied.

Kana skillfully buttoned the blouse, nude lips tight. "Australia."

"The chief of operations is the keynote speaker for the annual conference in Sydney. Research Team Beta is still sanctioned in Melbourne."

"Vietnam."

"Research Team 17 moved from Thailand to Vietnam. The politics are becoming too strained."

"What beach can I visit that isn't infested with some sort of Ambrose Inc. meeting, conference, kiss-assing countries' embassies or militaries?" Josephine's reach touched every corner of the world.

"Would a lake be sufficient?"

She turned around, the urge to cross her arms subdued with years of training. Instead, her chest puffed out as she pushed back her shoulders a centimeter.

"Find me a beach."

Oliver's indifferent eyes lowered as he pressed a hand to his heart with a slight bow. Josephine trained her dogs well. Oliver had been her glorified butler and nanny since she was three.

"I will send the itinerary details." He knew what she wanted —a place without company-affiliated personnel within a hundred kilometers. While Ambrose Inc. wiggled to nearly every continent, there were thousands of beaches, not even close to an impossible task.

If only all the world's men could be like Oliver. So dutiful. "Where have you been? It's New York in September, not cool enough for the turtleneck and wool slacks."

Oliver smiled the fake smile, a false placating gesture. "Offering my assistance in Europe."

"What was her recent order? Make sure you woo the president and allow the pharmaceutical law to pass into the EU?"

"Her last order was against the Title Sixteen law in Switzerland."

The heels of Kana's boots clicked as she approached the older man. He'd told her more than she expected. Northern Europe. This close, she could smell the hints of rich aftershave, but there was no other distinct scent to hint at his whereabouts. "All your focus is back to her. She must have you running her errands now I've escaped the nest." She mockingly patted his chest.

Oliver grabbed her hand and stepped back. Kana, just as fast, pushed back the sleeve of his sweater. Medical bandages were around his forearm, unable to fully conceal the veins lifted like tree roots against sidewalks. She'd often seen the tiny beech mushrooms, skinny stems, and bulbous tops curl out of his flesh as he practiced bloodletting.

The bandages lay flat against his skin; there was no evidence of fungi bent and curled up against the confines of his skin. He wasn't overusing his ability to make portals, so she supposed Josephine wasn't running him to the ground.

Oliver was a prime example of an A.E. Potentia success story. With a series of tests, he'd been identified as hosting the dormant parasite, an ideal candidate that hadn't gone through the Fever during puberty. And with a single dose of Dr. Ambrose's concoction, he went through a forced Fever and survived the grueling, life-threatening stage. Out from the flames of hell emerged a man with an inhuman ability to rip wormholes for transportation purposes. He was an exception, since A.E. Potentia was no longer sanctioned for anything other than military use. Countries couldn't have any old-Jane and old-Joe ripping portals, pushing things with their minds or passing through solid objects.

"Kana," Oliver warned. He rarely used such a cautionary tone to remind her of boundaries. Kana retreated to the chaise lounge, where her handbag was tossed.

"Do your job. I want to be on a plane before the end of the night," she said dismissively. The atmosphere altered, and a layer of thin fog tickled her flesh. Kana closed her eyes and inhaled. The coil of energy was simmering like the delicious burn of a strong whiskey. It had been too long since she absorbed a User's power. With the last specs of water gone, she knew Oliver had disappeared, returning to Europe or locating Bexley in California. He would carry out her orders. He always did.

Chapter Two

OLIVER PROMPTLY SENT the flight details. The bastard picked Washington State, a private beach home near the Long Beach Peninsula, probably one of the least exotic beaches. It was a slight to her for the sleeve incident. He could have at least picked Ireland if he wanted to leave her on a cold beach, but he was never spiteful to the point of dropping her off in Greenland.

She stretched out her legs in the first-class pod of the plane. The other passengers shuffled and the dragging of their carry-ons into the back of the plane was like rattling loose change. Oliver purposefully chose to not use a private jet either, making her take a commercial flight.

Her phone chimed. Speaking of the devil, Oliver sent a single message with an image attached; it was a simple, unassuming card from Italy with all the proper stamps. The postcard looked identical to the ones she and Bexley wrote during the brief summer, down to the ink smudge in the corner and the smear of words as Kana's left hand moved across the narrow space. The overly circular handwriting gave away the young age. It was a silly activity to send a postcard to a family member.

Normally, she had a firm grip on her memories, but the faded image of the centuries-old villa rooftops along the beautiful Amalfi coast coaxed her back to her thirteen-year-old body. She sat on a stone wall, warmed from the blazing summer sun, with more history than the American colonies. Her skinny legs dangled off the edge as she scribbled on the back of books. Little did she know that in a few hours, she and Bexley would be in a series of truly unfortunate events, and this would be the last time she saw the stunning blue hues of the ocean. The skeletal memories clawed through. Screams ricocheted in her ears, and the plunging squishy sound of knives sliding through bodies resurfaced. Each fragmented bone of memory breaking her attention further, doubling with her stuttering breath.

Kana's fingers pinched at the delicate skin of her right thumb, peeling away the thin top layer, chunk by chunk. She changed her mind, jamming the memory back, the faint lemon and bergamot of the southern Italy region dissolved as she buried the memory under mental cement. The idea of the beach held no interest. A hike through the wilderness seemed like a grand idea.

———

THE HEADY WOOD AND ZINGY YUZU FRAGRANCE curled in the air. The stick of incense was a fine gift from the Japanese monarch. Oshiya, much like many modern countries, had a constitutional monarchy; the family was as symbolic as the stamped profiles of men and women on the currency. Somehow the monarchy simultaneously held incredible value while having none at all.

The yoga mat made a sharp snap as Kana flung it into the air, and the strip of foam settled below the wall of windows overlooking the lake. The flight stewards put up an annoying fit, saying the plane's loading bridge was disconnected and passengers couldn't leave or some nonsense. Kana sarcastically questioned if dropping the word *bomb* would get her off the plane. The dramatics erupted after that, and in the end, a simple threat to contact Richard Benowitz, the airline CEO, and a promise of paying for everyone's flights, let her walk off the plane with only an hour of wasted time.

The doorbell rang, the sound slicing through the wood and glass house. This was exactly why private lake houses were superior: no pesky neighbors. The spontaneous change of plans meant the best she could come up with was a collection of lake homes, all spaced apart to create the illusion that there was only one home for kilometers. Whoever was at the door left after jamming their finger against the doorbell four more times, ticking her off.

She opted for a jog. The muscular definition in her abs diminished under the soft flesh, evidence of her slacking fitness regimen. Three weeks ago, she had been in L.A., meeting with the producers of her entertainment company to track upcoming projects, clinking wine glasses at the booked floor of the rooftop bar. When a firework went off, beads of cold sweat had bloomed faster than her accelerated heart. She locked herself in the nearest bathroom to calm her wretched mind and body. There wasn't enough oxygen, her scrambled egg mind unable to parse through her rational consciousness pointing out the rich oak stall door, the brass handle, the artificial candle scent, the sound of the soft jazz playing through the speakers in the corner of the bathroom as she tried to ground herself. She was safe.

By the time she reached the trailhead, she pressed one hand into her knee as she leaned over, swallowing through the pre-vomit sweats. Maybe pushing herself to do mini sprints wasn't the best idea. As she came down the wide bend of the trailhead to return to the lake house, the trees appeared longer and taller with the added shadows. The clipped flashlight on the collar of her jacket lit the padded trail, but it was a warm ember color emanating from the lake shore that caught her attention. Someone had started a bonfire.

The motion detecting lights staked along the property's

perimeter blinked on as she approached the long driveway. Through the extensive sheet of windows in the front of the lake house, a figure moved behind the kitchen countertops.

Shit. She ran without a pause, not needing to consider what to do next. The intruder saw her. The lights encircling the house could have easily been mistaken for a landing strip, illuminating the path leading straight to her. Someone had broken into the house. She highly doubted the heiress who greenlit the use of her lake house had decided to pop in for a visit, and the intruder didn't drive up based on the absence of a car near Kana's parked rental. An unknown person was dangerous, but as long as they weren't a User, everything was OK. She pivoted and retreated to the trailhead.

Murphy's Law was in full swing with a sweet artificial taste of white chocolate on the tip of her tongue. Fuck, the unusual flavor meant there was an Idu, just her luck. She forced her legs harder, faster. She would have a better chance with the mess of woods offering more coverage.

A projectile blasted through the air, causing her to stumble forward. She grabbed her left side, where the object—which may have been anything—pushed to an accelerated speed and pierced her flesh. Her body was stunned, even as her palm became slippery. She yanked at the bits of energy in the air, the taste of overly sweet chocolate, siphoning what she could.

The padded earth slid under her foot, and she geared up her strength because if they wanted her dead, they could have shot the back of her head. A second shot, the resounding pop of a gun, and a bullet smashed into the thick body of a tree just ten centimeters away from her left ear. A clear warning. She couldn't run.

Two silhouetted bodies stalked toward her, one casually tossing a small round object in the air, a gun in the other hand, while the second person remained near the porch of the house. Both were too tall and broad shouldered to be women.

"Go on," the slender man said. His voice had a drawl at the end as he waved the gun in a shooing motion toward the house. In the shrouded darkness of the night, Kana noted his lack of a mask. The half moon offered enough visibility to see the long, thin column of his nose bridge and the slim, parallel lines of his lips—a rat face.

She didn't demand to know what they wanted. They always wanted one thing: A.E. Potentia. As if she carried the drug on her like a tube of lipstick. God, people never learned!

Another pop of the gun sent her jerking away to the right as fragments of wood splintered near her right arm. She followed instructions. The clomp of heavy boots was a loud shadow behind her as she shuffled toward the lake house, her hands pressed over her bleeding abdomen.

The air to her right dampened, like wet jeans weighing down against her body. She swiveled to her right to witness a third form push out of the fracturing space on the pebbly lakeshore at the bottom of the staircase behind the lake house. A severe frown lined her mouth, partially in disappointment that she was too far to suck up any of the residual portal energy, but also worried by the additional assailant. A Passive Tomi and an Active Idu were not good odds. If they were already Users, A.E. Potentia wasn't their goal. She swallowed back her initial assumption of their reasons for her predicament.

"Faster," the beanpole of a man ordered. With the light from the side of the house, she glared at his pinched rodent face as she descended the steps, closer to the newcomer. The second man remained further back, not having started down the steps.

The third man, the portal creator, looped his arm through hers and dragged her to the bonfire. She swallowed the shock of pain, all too aware of the hole in her body, but it was futile to fight this beast of a man who was larger than the other two men and smelled like a dusty ashtray.

As they approached the impressive bonfire, with logs half her arm span, the crackling of wood and blazing orange flames crafted a summer image, and if not for the terrified, tear-stained faces of the people seated on the logs, it would have been an ideal summer night. A waif of a woman and a balding man with an impressive handlebar mustache pressed their children—one teenage boy and one younger-girl—between them. Two older men, the oldest of the two in his early fifties, their hands interlaced and quivering, whispered to each other.

All eyes zeroed in on Kana's bloody hands clutching her side. The family leaned away from the bear of a man dragging Kana over to them; it appeared she was the only one harmed.

"Now our esteemed guest has arrived." A woman's mocking voice, too syrupy and high-pitched, announced herself. Dressed in black cargo pants and a jacket with deep pockets her hands were hidden in, like the other three attackers, she strode back and forth behind the hostages, an impatient lioness.

"Christ, how many of you are there, a football team?" Kana muttered. A team of four seemed excessive. The other strangers around the fire looked at her like she had lost her mind.

"Are you sure this's her?" Bear asked as he pressed a hand between her shoulder blades, causing her to stumble until her knees crashed onto the rocky shore. The mustache father released his daughter and grappled with sweaty hands to help Kana onto the log beside theirs.

"She don't look like the pictures," Beanpole man quipped, stalking around the fire to get a better look at her face. "Aren't her eyes bigger?"

"Great, now you're racist," Kana said with an eye roll. Most people recognized the sharp red eyeliner; without her signature look, most people had a hard time identifying her on the streets.

Her gaze swept over each attacker. The fourth team member had yet to speak. Unlike the rest of the team, he did little and remained quiet with crossed arms as he stood beside the portal creator, Bear. The rest of the team made subtle eye movements to look at him, as if seeking approval.

"What's your name?" Beanpole asked. He was slimmer than the only woman on the team, who was closer to Kana's height, and through the dancing shadows and loose pants she could see the woman was packed with muscles.

"Christina Yamaguchi," Kana spat. Jesus Christ, he really was a dunce.

"See I told you she isn't—" the beanpole began, but the woman punched him. The crunch of her brass knuckles smashed into his face, and his head whipped to the side. *Damn.* The woman was the hothead of the group. The other hostages cowered, the little girl sobbing at the show of violence.

"You dumbass," she growled, "that's an Olympic ice skater."

Beanpole spat, globs of blood and saliva splattered on the shore.

"It's her," the no-longer-silent fourth man said with finality. He was the alpha of their little ragtag pack, and he was utterly unremarkable. Another white man of average height and average features and a face that could be any generic plain-old-Joe face with some stubble.

All gazes turned to her, and the other hostages tried to place her soft features. "If she's the one you want," the mother croaked, her voice broken by the sobbing and screaming she must have done hours earlier. The wash of horror on her son's face and her husband's was a bit comical. But Kana didn't put it past the woman. She might as well sacrifice one person and save her family.

"Unfortunately, Miss Ambrose isn't known for being cooperative," Average Joe said.

There it was, her name, the name everyone recognized. Again, eyes fell on her face as if trying to piece together the magazine covers, the headlines, and the articles plastered with her face since she was a baby. It was like a light flicked on in each of their heads, not just placing her identity, but realizing they were hostages with Kana Ambrose. The wind shifted and Kana tucked her head down as the smoky plumes burned her eyes.

"What do you want?" The man seated beside his partner dawning a vintage Prada blouse asked.

"Josephine Ambrose," Average Joe said, looking only at Kana as if saying the request would incite an immediate response.

She barely stopped from rolling her eyes and cursing at them. "You got the wrong Ambrose," Kana hissed. "I don't touch anything scientific. Don't you know I dropped out of both Harvard and Oxford?" She sneered. This wasn't a random group of old friends who decided to try to take Kana Ambrose one night over a poker game. The posture was stern, straight lines, not a hunched shoulder—military, and since two of them already showcased their abilities, it was a safe assumption that more of them were Users.

"As you well know, Dr. Ambrose is impossible to reach." Average Joe said.

Kana inhaled deeply through her nose. "I don't know how to tell you this. I've been kidnapped at least six times. You're going to try to send a video, maybe cut me up a bit, and send it to the president, but let me tell you a little secret, she doesn't give two shits about me." She spoke slowly and clearly, maintaining direct eye contact with Average Joe.

"Cared enough to send people to pull you out of those kidnappings," the woman growled back. Kana grinned. Her teeth flashed red-orange, reflecting the flames.

"We are lucky seven then," Bear said.

"See if she's finished," Average Joe ordered, and Bear answered. The gentle dampness tickled Kana's skin as he started using his Passive ability. Distinguishing between the different types of Users was a fluke; sucking up the expelled energy, that was unique. She needed every drop if she was going to make it out of this alive. They might be able to create temporary wormholes, push a penny at a speed that could blow someone's head off, and walk through walls, but she had her own magic trick. *Don't let them know*, a haunted warning rose.

"You're all Synthies and served, must be army or marines," Kana said casually. Good ol' America was the highest consumer of the synthetic drug, which made them the most profitable customer. There was a tentative political partnership with the mighty USA. Oshiya was one of those outlying countries Europe had conquered, to then be shoved out, and America had swooped in to assist with gaining independence just a little over a century ago.

Pain shot through her scalp as the woman snatched a fistful of Kana's hair and yanked her up to expose her throat. A vague shift in her peripheries as Beanpole moved, the flavor of old dusty chocolate that Kana clocked as Beanpole's power barely touched her tongue as a thin, long object soared through the air and into the woman's hand. Kana licked her lips as she tasted runny eggs along the sides of her tongue. The woman's Idu power tasted awful.

Kana's heart thrashed as cold sweat beaded down her armpits, her snippy confidence cracking. A dozen threats were made against her, and each time, her adrenal gland kicked into overdrive. She was still human after all, even though the tabloids loved to say otherwise. Her kidnappers had kept her alive this long and only now began to reveal what they wanted. The woman wouldn't slit Kana's throat, even if she wanted to.

"Call us Synthies one more time," the woman hissed. Her breath smelled like stale garlic.

The woman proved militaries liked having a team of each User: Burly-Bear to make portals; Beanpole and the woman were physic manipulators, who could alter the speed of an object in motion; so Average Joe would be a Sori, able to move through mass and round out the team's abilities. Why did they need

Josephine? A.E. Potentia was useless to them if everyone was a User, Synthetic or Natural.

"*Syn-thie*," Kana antagonized, enunciating each syllable, knowing she was poking the bear. There was a distinction between a Synthetic User and a Natural User, and the fissure between the two had widened in recent years. Synthetic Users became a lesser title, while Naturals elevated themselves to a higher pedigree.

The woman dug in her fingers and yanked at Kana's scalp, pressing the machete against her throat. A single wet line rolled down Kana's neck like a raindrop sliding down a car window. A loud crack from a collapsing log drowned out the horrified shrieks and cries of the other hostages. Everyone was pointedly avoiding her, not wanting to see her throat being slit open.

Chapter Three

"Lotus," Average Joe warned, and by the lengthy silence their argument was nonverbal before the woman lowered the machete. Kana let out a puff of air, her neck cramped from the forced angle. The woman's code name was Lotus. She seemed far from peaceful.

By the wavering fire, Kana observed the portal. Deep clefts spanned outward like someone had smashed an invisible sledgehammer, and the space caved inward as Bear's boots crunched over the lake rocks. He was an advanced Tomi; it was difficult to split portals without having an anchor, which was why most utilized walls or doors as their pinpoints.

"Rogue, you have to help Winter. She should be done playing with Mr. and Mrs. Smith," Bear announced. Someone failed at suppressing a choked wail. Judging by the violently shaking wife, she must have been close to the referred couple. Beanpole, code name Rogue, went off, fading into the darkness as he stomped across the shore, muttering under his breath about how he always had to deal with the mess until his retreating back bled into the night. Kana was more concerned with another member of this team, which meant another person to escape from, and Kana was not liking the odds—a team of five, while not the largest group Kana had dealt with, was more than normal and more than necessary.

"I don't understand the point," Kana said. "Holding a gun to my head and demanding an audience with Josephine isn't what you really want." Did they spend all this time and effort tracking her down to send a hostage video? Whatever they wanted, they were banking on the exchange to happen immediately. If they wanted her long-term, they could have trapped her in the lake house or moved to a secondary location. Silence met her as they waited.

Rogue ambled beside the elusive fifth member: Winter, a woman. Unlike the others, her hair was long and scraggly, in desperate need of a deep conditioning and gloss treatment. The family and couple leaned back from the oncoming person. The crusted blood covering the lower half of her face was disturbing.

Winter was a sick Synthie. The Hunger stage was evident by the smell of blood, soaked against the front of her poncho like a bib. Poor Mr. and Mrs. Smith. Kana imagined bits and pieces of them slowly being dissolved in Winter's digestive acid. Winter must be close to a Rabid state, if she wasn't there already. Could this situation get any worse?

"Who shot her?" Winter asked, the woman's eyes almost invisible under the wall of bangs, far too thick to be real.

"Do you even have to ask?" Lotus retorted. The sharp edge to her voice softened to a familiar tease as the ex-military pointed the tip of her knife at Rogue.

"What? I wanted to test and see if she's like me." Rogue shrugged.

"I can't help you," Kana repeated to the newest member. Winter seemed to hold a high status among the group, much like Average Joe, and the rest of the team yielded to her presence. Winter moved as if weights shackled her legs. A pant hem at least fifteen centimeters too long dragged along the pebbled shore until

Winter stopped, placing herself immediately behind the father. Kana's palms were sweaty as she thought about what was hidden under the ill-fitted poncho with its unusual humps and lumps.

"Call her," Winter said. Her gentle, feminine voice didn't match the exhausted face. Up close, Winter looked more like a melting wax figure. The family across from her trembled, the father gritting his jaw as the soft muscles of his biceps strained, as if he were fighting to stay as still as possible. They had no idea how dangerous a Rabid Synthie was, but they could sense the bloodlust, the inherent deep-rooted feeling she was wrong.

Small pebbles clattered to Kana's right as Rogue came beside her and pulled a small burner phone from his back pocket.

"She won't answer," Kana said, dismissing the compact device.

"Just call her!" the mother screeched, pressing her daughter's face against her stomach, as if hiding her daughter's face would protect her. "What the fuck is wrong with you? Call her and end this!"

"She doesn't own a cell phone, or have a landline," Kana said coolly. Lotus looped her arm under Kana's left armpit and hoisted her up. Her teeth smashed together as she held back the painful groan, reminded of the torn flesh and muscles in her abdomen.

"Call her PA, her secretary, the VP, chief of staff." Lotus smashed the phone into Kana's hand.

"She doesn't have a PA, an executive assistant, or any secretary. If you did your research, you'd know she doesn't even have a lab assistant. She. Works. Alone."

Rogue bent down and picked up a dime-sized rock and casually tossed it once, twice, and on the third toss he threw it underhand at Vintage Prada. The pebble lifted into the air at a normal speed, but as soon as gravity pulled the object down, it shot through the air nearly three times faster than a bullet.

Vintage Prada screamed as he crumpled forward, clutching his right knee, fresh blood squirting between his fingertips as the small rock blasted through his flesh and bone. The older partner flailed his arms, his hands flexing around nothing as if he was unsure if he should grip his partner to comfort him or if it would cause more pain.

"Call," Lotus repeated, "or the kid's next." Rogue picked up another rock, his eyes trained on the teenage boy. The family exploded into hysterics. The mother transformed into a banshee, reaching out to hold her son while the father tried to push his son behind him, forgetting about the looming predator.

Kana took the phone and dialed. The computerized ring roared over the crackling fire. Lotus laughed a dry maniacal sound. "Already knew to hit the speaker. Must be hard being an heiress, the princess kidnapped again. Shit, you weren't kiddin'."

The phone rang a second time. "So you know not to say anything funny, no code phrases, rich bitches like you have a dozen of them." By the fourth ring, she was sent to voicemail.

"You have reached the voicemail box of 510-222-4554. The voicemail box is full. Please try again later. Goodbye."

"Who did you call?" Lotus demanded.

"The only person close enough to be an assistant. Do you pick up an unrecognizable number?" Kana snapped. "Give me my phone. He'll pick up if I call him from my phone." She knew Oliver wouldn't answer if she used a burner phone. She also knew to call that number specifically because that was the phone connected to the US phone number, and he would at least know she was still in America. Her eyes went to Bear, the portal creator. Bear's hooded gaze went to Average Joe, awaiting his final decision.

"So someone can track your phone? I don't think so," Lotus sneered.

A guttural groan that sounded like an old house's bones creaking was barely audible over the frantic exclamations from the hostages. Kana caught on to the way Lotus was quick to drop her bite, her eyes flitting over to her sick partner. It wasn't just Lotus.

All the other members subtly shifted. Average Joe's left cheek twitched, while Bear's face curled into worry. Winter was important to them. Whatever they wanted, it had to do with her.

"Where is it?" Average Joe asked, his decision final.

"Somewhere in the cabin." Kana shrugged. "I don't keep track of it. Maybe the bathroom."

Average Joe gave a nod, signifying Bear could leave. Kana eagerly licked the sweet dampness in the air. If only she were closer, she could chug more. The longer she could stall, and push them to use more of their powers, the better chance she had to form a plan and have enough energy to escape.

"Try someone else," Lotus hissed.

Kana called six other numbers which inevitably went to voicemail before a portal opened and Bear tossed Lotus her phone.

"A whopping three contacts," Lotus announced as she tapped away. "Oliver, Bexley, and Pip. Are you sure these are people? Sounds more like dogs."

Average Joe plugged in a dongle that connected to a compact device resembling a portable charger. He stared down at something on her phone screen before he tossed it back to Kana.

"When Oliver answers, what exactly am I supposed to ask for? I need Josephine on the next plane? He can't promise that. God themself can't get Josephine here if she doesn't want to come."

"Find where Dr. Ambrose is first," Average Joe said.

Oliver answered after the first ring. "Yes," he drawled. It must be mid-afternoon in Europe if he was still there.

"Is Josephine still in Oshiya?" If Oliver questioned why she was calling him, he would know exactly what predicament she was in. Kana never willingly requested information about Josephine. She imagined him using his second phone, calling in a retrieval team, except she wasn't at the Washington beach. He should have received a note that she missed her flight. Fuck, her abrupt decision to change course in Oliver's selected destination has placed her in a worse position. She needed to buy time and drop as many hints as possible. Average Joe hijacked her phone, maybe to scramble her number, or have it bounce around different points. Whatever he did, Kana couldn't rely on Oliver accurately using her phone or the number.

"As far as I know, she hasn't left the newly built research base," Oliver replied.

"I have a friend who needs to speak to her." Kana looked at Average Joe, with a lifted eyebrow as if asking them, now what?

"Your friend will have to wait," Oliver continued. There was a barely audible *tap, tap, tap* of his thumbs on a screen. "You and I know she runs a tight schedule."

Code word: schedule. Oliver wanted to know how many were an immediate threat.

"Thursday, she has events. Who has been in contact with her?" She dropped the answer: Thursday equaled five assailants.

"No one right now."

"What about Llangorse? He's just as reclusive as her, locked in the northern lab. Call him." Kana was sweating. She was sure the code word came out naturally. They couldn't know Llangorse was a hint for a lake. The name came from the lake in the tale of *The Sword and the Stone*.

Oliver's next question would help narrow down which lake. If he mentioned *John*, that meant East Coast. If he said *Chester*, that was West Coast. It was probably sad how easily she and Oliver exchanged the memorized codes.

"He's out of the country. I can call John, his plane is due to land in a few hours."

Kana's response would have to either offer the number of syllables or spell the name of the lake. "What about Frank Sr.?" Kana asked, cuing Oliver to start talking for a while as she came up with a phrase that would use the letters in the name of the lake.

"Frank Sr. is on his yearly yacht tour. He's holding interest around the South China Seas this year, his research has borne fruit which he—"

Kana watched the determination set in Vintage Prada's pained expression, and before she could say anything, the idiot shouted.

"Help us!" Vintage Prada wailed, "Lake Wal—"

A rock obliterated his face; skull and brain matter exploded all over his partner while smaller pebbles speared through his mass, leaving his body looking like a colander.

Chapter Four

Hell broke loose. The partner screamed, falling backward, with lumps and chunks of body matter splattered over him. The father used the distraction to tackle Winter, sending his fists flying and shouting one word, "Run!" The teenage boy did something —maybe threw sand at Bear before trying to kick or grapple him while the mother and daughter ran down the pebbly shoreline. That was the one plus to having other hostages. They caused more disruption.

Kana twisted, and her sneaker collided with the side of Lotus's kneecap. The military woman's piercing screech was cut short by the satisfying crunch. The Synthetic User's leg buckled, and she crumpled forward, barely catching herself before Kana drove another brutal kick into her side, sending her sprawling into the dirt. Kana didn't wait to see if Lotus would rise. She sprinted toward the spindly tree shadows. Behind her was the sound of ragged breathing, strangled screams, and bone cracking and crunching. Average Joe shouted something, but she didn't dare look back.

She didn't get far, two strides into the tree line, when a taste of slimy egg yolk on the roof of her mouth warned her Lotus was about to launch something. Kana was lucky. She twisted at the right time, at the right angle, and the fired bullet grazed her arm. A theatrical scream and she fell dramatically face first, holding her arm as if she were shot.

Lotus stalked over and kicked her back. Kana tried to ignore the pain as she rolled onto her side. "Little cunt," Lotus hissed as she aimed the gun at Kana's thigh.

Kana swung her other leg, crashing into Lotus's shin. She might be rusty but she hadn't spent hours of training to die at some lake. She moved out from under the pointed barrel and threw a punch to Lotus's throat and another kick to her gut as she tried to grab the gun.

Lotus smashed her fist into the side of Kana's face. The pain stunned Kana, a punch to the face was always jarring, but Kana had the sense to keep attacking, not allowing the hit to stun her any longer. Her hands at least knocked the gun away, not that it mattered. The pissed-off ex-military Synthie woman reached into her pocket. Kana braced herself as the egg cascaded on her tongue. Lotus could have a handful of tacks, and with enough force, Kana could easily end up like Vintage Prada.

Don't let others see you. A warning that passed through Josephine's lips now morphed into Kana's consciousness. Now or never. She exhaled as Lotus threw a collection of nails, syrupy yolk dripping in Kana's mouth as Lotus's power kicked in. Kana hurled her stored energy; it was like forcing herself to unsteady her vision until the natural focus blurred. Her wave of power gripped around Lotus's whip-like force and redirected the trajectory. The nails blew back. Lotus, shocked, was forced to the ground while Kana used the precious seconds and lunged for the gun.

Lotus recovered from her surprise, but Kana fired the rounds without hesitation. The first bullet hit Lotus's torso, but the other three, two of which would have hit Lotus's head, slowed as if passing through water. An explosion of white chocolate and eggs battled in her mouth as both Lotus and Rogue pushed at the bullets, slowing the bits of metal until they were suspended in midair. Lotus moved out of the way, clutching her bleeding stomach.

"*Sheeet*, she nearly got you," Rogue said, out of breath, behind them. Kana siphoned as much energy as she could as Rogue maintained the bullets glacially moving through the air. The longer he maintained the hold, the longer she could refill her battery.

The adrenaline pounding against her ears dulled as the chaos down by the beach amplified; the screams became louder as the immediate threat of death faded to the background. "What are you waiting for?" Lotus screeched. "Shoot her!"

Rogue held up his hands, and the suspended bullets dropped to the ground. Kana scrambled for her next move. The gun was useless; both Rogue and Lotus could push back any bullets. She had enough energy for maybe two more attacks. Her best bet was to escape long enough for Oliver to find her, but how could she escape from Lotus and Rogue?

A dragon roar shredded through the air. "Fuck, not again!" Rogue cursed, his adrenaline-high flushed face paling as he ran back to the beach. A silhouette moved in the far right of her vision, but she was too slow. Kana screamed as a knife slid into her back, somewhere under her right shoulder blade.

"Lotus!" Average Joe shouted as he stormed into the sparse trees. "Get the medical kit, fix her!"

"If you haven't noticed, I've been shot," Lotus hissed, flashing a bloody palm to Average Joe. Kana only wished she'd had better aim and had hit a major organ. More words were exchanged, and the heat in Kana's back was becoming unbearable.

"Her life is worth more than yours."

Lotus's jaw clamped shut as she grumbled like a dog with a muzzle, but obediently dragged Kana back to the orange flames and the epicenter of the chaos. Kana blinked, trying to keep her focus, but it was hard when she couldn't stand straight. The knife was very much still in her back, and each movement made that evident as the steel sent pain with every breath.

"I—" Kana's teeth chattered. Shit, had she lost so much blood already? Her vision faded and locked onto a black humped mound, hovering over an open human chest.

The creature wasn't an animal. Those were human hands, shoving handfuls of slippery hunks of large intestine into its mouth. The slurping and gnawing added the perfect soundtrack to the horrific scene. The torn bodies lay sprawled around the bonfire like decimated crabs at a Seafest, legs, arms, and torsos tossed aside.

The clip-on bangs had been knocked off, the wig was half askew, showing the conglomeration of body parts: a tongue grew out of her forehead, three fingers poked out of the side of her neck, divots and bubbling of skin marred the rest of the neck. Winter was drowning in the Hunger, an insatiable appetite for human flesh, slowly disfiguring her body as she consumed more humans. She was truly Rabid, and this was worse than anything Kana had seen. She'd only seen one other Synthie inflicted by the Hunger, just at the start of a Rabid state, the flesh of his palms shredding away like grated cheese to reveal misshaped chunks of cartilage, the curve of a knuckle.

Kana's vision became filmy as she swayed, left then right, the blaring clash of noises, shouting, the tension of panic between the team members dampened by the smell in the air. She felt like she'd crawled inside an animal carcass. Winter looked up and edged closer to her. The woman moved oddly; her spine swayed unnaturally as if the bone were softening. Kana had been so focused on the deformed woman that she overlooked Rogue, who stood a few meters to the side, his face dripping with sweat. The artificial milky chocolate was a solid mold over her tongue as Rogue pressed layers of his energy against Winter.

He was purposefully slowing her movements. But beneath

the white chocolate encasing, there was an unusual fizz, like little bits of candy popping in her mouth. Kana backed away from the approaching Rabid Synthie, whose eyes were no longer focused in one direction, the left eye moving off to the right, the right eye lifting to the sky.

The military team moved closer to Winter.

"We're losing her," Bear said, shaking his head. A gust of wind dragged the poncho off of Winter's body. Kana barely registered the loose sliding skin that looked like thin wet plastic against glass, because something else distracted her as she tasted the tiniest drop.

Wow. Winter was expelling a lot of power; it layered sticky like peanut butter along the edges of her tongue. She absorbed a little more. The flavor was gag worthy, rancid like stale natto. Her heart rate spiked as she gulped more of Winter's power. It tasted awful, but she wanted more. Her body was alive, wired as if all the blood in her veins had been replaced with pure bolts of energy. She felt great—better than great. The twenty-three-centimeter knife sticking out of her body didn't feel like anything. Her hand touched the small hole in her left side from the bullet wound. She wiggled her pointer finger into the hole, and a small bubble of laughter escaped. Her throat bobbed as she gulped more of the syrupy energy. How could no one else feel it?

A child's soft giggle echoed around. Did the little girl survive? Kana's hand covered her mouth—the sound was from her. The smell of iron filled her nostrils as she tried to stifle her cackles. Kana couldn't remember being stabbed in the back, though many people told her she was a backstabber. Her hand reached around, and her fingers grazed the handle of the knife.

Someone tried keeping her hands away. "Has she lost her mind? Stop her!"

Yes, she'd lost her mind. Her brain felt like it was deep fried, and now she had a knife in her hand. Everything was warped; she was peeking through a camera lens that intermittently zoomed in and out, timed with her beating pulse.

Blink: she was swimming in the Mediterranean, watching fifty yellow fish swim like a tornado around her.

Blink: she walked through a botanical garden, staring at cotton candy hydrangeas.

Blink: she threw her head back and laughed as she danced around a bonfire in Vietnam, the bucket of alcohol sloshing around her wrist.

Reality overlapped like a delicate layer of chiffon, the rest of her mind trapped in the humid air suffocating her, the drunken laughs and screams of the partygoers on the beach melded with the orders and the screeching Winter. Kana squeezed her eyes closed, willing her mind to stop tilting and shifting as she stumbled and fell. Her sticky, wet back hurt.

Bodies blocked the Vietnam dragon dance. Rogue growled, "Black! This ain't workin', where the hell is Lotus? I can't hold her back."

"Plan B. Get the girl to the car," someone ordered. "Rogue, you and I will subdue Winter."

"Winter's fightin' me. I'm reachin' my limit," another voice huffed.

Kana's eyes widened as a gigantic man blocked everything in sight, crouching in front of her. His face was regretful. Kana wondered why he was looking so sad at a party. She never understood the poor bastards who get sad and mopey after drinking.

A roar sounding like a pissed-off grizzly echoed into the bleak space. Kana jerked, her thundering heart skipping at the animal war cry and more shouts and a lot of *fucks* as the thick arms lifting her vanished. The hard, rocky shore ground into her back as she caught sight of the deformed dragon skittering on its hands and legs before leaping onto the man. The pale face ripped into the man's jugular as it sunk its fingers into his eye sockets and ripped the delicate blobs out. Another wave of pure bliss and power drowned Kana's lungs, sending happy tingles to every crevice of her body. Jesus motherfucking Christ. Kana grinned, basking in the high. She was so out of her mind. This was better than the nebula weekend when she thought she had exploded into a star. She stared at the looming nightmare above her, the legs and arms planted on either side of her prone body, like a dog.

Kana tilted her head as the creature lifted its hand; thick droplets splattered against her face, blood and saliva. She attempted to raise her hand, wondering if they were going to shake hands in a greeting. The tongue on the forehead wiggled, licking the creased forehead skin while the dragon's closed fist raised and pounded down.

Chapter Five

Kana screamed. Her vocal cords snapped, one by one, as the cry of pain rocketed out of her throat. The thin, delicate skin of her body stretched like a balloon, filling and filling until she popped; the bottled-up power she guzzled exploded, and the sweet reprieve of unconsciousness came knocking.

The digging of the small rocks along her side hinted that she lay somewhere. The high melted away, and even as she clung to the numbness and tingling sparks of happiness, hot, fiery waves of pain rolled in, getting stronger as she became more aware. Well, she was somehow still alive. Her half-open eyes stared at the glorious night sky. The Milky Way and the millions of stars stared back. If this was the last thing she saw, it wasn't so bad.

Lucid moments were bolts of lightning, destroying her body, sending rackets of pain to every strand of hair and every layer of skin. A hand pressed into her stomach, another moved her shoulder. Her brain couldn't string together the litany of curses before she passed out again.

A voice said, "Keep her awake." The whoosh of thundering air swallowed her words, and a single string of consciousness told her it was the whipping of helicopter blades.

A gloved palm tapped against her face, then hit her a little harder. She opened her eyes to send a glare at whoever dared slap her. Someone else jostled her, lifted her, and she screamed. Her hands flailed for anything to stabilize her. But the moment lasted less than a second before she dove head-first back into the open arms of darkness.

Oliver deserved a reward. She knew an extraction team reached her in time because she was in transition to whatever destination had the best doctors. A quaint summer getaway would do nicely. He'd always liked Norway, not most people's conception of a summer home, but she supposed she ought to buy him one. Another jerking motion and she screamed. She didn't know if any sound came out; her throat was raw. Maybe she'd downsize that summer villa to a cottage. Why wasn't she pumped with painkillers by now? She needed the blissful numbness to soothe the feeling of being dipped in lava and acupunctured with icicles.

A hand clasped around hers, larger and strong enough to handle her chokehold grip as her nails dug into the gloved hand. Her eyes slit open as a voice in the muffled background strung out a long list of anatomical and medical terminology. She moved fast on a thin mattress with wheels. The gurney rolled over a lifted section of ground, cueing another cry of pain.

Rattle, rattle, the metal bars of the medical bed bounced around and she was wheeled into the second bane of her existence: hospitals. When was the last time she'd gone to a hospital? She was sixteen, and solidifying one of her goals to make it two years without being kidnapped or sent to the hospital. That New Year's resolution almost worked, until some crazed activist shot her a month after her eighteenth birthday, the twinkling lights and carolers' Christmas tune cut with screams. Merry Christmas to her.

Someone covered her nose and mouth with an unknown object. Her eyes flew open, awful overhead hospital lights blinding her as she jolted up. Hands, more than two, less than five, shoved her down before she could sit up. She thrashed like the final escape attempt of an animal caught by its predator. Her hands clawed at the mask, her body twisting and jerking, the monitor clipped onto her finger flying off, silencing the irritating high-speed beeping as a memory sunk its fingers into her eye sockets, and there was pressure around her face. She couldn't breathe.

"Stop." The voice overlapped with her internal shouts to stop. Tears leaked out of her closed eyes and relief reflected in her limp frame as the pressure on her face lifted. She was too old for this. Sweet, sweet unconscious returned.

Unfortunately, the tiny peephole of lucidity in her comforting darkness became larger, the size of an envelope slot, and then, to her grave dissatisfaction, a floor-to-ceiling window she couldn't ignore.

"Kana, you can't continue to sleep. You aren't in a coma."

Kana's head was clear enough to recognize Oliver's haggard voice. She evened her breathing, thinking about the beach; digging her feet into the warm sand, and watching the briny ocean lap around her shins. A Mai Tai sounded good. The chilled glass, the ice cubes clinking as she took a sip.

"Stop pretending, your brain activity is monitored." Oliver sighed, an action he rarely did, even when she was kicking and screaming during her rebellious preteen years and throwing fire torches at him. Literally sticks of fire. Some new-money tech heiress's sixteenth bash had been Hawaiian themed, and Oliver had pissed her off for an unmemorable reason, so she'd picked up the nearest torch and threw it at him. He hadn't sighed or complained.

"Mai Tai," she croaked.

There was a movement of suede shifting and an exhale of amusement. Another person was in the room, which was surprising. She sniffed, keeping her eyes closed. Bexley favored a distinct coconut scented product, so it didn't matter how often she changed her perfumes; she used the same hair conditioner, and this wasn't her. In fact, she couldn't catch a specific scent.

"You can't drink while in recovery," Oliver chided.

Kana visibly scowled as she pulled the hospital sheet over her face and cracked her eyes open. As expected, the god-awful fluorescent lights were beaming down in all their glory. Before she could tell Oliver to shut the damn things off, someone stood and moved across the room, and the lights blinked out.

"This hospital has competent staff," Kana commented, as she finally opened her eyes.

Oliver lounged across from her in a sofa with a newspaper between his hands, little reading glasses drooping down the long slope of his nose and a pair of snazzy red suspenders.

"You look like an old man from the fifties." Her voice cracked as she licked her crusted lips. The circular table to his right had a white ceramic mug with coils of steam lifting into the air. His laptop was halfway closed, a stack of documents atop his leather portfolio.

"I am an old man," Oliver said, and with a fluid movement, he snapped the newspaper in half and placed it on the arm of the sofa. "And you are speeding up my age. I didn't get this premature white hair without a reason."

Kana was about to joke that she was closing in on her ninth life when her periphery caught sight of the figure to her left. "Who the hell are you?" Kana demanded as she turned to face the person seated in the corner of the space, away from the window, but angled at the door.

The young man in question was not part of the hospital staff, unless the hospital had begun staffing personal security guards. He wasn't wearing a uniform per se; the cotton shirt still had creases where it had been folded in a drawer, his khakis screamed IT and didn't go at all with the heavy-duty boots. Nothing a nurse or doctor would wear. His face remained neutral, but she could smell military or police from kilometers away.

Her gaze caught the curtain material, dual layered, a thin pearly sheet, and a distinct royal blue linen. There was only one hospital with these curtains. They may have altered the furnishings, and the velvet couch was a nice touch, but she knew where she was.

"Pull the curtain," she drawled, her eyes unblinking at the man. His age was hard to pinpoint. Older than her, maybe late twenties. If he shaved the scruff, he'd shed years. Young but old, the kind of old that came from seeing shit go down.

"Kana," Oliver said, exhausted. He dared to say her name like he was returning from a ten-year war. She was the one who'd probably had multiple surgeries.

"I. Said. Pull. The. Curtain," Kana repeated, pausing between each word. Neither man made any effort to move. Fine. She flung the blanket off her body and moved to swing her legs off the bed. Tight gauze trapped her entire torso, causing discomfort. Her body rebuked the entire movement, but she wouldn't show pain. She refused.

The unknown man conceded and pulled the curtain.

"Kana," Oliver said as he tentatively crossed to her side.

She stared, her body involuntarily trembling as she forced her posture straight. The metropolis sprawled before her eyes. The iconic Oshiya tower, fawned at and adored by architectural enthusiasts for the feminine curvature and the masculine tip. Off to the far left was the eyelet lace bridge structure that connected the city to the Ruushi district. They were on one of the top floors of the hospital, reserved for VIP admissions, and certainly high enough to see a peak of the ocean on the horizon.

She wanted to roar, pick up the bedside lamp, and smash it through the window. She would rip out the tubes and IVs in her arm and leap out of the window. This was the one place she never wanted to be again. Out of every hospital in every country, she'd been brought back to Oshiya. The country that took pride in its goddess, Josephine Ambrose.

Josephine could spit in someone's face, and they would thank her. She was beloved by the public, more adored than the president and the royal family, according to the annual polls. Which said a lot about Oshiya's citizens, speaking to either the distrust and lack of support for their president and ancient monarchy, or the efficient PR team Josephine paid.

The unrestrained tension was close to rupturing. Oliver took another step toward her, but maintained a respectable distance. Best not to get too close. "The injuries were extremely difficult. You needed the specialists here, the ones trained and well-versed with Synthetic attacks."

"I was stabbed," she said in an even voice, the undercurrent of anger seething below the surface.

"And shot," Oliver added.

"Neither of which requires a specialist," Kana hissed. "I could go to any ER doctor in any country. Why. Am. I. Here?" She demanded the last question, ignoring the young officer keenly watching their interaction.

"You don't remember the third attack. That's for the best. What matters is a call was made and you were pulled from death's doors."

"Congratulations, they did their fucking jobs. They're getting paid a millionaire's salary to work here."

"Kana, what are you doing?" Oliver asked as Kana squeezed the needle and pulled out the IV without hesitation. "Kana," Oliver warned.

"Stop saying my name." Kana's voice rose as her socked feet touched the hard floor. "You said I was free from death's doors, so I'm leaving. I'll stay with Bexley in San Diego and dutifully visit the post-op doctors at the UC hospital. I know the drill."

"The president is requesting an audience," the stranger said. "He wants you in better condition."

Kana tested her strength, ignoring the young man, and

grabbed the pole with the second IV to help stabilize her weight as a crutch. "He can FaceTime me."

She shuffled her foot forward and immediately had to wrap her left arm around her stomach, hunching forward as pain drilled through her core. Oliver was at her side in two strides. She hated that her weak body gave in, and she let him lead her to the edge of the queen-sized medical bed.

"How many times have we been here?" he asked softly as he sat beside her.

A surprised laugh escaped her. She winced as her ribs constricted. "Close to ten. Are we including the times you were injured or exclusively me being trapped in these hospital rooms?"

"Including both of our trips, it's been sixteen visits."

That's depressing. That was more than half her age. "Don't get sappy on me, Ollie," Kana teased, sweetening the nickname. "Going down memory lane and the obstacles we've overcome together doesn't change anything. I'm an adult. You can't keep me here without my consent, or is that why the security detail is here? To keep me under lock and key with a guard dog?"

"His name is Spencer, and he is here because situations have become more complex," Oliver said. He clasped his hands between his parted legs. There were nine uneven creases in Oliver's pants and normally pristine, crisp shirt. His facial hair, while trimmed, was thicker than she'd seen it in some time.

"It's always complicated."

"The incident was leaked to the press. Specifically, you being the only survivor."

Kana felt an insidious, tumor-like migraine inflating. It was always a PR problem.

"How bad? New Year's Day of twenty eleven?" she asked.

"No."

Her lips pursed as she stared deep into Oliver's hazel eyes. "Italy twenty thirteen?"

His nostrils flared.

She closed her eyes, inhaling the stagnant hospital air. Of course, it was going to be like the Italian summer of 2013. That postcard was a terrible, ominous warning. "It better not be Lenny handling PR. I want Tanisha or Molly. Hell, both of them are better than Lenny."

"It's handled."

"What's my timeline?" Kana ran her tongue along the scar inside of her cheek, trying to not draw attention to the fact that there was a wet feeling on her right side. Her hand was still protective around her midsection, and yep, those were small wet droplets leaking through the gauze and starchy medical top.

"Doctors estimate two months to make sure the internals are healing. Luckily, there were no broken bones, and therefore not too much physical therapy."

It was a bitch when she had broken bones, recovery took forever in those instances, but two months mandated hospital recovery for a gun shot and stab wound was unacceptable and unnecessary. There was another reason she was ordered to stay longer. The sooner she could skip from the hospital, the sooner she could plan her escape from Oshiya.

"I want to speak with the doctors. And Dr. Lee. Also, I think I pulled some stitches." She held out her hand, her fingers stained vibrant red.

Oliver shot up from the bed and ran out of the room, the sliding doors whooshing, a gust of air crinkling the newspaper.

"So dramatic," Kana muttered as she reached for the call button and adjusted to rest back against the wall of pillows made of plush, down feathers.

"What did they promise you?" Kana asked, turning to face the military man.

He hadn't returned to the chair in the corner, but stood in the other corner, diagonally from her and in line with the door, strategically placed in case Kana attempted to run. Not that she could get far.

He didn't respond and maintained a bland expression.

"Or did you just get the short end of the stick? Because I'm betting you are not here willingly. I'd guess you were part of the retrieval team, and orders from above demanded someone stay with the victim, and you are the youngest of the team. They really love forcing the fresh recruits to do the babysitting jobs."

He didn't alter his stance, no shift in weight, no finger twitch, and his face was free of tension. He was good, but she kept fishing. He wasn't unattractive, his features weren't perfectly symmetrical, his mouth and jaw seemed titled just a little to the left.

"If you weren't on the extraction team, then you must have done something naughty. Am I your punishment?"

That earned a brief moment of surprise in his expression. His eyes awakened, like a caffeine addict smelling the first scent of brewing coffee. She grinned at the deviation in his behavior.

The door opened, and four white-coated doctors arrived and stood in a single file line at the foot of the hospital bed. Oliver brought up the rear and returned to his perch on the sofa. Kana's face cooled as she neatly crossed her hands over the hospital electric blanket and carefully looked over each person. One was closing in on sixty, the two in the middle of Oshiyan heritage, one darkly tanned, the other fairer, and the last a short, curvy woman with a head full of impressive curls. Dr. Lee, a woman with incredible hair stronger than a horse's mane, was notably absent.

"Who was a part of the surgeries?" Kana asked.

The four doctors all glanced at each other, but they looked at the eldest man who had entered her hospital room first. He must have given a subtle hint, because three of the four raised their hands.

"Out." She jerked her chin up to dismiss the man closing in on sixty.

"I'm the chief medical officer," he sputtered. His mouth opened and closed, the deep lines in his forehead wrinkling further.

Kana zeroed in on him with her frosty expression. "You must be the acting chief medical officer, because Dr. Lee has served this hospital for the past fifteen years. You'll get a handsome sponsorship from Ambrose Inc. by the end of this quarter." Sponsorship, a cleaner word than bribe for the bureaucratic bullshit. "Get out."

The green chief medical officer chuckled as if she were joking. "Dr. Espinoza, call the nurse. We'll need to redress the wound and—"

"Did I make a joke?" Old men always assumed any order she said wasn't real and should never be taken seriously. "Or did you blatantly ignore my order?"

A cold draft blew through the room. Kana could tell the other three doctors tried to still their wiggling mouths.

The vein in the elderly man's neck bulged, and his pasty face reddened as he swiftly left the room. "I have a board meeting to attend. Report back," he said briskly.

"Who signed the revised Title Six NDA?" Kana asked, returning her attention to the remaining three doctors.

The soft woman didn't raise her hand.

"You are excused."

The remaining two doctors glanced at each other.

"Why are you still here?" Kana asked, eyes boring into Spencer.

"Spencer, let's get some coffee," Oliver offered. Spencer didn't have enough clearance to be in the room with her doctors. Good to know.

"Your stitches need to be examined," the woman doctor commented.

"I want the quick summary of my situation, and then I want the best-case scenario for recovery."

The remaining doctors side-eyed one another. The woman took a hesitant step forward, seeing as the male doctor didn't make any movement.

"Did you step forward because you're the most skilled at

stitches or because you assumed, as a woman, I'd be more comfortable with you?"

"Um." The female doctor hesitated.

"Aside from the two penetrating injuries, the first was a wound similar to a gunshot, a small object entered and exited your right lumbar region," the male doctor started.

The female doctor removed instruments from a medical drawer, ripping open the sterilized equipment.

"No major damage from that wound, and the graze to your left biceps required a total of six stitches. The second major injury was the stab wound cutting through your right side, which managed to miss your stomach. It should have gone into your kidney, and you would have died, if you had one on the right side. Most of the internal injuries were along areas of your large intestine."

The female doctor pushed up Kana's medical top and cut the layers of bandages and gauze.

"The most concerning wound was the forceful blunt injury." The doctor frowned, accentuating the two parallel creases from his nose to the corners of his mouth. "Rarely has this come up. Most people don't come into contact with a Rabid Synthetic User that destructive." He cleared his throat and reviewed the medical chart.

"The wound pattern was unlike anything we've seen. There is severe bruising as if there was a lot of pressure against your abdomen, but it didn't last long. It would have split you open if it did."

The doctor peeled away her bandages. Kana's abdominal muscles trembled. The skin was an ombre black, instead of regular bruising with blue and yellow and green. A line of small, neat stitches ran along two parts, one straight down and the other further on her right side from the bullet wound.

"You took samples of my skin." Kana said.

The doctors were silent.

"I want the results immediately. You will not share any findings." Kana allowed her order to hang in the air before she asked the question she really cared about. "When can I check out?"

"At least a month. We would prefer if you stayed two months."

"No, get me the treatment and recovery plan. I'm checking out in a week."

Chapter Six

"Send the profiles of those two doctors," Kana said as soon as Oliver returned with a nondescript coffee cup in each hand. She took a gulp; her face scrunched. Half of her wanted to spit it out, but it was too late. Most of it was down her throat and she hacked, droplets caught in her lungs. Tears formed in her eyes as someone plucked the offensive drink out of her hand.

"What the hell is that?" Her small fist hit her chest while she coughed twice more.

"Green tea. You are on a strict diet, no drinks with over thirty milligrams of caffeine." No alcohol and no caffeine. If they wanted her to recover, she needed some pleasures in life. A happy patient made for a faster recovery, and all that.

"There was a lovely summer home in Marienlyst, Norway, but it just disappeared with that tea."

Oliver, unfazed by her childish antics, settled in the chair halfway tucked beneath the rounded table and sipped his coffee. She knew it was coffee, by scent alone.

"It's green tea or decaf," he said with a pleased smile.

Goddamn, she hated Oliver sometimes, and only because he

knew her too well. Decaf was an abomination to humanity. She didn't want to look at his smug face right now.

"Go and tell Bexley I'm fine. Even if I wanted to escape, I'm sure there's a code magenta in place."

"Code magenta?" Spencer echoed. His eyes went to Oliver for an explanation.

"You must be really new. The big, bad temporary chief medical officer didn't give you the special hospital code?"

"It won't be necessary to put the hospital on a code magenta alert. Spencer's going to be keeping you company," Oliver chimed in, a little too cheery for her taste.

"They created a color code exclusively for you," Spencer concluded, failing to keep the curiosity hidden.

Kana's lips peeled back. "A lot of things are created exclusively for me, darling,"

"Spencer, please excuse us for a moment. She's starting to use pet names."

Spencer obeyed and exited the hospital room.

Kana growled, "Oliver." It seemed Oliver was also losing his patience. "It looks like you are forgetting your place." Oliver's face darkened, and the tension thickened between them. His only duty was to make sure she was happy. Of course, he had other responsibilities. His job description was a whopping twenty pages. Sure, he was responsible for carrying out Josephine's orders and attending to her whims, but his priority was Kana.

Neither said a word. Oliver leaned back in the chair, his right leg casually tossed over his left as they stared each other down. Kana stewed, her entire torso itching as if her skin was a giant scab, the dried and healing edges itchy beyond belief, not even counting the actual intestinal pain. The pain meds were wearing off, or her attempt at standing and moving did more damage than she expected. *Fight through the pain.* She couldn't let the exhaustion or pain cross her face as her internal mantra started back up —*show no weakness.*

"You had me worried," Oliver began. Great, so he was making the emotional speech.

"You may not be physically rolling your eyes, but I can see your dismissal. Is it so hard to believe that I'm concerned about your well-being?" His steady gaze was genuine and Kana internally recoiled like a cat being flicked with water.

"Maybe in three years I can forgive the transfer to this hospital, even though you know why I can't be in Oshiya." It had taken years for her to legally leave the country. Illegally, it would be easy, just charter a plane or boat and loop around the stringent border patrol. Her film production company had more purpose than to bring in income.

"Your records are sealed, the protections for child cases are immense, naturally. With Josephine's power and pull, you have nothing to worry about."

His flippant brush-off of the Event was fuel across the dying flames. This wasn't about the records being sealed; it was about their existence. The Event was a leash that someone, Josephine or the president, could use and hold over her. She was losing her grip, and she didn't want this discussion to devolve; there was a larger point that bothered her.

"I can't begin to understand why there's a guard dog," Kana said, coolly.

"The president has requested an immediate audience with you after you are well enough to stand and walk." Oliver pointedly avoided the mention of the bodyguard.

"And he thinks I'll run out before I grace him with my presence." Kana scoffed.

"Yes," Oliver said, "because you have left the country when he asked for your presence on numerous occasions."

"Only twice." Kana sighed, settling deeper into the cocoon of pillows. "If all I have to do is meet with the president, then last time I checked, he has two functioning legs and arms."

Oliver flipped the page of a document he was reviewing, his

eyes flitting over his spectacles as he said, "Unfortunately, he needs to speak with you in the White Room."

What an unexpected choice—the White Room; there was an enormity around those two innocuous words. It was supposedly the most secure room in the nation. Rumor had it that it was because the room's location changed to keep portal-ripping Naturals or Synthies from entering. Did she dare she admit her curiosity was tickled?

"Does it have to do with my attack? I've never seen a Synthie that far off the deep end." The moments before her stabbing, Winter's deformed body was a sight. The Hunger caused the Synthetic User to turn to human meat, and the host's body became a tumor, growing extensions of the consumed person. She grinned. "Maybe I will meet with the president. It seems something is happening to the Synthies. It makes me wonder: why not speak with Josephine?"

"My clearance for the nature of the president's internal workings doesn't extend to why he has demanded a meeting with you. The investigation of your attack is underway. Spencer is to make sure another fringe group doesn't get violent." And attack her again.

"A bodyguard won't stop anyone. Halloween of oh-nine?" While not considered a holiday in Oshiya, it was readily adopted as a festival. When Kana went trick-or-treating, it was one of the few days she could put on a mask and be anyone else. The Halloween of '09 was ruined when her bodyguard was assassinated the night before. The man she walked around the neighborhood with in a Spider-Man costume wasn't who she thought.

"He won't be wearing a mask. There's no risk of him being swapped."

"June third of oh-six?"

After her second kidnapping attempt, Josephine had requested bodyguards. It looked bad if her daughter continued to be kidnapped every year. The bodyguards sold her out. It only took one to realize her value and her proximity to the drug.

Oliver extended his legs, and an audible pop reminded Kana of the knee surgery he needed after one of the attacks ended with both of them hospitalized. "Won't be an issue. He's been properly screened. Personally selected by the president."

She laughed dryly, which did little to validate the watchdog. If anything, she suspected Spencer more, knowing that the president wanted him out of all the other military goons at his disposal.

With every blink, her eyes closed for longer periods. "And someone needs to make sure a nurse or doctor doesn't get too happy with the drugs," Kana mumbled. It was a delicate line between the high of the opioids and being coherent enough in case someone had nefarious intentions, but she might have said, *nd surree doc drugzzz—*

———

Oliver was still in the room when she clawed out of her morphine twisted dreamscape to catch his listless voice. "—our liability is capped." The supple fabric of the armchair moved. Silence, then, "No. Finalize the terms. I want to review the three amendments before production continues." The dull thunk as Oliver's phone hit the oak table and the soft repetitive clicking of fingers hitting keyboard keys sent her back to sleep.

The fluid scratch of a sharp point against paper was a strange comfort. Her eyes were thin slits, just enough that she caught Oliver scribbling along the stack of documents on the small desk across from her bed with a familiar pen. "That isn't the Pelikan from nine years ago?"

Oliver lifted his eyes and raised the pen higher to show off its body, and the flecks of iridescent color confirmed her suspicion. "Of course, why are you surprised?"

There was a warm, uncomfortable feeling against her sides.

"There are a dozen better fountain pens—you could easily have a rare Montblanc."

He gently laid the pen down. "A young lady I'm rather fond of tossed me a bag as she returned from a trip to Europe with a breezy 'happy birthday' in passing. When I asked about the gift, she said all gentlemen have fine pens. I find this pen is more than fitting to complete its tasks and holds more value than a rare Montblanc."

"Why are you still here?" she asked as she pushed herself up, rubbing her eyes. Whatever drugs they gave her were making her eyes shriveled raisins and her mouth a hot, cavernous sewage drain.

"Toothbrush and toothpaste." When was the last time she'd brushed her teeth?

The hollow tap of a plastic cup landing on the end table made her turn. Spencer stepped away from the compact table with a lax expression. She plucked up the plastic cup with the folded toothbrush with a globe of toothpaste nestled between the bristles without a word of gratitude.

"Bexley sends her regards," Oliver said as he finished tapping on his phone. "It is in everyone's best interest if she doesn't visit at this time."

"Where's my phone?" she asked, shoving the toothbrush into her mouth.

"When you're discharged, there's one waiting in your apartment." Oliver slid his laptop into the leather briefcase embossed with a Hermes logo, a Christmas gift she'd shoved under the white Christmas tree five years ago. Kana scrubbed her teeth, her eyes moving over the small overnight suitcase beside the chair and his neatly folded trench.

"All the essentials have been brought, and the loft is cleaned and ready for you. You'll find the files on the doctors here." He gestured to the tablet on the minimal desk between the two windows. "We are still in blackout. There won't be any internet or data on the tablet."

Never mind the drag of his hand down his face and the indents of exhaustion, Oliver, as always, took care of everything. She accepted the small cup of water that appeared in her right field of vision as she swished and spat into the empty cup.

"You know how to reach me." Oliver spoke, but not to Kana. His gaze locked off to the right, where Spencer hovered. Oliver didn't say any parting words as the wall crinkled and he collected his belongings and left through the portal.

"Finally," Kana sighed as she set the frothy spit cup aside. The day was already improving. Her teeth didn't feel like there were two wool socks on them, and Oliver's overbearing presence was gone.

"Tablet." She held out her hand with an expectant look at Spencer. After all, she was the one incapacitated.

He remained still for three seconds, as if being told to retrieve the tablet for her was a chore, but eventually he crossed the room and handed her the thin piece of technology. If she were fully able and moving, he would have definitely seemed like the type to question or put up more of a fight.

As Oliver said, the internet was nonexistent. There were only two files on the home screen. She opened the first file. Larry Stacy Cohen was a fifty-seven-year-old medical doctor, specializing in trauma and gastroenterology. His father was an Oshiya native who passed away from a heart attack two years ago. His widowed mother was from America, the great windy Chicago. Kana wanted to skip the boring educational stats, but there could be a useful secret. Dr. Cohen was a rather boring man, following his father's expectations to a T. He'd been sent off to an elite education at Oshiya's top academies by the time he was five years old and left the motherland for an extended time for his early acceptance into Johns Hopkins, after which he returned to Oshiya where he hadn't left since. He had a wife, only five years his junior, with two very blonde offspring.

The next section detailed his internet history and she found a few goodies there. There was the expected occasional porn search, which was quite vanilla considering what she'd seen on other people's profiles. The spiciest repeat offender was threesome action.

She checked his bank records, and even that looked quite clean. No flagged incoming amounts for more than his standard salary, including the multiple bonuses. She was only on page ten of the sixty-page report.

"What do we have here?" she asked herself, pleased. Every other year, the good doctor went to Croatia without his family. According to his assets, he didn't own a home or property there, and no rental fee was shown after he arrived. She bookmarked the file for further details.

"I want a bath. Get Nurse Merriwether and only Nurse Merriwether."

She dragged her finger down the screen and opened the other doctor's profile. Dr. Espinoza.

"You have a call button."

"That I do."

He didn't say anything else, and remained in his chair. That was fine. She always got what she wanted, and she needed him out of the room.

Kana pulled a corner of a stitch. She wasn't an idiot, as the press liked to portray her, and she knew enough about anatomy, so she irritated a corner of her left side to add a wash of color. She waited for the fabric of the hospital tunic to absorb the blood, and then her stellar acting kicked in.

She jolted up, clutching her side as she rolled over and hit the nurse button. She added a few curse words, and to top it all off, she dredged up the incident of '11 from her mental Pandora's box.

She didn't remember much after the attack, but the spike of terror at the oxygen mask placed on her was enough to send her heart rate through the roof.

"Dr. Cohen," she gasped as Nurse Merriwether threw open the doors with such force that Kana wondered if she had a battering ram. Spencer moved with the nurse to Kana's bedside.

The nurse thrust the sheet away and a pool of blood the size of Kana's palm stained the top. Kana had hoped it would be bigger, but this would do.

Nurse Merriwether was plain, but her intellect and skill were far above average. Her hair was the color of brown grocery bags and was laid in a low bun against the nape of her neck. There were more uneven, graying stripes than Kana remembered.

She gritted her teeth and groaned meekly. With speed that only came with decades of experience, Nurse Merriwether adjusted the IVs and machines and wheeled Kana out in under a minute, an impressive feat given the size of the hospital bed.

Unfortunately, Spencer followed the wheeled gurney. Not great, but Kana eyed the double doors that led to the surgical and operating rooms.

"Stay," the nurse ordered as she tapped her keycard against the slim black box, and the doors swung open.

Spencer obeyed the nurse without a word.

The gurney rolled between the polished vinyl floors and the muted white overhead lights. Kana's muscles strained. Her heart rate ticked faster as she smelled the sanitized air. Her stomach somersaulted, and her heart twisted as if someone were trying to pull the organ through her ribs.

The doors sealed shut behind them, and Nurse Merriwether rolled Kana into a different hall before stopping the gurney with a dramatic heaving sigh.

"Kana." The head nurse clicked her tongue as pencil-filled brows arched with disapproval.

"You know how it is." Kana shrugged. "They want me here for two months."

The nurse tsked, but rolled Kana down the end of the hallway and into an empty operating room for privacy.

"Your wounds are strange, and you know how dangerous strange is around here." The nurse had bags under her eyes. Her voice echoed coldly in the nearly empty room. The lone operating table and glaring operating lights overhead cast large shadows across her prominent bridge bone.

"What do you want?" Kana asked as Nurse Merriwether opened a drawer and plucked out gloves and a suture kit. "You are tired. A vacation, time away from this place? Take the family and visit one of my homes."

Nurse Merriwether shook her head. "As lovely as that sounds, work isn't the problem. I couldn't leave, it helps keep me busy."

"Ah, is it the useless husband? I know superb divorce lawyers."

Nurse Meriwether laughed, a brittle sound. The deep frown lines etched in her cheeks deepened as she leaned over Kana's torso, shoving up the hospital top to expose the ripped stitches.

Kana remembered this joyful woman holding out lollipops and humoring Kana during her rounds when young Kana found herself bored in the hospital, which she'd visited more often than anyone should in their lifetime. Nurse Meriwether taught her important life skills, like the main bleeding areas on a person's body, how to stitch banana peels, and ventriloquy with the yellow and purple stuffed bunnies from the Pediatrics Wing.

"Keith's fine. He's too afraid to leave me, and when I'm ready to, I'll leave him."

Kana grinned. He should fear her. "You're too good for him."

Nurse Meriwether finished with Kana's torn stitch and slapped on a new bandage. "A compliment. How rare. What do you want?"

"Give me a ten-minute head start."

The nurse crossed her arms over her chest as she pushed back on the stool, drawing one leg over the other. The pursing of her lips screamed absolutely not.

"Seven minutes. With discretion about who assisted me, of course," Kana negotiated.

"You see the color of your skin." The nurse pointed to the edges of Kana's stomach, which was still an irregular black, like slick oil.

"And the doctors took samples and will run a million tests. The researchers are probably getting wet just thinking about the sample. I don't need to be here for any of that," Kana countered as she swung her legs around the side of the gurney.

"What about your bodyguard?"

Kana waved her hand as she stood up. The cold linoleum bit into her bare soles as she moved one foot forward, testing the limits of her body. "That's why I need some time. I'm just going to a safe location." Kana cautiously took three more steps. Not bad, her skin felt like a shedding snake's, but the pain was manageable, and that was the most important thing.

"Five minutes," the nurse countered and tossed the latex gloves into a trash can. "I've seen you grow up, Kana. I'm only allowing this because you are the most stubborn person, and if I say no, you'll do something even more dramatic. Use your contacts, be safe, and you'd better see a doctor at least twice a week."

With the head nurse's blessing, Kana rushed as fast as her body permitted. She was in the West Wing, since Nurse Meriwether had pushed her past operating rooms one through ten. There would be a locker room at the end of the hall if she made a right. She grinned as she pushed through the locker room door, snatched a white coat off the wall of coat hangers, and pulled on a face mask.

By the time the elevator digits flicked to level three, the alarm went off.

"Hold the door," Kana ordered as two hospital employees in purple scrubs came through a side door.

One girl obeyed Kana's command, squinting with confusion at the blinking light. "That's not the fire alarm," she said as Kana exited the hospital, and the door locked behind her.

She didn't have her phone or wallet. She could go to the loft Oliver had prepared, but that would be the first place they'd check. Vyolette lived close to the hospital. The socialite was rarely in her estate, but Kana was confident she could work magic with the posted guards. Or maybe she'd sneak in. There were at least three easy points of entry into Vyolette's home. Kana hurried down the last few flights of stairs.

"That's rather impressive. You work quickly," a voice said casually from her right side. Kana tried not to deflate. Spencer's voice contrasted with his rather typical appearance. A hint of a darker resonance colored his voice.

The surgical mask was blowing hot breath back up her nose, already fatigued after only a few minutes of walking. She didn't appreciate Spencer's lackadaisical air.

"I wanted to see how far you would go, but the doctors gave strict instructions that you need to stay in the hospital for another few weeks. Next time, pay attention to the security cameras. A doctor walking around barefoot is obvious." His chin lifted to point at the camera right below the door she stood under.

Kana yanked down the mask. She wasn't an idiot; she didn't expect he had immediate access to the secured cameras. That was her mistake, and one she wouldn't make again. "What do you want?" she asked.

"I want this to be over." He gestured to the space between them.

Kana lingered in the silence, trying to decipher what he meant, because despite his nonchalant stance and smooth features, the words were the exact opposite: strict and harsh.

"Instead of dragging me back into the hospital room kicking

and screaming, how about we visit the president? I'm well enough to walk, with a clear mind. What more could he want? The sooner I meet with him, the sooner this is over."

Spencer's face was surprisingly difficult to read. No softening of tension, ready to argue. "I'm driving."

Chapter Seven

She chose silence during the ride to the president's estate, content with angling her body to face him in the passenger seat. He was younger than she had initially estimated; outside the hospital lighting, and up close, his jawline appeared cleanly shaven, the rounded curve of his high cheekbone softened by a healthy layer of baby fat. If he went straight into the corps or was accepted into the military academy after secondary school, he had maybe two years in the field. Still a fresh recruit. Even if he'd been sent out on every assignment, he would have a low total of field hours. Which begged the question—what exactly made him special?

He handled her scrutiny well. Not a twitch in his hands on the wheel or a nervous flit of his eyes. Most people didn't like being blatantly stared at, and the itchy uneasiness was easy to spot in their involuntary ticks. He met her gaze at a stoplight. His eyes were a shade of brown, akin to her favorite rich suede jacket, with slits of dark moss woven throughout. "Do you have a question?"

"I don't," she said. The other reason she'd focused on Spencer was to distract herself from the scenery passing by.

Beyond the tinted car windows, if she differentiated the

moving blobs of color, she'd see the neatly trimmed bushes and hedges along the street dividers. The blue-paneled rectangular street signs were mounted on the exterior of the buildings, and there wasn't a single soda can, stubbed cigarette butt, or crumbled fast food bag on the sidewalk. The influential district had a painted and glossed face, inviting anyone to stop and take a picture of its glory. Dubbed the cleanest city in the world two years ago, Kana wished they could peel back that pristine face and peek into the rotting muscles and rusted iron. Oshiya brought about heartburn, an ache that made her squirm.

Spencer caught her movement. "You had a strong reaction when you first awoke in the hospital. Does being here bother you that much?"

Kana silently laughed. "Does a bird wish to be caged? A ridiculous question. I have my reasons for not wanting to be here, just as I'm sure you have reasons for being delegated as my escort, and it must have been an abrupt order. You haven't been in Oshiya for too long."

"Why would you say that?"

Kana smirked. "The most obvious is your tan. You've been baking in the sun for at least two months, and I can't imagine a field officer visiting tanning booths." Oshiya was on the cusp of leaving spring, the perpetual warm rain and typhoon season near the exit doors. She doubted he was off on an early summer holiday, lounging on Myrtos Beach, browning like a nut. "The other tip-off was that when you handed me the cup of water to spit the toothpaste, you pressed your left hand under your extended right hand, and when the new chief medical officer came in, you placed your hand over your chest, all small actions you've picked up being somewhere in the Middle East. I hope you at least tried Knafeh."

"That's . . ." He was lost for words. "Perceptive."

Kana lifted her chin, preening her feathers. "Don't hold back your utter surprise."

"But you're wrong," he finished.

The tip of her tongue pressed against the back of her teeth, a snake curled and ready to strike.

"You were mostly right. I was away, but returned to Oshiya over a month ago. I've been landscaping my childhood home. That's maintained the tan."

"It must have been urgent if you were pulled out of the field. A national security threat? Assassination attempt?"

"It was. My parents needed me, and it's been years since I was home for Aurhysen."

Aurhysen. The word blossomed, a gentle vibrating hum from Spencer's throat. Kana forgot about the celebration. She hadn't heard anyone even speak of Aurhysen in years; it was one of the two holidays reserved from the old traditions of the dead, original inhabitants of Oshiya.

"The parades seemed more extravagant, and the light show near the harbor was more beautiful than I remember. I forgot how it felt to be in my childhood living room, with the coffee table and its wobbly leg, everyone together crafting their orbs. Fresh bread baking in the oven, the stew simmering in the large pot on the stove. It was an unusually cloudless day and night, ideal weather for Aurhysen." Spencer trailed off.

"I didn't ask for your life story." Kana cut in before he could weave any more of his reminiscing and turned away from him. She didn't like his gooey-sweet sentimental family traditions, as they contrasted with her nonexistent ones. Only once did she remember standing in a private boat with a nanny, witnessing the highlight of the Aurhysen holiday. The bobbing, glowing glass orbs looked like dollops of light, pushing and pulling further out to sea while the floating lanterns rose in the sky. There was one distinct moment when the endless horizon truly became a black infinite line as light on earth was highlighted by the drifting orbs, the sky alight with hopes and prayers lifting to the heavens in the paper lanterns.

Josephine and, by extension, herself, celebrated holidays when the Ambrose presence was required for galas or a public appearance; otherwise, Kana had spent her days in the glass and marble estate.

They finally left the main district and headed up the curving valley to a less densely populated area. The main roadway was freshly paved, the only smooth and unblemished part of the smaller, outlying suburb, with long concrete and cinder block homes. The spindling roads, shooting off the pristine main road leading to the compact residential areas, were dry, cracked, and pitted. The lush greenery was gone until the car moved up a hill and through the valley pass, where the presidential estate was nestled. Spencer pulled up to the first of the two security gates and rolled down his window.

"Do you have an appointment?"

"Kana Ambrose is here to meet with the president," Spencer announced, handing the guard his driver's license.

The guard leaned down and moved closer to the window. Kana arched her eyebrow at the guard.

"You're new," she said, and blew a kiss.

The guard straightened as his cheeks pinked, and the tall gates split.

"You enjoy flustering people," Spencer commented. The gravel crunched under the tires as he turned around the obscenely large fountain and up the driveway.

Kana didn't dignify that with a response; it was a comment on her character, and she didn't have problems with the observation. It was fun to see people's reactions. Spencer stopped at the front of the rectangular building inspired by Georgian architecture, an echo from the time the British invaded, before they were shoved out and Oshiya was conquered by the French for a short stint. A dozen staff were lined up like servants from the Regency Era, with one staff member on each step, feet angled toward the car, and hands neatly folded in front of them, suggesting that the guard had alerted the estate.

Spencer let out a low whistle. "The welcoming committee?"

She couldn't stop sinking further into the chair. A tightness constricted her chest as the fight-or-flight response kicked into action. Past Kana's overconfidence was a real bastard, and now that her current self faced the presidential estate, she hated this feeling of weakness.

A man in a pressed pants suit, with a collar that encircled the neck and a single diamond cutout that dipped between the collarbones, a fashion nod to the traditional collared tunics, bent and opened the passenger door, a gloved white hand to his chest. She sucked a silent breath through her teeth as a familiar woman appeared in front of her.

"Miss Ambrose," the all-torso woman said indifferently.

"Laura," Kana said curtly, and wrangled her composure, sliding the heavy mask in place and letting the butler help her out of the car. The older woman had the tight face of someone who maintained strict dermatology appointments and, while well executed, cosmetics couldn't stop the aging process entirely, leaving an artificial face behind.

"It was entirely unnecessary to bring everyone to greet me. Dismissed." Kana continued with a wave of her hand.

The staff glanced at Laura with silent questions, as if they weren't sure whose orders to follow. Laura, the president's executive assistant and right-hand woman, or Kana Ambrose. Laura gave a minuscule nod, and they retreated up the stairs, their footsteps perfectly in sync.

"We heard you returned to the country. Will you be staying in the guest estate?" Laura inquired.

Kana barked a laugh. The sound was strangled because of the constricting bandages around her torso. The exertion bounced through her body, causing the world to fade around the edges, and blood soared to the crown of her head. A large hand pressed against her back, between her shoulder blades, to steady her. She instinctively stepped forward until the warm touch was gone.

"That's the funniest joke I've heard in a long time." Kana wiped a tear from her eye.

The pinched mouth and narrowed eyes were always a delight. Laura's stink face never got old.

"If he thinks I'm going to be staying on the presidential estate, not only is he delusional, but he's overstepping his boundaries. I'm here because he demanded my presence in the White Room."

Laura coughed, and her icy eyes slid to Spencer, just half a meter beside Kana. "I was unaware he requested to use the White Room," she said in a perfected, low whisper voice. Not even Laura knew? That was surprising.

"Would you like to freshen up or have some breakfast? He's busy at the moment, but his schedule can accommodate a meeting in about two hours."

"Bring fresh coffee and clothes to the guest room in the East Wing. I'll be in the Teal Room."

Kana climbed the steps, ignoring the repeated skewering of pain, and focused on the sensation of the stiff hospital fabric against her skin as she moved beyond the circular entryway and made an immediate left.

The guest room was, unfortunately, at the end of the hallway, tucked in the far back corner. She stared at the elongated hall as if trick mirrors were warping the space to make it endless. Her skin broke out into a cold sweat. This was a familiar hallway, one she had run through when she was a child. Her socked feet had slid across the polished wood like an ice rink, as she dodged the stiffly dressed adults.

"You don't need to force yourself." Spencer's voice popped her nostalgia. He was a respectable distance from her, trailing like an obedient dog.

She forced her shoulders back and moved forward. The first few meters, she gritted her teeth and mentally told her leg to lift and slowly step down. She refused to distribute her weight against the walls or grab the edge of a table or one of the ornate vases that stood to the height of her collarbones. What felt like ten years later, she made it to the room, sweating profusely, closing the door in Spencer's face. She collapsed on the closed toilet seat and pressed her head into her palms as she breathed and waited for the spots to settle.

There was no blood seeping through the bandages, but the flesh under her splayed hand was hot. She splashed water on her face and stared at herself. This was not exactly her best moment. Her skin was a pasty green, her lips peeled like a drying tangerine. Vogue wouldn't be making any calls anytime soon.

She rubbed her eyes; the whites blushed red, the dark sagging bags under the delicate tissue became more prominent. Her fingers itched for the red eyeliner, the wand of concealer, the compact of blush, her war paint to transform into Kana Ambrose, not this reflected disaster.

Neatly folded at the foot of the bed were sweats and a hoodie. She kicked off the hospital pants.

"Miss Ambrose," a feminine voice called after a polite knock.

"Enter," Kana said while she hauled the cotton sweats over her hips.

A young woman—barely a woman, she looked shy of twenty—carrying a silver platter with a teapot, a bowl of sugar, and a tiny cream jar, entered.

"If that's not coffee, I don't want to see it."

The girl balked as she paused in the doorway, her torso leaning away from Kana. "The gentleman outside sent back the coffee."

Of course he did.

"Go back, refill the teapot with green tea, put a shot of espresso in the milk container, and in your pocket carry one of those cans of double-shot espressos I know they keep in the kitchens." Kana shooed the attendant away.

Six minutes later, the girl returned, minus the creamer container, because, naturally, Spencer checked the pots and containers first. "Perfect," Kana clapped her hands as she popped open the can and was about to take a swig when she noticed the label—decaf. She balked. On principle alone, she wouldn't drink this abomination.

"He asked if you told me to do anything else besides switch out the tea." The assistant bumbled nervously.

"You can't lie?"

"He's a bit—" She paused, and her face reddened. The woman was close to Kana's age, and here she was blushing like a teenage girl caught making eye contact with her high school crush. Pathetic. She dismissed the girl and called for Anne, the executive chef, instructing her to send over fresh coffee through the servant staircase from the East Wing while she sent for Lawrence, one of the oldest groundskeepers, to sneak a thermos through the window. Her attempt was thwarted, and she stared at the empty tray with a note. "Sincerest apologies - A.L." was scripted perfectly with Chef Anne's initials. Kana squashed the note and collapsed on the bed. The battle for coffee wasn't over. As she thought of other ways to trick the coffee dictator, the exertion from walking took a stronger toll than she imagined.

The rotary phone on the bedside table rang, and Laura gave succinct instructions to meet at the elevator in the eastern corridor. Kana walked out of the room, ignoring Spencer and the smugness wafting off him—the bastard.

She straightened her face much like smoothing a napkin over her lap. The estate was rather quiet. Normally, people ran around with papers, folders, tablets, or all three, speaking through their little dangling EarPods that were like extensions of their ears. A man and woman in identical suits spoke softly to one another, a thermos in each of their hands. The woman noticed her first. "Miss Ambrose," she said politely. Her ID badge was tucked into the front pocket of her blazer. The man failed to hide his surprise.

"Miss Ambrose," he exclaimed. "What an honor to meet you. My god, the stories about what happened at the lake. The last we heard, you were in the hospital, being treated for severe injuries. The press does like to exaggerate." He spoke with such casualty, like gossiping among friends. Everyone looked at him as if his eyeballs had rolled out of his sockets.

"Who the hell are you?" Kana asked with a curl of her lips.

He realized his mistake and blubbered a string of apologies. The woman thankfully led her coworker away. Despite Oliver's assurance that PR was controlled, she needed to call Tanisha and confirm because it seemed like things were not at all handled.

"I heard you were here," Laura said, appearing out of nowhere. How she managed to walk without her heels clicking away was a real feat. "Come, he's waiting for you." Laura led them to the elevator, with Spencer dutifully following.

"He's coming?" Kana didn't realize the invitation was extended to the young man.

Laura's dark eyes moved from Kana to the space off to her right, where Spencer stood. "Yes, he requested both of you." She hit a series of buttons: Floor 1, Floor 2, Floor 2, Basement 1, and the emergency button.

Chapter Eight

The back of Kana's mind tingled at the prospect of seeing the White Room. Josephine had frequented the highly secure vaulted room numerous times, and if anyone knew how often Josephine visited the White Room, it would only add fuel to the old rumor of a perceived relationship with the president. When he was re-elected four years ago, his campaign opponent started a lovely rumor that Kana was a product of his and Josephine's affair, which was ridiculous given one look at Kana, who lacked European features. Both Josephine and the president were native Oshiyans, with slim, tapered features and a mix of sharper cheekbones and protruding brow bones from their western ancestor's repeated conquests of the island. Physically, Kana inherited none of Josephine's attributes unless she smiled, her likeness reflected in the curves of her eyes, cheeks, and lips. Yet, people claimed that the president's great-great-great-great-grandfather on his father's side was Japanese, as if the recessive physical characteristics had presented themselves in Kana. The second and more popularized rumor was that Kana wasn't Josephine's biological daughter, but rather that she was adopted from a scientist colleague. Another claimed she had been kidnapped abroad, another that she was a

surrogate daughter, or Josephine's third cousin. The people loved
to speculate.

Kana gave little thought to the rumors. She knew the truth.
After watching variations in the picturesque families moving in
and out of her life—the stiff husbands with one arm around the
trim waists of their wives, the other hand clasped over the
shoulder of the child—young Kana looked around to find herself
alone, and wondered where her father was. Before the idea of
genetic testing and ancestry festered and made its way to the tip of
Kana's nine-year-old tongue, Josephine left a folder on the closed
lid of the grand piano.

There were three pictures. First, Josephine on the far right,
standing shoulder to shoulder beside two young men, the three of
them in a variation of straight jeans and loose t-shirts. She had a
thick textbook pressed against her chest, her stoic face stared at
the camera. In the second picture, Josephine was among a group
of seven, probably three years had passed, and she was only the
second woman in the gathering. The group was posed on the
great plains of Mongolia. And the third was a picture of the same
group of adults crammed inside a hotel room with laptops and
papers covering every surface, bottles and ashtrays full of broken
cigarette butts on the windowsill and atop books. It wasn't hard
to notice there was one man in all three pictures.

Her father was a man of no great importance, Josephine
explained; his scientific rigor was acceptable, but he lacked inge-
nuity and original thought. He felt he couldn't raise a child, and
Josephine had little money to her name. A.E. Potentia wouldn't
be released until Kana's first birthday, and the empire barely had a
foundation. Josephine wanted to feast on the world, swallow it
whole until emptiness wasn't a word she knew. He, by comparison, was meek and settled for a mundane position at a second-tier
university. There were additional documents: Kana's birth certificate, hospital records, and invoices and research papers; it was a
paper trail to prove Josephine's involvement with Takeshi.

When Kana was seventeen and her distrust in Josephine hardened to a diamond form, she learned how easy it was to falsify records with the right contacts and the right amount of money. She left for a quick trip to Japan under the guise of accepting an invitation from a prominent figure's daughter. The Oshiyan government wouldn't let her out of the country otherwise.

Takeshi was exactly as Josephine described, and the stark truth gutted her. He had a head of thick hair, the edges turning white, and a stalky, slouched frame dressed in polyblend black slacks and a white button-down. He was identical to all the other men, down to the way the thin cigarette dangled from the corner of his mouth. His face was a passive haze, the look of a person who had accepted a cyclical, mundane life, until his droopy eyes caught someone across the street. A slow warmth like the caress of the first minutes of dawn crept across his face, and Kana saw fondness, happiness, love, and all those gooey emotions poets scribbled on about. He held up his hand, and a girl greeted him. A long sheet of black hair blocked most of her face from sight, but by her lanky frame and uniform, she had to be his daughter or someone of equal importance. Kana left. There was nothing for her there.

———

Tap, tap, tap. Nausea rolled through Kana like the dense morning fog, the triplet sounds triggering the memory of dull nails tapping against the butt of a gun. Kana diverted her attention to the pearlescent color of Laura's trimmed nail as it moved across the screen of her tablet, and the smell of the woman's dark vanilla perfume. The elevator landed smoothly on the destination level, and with a sharp ding, the silver doors opened to an empty beige room, a room that could be any doctor's office.

"Exit this room, make a right and at the end of the hallway, there will be security, then a car waiting. Expect to be blindfolded," Laura said as Kana and Spencer exited the elevator and the doors softly closed behind them.

As Laura said, there was a security detail, a man and woman lounging in swivel chairs with flaking leather at the end of the hall, which led to a compact room with a boxy X-ray machine and a full body scanner taking up most of the space. Beyond them were two frosted sliding doors. Security was not as extensive as she thought, maybe because they knew her face. They ran her biometrics—fingerprints and optical scans—then she stood in a more advanced version of the body scanners used in airports.

The woman waved Kana through after one brief look at the machine. There was little to hide in the sweatshirt and sweatpants. She wasn't even wearing underwear. But the woman held up her hand. "The pen." Kana clicked her tongue as she reached into the sweats pocket and tossed the ballpoint pen at the security guard.

Spencer removed his jacket, the gun holster strapped around his broad shoulders, two knives strapped on each ankle, and a thin spool of wire from his back pocket. Kana stood at the end with a *Really?* expression.

"What is this?" The guard held a vial about the length of her pointer finger and containing a clear liquid.

"Arsenic," Spencer answered without a blink.

"And this?" The other guard held a small pouch and shook out the contents into his palm. The steel nuts and bolts reflected in his hand.

"What it looks like. Nuts and bolts."

Kana internally rolled her eyes. Only Idus carried around random projectiles like that.

"Any explosives on him? He's got every other weapon. Do you have one of those trick cap teeth?" Kana drawled as Spencer stepped into the scanning machine.

"Clear," the woman analyzing the machine image announced. Her guarded eyes locked on Spencer.

"You can collect your items when you return from the room."

She pushed open the door, revealing an underground parking lot where a black, four-door car awaited them.

Kana eyed the driver, a lanky forty-something-year-old with an unfortunate receding hairline. He had an apologetic smile as he held up two blindfolds. She gulped, unable to stop her reaction, as she forced her hands to unclench. Her eyes swept from the driver to Spencer and the tinted windowed car. The paranoia and whispering voice told her this was a setup. *Never get into a car without a weapon*; had she become so soft that she'd convinced herself that life was normal? There were three men; she was outnumbered. Hell, Spencer could take her. This was a hoax, another ploy to get her. The loose gathering collar of the hoodie felt tight. It shouldn't, the bulky material hung loose on her body, but she was suffocating. She didn't realize she'd taken a step back, too busy berating herself for not snatching a scalpel from the hospital until Spencer's hand touched her back to still her.

"You are safe." His tone was not comforting, not in the soft way a parent might speak to a child. He simply stated a fact, and that was enough to keep Kana's initial snarky remark at bay.

The driver tied the blindfold over her eyes. She bit the inside of her cheek while Spencer stepped closer, until the warmth from his body seeped into her back. At that moment, he placed a small flat pocketknife into her hand, and parted from her. Kana was slightly impressed and made a note to figure out how he got that under security's nose.

The journey to the elusive White Room was exhausting. She lost track of how many times they changed cars and drivers. At one point, she swore the driver merged on and off the same highway at least five times. Eventually, the car stopped for the last time. The deafening rush of cars above blared as soon as the door opened. The whoosh of the wind as it tunneled through the underpass nearly knocked Kana over and then nothing, all sensory stimulation ceased. Someone brought them inside, and instructed the removal of their blindfolds after sealing the door behind them.

"Finally," Kana muttered, one hand ripped the blindfold off, while the other hand molded around the knife hidden in her pocket. In a fluid motion she could flick the blade out and smash it into the first person that dared to touch her.

The one light fixture was bright enough to burn her eyes. They were in a short hallway with gray concrete, no ceiling or floor tiles, and one white wooden door on the other end. One sniff told her it was *bocote* wood, and probably Oshiyan *bocote* wood.

Kana twisted the doorknob and held her breath. Would it be an inner sanctum with dark artifacts, a pretentious bookcase with first edition books behind glass and temperature-controlled shelves, or a dragon's lair with a collection of shiny gems, gold, and priceless artifacts?

"This is underwhelming," she said as soon as she crossed the threshold.

A scratchy record player played Seimon Yoh, one of Oshiya's most prevalent jazz revolutionists. The room was the size of a modest entertaining space, with a blend of contemporary and classic styled furniture pieces, two antique leather armchairs facing a velvet couch. She didn't like the modern art fixtures flanking the electric fireplace. Over the mantel hung an original painting by Davidson Buchaaun, a contemporary Oshiya artist from the early '90s. Fitting the concept of a ghost room that moved locations. There were no bookcases, the white walls had a few framed art pieces, and the only other large item was the desk at the other end of the room. And there he was.

"Kana." The president beamed, pushing himself out of the chair behind the grand desk. "My dear, you haven't aged at all." He crossed the space with open arms.

Kana couldn't say the same. He'd lost his sun-kissed tan, and it seemed he spent less and less time outside. His hair was more salt than pepper, and thinning. He'd softened around the edges, expanding outwards like a half filled water balloon.

A hard plastic smile locked into place as she met him halfway, letting the knife sink into the fabric pocket. There was an air about him that was hard to pin down. When she was younger, she described him, with the devotion of the British loving the Queen, as close to regal. Now older and wiser and able to see through people's personas, she was immune to his charisma.

"Victor," Kana said, catching a flash of annoyance in his gaze at the use of his first name and the omission of his title. A lingering reactive recoil caused her to slide into herself for a moment, but he insisted she use his name growing up. She straightened her posture; she was only doing what he requested, after all.

They hugged for a brief moment, the type of hug where each person consciously tries to have as few parts of their bodies touching as possible. The smell of his spicy cologne sent her on a high-speed rail of memories, smears of color and silhouettes indistinguishable from one another.

She stepped back as he turned his attention to Spencer. "Nolan," the president said. He walked around Kana to where the bodyguard stood at the end of the burgundy sofa. The president clapped the younger man on the shoulder, the gesture both familiar and a power play. Nolan? Nolan Spencer. The name rolled silently in her mouth. He looked more like a Spencer than a Nolan.

"Mr. President," Spencer said with a salute, a hand to his heart as he bowed before they shook hands.

"I trust Kana hasn't caused you too much trouble," the President said breezily.

Spencer placed his hands behind his back, and his posture fell into that of a good soldier standing at attention before his commanding officer. "She has not."

Kana rolled her eyes. It was always fun when people talked

about her when she was in the same room. "Was it necessary to hire a shadow?" Kana asked, deciding to start the conversation with Spencer's abrupt appearance.

"There is much to discuss. Come sit." The president gestured to the armchairs across from Spencer's claim on the sofa, blatantly ignoring her question. "I would offer drinks, but," he paused as he looked at Kana, who was injured, and then at Spencer, who was on bodyguard duty and needed a clear head. She alternated her weight from foot to foot, not liking how the air felt stagnant, as if she were in an airplane, sealed away with recycled oxygen.

"How long has it been?" he asked, one leg crossing over the other, lifting the hem of his tailored pants to reveal socks with Oshiya's flags embroidered into the fabric.

Kana ignored the offer to sit. Instead she stayed where she was, keeping the well-worn mocha leather armchair between them. "Only two years," Kana said, not nearly long enough.

"Feels like a decade." He sighed whimsically as he leaned into the seat, his eyes warming as he went to memory land. "Do you remember—"

"I'm not here to reminisce," Kana cut in.

The president tensed, and a shock went through the atmosphere as he did so. Maybe she pushed the limits a little too much, but she refused to apologize. "The kidnappers were ex-military, American Marines, and they wanted to see Josephine," she said. "Why would a team of Users need to see her? While it was an unfortunate situation, I don't need a bodyguard and haven't needed one in years. He is dismissed."

He loosely interlaced his fingers as he set them on his lap, while the corner of his lip ticked. "He's going to follow you until the task is done," the president said in a polite, political tone. The lower half of his face pulled taut to mask his displeasure.

He had a task for her? Kana held back the urge to touch the scar tissue in her cheek.

"I'm not at your disposal to assign tasks to," she said with as little snark as she could muster. She wasn't a soldier he could order and hand off duties to.

"You are a citizen of Oshiya, and your president is requesting your help. Call it a favor if that appeals to you more," he continued, with a touch of sweetness in his voice. Kana's skin prickled, her body coiling tighter and tighter. He wouldn't dare to blackmail her. He possessed too much power to stoop that low; it was beneath him. Good thing Oshiya wasn't a dictatorship. She held back that particular comment with great effort. She seesawed with the notion of outright refusing and walking away, or maintaining the amicable false pretense.

"When was the last time you heard from Josephine?" he asked with an expectant gaze in his golden eyes.

Kana's shoulders locked uncomfortably. "I like to keep our relationship nonexistent."

"She hasn't reached out in an obscure way?" he pressed.

Kana's mouth drooped into a scowl. "If she did, I missed it. I'm not her keeper. If you've brought me here to discuss Josephine, you've brought the wrong person. Oliver is more helpful. Apparently, she's still ordering him around the world."

"She's been missing. No one on her estate has seen her, and the labs have no footage of her in any of the facilities."

"She probably went on a research retreat, or is locked away in one of her think tanks. Give her a few days, she'll come out of hiding." Kana brushed him off with a scoff. She liked snooping through Josephine's research, and if she could locate one of these special think tanks, it was like finding gold at the end of a rainbow. The thing was, Josephine only worked in her labs when it was time to rigorously test her ideas. The woman spent most of her time brainstorming, working out the parameters around her theory, and while she was brilliant, she was not a computer and needed to visualize and scribble down the thoughts that came from her speeding mind. Josephine was strict. She only stayed in one vaulted think tanks for twenty-four hours before she cleaned house and moved on, too paranoid about others finding her brain dumps.

"My dear, she has been missing for over a month. When I say no footage in any facility, I mean all facilities worldwide and all of her properties. She hasn't left the country."

Kana was about to ask how he could be sure, but he had the military at his fingertips. With far more resources and manpower, he could thoroughly look at over a hundred possible locations, yet he still couldn't find a trace of her. Kana forced her mouth to remain in a flat line as the edges pushed, wanting to pucker. If all his resources couldn't find Josephine, Kana was the last resort. Her eyes zeroed in on his mask of pleasantness.

"And you think I can find her?" Kana asked. What an absurd request.

"You're the only one that can." He certainly said that with a great deal of effort, as if stooping so low as to ask her for help was abhorrent. "She was working on something new, groundbreaking. We were going to have a meeting in this very room, but she never appeared." He spoke with one hundred percent confidence, which only caused more doubt for Kana.

A jolt of pain made her lean forward. She fought to keep her hands at her sides as she nearly reached to grip the back of the loveseat for support. Fucking hell, she should have sat. The abdominal flutters weren't tender anymore, rather sawing pain, but she couldn't concede and sit now.

"And you think someone kidnapped her?" she asked, ignoring Spencer, who subtly moved closer to her. Spencer observed her, somehow able to keep his weighty gaze un-burdensome. It was common for men to look at her, and it never failed to make the hairs at the nape of her neck raise.

"It's a possibility, but slim. You and I both know if someone were able to snatch Josephine Ambrose, they would be making ridiculous demands like my resignation, the death of monarchy, and to rule of the country."

Kana agreed. There was no way someone wouldn't claim the kidnapping.

The president allowed silence to fill the room like liquid, spreading into every crevice of space between them. Kana's agitated gaze scanned his lightly wrinkled forehead and down the long slope of his nose. The tiny mole under his left eye annoyed Kana, as it was placed right in line with his pupil. Of all things, his mole had a rather popular fan account on social media. Ridiculous.

He wanted something else. Sure, Kana believed Josephine had discovered something. Aside from creating the revolutionary synthetic drug, she contributed to smaller scientific research outside of genetics and virology to secure her second PhD, and was working on a third PhD in entomology. The woman never stopped researching. Scientific discovery consumed her and left space for nothing else to occupy her mind or heart.

Josephine went off the radar occasionally, but not completely. The obsessed researcher needed her equipment. Even if she went off to the Alps or Mount Kilimanjaro, she'd need a spot for her centrifuge, electrophoresis analysis equipment, chemicals, and a dozen other gadgets that cost fortunes. There was always a money trail somewhere.

"And you have no idea what project she was working on," Kana clarified.

"Officially, she was looking at cancer cells." Naturally, Kana was sure Josephine dabbled in actual work that could help the population, but it wasn't for humanity's sake; Josephine could create a biomedical weapon if she wanted.

"Unofficially," the president tilted his chin up, the overhead light no longer casting partial shadows over the planes of his face, "creating a second version of A.E. Potentia."

Chapter Nine

"How loyal is Josephine?" Kana asked in a measured tone. In a world where the concept of black and white ruled, people's perceptions faded those stark colors to tones of gray. Josephine expected loyalty, and despised it when the notion was a malleable concept to other people. Kana caught the president's hesitation and the twitch of his brows. He was much like Josephine in that way, yin and yang in values, and not tolerant of others mucking the lines.

"She's loyal. Even when other countries offered her deals beyond your wildest imagination, she turned them all down, to stay here, our home, Oshiya." He punctuated *here* with a stab of his pointer finger into the arm of the chair. The odor of patriotism seeped out of his pores, but he was right to an extent. Menial monetary gains didn't sway Josephine.

Fine. If he didn't question her loyalty, they were back to square one. "Again, why do you think I would know where she is? You have a country with more resources."

"And I've exhausted them. The only clue we have is this." The president made his way to his desk, and when his back was turned, Kana flicked a piece of hair over her tense shoulders. The deep tissue ache from holding her tense frame was nearly unbearable. Her eyes caught Spencer standing by the curved snout or odd loop of the contemporary statue, standing at attention like a silent relic of a knight in armor. If this was such a private conversation, to the extent the White Room was required, Spencer had exceptionally high clearance. Oliver would need to send over a profile on Nolan Spencer.

The president unlocked a drawer and set an intricately painted wooden box on the center of his desk. As she approached the object, she attempted to maintain her gait as naturally as possible through the mounting pain as the pain medication evaporated out of her system.

Pearlescent accents highlighted the painted folk-style floral pattern, and the intricate lines of the gilded leaves were faded and chipped.

"Do you recognize this box?" the president asked, scrutinizing Kana's face.

Kana didn't, and she said as much. The room was silent as the needle from the record player lifted and the record silently spun.

"One of Josephine's last transactions before all her bank movements ceased was to a security deposit vault."

"You obviously have no problems with breaking into a person's secure bank. I hope you had a warrant," Kana said. Her eyes moved from the president and back to the painted box. "Crack it open."

The president ignored her first comment and opened the wooden box, removing a small square sheet of paper. A doodle, so terribly drawn that only a child could have accomplished such a poor rendering. The purple ink had aged and faded to pink in some areas. A picture she didn't recall doing, but that didn't mean it wasn't hers. She used to always doodle and sneak drawings around the house, research labs, or between pages of Josephine's notebooks. This was why they assumed she could help them, all because of a childish drawing found in a security deposit box?

"I want you to look for her, and I believe this is a clue. Think of it as a scavenger hunt."

A scavenger hunt which Josephine had planned didn't amuse her, and she certainly didn't want to participate. "I want to go to my house in San Diego."

The president set the drawing back inside the box and shook his head. "Unfortunately, you are grounded. The lake incident has sparked some claims that Ambrose Inc. has orchestrated the entire hostage situation."

Kana's face broke like an egg cracking over hot oil. There was too much to unpack in those few sentences. *Grounded* was synonymous with being locked in the ivory tower of the city. After the time an extreme fringe group in northern Russia had gone after the Ambrose family, authorities issued the grounding orders. Then there were the researchers in China trying to infiltrate Josephine's labs, or the cartels in South America—someone somewhere in some country was out to get them, and the president was always quick to slap that grounded label. And now there was an accusation that Ambrose conspired in the hostage situation.

"I was assured the press was handled," Kana said, crossing her arms across her chest.

"It was, but it would seem someone leaked that the attack wasn't random, and your sudden appearance put the other people at risk."

"Are they victim blaming me?" She couldn't stop the bite in her question as her blood stirred, cranking in temperature with every heartbeat. The press was a consistent pain in her ass, eager to paint her in any bad light. She could do no right in their eyes.

The president remained neutral, not at all bothered by the news. "The family that was killed"—that's right, there had been kids, and the snuffing of young lives had a greater impact on Kana than the adults—"were important politicians, and the second couple, whose remains were found in their cabin, had ties to important pharmaceutical moguls. Allow the media to settle down before anyone demands your extraction."

Extraction. The final word resounded like the chime of the twelfth hour. "That's a load of bullshit! Who would even dare press charges?" Kana slammed her hands on the president's desk. Her vision melted into white light, and her flushed face could have been mistaken for anger, instead of pain.

"It's best if you stay on our soil. Help us by looking for your mother. For now, Josephine's disappearance hasn't been noticed. Spencer will be accompanying you in case another fringe group attempts another attack. It's best to have one of our elite close by." The president's eyes moved to the audience in the room.

She needed to know how bad the press situation was. Out of reflex, her hands went to her pocket in search of her phone, a list of demands for Oliver ready in her mind, because the situation was not at all handled; it was hemorrhaging. The abrupt movement sent searing hot pain throughout her body. She needed to leave the room in the next five minutes. She had reached her limit. There was no way in hell she would pass out in front of the president.

"What do I get for this favor?" The question passed through clenched teeth.

"In return for finding Josephine, you'll get a carte blanche."

An explosion, as if the big bang reduced bits of her brain matter into specs of dust. She must have blacked out from the pain, because she was processing his promise with multiple system errors before she came to her senses.

A carte blanche. Now, Kana was interested.

The president smiled, knowing that she wanted this carte blanche, and badly. "Spencer is bearing witness to my offer. Anything you want within reason, naturally."

"My newly acquired shadow could die at any moment."

Kana picked up the fountain pen stabbed into a diamond block on the president's desk and wrote, *If Kana Ambrose locates*

Josephine Ambrose, she will be given a carte blanche from the president of Oshiya.

"No contest. If we involve lawyers to make this an official contract, how long do you think it would take before we settle on agreeable terms?" Kana asked, and while she had waves of pain, sweat gathering like the misting Pacific coast, and her mind fraying, she was coherent enough to know she needed this promise documented. "Sign." She flicked the pen to the president. His lips turned in an amused smile, one a father would offer to his pouting child.

With a swish of his wrist, he signed. "No contest. I agree to your terms."

"I'll consider your offer." She was in no rush to begin this ridiculous search for Josephine. If she were grounded, fine. She'd entertain herself in the meantime. "If I'm going on a wild goose chase, I need to be out of the hospital."

The president smiled as he closed the box and slid it to Kana.

"And if I need to fly to London because she left a postcard of Big Ben?"

He smirked. "Arrangements will be made, but I have full confidence that she hasn't left the country, and whatever game she is playing at is staged here. It's good to see you," he said, ending their meeting. She didn't extend the same fake pleasantry. This conversation was over. Instead, she inclined her head and took her exit. She heard a faint movement as Spencer took her place before the president. She wanted to look over her shoulder. What silent conversation were they having right now? But if she looked, it would indicate she cared. She didn't care. She was suspicious. There was a distinct difference. The president claimed Spencer's presence was for protection, which may be true, but he was also her watchdog, making sure Kana followed through with the president's request.

They left the White Room, and thank god, the route back required two car changes. The security returned Spencer's weapons in a plastic tray. He held out the painted box for Kana to hold. She didn't take it. If she wanted the box, she would have taken it. Instead, she watched him scowl at her as he set the box on the table's edge and geared back up.

A sharp pain caused her to stumble as she entered the elevator. "Hospital," was the only word Spencer said as they stood at opposite ends, the space between them vast and almost silent except for Kana's hiccuped breaths. The handrail was slick with her sweat as she gripped the metal bar, slouching to sag into the wall. She had to focus on anything other than the pain. Her mind scrambled for something to distract her until she arrived at the hospital with the sweet drugs.

Josephine. That name was too easy, a bomb trigger over the past few years Kana had managed to dodge, but now, her name cropped up like an infestation. Among the stained images of gilded homes, trimmed gardens, and trips around the world, the first real memory Kana had was sneaking into Josephine's lab, which seemed appropriate. Kana was curious about her mother, who spent more time in the chrome and white rooms than with her. Tucked between the lush headboard and the mattress was a compact notebook where Kana scribbled and drew doodles, and on one page was a list of names, a ranking of sorts: Oliver, Nanny, Chef, Thursday Tutor, and it was a toss-up between the personal driver and Josephine for the fifth spot. She must have begged Oliver to bring her to the lab; there was no way she could have made it to the undisclosed location. Once there, she found herself in a fishbowl with two walls made from the glossy whiteboard coating. Scribbles of formulas, half-formed ideas, most of the time just single words bloomed in random areas. The center of the space had a giant square counter with sleek machines, some bulky, bigger than pint-sized Kana.

A hand that felt like it descended from a giant in the fairytales that her nanny read gripped the back of her neck. "You slinky little kitten."

Kana squeezed her eyelids, shoving away Josephine's shadowed voice. The rapidly drying cement of exhaustion made it harder to keep herself upright. She needed a little pick-me-up, a shot of energy. Curious, she tapped into her internal battery pack.

That was a mistake.

Crippling pain raked throughout her body, as if a machine gun had just fired dozens of rounds into her sack of flesh and bones. She blacked out and came back just as quickly. The handrail was no longer in her grasp. A flat surface pressed against her cheek. The lifting stopped, and a slow, loud alarm blared. Then the momentum continued, and a disembodied voice broke through the alarm. "Is everything alright?"

"Get an ambulance," Spencer responded, voice not inflecting at all, cool as a cucumber.

"Kana, move your arms." He spoke clearly and patiently, not soft and gentle, because she wouldn't be able to hear him if he did with the turbulence of blood adding pressure to her skull. A hand pried her arm away, one she didn't realize she'd wrapped around whatever was causing her pain.

Spencer was checking for blood, but the pain wasn't a reopening of her wound. Her power source was like cracks in her body with lava bubbling out and decimating the rest of her insides. "Sick," she managed before she rolled onto her side and puked.

Chapter Ten

"I'm fine," she grumbled as paramedics lifted her onto a gurney, the rough straps locking her into place. She glared at the distorted faces peering from the windows overlooking the back courtyard where the white, boxy van was parked. The front half of the roof was solid, thick glass, glowing red in swooshing motions like a concentrated lighthouse beam.

The paramedic tightened the strap across her chest. "Blood pressure is low. Ninety over seventy, heart rate elevated to one twenty-three, O2 levels eighty-nine." The woman twisted to her left for the oxygen mask.

As Kana's heart revved into overdrive, a strong and finite, "No," stopped the paramedic nurse. "No oxygen mask," Spencer said as he sat on the bench. "If her levels don't reach ninety-five in five minutes, we'll consider the oxygen."

Kana relaxed on the gurney, relieved that the mask wasn't going on. Oliver probably gave Spencer a file: "All the Things to Know About Kana and Her TRAUMA." That file must be a doozy. She was a tiny bit impressed he remembered the anecdote about nothing on her face.

Behind the thin flesh of her eyelids, she imagined the beach, the meditative swish of the tide drawing in and out as the ocean waves frothed close to her toes. *One, two, three.* She counted the beats of the waves to even her breathing pattern.

"We have a note to return you to the Ambrose Hospital," the paramedic said, looking up from her tablet.

"Make it quick," Kana sighed in acknowledgment.

After being poked, prodded, scanned, and returned to her private room, where she slept for the next two days, she felt better. Better was optimistic. Fine was a worse, blanket term, so she was well enough to replay the unexpected conversation with the president and, more importantly, his offer, a dozen times over in her mind. A carte blanche from the president was a gift too good to turn down. They both knew what she would ask for. The Event to be wiped, her citizenship denounced, giving her a clean slate that would provide her with the necessary freedom from Oshiya. A clean cut. Kana tossed the cotton sheet over her head to hide her twisted expression from Spencer, who remained silent in the corner of the hospital room.

The Event was an accumulation of unfortunate micro-occurrences, but wasn't that just her life? She was six and a half, and the first mistake was when one of her tutors taught her memorization devices, mnemonics, acronyms, mind maps, and the like, because children, with their elastic minds, had better memories, and Josephine would be damned if she let that natural enhancement go to waste.

The second important event was on the island's eastern side, where Oshiya's national security had been working diligently to neutralize a data leak. A single strand of encrypted code that floated off, whether by human error or by malicious intent, it was never determined which.

Through more random and inexplicable events, six-year-old Kana and her nanny had walked through the Kkoulleuge district

—an affluent area illustriously known for the highest concentration of gardens and botanical buildings condensed in one city. Surrounded by potent perennials and bees that frightened her when they skirted around her powder blue dress and hovered over the white bows in her hair, she watched a funny man across the road. He didn't stand out, dressed in a pressed cotton suit the color of sage, and a silk pocket square tucked perfectly in his breast pocket. It was in the lines of his form, the slouching and alternating crossing of his legs, that made it seem like he was in someone else's clothes.

The man folded the newspaper, picked up the coffee cup on the bench, and threw the items in the trash. The nanny held Kana's hand as they crossed the road to pass through the arch of wisteria. Unfortunately, the next moments tumbled the dominos: a year one primary class with their little yellow hats and matching backpacks made their way to the arch tunnel, another man attempted to cut through the miniature children, and a dog barreled through the gardens with a woman screaming commands. The dog split Kana from her nanny, and the orange leash flapping in the air like a snake knocked over the trash bin. Children screeched with delight, and a glint of metal caught curious Kana's eyes, and she found a smiley face thumb drive.

There was, of course, more. Kana watched Josephine insert those thin metal sticks into laptops, and when she got home, she did the same. The laptop screen was black with a string of codes. It was like the memory games her tutor played with her. The code detonated, leaked acid out of the thumb drive, causing a chemical reaction that made the laptop combust. Military personnel descended upon the estate like an attack of killer hornets and questioned her for two days, and the decision for Kana to be flagged as unable to leave the country was made, and that was the end. Technically, Oshiya was a republic, and while the president couldn't force anyone to do anything, his power and reach were a constant thorn in her side because the string of code burrowed in her head had been flagged as a national security threat. Kana's leash was a noose.

The president was a businessman. The tentative request appealed to him because Josephine was a bigger security risk than Kana, and if she couldn't find Josephine, oh well, Kana would figure out how to get away from the country one way or another. She had far less to lose.

With her mind made up, she maneuvered to sit at the narrow desk; her ass was numb from the hospital bed. The window was open enough for Kana to view the silhouetted cityscape beyond the flutters of the curtain fabric. Her fingers twitched, curling around an invisible cigarette. Being in a hospital always brought back the desire to fill her lungs with smoke. "Tell him to allow me to be discharged. I'm not going to play their game in this godforsaken place," Kana said to her shadow.

Spencer had the means to contact the president, and she would use him as the errand boy. The president made the call, and she had the green light to leave the next day. After being told a dozen times how to care for herself, she was vibrating in the hospital room.

"I'll come for the weekly check-up," Kana lied as she tapped her finger against the propped railing of the bed-gurney. Dr. Cohen's eyes moved to Spencer, who stood near the window frame closest to Kana's bedside, but still between the two people in the room.

"He's my driver. He'll make sure I come. Remember, I want the results as soon as possible. I don't want them to go to anyone else."

"I can't promise no one else will see the results," Dr. Cohen said as he clicked his pen twice.

"You can, otherwise I'll be telling your family about your lover in Croatia. I believe he went to the same graduate school for a master's program."

Dr. Cohen became a black and white caricature, all color gone. Kana swung her legs off the bed and slid her feet into the leather sandals. A vintage Prada trunk had been delivered hours earlier with three sets of clothes, lingerie, and a bag with her favored perfumes for the last of spring.

"Now, this wouldn't be devastating if you hadn't been caught five years ago and promised your wonderful wife you'd ended your other relationship. I expect your complete secrecy." Because based on the details from Dr. Cohen's bank transactions, he loved his wife. It showed in the purchase of the concert tickets to that old retired pop star she'd probably adored when she was in high school, and the supplies to build her own greenhouse, and the trip with her dying mother around the Mediterranean. And they said money couldn't buy happiness. Mrs. Cohen received excellent care and lacked nothing, yet loving more than one person proved a difficult problem, particularly given his wife's strict belief in monogamy. A secret partner was his ugly secret, a tale as old as time.

Kana smiled as she patted the doctor on the shoulder. "That's only surface level. Imagine what I can do with all the free time I would have if I were stuck in this hospital," she threatened.

She pulled on a baseball cap and offered the doctor a last smile before strutting out of the room and to the car. Spencer, the polite gentleman, opened the passenger door. He'd ditched the painfully obvious black sedan that screamed *I'm carrying an important figure* for a modest Lincoln.

"What's your actual mission, Mr. Spencer?" Kana reached over the rearview mirror and popped open the roof compartment, where she found a pair of aviators. She slid them on her face, but glasses never fit properly over her flat nose bridge. "You were a serene summer breeze inside the White Room. I imagine less than a dozen people have ever been inside."

"Quite the contrary. I've never been inside. I thought it was a myth." Spencer, Mr. Goody Two-shoes, diligently used his blinker at every turn, properly slowed at yellow lights, and did full stops at each stop sign.

Through the tinted shades, she couldn't spot any micro-expressions that hinted at a lie. "You seem to know the president," she pointed out.

"That is the third time I've met him," he said, carefully looking over his shoulder and turning right.

She hummed as she reached over and fiddled with the radio until smooth jazz serenaded them for the drive.

Architects had shaped the exclusive gated neighborhood, Haetan Ridge, at the fringe of a small valley, with the entire back section facing the open ocean. Much like the other districts, no commercial building could be taller than thirty-four meters. Haetan Ridge was a boutique condo complex designed at an incline, like the slope of a roller coaster. The long driveway, gardens, and the first floor were wide and curved to bend around the natural curve of the cliff, and the higher the floors went, the building narrowed. Each tenant had their own entire floor. The penthouse was at the peak height, exactly one meter below the required zoning.

Kana caught the tick of Spencer's brow as she hit the number five, and not the highest number on the panel, twelve. She owned the twelfth floor penthouse, but Oliver had cleaned up the fifth floor which she also owned because trying to escape from the rooftop was not ideal.

The elevator door opened to a pale stone hallway with light crema-brown wood accents. Two doors stood like twins side-by-side in the left hallway, while the right wall had nothing but taste-less paintings and a bolted-down narrow table. She flicked up the keypad outside her door, pressed her pointer finger on the narrow black box reader, and punched 7-8-0-4-4.

"Order anything," Kana said as she kicked off her sandals by the front door. The extensive flat was earthy in tone: a polished dark stone floor, a sage green wall, and high wooden beamed ceil-ings. There was little delineation between the space, and large gaps of nothing made the space feel stilted and incomplete. There was no kitchen or dining table, and not a single chair, just two stools tucked under the concrete kitchen counter. The L-shaped sofa stood atop a large rectangular alpaca rug, with an oblong cedar coffee table in the center. An impressive collection of plants was vibrant and thriving, clearly recently placed in their new home, since Kana only had fake plants that needed dusting.

"Guest room is the door to the left, but I'm sure you knew that already!" she shouted over her shoulder.

The cleaner had fanned out a tasteful list of takeout menus, organized by color and height. The lingering scent of the mint and eucalyptus cleaning product still hung in the air. Her bed was made with her favorite brand of silk sheets and duvet. She yanked open the closet doors to find the wardrobe with her clothes from the hotel in New York City, all neatly hung, with shoes shined and displayed, and a crystal bottle of perfume placed in the velvet shelf of the vanity. Just as Oliver said: the flat was spick and span and ready for her arrival.

The vintage rotary phone made a zipper sound as she dialed the Chinese takeout place. "A number three and a number eleven, extra spicy, and double those peppers," she ordered as she slid onto her bed like a snake, sinking into the silk. Her hand reached over to the end table where a palm-sized chrome remote lay, and with a press of a button, the back floor-to-ceiling windows split in half, cranking apart to leave a massive opening for the ocean breeze, the warming winds bringing summer and the faint rose scent from the wild roses native to Oshiya. They were more resilient than other roses, wild and able to grow along the cliffy terrain. Her brain told her to hate every bit of this, but her body relaxed further into the bed, the comfort too hard to resist, and she slept.

THE LITTLE TAKEOUT BOXES WERE LINED UP PERFECTLY on the polished concrete kitchen countertop with a single packaged sweet sesame ball shaped like a bow, the restaurant's specialty treat resting like the topper to a gift. She picked up the boxes and tossed them in the trash as she called in a new order.

Out of habit, she lifted her left leg to hug it to her chest, but her torso shrieked, the wounds protesting. She lay on the couch with one leg outstretched on the coffee table, her ankle twisting slowly like the second hand on a clock. An old sitcom played quietly in the background, but it failed to hold her interest as she mindlessly ate her noodles.

This cycle went on for a few days. Kana lazed around the flat, moving from her bedroom to the back deck to the kitchen like a cat chasing the sun. The brown bags, plastic lids, and napkins from a dozen restaurants filled her trash can. Her body was in constant flux; either she felt supple and fuzzy, riding the high, or trapped, the pain leaving invisible scorch marks after a blaze. The little amber bottle, a quarter full, sat on her bedside, the white pills offering relief. She knew someone had removed some pills. Kana supposed it was a valid concern. Oliver had sworn she was on the brink of addiction when she was only fourteen, and must have warned Spencer to monitor her drug intake.

She iced out Spencer, which, surprisingly, wasn't difficult. He seemed just as opposed to the living situation, and spent as little time in her immediate space as possible. At one point, she wondered if he was in the guest room, and the notion of tiptoeing to check bubbled to the surface, but she quickly smothered the curiosity. It wasn't like she was super interested. She just noticed how silent the last day had been. Occasionally, she heard the thump of the refrigerator door close, or the electric kettle boiling, silverware clinking, but nothing for the past day.

When she crept out of her bedroom, the expansive living

room was empty, with only the comfort of the shadows and moonlight. She rocked onto her tiptoes and craned her neck across the space to the dark hallway. There was no looming figure waiting, trying to catch her if she snuck out. A late-night walk, that's all she wanted. She tiptoed around the kitchen island and turned the corner. "Fucker," she hissed as she jerkily shot backward, avoiding the near collision with Spencer.

"Do you haunt the halls at night?" She added another step back, and her left eye twitched at the discomfort in her abdomen, but there wasn't pain, so the doctors were right. Rest was doing her good.

"Water," he said, as he moved forward so the tall glass he held was visible in the slant of moonlight from the back windows. The rest of him remained shrouded in the shadows.

With a hum, Kana edged back again. Spencer lacked physical intimidation; at 178 centimeters, he was not particularly tall, nor was he built like a linebacker. Kana had confronted men over 193 centimeters, men stuffed full of muscle, and men who were none of those things yet carried themselves as though they deserved it all. Physically, Spencer was average, but his eyes left an uncomfortable knot in her chest.

They possessed a magnetism that was, for lack of a better term, intense; very few people had that precision without revealing what they wanted. Men were grossly simple, and their leers too obvious, but not Spencer. She didn't like it, because he wanted something from her. She couldn't figure it out, yet.

"You don't have to repurchase food orders. I'll let you pick them up," he commented out of the blue. Kana paused and looked over her shoulder, a silent invitation to continue speaking.

He moved to allow the moonlight to shine on his features. Kana narrowed her eyes.

"If I wanted to poison you, I would have switched the painkillers," he said.

"I don't know what you're talking about," she lied as she

returned to her room with stiff shoulders and a clenched jaw. He caught on quickly, realizing that she wouldn't accept food or drinks from him. Call it a habit, or learned behavior from her mistakes. Someone who was supposed to be caring for her had drugged her one too many times, and it served her well to handle the delivered food herself.

Chapter Eleven

Boredom was a time vortex. It was endless at times, with five minutes feeling like five days, while ten hours flicked by as easily as turning on a light. Normally, the internet was the culprit. How easy it was to be bogged down by useless videos, marketing techniques, and the lives people wish they were living. But she was still under blackout orders. The media circus ran rampant for juicy stories such as Kana's survival. Oliver left a phone for her, but it would be best if she didn't go online. There were only so many films she could watch, and books were a bore. Only a fraction of her was worried about a potential impending attack. The president was full of shit, and the excuse to have Spencer around as a protector only added to the steaming pile, but Kana kept a pocketknife on her, just in case.

Kana left her loft three times, and each time, Spencer not-so-subtly followed. Her flights of fancy were limited, as she became winded after walking a few blocks before she was forced to return to the endless loop of dullness.

She peered through the opera binoculars that once belonged to two Golden Age Hollywood starlets. The rare ivory glinted against the morning sun. A family walked down the beach, the mother's statuesque figure apparent even in the oversized silk robe she wore. The youngest child, a boy, ran ahead, clouds of sand kicked up behind his tiny feet, a Doberman running beside him. A third figure jogged up and reached out to grasp the mother's hand. Kana blinked and stood up from the chaise lounge on her back deck, the chiffon of her robe parting as she leaned over the ledge. This was who Kana was waiting for.

The daughter's hand was blue; her body was covered from head to toe, with her hood up hiding the final transition: the girl's healed skin blue from surviving the Fever. A physical sign that lasted nearly a year, letting everyone know exactly the kind of pain she had gone through and come out victorious. Kana tried to see more of the teenage girl, but it seemed the family didn't return the same way they came. Disappointed that the one interesting thing was gone, she retreated inside.

The following morning, the painted box was on the kitchen counter beside a glass of freshly squeezed orange juice, then on the patio chair where she normally lounged during high noon, and then inside the porcelain bathroom sink. Each time she found it, she dropped the box against the closed guest room door.

She nearly stepped on the edge of the box the next morning as it stood outside her bedroom door. And so the game of hot potato continued until one random evening, with the live audience on TV howling into fits of laughter at a well-timed joke, Kana flipped open the box that sat on the coffee table.

She slapped the small paper onto her forehead and stretched back on the couch, willing the inked drawing to sink past the banana-yellow paper and into her mind. If the drawing was the only important item, why use the box?

The box was important then. The president had probably run an analysis on the box. If a painting were hidden under the painting, they would have found it; if there were a secret compartment, someone would have found it. Surely, the president had the wood species, paint type, and every component analyzed, from the compounds to the location of its possible purchase.

Her eyes opened, and she turned to look at the box. The square paper fluttered off her forehead. The answer, or a part of the answer, was not in the minutiae of the construction of the antique. The box looked like a generational gift passed down the family line or found in a European market. Sighing, she went over and picked up the box. The weight was more than she expected. She turned it over, staring at the engraved stamp: *Milan*.

Her jaw stopped moving as an idea clicked. The box itself wasn't familiar at all, but rather a placeholder for a memory, with the note as a target for the exact memory.

As with most children, random bouts of interest came more frequently than the hours on a clock. When she was seven or eight, she found flipbooks fascinating. She was adamant about creating mini books and doing stills on each corner of a Post-it. At some point, she wanted to level up and attempted to do a dog after completing two Post-its with simple smiley faces. Her nanny took her antique shopping to the largest dump of people's unwanted things, which happened twice a year. The biannual affair, known as Guiles 113th Antique and Relics Fair, was uncreatively named—it spanned 113th Street, which was a five-block stretch of road. Guiles was the surname of the inceptor, and shared the name of the local park that was a landmark for the entrance of the fair.

Young Kana picked out a pretty jewelry box. Her bright orange sparkly nail polish was a striking contrast to the powder blue box she lifted closer to her face to inspect.

"You certainly have an eye for beauty," the nanny—Selena, Marina, Lina, the nannies changed too frequently for her to keep track—commented. But Kana remembered this nanny because of her habit of changing her hair with the seasons. Not a basic blonde for summer or rusted red for autumn; no, this nanny went for teal blue in summer and silver blonde in winter, with tips of royal purple.

"This looks like it's from Italy. See, you can see the inscription here." The nanny, with pearl clips holding back the wavy blue hair behind her ear, looked more mermaid than human. The woman turned the box upside down to see the engraved name of the maker. It had been crafted in Florence. They returned home with a bag of little treasures. Kana impressed with miniature zoo animals and an old calligraphy set, while the nanny selected a crystal vase to hold the fresh bouquet of warm sunset-colored flowers.

"Kana." Josephine's voice was a bullet through the large entry room.

The nanny had nearly cut her finger with the flower shears as she was trimming the stems in the sink. Her thick lashes fluttered four times, as if she couldn't believe the unexpected visitor.

"Madame, we—" She scrambled to find her words.

"Stop ruining the Post-its." Josephine blew in, not in her usual lab coat and comfortable shoes, but in clacking heels and a luxurious gown, a wave of fire fanning around her.

"I don't want to see anything until it becomes proper art. I will pay an art professor or send you to Italy to learn from the masters. No more of this trash." Josephine never raised her voice, and when she spoke, her lips moved only the amount necessary. She tossed the yellow Post-its with the dog renditions onto the counter.

Josephine pressed her phone to her ear. "Yes, I'm here. I want another test done tonight. Did I stutter?"

The front door shut behind her, and the traces of her custom perfume, a mix of basil, dark berries, and oolong, lingered in the cold air.

"Your drawings are wonderful." The nanny rushed to Kana's side where she continued to say how impressionistic the dog was, but Kana wasn't listening. She stopped drawing shortly after.

The Guiles 113th Antique and Relics fair was the answer. Kana found the phone Oliver had left, intending to search for the exact day the antique market started, but her eyes locked on the search engine's top headlines, most from trash sites and magazines:

"Ambrose Heiress Conspiracy for Monopolization?"

"Kana Ambrose's Final Girl Sequel"

"Ambrose Heiress Hostage (Again)"

"Kana Ambrose Investigated for Involvement in Lake Slaughter"

Hot air blew out of her nose. Her hand, clutching the phone, trembled as she refrained from launching the object across the room. She wanted to scream, or at least break something. Ripping into her past and turning her life into a horror movie mockery was the height of journalism these days. They'd really stooped low. She shoved her arms into a jacket, pulled the hood over the baseball cap, and stalked out.

The gated luxe condos and beyond were well lit. Haetan Ridge's neighborhood was crafted with minimalism in mind, and the streetlamp posts, each bulb built into the flat rectangular head, sent a trapezoidal yellow glow against the 2 a.m. black backdrop of the bare, narrow sidewalks. The sidewalks were hardly used; everyone in the neighborhood had at least one car, including the children, and discarded models remained in the underground garages waiting as gifts. The sidewalks remained necessary for the occupants to reach the various staircases down to the beaches. She stepped over a rope with a Private sign. The small nook was on private land and rarely visited by strangers.

She dug her feet into the soft sand, the crashing waves, a redundant white noise. If only it were a full moon. She'd like to see more of the ocean at night.

"You shouldn't go too far."

Kana's heart seized while she shook at the abrupt words. "I should have checked for video cameras," Kana muttered.

"There aren't cameras in your home. The doorman tipped me off," Spencer said.

"I'll have to toss a bedsheet off the balcony and shimmy down next time."

"I wouldn't try until you're fully healed."

"If I wanted to escape, I would be sneakier than a knotted bedsheet."

"I have no doubt about that," he replied.

In the darkness, Spencer's undefinable outline looked less human and more like a boulder. She wiggled her toes in the sand as if they were little crabs burying themselves.

"Are you a Natural or a Synthie?" She stared at the general shape of his head.

"A Natural."

"Active or Passive?" He chose not to answer that question directly, even though she knew he was an Idu.

"Oliver didn't provide a thorough profile on me?" he asked.

Kana ignored his question, because she'd forgotten to ask Oliver for Spencer's file. She was too concerned about the doctors leaking or selling her information either to Josephine or a third party. She'd forgotten to dig into her newly acquired shadow.

"Do you always lie?" she wondered.

That gave him pause. She wished she could see his expression. She bet he was more open in the darkness. People reacted differently if they thought no one could see them.

"No, I haven't lied." His tone remained smooth, but the edges were softer with sincerity. Oh, he was good.

"How'd they recruit you? The military likes to make their soldiers." Ever since A.E. Potentia had been mass produced to two hundred or so units—and even that was misleading, since less than two hundred were produced in a year—militaries around the world had been eager to strengthen their people.

He was quiet again, not offering a response.

"Do you have a tragic past? A young orphan embarking on a

hero's journey as he gets sucked into the jaws of death and signs his life away to the military?"

"You seem to have a distaste for the military."

Kana snorted. "It's ironic that Josephine created a bioweapon of sorts, I know."

"I voluntarily enlisted, and my story is bland. No tragedies or hero origin stories."

Kana leaned back, about to cross her arms behind her head, but the raw stitches protested. She'd be the judge if his history was as white bread as he implied.

"I grew up in Kkileyo, a low middle-class suburb, a town with less than ten thousand people. The lines of separation enough that people knew of each other but not directly. It's a far cry from any of the larger cities, lacking the charm of the coastal cities or the beauty of the valleys and mountains, but it's home," Spencer said, pausing long enough for Kana to interrupt. He was willing to divulge pieces of his past so readily. Most of the time when people blabbed anecdotes about their lives, she could care less, but that snarky inner voice barely scoffed—odd. For some reason, she wasn't annoyed.

"I lived in the same home for my entire childhood and would have stayed longer if I could, but as you said, I signed myself away and entered the academy. I've come to find that building expectations is unavoidable, and they are easy to crumble, but people are capable of surprising you."

She disagreed; people were exactly what she expected. "Am I the heiress you expected?"

"Yes, and no."

Kana grinned. "Did Oliver tell you to keep your answers vague? I'm sure my vetting isn't anywhere as bad as his." That earned a breathy chuckle, as if he'd tried to stifle the sound.

"Your friend had interesting interrogation tactics."

"He wants to make sure you, me, or both of us don't end up in body bags. The last round with a guard didn't end well for him." She'd made sure he didn't assault anyone in the future. "It's less of a hassle if Oliver just lets me be alone."

"He cares."

Kana rolled her eyes as a tiny white dot of light moved at a snail's pace along the night sky.

"You haven't been around this part of society," she said. "So I'll tell you a secret. People don't care, not really. When they want something, they'll take it. They'll be ruthless and unyielding. People with more money and influence tramp through whatever they want, to get what they want. But those aren't the ones to watch out for. You can see those cocks coming kilometers away. The people you need to watch out for are the gentle ones. Those are the tricksters, showing kindness to soften their selfish greed, and what's worse is sometimes they don't realize they are doing it."

Spencer had no comment. He silently sat beside her. His probing eyes eased off her form and turned to the black ocean.

Chapter Twelve

Kana winced as she tried to sit up, and like a baby learning how to move, she ended up rolling onto her side awkwardly before pushing herself onto two legs. The conversation with Spencer quelled her rampage for now. She stalked back to the gated complex, pausing when she entered through the front doors, sending a razor side-eye to the doorman. His Adam's apple bobbed as he swallowed.

"Good evening," he said politely, his hooded eyes glued to the computer screen at the concierge desk. She would speak to the owners more carefully about the discretion clause. Spencer could have held a loaded gun to the doorman, and he shouldn't have told anyone her whereabouts.

Spencer's slightly distorted reflection in the metal of the elevator doors showed him to her left—a thoughtful expression contradicting the sharpness in his eyes.

"Don't have him fired," he said, meeting her gaze in the reflection.

The elevator chimed, and the doors opened. Kana jabbed at a button that sounded like a typewriter. Spencer made a move to the left to enter. She mimicked his movement, not allowing him in.

"How presumptuous of you. To think I would have someone fired who explicitly knows to be discreet because of the clientele that live here, and yet he still blabbed about a resident's whereabouts. I wouldn't dare," she commented sarcastically. Spencer moved to his right, and she moved to her left.

"There are two kinds of people, one that tramples on everything in their path and another that uses kindness like a honey trap." He threw her words back at her, not maliciously, only factually, and she couldn't fault him for that. The closing elevator doors cropped the image of Spencer standing in the lobby closer and closer .

"Enjoy the exercise." She tilted her chin to the staircase as the doors closed between them. So maybe pressing the button for every floor to delay it returning to the lobby was petty, but she did it anyway.

She locked the door to her apartment behind her, kicking off her sand-crusted sandals and leaving behind a trail of her clothes as she stripped and climbed into her porcelain claw bathtub.

Her abdominal flesh was ruined. The bandages hid little, and the spindly lines of black flesh peeked out. She'd need to make an appointment with Dr. Park in Seoul to fix the scarring. Crop tops and tasteful bras under blazers were out. She wasn't sure how destroyed her muscles were. She clicked her tongue as she sank deeper into the milky liquid, the aroma of rose and vanilla filling the bathroom. The antique fair would be a distraction to prove if her memories linked together as much as the president believed. If Oshiya didn't already know of her return, they would tomorrow morning.

————

DRESSED IN PERFECTLY TAILORED LINEN PANTS AND A tightly crochet top with a low back, just enough to let the bruising peek through, she breezed into the open living space, the spark back in her step.

"I will not have you prancing around like an assassin. Blend in better," she said. Spencer stood in the open kitchen watching the electric kettle boil water. The gray tab of the breakfast blend tea dangled off the side of his thick, amber glass mug. He must have incredibly sensitive hearing, or he'd lied about cameras in the apartment, because he was already dressed in heavy cargo pants holding more weapons than she cared to know about. His shirt was a form of nylon fabric, clearly lacking breathability.

"If you went to a comic convention, you'd win a prize for your tactical outfit."

Spencer raised his eyebrows. Kana eyed his Chelsea boots, a vast improvement from the military lace-ups, and the least offensive part of his outfit.

She opened the fridge and found a glass container filled with a thick green smoothie. Oliver had had a lot of time with Spencer in the hospital room if he'd told Spencer to prep her morning drink. In the absence of coffee and alcohol, this was a peace offering.

"Have you been away from Oshiya for so long that you forgot the late spring heat?" she asked. Oshiya was renowned for a distinct time frame between spring and summer when the wind and ocean currents created an unusual vortex, and the country was stuck in an oppressive heat wave.

The screwed lid clunked in the copper sink as she breezed by, returning to her closet to find appropriate accessories. If Spencer passed out from the heatstroke, he couldn't say she didn't warn him.

"Damn," she exhaled as she took another sip of the smoothie. He'd made it perfectly. A quick text to Oliver for Spencer's file was sent with a whoosh from her phone as she dragged the tip of her manicured nail on the glass top, scrutinizing the shape of her sunglasses display.

Check the tablet, was immediately sent back.

Kana checked her appearance in the antique mirror. Under the layers of skincare, her face was plumped, cheeks and the tip of her nose kissed with rouge, and her lips shiny, each layer fortifying her walls. She pushed the sunglasses up her nose bridge with her middle finger. The flash of cherry-red on her nail matched her signature red eyeliner. She looked like herself.

Her phone chimed, and the tapping of her nails across the screen matched the beat of the heels of her sandals as she exited the apartment, reading a message from the doorman confirming her ride to the antique market was waiting out front. Spencer took her advice for the thinner T-shirt, but kept the ugly pants.

"Unless you want your face plastered on every newspaper, website, and social media account, stalk the driver from a distance," Kana said over her shoulder as she spotted the black car. Spencer's stride shortened at the sight of a bald doorman, who was a decade younger than the one from last night.

Spencer did not follow her into the taxi, thank god. The driver, a man in his late fifties, silently drove to the destination. "Miss, there is someone following the car," he said ten minutes into the drive. The driver's nervous eyes flitted to the rearview mirror and returned to the road ahead.

Kana turned around to look out the back window expecting Spencer's generic black car, but it was someone on a motorcycle. She would have assumed he was an enemy if she hadn't seen Spencer in the changed navy cotton shirt.

"Ignore him," Kana said, turning back around. "Park two blocks away at the corner of Cornell."

The driver obeyed and pulled along the curb. She handed him a hundred note bill, the paper crisp, and his caterpillar brows lifted as he tipped an invisible hat in gratitude. She took in the bustling and chaotic collection of people and tents. The line of food trucks sent wafts of greasy oil, smoking meats, and spices, overpowering the smell of the ocean. The silk tie around her hat tickled her neck as the sea breeze kicked through the streets.

"Double shot," she said, ordering a coffee and ready to punch anyone who might try to stop her.

The barista gushed squeaky compliments about Kana's appearance. Kana ignored her and forced the burned coffee down her throat.

Along the sidewalk, tarps were splayed out with piles of stuff closer to garbage than treasures: yellowing and moldy books, tarnished sterling silver rings and necklaces, and broken childhood toys. Then there were the white tents and boutique stores were trying to sell their handmade goods or items purchased from other estate sales at double the price.

A trio of girls brushed past her, and she felt their two-second analysis. It was quite the superpower women had, to be able to gloss over strangers. *Yes, she has a good sense of style, no, she can't dress for her body; good, my legs are skinnier, her legs are too skinny; she has a smaller waist; she's taller, she's shorter; she's wearing too much makeup, she's not wearing enough.* All these comparisons happening in milliseconds to form one final thought: she's pretty or she's not.

The analysis happened in a single glance, and, used to the appraisal, she had the mental fortitude to ignore whatever envious or confidence-boosting conclusion the girls and women made around her. Men were simple-minded, and she suspected they ran through three comparisons before coming to similar yet different conclusions about the surrounding strangers.

She remembered the antique fair being more. Or was her memory colored by the yellow sunshine view of the world the nanny had, starkly contrasted with what Kana was usually around?

"What a stunning young lady," a man with an unkempt beard

said as he beckoned for her to come closer to the broken chande-liers and candlesticks he was selling.

Kana blatantly ignored him. "Come, take a look." He maneu-vered himself into her path with a few strides, his hairy arms outstretched to block her path, deliberately ignoring her disinterest.

"You have nothing of value," she said coolly. "If I wanted to buy your garbage, I would have stopped." For a second time, she took a step forward, but he didn't move.

He sputtered, the wiry hair of his moustache nearly hiding his thin lips opening and closing. "You bitch, this is silver and copper from places with more history than you'll ever know."

"Don't even try to pawn that off as actual silver. I can smell the metallic alloys from here. Any appraiser would walk by your minuscule corner, *c'est un vrai blaireau.*"

His face enflamed, the meaty neck muscles coiled, and through her shaded view of the world, she could see his hands twitch at his side, so easily riled by a simple observation. She wouldn't walk around him. He would move for her. She lowered her sunglasses until the curve of her eyes could be seen. The recog-nition was immediate. His slow, tiny brain put together who she was and he lowered his head as he stepped away. She slid her sunglasses back into place and sauntered on.

The single interaction with the vendor was a drop in a pond. Kana could hear the clicking of the keyboard and a whooshing sound as someone angrily posted about the exchange. As she reached the end of the block, people no longer ignored her.

There weren't phones out yet. No one confirmed that Kana Ambrose was browsing the antique fair. She nearly forgot the reason she was out in public. The climbing heat and humidity raced as the sun moved across the sky. She eyed a stand selling slushy alcoholic beverages. Between the dozens of bystanders' looks, it was hard for Kana to discern if her shadow was still trailing behind her. He was, she was sure of it. He was nothing if not a listener, a rule follower, a good soldier.

She was about to stand in line when she saw the fluttering marigold yellow of a woman's silk shawl. Kana's feet carried her after the woman, who turned out to not be a woman, but a lithe man. She lowered her sunglasses, the burning sun blinding her for a moment, but the shawl was unmistakable: hand-dyed silk with intricate beadwork around the hem, the shape itself a mix of a cocoon and draped cape. To an untrained eye, it was an odd creation, one that plucked at a memory.

"What are they doing?" Kana had pointed to the women with their pants rolled up to their knees as they stood in a river, strips of cloth stretched between them. Josephine had a meeting with a Japanese company and a visit to the ambassador.

Nanny Brent—or was it Brandon?—an eccentric man who spoke fluent Japanese, English, and Arabic, was charged with taking young Kana on a tour through Akito.

"Shibori is a traditional dying technique," Nanny B informed and went on an educational rant about the traditional history, but Kana stopped listening.

At twelve, Kana had a trained eye for unique things. Nanny B said as much as they stopped at a textile artist who blended the traditional silks and dying method with bead and knit work.

"I want the indigo one." Kana pointed to the naturally blue dyed piece of fabric. Nanny B translated, and the woman said something quickly. The gentle curve of her brows hinted at doubt.

"She's not selling any of these. They are for a display. There's a competition in the neighborhood."

"What does the winner get?" Kana asked.

The artist spoke an octave above a whisper to the translator, but her face was tight with strained politeness. She made sharp gestures with her hands and Kana caught the sense she wanted them to leave.

"Aside from acknowledgment of their skill, a gallery in Tokyo."

"I'll get her a gallery in New York City, Tokyo, and Milan. I want the shawl."

Kana slid around the throngs of people, pressing a hand against the back of her hat as the wind picked up. From only the lines of his back and narrow walking gate, it was too difficult to know if she recognized the man with the shawl. He eventually slowed and paused in front of the bottom floor of an outdoor mall. This area was designated for textiles and accessories, according to the hanging banister draped across the sloping archway entrance. The tall cathedral-high ceilings created the illusion of more space as tourists and locals squeezed through the pop-up tents.

The stranger's left hand pushed aside a thick beaded curtain that acted as the door. The two-and-a-half-centimeter thick beads created a hollow rain sound as they clanged against one another.

Fireworks of colorful fabrics piled on tables and draped from the ceiling and benches were hard to peruse because of the inundated space. The compact store sold scarves and shawls, but none were in the style Kana recognized.

"Let me know if you need help," he said and claimed a seat on a stool in the corner while balancing an iPad on his lap. His free hand pushed the sunglasses on the crown of his head, parting the shag of bangs out of his eyes. The store smelled of onion and a honey glaze, and judging by the long kebab stick resting inside the trash can, the man had just finished a snack.

"Your shawl," Kana said, "it's unique. I don't see that style being sold here."

Kana didn't recognize the man, but she could have met him before; most people were unmemorable. He embodied the standard Oshiya features: a longer nose, upturned large eyes, and a small mouth with thin lips.

He smiled, his eyes curving in delight. "A recent gift. It's a beautiful thing, isn't it?"

"Is it a Fuku Yamuzuki?" Kana stepped further towards the stool where the store owner sat.

The man's mouth parted in shock. "Yes, it is. I'm surprised you knew."

Kana removed her sunglasses, biting the tip of the earpiece.

The man's back straightened. His eyes fluttered rapidly three times as his jaw tensed and relaxed. "Kana Ambrose," he said.

"Who gave it to you?"

He set the iPad on the small desk and shook his head. "I don't know. I found it wrapped in a box when I returned from a lunch break during the initial setup of the stall. My coworker said a courier just dropped it off. There was a note that asked me to wear the shawl for the entire antique fair. My partner has a stall at the other end, and I have to make trips back and forth, so I thought it was a bit strange that I was asked to wear a shawl in this heat."

"Where's the note?"

He rifled through the slim top drawer of the desk and held out a small business card note.

A Fuku Yamuzuki original. Please wear it for the entirety of the antique fair.

The sender had typed the note on a typewriter. She flipped the card over to find the other side blank, but there could still be a message.

"Someone sends you a mysterious box and asks that you wear the item and you listen to their demand?"

The man shrugged. "I looked up the artist. This is worth half a million yen, and that's a lot of money. I've never had anything so luxurious before."

"And?" Kana waited because there was more.

"Why are you so interested in the shawl?" He questioned defensively, his hand gripping the silk fabric. "I'm sure you could buy as many as you want."

Kana could. She was the one who sponsored Fuku and propelled her as one of the best up-and-coming artists. Her gaze swept over the vendor, concluding that he was a nobody. There was another incentive, possibly a payment after each day of wearing the shawl, but whatever it was, this nobody had been used as a walking sign to lead her to this shop.

"Take a long lunch." She handed him five one hundred note bills. There was something here. She just had to find it.

"A thousand," he countered meekly. Kana held back a scoff. If he wanted to negotiate, he should have balls and hold his ground.

Kana held up the bills. "Five or my bodyguards remove you and you get nothing."

He snatched the cash; the beads clacked against one another as he exited the shop.

The stationary fan moved the thick heat around the enclosed space. Kana felt beads of sweat running down the side of her neck. She paced around the store, her eyes roved over the products before she lifted the stacks of scarves, not finding any hidden message on the plastic table coverings.

She closed her eyes, listening to the loud vibrating whirl of the fan and the mindless noise outside the small store. A memory of the markets in Bali overlapped with the time in Delhi. The tinkling beads, followed by giggling, signaled customers arriving.

"Shop's closed," she said as two teenage girls with sweating smoothies in their hands gaped at her. Kana tucked her sunglasses into her crocheted top's low V-neck.

"Oh my god, you're Kana Ambrose!" the girl with the at-home bleached bangs shouted. She slapped her friend's hand as if to make sure her bestie was paying attention.

"Gigi, I don't think—"

"Can I take a selfie with you?" Gigi barreled on, running fingers through her long hair and trying to flatten the frizz, ignoring her friend who tried to rein in Gigi's antics. The girls, prim, plucked, and painted, fluttered about; it was easy to see how many compared young girls to preening cats or birds, delicate creatures in their soft, pliable clouds of pink and lilacs.

Kana stared at the girl with her frigid expression. Her gaze caught the long, beaded doorway behind them. A painted block design covered the beads, but parts were dull, as if two images had been painted together, like the stippled images in optometrist offices.

"We're sorry to bother." The friend moved to yank at Gigi's arm and tried to move to the beaded doorway, but was shoved aside as Spencer stormed in.

The girls shrieked like yipping puppies as they split to make room. "Get down," he ordered Kana, while he snatched one thin arm in each hand and tossed the teenage girls on their asses out of the store.

Kana's mouth became a battleground, mint and steel that tasted more like blood coating different areas of her mouth. She ducked in time to hear the plink of a small projection smashing into the thick base of the fan, and another plink as a second projection sliced through a pile of thin scarves.

Her body strained to absorb the remnants of the energy. The world around her became an alpaca sweater, tufts of fluff around the edges. Her absorption felt wrong. Instead of a smooth silk stream, it was erratic, as if electricity was charged in water.

Screams and shouts were the trigger she needed to scramble to her feet, but a muscular arm shoved her under the table. She took little sips from the buzzing energy, afraid to absorb any more, the fear of becoming incapacitated wasn't worth the risk of recharging her power source. But she would risk a little; she was barren, and while Kana rarely used her unique ability, she was never completely at zero. And she didn't like that if it came down to it, she didn't have any of her power to use.

"Stay," he ordered as more bullet-like projections came like raindrops, but not a single one hit as Spencer altered their path.

Unlike Spencer, Kana didn't listen to orders.

Chapter Thirteen

The cement dragged against her thinly covered knees as Kana crawled under the tables. Grunts and the pinging of metal against metal was barely distinguishable over the swollen noise of people stampeding, shouts and orders just outside the thin tent walls. The distorted shadow-silhouettes, visible through the thin plastic tablecloth, were like a shadow puppet action scene, and she wouldn't stick around to see who won. If she were lucky, Spencer was as good as the president boasted. If he wasn't, well, she didn't want to be here to find out why someone decided to shoot up the most populated antiquities fair. A final thud, the sound of a body collapsing on the floor, and a familiar pair of scuffed Chelsea boots approached the table.

"I told you to stay put." Spencer flipped up the tablecloth, a hint of a scowl set in his lips. He offered a hand, which she refused.

The extension of her torso agitated her healing wounds, but she brushed off the dirt patches on her knees, acting as if she didn't feel a stabbing in her gut. She eyed the man who lay prone against a table, half atop strewn piles of polyester scarves.

His white shirt was the perfect canvas for the dark bodily

fluid. Kana moved half a step closer to the dead man. The blood color looked strange. She was about to close her left eye when Spencer moved in front of her, blocking the man from her sight, probably trying to protect her innocence, as if she hadn't seen dead bodies before.

"Your nose." Spencer offered a scarf from one table.

Kana touched her face; her left nostril had mostly crusted blood. Her tongue licked her upper lip, tasting the thin stream of blood dribbling out of her right nostril. She caught Spencer's gaze following the tip of her tongue.

"A blood fetish?" she asked innocently, tilting her head down and peering up, making her eyes look wider and more innocent, but her viper smile remained in place. "You wouldn't be the first, and certainly not the last. There is something to be said about men volunteering to spill blood for their country. They acquire a certain taste."

The corner of Spencer's mouth twitched, almost amused by her baiting comment. "The police will arrive in less than five minutes." He stepped forward, picked up a scarf from the stack beside her, and moved to press it to her face.

Like a frightened cat, her hand swiped out to slap his hand away. She turned and snatched a different scarf, dabbing at her nose as she looked at the beaded curtain, closing her left eye to confirm the glimpse she saw before the shoot-out interrupted her. She reopened her left eye, checking to make sure Spencer was preoccupied. He bent down over the dead man, busy checking for identification.

The beaded design had a symbol that only someone with tritanopia could see. The thing was, the placement of the block of colors on the inside portion of the beaded doorway was crafted so that even if a colorblind person with tritanopia saw the image, they wouldn't be able to see the image fully. Whoever had painted it had known she had colorblindness in only her left eye. A person needed one normal eye and one eye with tritanopia to see the image. Josephine was clever, and admitting that fact left an acrid taste in Kana's mouth.

She plucked a pen with a tacky flower on the cap and scribbled a copy of the P symbol painted on the beads on the back of the shop's business card. She also drew the symbol for Scorpio, the Triple Moon, and the Egyptian Ankh icon, just in case someone stole the note.

She scrubbed her upper lip, getting rid of the crusted blood. Her right nostril had stopped bleeding, at least for now.

"Let's go," she announced, heading out the back door.

"Do we need to go to the hospital?" Spencer asked as they ducked into the nearest stall, one selling purses, as officers sprinted down the cleared, narrow street.

"No." That would always and forever be her immediate response, even before her fingers glided over her torso. There was no blood. The man hiding behind the center table with a mountainous pile of fake leather bags—the smell of the chemical adhesive and plastic fibers was heady in the warm air—jumped at their sudden appearance.

Her eyes fell on another beaded doorway, just like the shawl stall. This one had a painted design, but not of a P; an arrow pointed up, as if signaling the stall across the way, directing her to the storefront with the shawl. She needed to check other beaded doorways. Outside, footsteps thundered, voices scrambled over each other, but not loud enough to distort the evacuation orders from officers. Her hat was lost, but she tied the crimson splotched scarf over her head and adjusted the sunglasses on her face. She looped her arm through Spencer's. The muscles in his arm tensed at the abrupt touch, but he drew her a smidge closer as an officer popped inside the store.

"Sir, ma'am, is anyone injured?" The officer, so bland he may as well have been faceless, pushed aside the beaded curtain to inspect the tent. Kana ducked her head to her neck as Spencer answered on their behalf, and the officer directed them out. The stall owner swiftly vanished out the back, but Kana ignored the officer and moved to exit through the curtain of beads.

"Miss, we need you to evacuate the area." An officer with patchy facial hair held out his arm to stop her.

"My bag. I left it in one of the shops. I need my inhaler," she lied, forcing a thin, airy quality into her voice.

The officer's dark eyes flicked to Spencer, as if he would be the voice of reason and tell Kana to listen, and her lips pulled back.

"We will be quick," Spencer said. Kana shoved the officer's arm and walked out, unlinking her arm from Spencer's, rolling her shoulder as if his touch was an unwanted chill. For his part, he quietly walked beside her.

Identical black slacked, white T-shirted, and thick vested officers roamed like buzzing flies around the sealed off corridor. She selected a stall two spots to the left of the shawl stall and crossed the threshold. The hot space smelled like dye and plastic. Kana ducked her chin down to peer over her sunglasses at the beaded curtain. An arrow pointed to the left, and Kana bet that if she chose one of the stalls to the right, it would point right. Josephine had not only sent out the man with a Fuku Yamuzuki original design, but she'd also marked the doorways to lead her to the stall, in case she missed the walking clue.

"Miss!" Kana clicked her tongue as she snatched a cheap fake leather purse that had fallen off a display just as a female officer with a tight, painful ponytail appeared. "You need to evacuate."

"I was just getting my purse," Kana said as Spencer offered his arm. They followed the escorted civilians migrating from the outside mall pavilion. Men and women in uniforms rolled out red tape and barricades, blocking the encroaching news vans, while half a dozen police cars blocked off the fair.

"I'm starving," Kana said, throwing her arms behind her back and stretching her muscles as she dodged the massing onlookers trying to see what the fuss was about.

"We need to go to the safe house," Spencer said, squinting at the potential threats.

Kana continued her pace across the street, trying to find a decent spot for a driver to pick her up. The street light turned green, but not a single car could move. Traffic was bumper to bumper.

"I'm serious." Spencer's voice appeared close to her side as she stopped in front of a coffee chain and tapped on the screen of her phone.

Kana rolled her eyes. Like hell she was going to a safe house. "You can call your superiors. They'll do a thorough investigation of the person and find the threat was neutralized."

"Persons," Spencer corrected, his eyes sweeping the streets, lingering in the windows of the cars that were backed up.

She scowled as the driver rejected her request for a pickup. A motorcyclist squeezed through the traffic, giving Kana an idea.

"Kana," Spencer hissed.

"If someone tries to shoot at us, you can just . . ." She made a flicking motion. Her body skillfully twirled away as his fingers grazed her arm in an attempt to hold her back. She knew this city like the back of her hand, and deduced he must have left his motorcycle on the corner of 115th and Goyum, one of the few spots with parking near Cornell Street where she'd been dropped off.

"The area's swarmed with officers now. We're fine." She grinned at his irritated expression. His eyebrows did a funny jig as he tried to remain impassive.

"They didn't have problems attacking in a public area. They could regroup and try again."

"A possibility. A low one, so why don't you help me get out of the hot zone? Do you have a second helmet?" she asked, turning the corner to see the black motorcycle. He lifted the seat and there were, in fact, two helmets. She swung her leg and settled in the seat as he stared, dumbfounded. "Keys," she said, tucking her sunglasses into the front of her top, unable to stop the pleased smile as she held out her hand. She would have preferred to take the bike and leave Spencer, but there was a threat, and having him close was useful. Her outstretched fingers wiggled, waiting for the keys.

He leaned back on his heels and shook his head minutely. "I'm not letting you drive my bike."

"And I'm not trusting you to take me to the restaurant where I want to eat." She cocked her eyebrow. "You'll drag me to a tiny house in the middle of nowhere. I drive, or I'll wait here for a ride."

"How do I know you won't kill us?" He doubted her ability to ride a motorcycle. His lips thinned as he shook his head for the second time. Kana propped her elbow on the speedometer in between the handlebars.

"You'd rather fend off an unknown number of highly trained killers than let me drive your bike for a few kilometers?" she asked with amusement.

The muscle in his jaw pulsed as he did another sweep of the condensed area. His eyes flitted to the rooftops this time. People were walking by, but the area where Spencer had parked his bike was mostly quiet. The end of the block had a wooden barricade to keep vehicles from turning onto the side street. "Point to the gas."

Kana tapped the small bulging area above the speedometer. "Engine, ignition switch, foot shifter," he rattled on, and Kana pointed to each part without fail.

"Knowing the parts of a bike doesn't prove I can drive, trust me," she said sweetly, batting her lashes.

He sighed as he ran a hand down his face, and then through his hair as he offered her the extra helmet. "Is the restaurant less than ten kilometers away?"

"It's seven," she promised, pulling the helmet on and patting the space behind her. She held back her laugh as she flipped up the visor.

"Don't tell me your masculinity is being threatened, and that's why you won't let me drive," she said loudly and clearly. A few people looked in their direction. A woman covered her mouth to hide a smile.

He sat behind her, the weight of his frame causing the bike to dip. Even under the unbearable heat, his body heat felt different. She wondered if it was the residual energy tingling off his body.

"Hold on tight," she said as she kicked the standing brake and took off. The arms loose around her waist tightened, probably trying to be mindful of her injury. It took a minute to get used to maneuvering the vehicle, but as they said, it was like riding a bike. The dormant skills kicked in. Once they were safely away from the congested traffic, she felt the broad chest behind her relax just a little, as the open roads were easier to navigate as she revved up the speed.

"You survived," she said as she parked in front of a rundown old west saloon, with dusty window shutters and a tumbleweed glued to one of the front beams, sanded and spray painted for a more rugged exterior.

"Any new ulcers?" she asked, removing the helmet and wrapping the scarf over the helmet hair she sported.

"Surprisingly, no. The stunt with the merge was a bit close," he commented once the helmet was removed. "I'm impressed," he attempted to fix his hair with a smile. It was a small thing, a bit crooked in the corner, that gave an endearing attractiveness to his face.

"What if I told you that was only my second time riding a motorcycle?"

His face slackened in horror as she pushed on her sunglasses.

She laughed while tossing him the helmet and climbed up the steps. The restaurant went all in with the old American West saloon theme, and Kana could appreciate the effort. The wooded walls and old, mismatched sets of tables and chairs gave the owners an excuse to use creaky and tarnished furnishings for the kitsch interior. The waitress' uniforms were long skirts with lace trim—not at all accurate to the time; the owner confused the Edwardian Era with the Western saloon—and on weekend nights, there was entertainment on the stage in the corner. Five ceiling fans blew a mouthwatering smoked meat scent throughout the open dining space.

"Two people?" the hostess asked as her blue eyes went from Kana to Spencer, who entered behind her. There were two groups of customers in the restaurant, a couple seated near the bar on the far right, and a family of blonde-haired, blue-eyed adults and identical spawn. Tourists, based on the number of pictures the mother was taking with her phone and Polaroid camera.

"Yes," he answered swiftly.

The waitress in the long lace skirt sashayed to the center of the room, the clunk of her heels echoing. Kana counted four workers within sight: three women and a man visible through the swinging doors to the kitchen.

"If we could have that table." Spencer pointed to one in the corner, tucked away from the windows and half in the shadows.

The waitress smiled. "Of course. Celebrating anything special?" she asked as Kana claimed her seat first, dragging the tall rickety stool to the side so she could rest her back against the wall.

"Just a lovely day to eat some meat," Kana commented, sweet to the point of mocking the waitress.

"I hope you weren't down at the Guiles antique fair. There was a shooting," the waitress said as she handed them each their menu.

"Anyone dead?" Kana asked, her sunglasses still firmly in place.

"Not that I've heard." She fiddled uncomfortably. "Can I get you started with some drinks? A beer, or cocktail?"

"I'll take your top bottle of whiskey on the rocks."

"It's a little early to drink," Spencer said with a tight smile. The waitress nervously looked from Spencer to Kana.

"Ignore him. He's a very strict Catholic and doesn't understand the joys of day drinking," Kana commented as she handed the waitress her menu. She didn't need to flip through the five plastic pages of meat variations. "I'll have the Kobe, bloody."

"I'll need a minute," he said, scanning over the menu, purposefully skipping over the bulk of the menu and flipped to the last page, where there was the miscellaneous section of pasta, salads, and the like.

"He'll take the Limbo, regular."

"I don't eat meat. Do you have vegetarian options?" Spencer asked politely, looking at the waitress.

"Oh, well." The waitress's shifty eyes moved to Kana. "She's right, the Limbo would be the best alternative."

"Perfect, thank you." He handed her the menu back with a full smile. Kana swore the waitress swooned. She wanted to push her sunglasses down to see if she was blushing, but the tiny thing scampered away before she could check.

"A vegetarian. I'm learning so much about you today," she said, leaning back on the stool as she slid her sunglasses down to the tip of her nose to meet Spencer's eyes.

"You seem to have known that fact about my eating preferences," Spencer replied.

"I was observant." She crossed one leg over the other.

"And you can drive a motorcycle. That wasn't in Oliver's notes." Spencer mimicked her movements, throwing his arm around the chair beside him, relaxing a bit as his eyes finished their internal sweep of the restaurant, deeming it safe.

"Oliver is good, but he can't keep tabs on me twenty-four seven. A woman in Egypt taught me how to ride a bike in the four days I was visiting."

"Just a woman? You seem to be connected to royalty and political figures around the world."

"She was a journalist for the Al-Ahram, a widow and mourning mother after the attacks in Cairo," Kana said as she tapped her pointer fingernail on the edge of the sticky wooden table. He caught onto the past tense and didn't comment.

"No dead bodies," Kana said. "That's interesting, because I was sure there was at least one."

"The police won't prematurely release information to the public," Spencer said.

"Was it a duo?" Kana asked, trying to watch Spencer's calm expression. He said there was more than one attacker.

"There were three."

"Another military team? They like running in teams of three to four."

"Nothing for you to be worried about," he said. His dismissive undertone was like the dangling of a treat she latched onto. "You seemed to know the store owner where the attack started," he pointed out.

Kana smirked. Not a subtle change of topic at all. She made a mental note to request the police details from Oliver about the attack.

"I don't know the store owner. But you seem eager to move away from any discussion about the attack." She tilted her head. Spencer's eyes flicked over her shoulder to the person approaching their table. Kana pushed the sunglasses in place as the waitress returned.

"Your drink and water," the waitress said, placing coasters on the table, not looking at Kana, instead nervously glancing at Spencer. Kana wondered if she'd have the courage to slip her number to him. Her eyes trailed up and down the polyester uniform. She was cute, shapely with muscle, young, probably fresh into university.

"Thank you," Spencer said politely, and the girl's face flushed as she hurried off.

"She's going to give you her number," Kana said, removing her sunglasses a second time.

Spencer sputtered in his glass of water, cold droplets jumping out of the glass. The only thing to get him flustered was the mention of a waitress having an interest in him. Interesting. Kana sipped the chilled alcohol, which pleasantly burned down her throat.

"She won't," he objected after he composed himself.

"A bet," Kana proposed, swirling the amber liquid in the single block of ice. The speakers played American country music that had been popular a decade ago. "If I win, you tell me the real reason the president assigned you this gig, and if you win, well, you can have anything you like."

"The rewards seem disproportionate to the bet. Lower the stakes."

"You think you'll lose," she said, grinning as she sipped the whiskey.

"If I win, you listen to the doctor's orders," he counter offered and lowered his eyes to the drink. Boo, he wanted her to stop drinking. "And if you win, I'll answer five questions unrelated to my work."

Kana sipped her drink, and their eyes locked onto each other. In the dim light, his eyes were dark, nearly as dark as hers. "The terms of the bet: a waitress will give you her number as we pay the check. She assumes you'll pay and will write the phone number on the receipt."

He smiled, amused. "That's very specific. You could have made the terms the waitress will give me her number."

"Specificity makes it more fun."

"Deal," he said, and they clinked drinks. They stared at one another over the rims of their glasses. He wasn't a total pain in the ass, nothing like the stiff upper lips or loose lips of others, and he didn't feel the need to mansplain everything to her. His almost-hooded gaze was softer, as if he was enjoying their little banter.

"You seem rather young to be assigned to a classified super-secret task," Kana said. "When did you graduate?"

"Four years ago."

Kana leaned back, rotating her crossed ankle clockwise in time with the rolling ice in her glass. "That doesn't seem like enough time to get your field training hours and somehow catch the eye of the country's beloved president."

Spencer's expression was stuck in the lines of pseudo-politeness. He seemed to hold that modicum of pleasantness as his default mask. "You don't need to worry. I completed my required field hours." His words sounded tight, like he was balancing them carefully.

Internally, she giggled with glee. She'd caught onto something that irked him, or at least led to something important enough that Spencer was trying to hide his feelings, and she liked to dig until it hurt.

"Where were you stationed for your field hours?"

"I was a floater." A quick and vague response.

"I imagine the scorching deserts of the Sahara weren't the best places for field training. As much as I don't appreciate our military, what does field training entail?" Kana caught the tick of his jaw. So it was more of what he was tasked to do. Not all that interesting; she could guess what he did. "Very dangerous things, I suppose. Political moves and assassinations."

His neutral smile returned. "I'm sure you can understand being in uncomfortable places or situations. While the Sahara was not pleasant, being in a submarine was the worst part of the training. Have you ever been on a submarine before?"

There was a sensation of displacement, almost like déjà vu, where she felt the elasticity of her mind trying to reach for a memory. "Maybe once when I was younger. I remember the spaceship more. Both are equally claustrophobic." Kana prevented Spencer from questioning the spaceship comment, continuing, "When we finish," she waved her hand around, "this, will you return to the welcoming arms and warm bosom of the military?"

"If you're trying to fish for my motives, I can tell you I am loyal to the truth."

Kana slid her sunglasses back on, intrigued by his choice of words. The food was brought out, and Kana's small, neatly squared piece of Kobe beef smelled incredible. There was a single piece of flat bread made from rice, one ceramic sauce bowl filled with the honey soy glaze and another filled with whipped butter, and a neat bundle of asparagus shoots on the side for a splash of green.

Spencer's bowl of salad came with an identical flatbread-and-sauce duo, featuring cubes of tofu mashed and baked for a crisp top. "Plate." Spencer gestured to her platter as he pulled out a travel size spray bottle. She pushed the plate toward him and watched a cloud of fine mist coat her food and plate.

With a raised brow, she asked, "You don't think someone poisoned the food?"

He cut a small sliver from the meat, a part of the asparagus, and a portion of the flatbread. He remained quiet as he ate the food, his eyes focused on an invisible item in the center of the table.

"You haven't dropped dead." She made a grabby hand gesture. "My food."

"Did you find what you needed at the fair?" he asked as Kana sliced into the meat, the bright red bleeding through the crisp outside.

She hummed, the meat melting in her mouth. The craving sedated as she daintily continued to savor the taste. The note with the symbol in her pocket felt like lead. "He's an idiot," she commented, setting the cutlery down and reaching for her drink. Before Spencer could ask about who she was referring to, she went on. "If she doesn't want to be found, she won't be. The president doesn't want her, he wants her research."

"The president was right to believe you can find Dr. Ambrose."

Kana's crossed leg twitched at hearing Josephine's title. A knotted mess lodged in her throat like a furball she wanted to hack out.

"Desperate men are unsightly." Kana stabbed the asparagus shoot. The president got lucky with the box. She was sure it was a one-off. The realistic part of her said to blow off the president, enjoy the quiet for a few more days, then get the fuck out as soon as she shook her bodyguard off. But she'd been attacked so publicly. There was an urgency from the unknown groups that worried her. And if she continued, the carte blanche was within reach.

They ate silently, the scraping of forks and knives settling between them. When they finished, Kana ordered a car. She was fading fast. The table shook as her phone vibrated. One glance at the screen showed her ride had arrived. She set her napkin down and put her sunglasses back in place. Spencer followed her movements with no need for any more words to pass between them.

The air was still gross, but the sun was lower in the sky, leaving a whisked passionfruit color behind. Spencer popped out as a silver car pulled up, the saloon doors flapping in the wind. "You were right," he said as he held out the receipt. "But it wasn't our waitress."

Kana plucked the receipt from between his middle and pointer fingers.

"She added a cute little smiley face, but if you recall . . ." She stepped down the saloon steps and yanked open the door of her ride. "The terms were 'a' waitress, not 'our' waitress."

Chapter Fourteen

After the antique fair fiasco, Kana had spent the last few nights lounging around the apartment, digging through her memories. It took less than one minute of searching to discover the symbol stood for Pluto. The hard part was understanding the significance of what Pluto meant and why Josephine purposefully left that clue for her.

She wanted to lay in the massive clawfoot tub, but the doctor had restricted her from too much water exposure until the stitches started falling out. Instead, she dragged a throw blanket out to cover herself on the chaise lounge. She twirled the business card back and forth, the ♇ symbol winking at her.

"What are you trying to tell me?" Kana asked the night. Thinking of the demoted planet and the solar system led her to think of Vyolette. There had been a Sweet Fifteen party (every year was a Sweet-something in Vyolette's childhood, and Kana was ten at the time) where she revealed the laguna her father had bought her and unveiled the observatory. It was one of the best locations for stargazing, with the fourth-best telescope in the world, and the largest and closest telescope she could access.

Kana had to find wherever Josephine was holed up, erase the

Event off her record, spend the rest of her years away from Oshiya, and build her name. Josephine and the president could go about their scheming and Spencer could propel back into the active roster, and everything would be as it should.

Spencer. Her lips tilted into a smile. What a little snack.

She'd skimmed Nolan Spencer's file that Oliver had sent and found that Spencer had told her the truth when she asked about his history. He came from a typical nuclear family in the middle west district of Borralyo, a small suburban industrial area. After completing secondary school, he received a handful of scholarship offers for athletics, but went to the military academy. He earned top scores in nearly every category, and they swiftly transferred him to the North Point base, notoriously known as the crème de la crème for prospective combat youths. It was a soldier academy.

His record was redacted, and paragraphs and pages were solid black. She had to scroll down until last year, when it seemed he'd either been discharged or put on "light duty" and was no longer sent on those super top-secret assassin missions. Kana didn't care much for the dark and dastardly doings of the government. If a person imagined it, a government was doing it, and probably in a less efficient manner.

Spencer was a rather wholesome person. His most-played genre of music was soft alternative pop, followed by guided meditation and a range of rap bouncing around different country borders. According to the video streaming graphs, he watched documentaries and romantic comedies, and even then, he'd only watched four films in the last year. The initial dark web sweep came up empty. Was he a monk or someone off the grid? Most likely paranoid, and he knew how to hide his searches. The next graph displayed the number of books he'd read, and his increased visits to the local library in Kkileyo verified what he'd revealed to Kana that night on the beach. He was back in his hometown.

An unknown number flashed on her phone.

"Yes?" she answered, one hand reaching to throw a blanket over her chest, as the night wind twisted through the balcony.

"This is Dr. Cohen." He sounded tired. "The lab came back with the initial results, and . . ." He paused, and she heard a faint shuffling and a clinking of glass. He seemed like a bourbon man. "The results are . . ." He struggled with finding the words.

"Spit it out."

"Are you a Natural or Synthetic?"

Kana's teeth clicked.

"I'm only asking because your file says you are neither, but that can't be possible. The reaction from the Synthetic User caused an odd response in your system. We've been running studies on the way Synthetic Users and Natural Users bend reality and the differences in their energy frequencies."

Kana knew exactly what he was summarizing; Ambrose Inc. was funding those studies.

"Hypothetically, let's say I'm a Natural," Kana said.

"If you are a Natural," he said carefully, "the Synthetic User was a lot of negative energy, and your body was a positive energy, like magnets."

"We attracted one another. Is that why my stomach looks like char?"

"Undetermined right now. Your white blood cell count is too high, since it's fighting off an infection, but you aren't exhibiting any outward symptoms." He paused. "You, out of everyone, must know the construction of a Natural compared to a Synthetic is different. I'd advise not to use any power, at least until you've healed."

"And let's say, hypothetically, I'm a Synthetic."

"I can't say for certain whether the reaction was because of your designated status. It would be helpful to drop the smoke and mirrors."

Kana would do no such thing, and asked a different question. "What tests are you running?"

"A sample tissue result was returned, and whatever it is, it isn't necrotic. Your hormone levels are abnormal. It would help if we had a sample of the attacker."

"I'll see what I can do. I expect the results to be destroyed."

Kana hung up and messaged Oliver to monitor Dr. Cohen's internet use, both personal and business related. If he saved anything, she wanted to know about it. A ripple of hunger gurgled through her stomach.

She pushed open the double doors, expecting to see Spencer stationed outside her bedroom, maybe hoping to catch him eavesdropping. Only an empty living space greeted her. She shrugged into a thin sweatshirt, the kind worn down from decades of use, and walked to the nearest fast-food chain, ignoring the quiet shadow following her. She didn't acknowledge his presence, and it turned out he wasn't in a chatty mood either.

The teen at the register looked with zero subtlety at Kana, as if trying to place her. Without makeup and her signature red eyeliner, she was unidentifiable. The boxy Clark Kent glasses were for her amusement. The less glamorous version of her could pass as anyone.

The takeout bag crinkled as she sat crisscrossed on the beach and unwrapped the double patty burger.

Could Josephine have put a clue in Vyolette's telescope? That seemed outrageous, and something the woman would do. The observatory was at the far end of the property, a gift from Vyolette's father to his mistress. Was Spencer proficient in breaking and entering? The easiest answer was to send Spencer with her demand to the president, but she'd rather not ask for the president's help and give the man any inkling as to what she was discovering. Kana sighed, giving in to the fact that she had to be there. If there was a clue as specific as the Pluto symbol, then she was forced to investigate.

Portal creation would be handy right about now. She could pop in and out; it was the closest thing to teleportation. But she couldn't create portals, and no one except the creator could migrate through one. Plus, Vyolette's security had half a million cameras. The best option was to attend Vyolette's summer party. They shut off cameras during those lustrous parties and permitted discretion. The event to welcome summer happened in three days. She swallowed the last bite, licking the salty residue on her lips as her message was sent off with a whoosh. There was a sense of dread floating off with the single line of text, like swimming in the open ocean, the dark, immeasurable depth below holding sharp-toothed predators, jaws gaping and ready to gnash and rip apart her flesh.

———

THE NIGHT BEFORE THE SOCIALITE REUNION, KANA prepared to engage with that part of her past. The red light from her LED mask dimmed, and she tossed the contraption off. She narrowed her outfit selection to six options.

"What is this?" Spencer asked as he held up a silk halter top. Kana knocked the fridge door closed with the edge of her hip, her smoothie in hand.

"If you're going to be attending the event, you need an outfit, and frankly, your closet and taste won't do."

"This is yours. Why is it the guest room?" He held out the hanger. The material of the blouse was like liquid as it fluttered between them.

"It's, in fact, yours. Gender neutral clothing items are normal," she said, hiding her glee as he scratched at the spot where his sideburn and ear connected. "Men can wear women's tops and women can wear men's tops." Kana held back her bark of laughter. Spencer's face said he couldn't decide if she was joking, and he tried to hide the horror. "Shall I make another jibe at the social construct of masculinity?" she asked, leaning into the back of the sofa. That didn't bait him.

"Try it on at least," she urged.

"No," he said.

"I won't drink at the party if you try on the halter top," she offered.

His eyes went to the silky top and back to her. "Tell me why we need to attend this party. It's an unnecessary risk."

"You don't question; you're Kleo Fellows." Spencer remained unimpressed. "The pink-haired girl in Tullsom's mystery series?" Kana was surprised, because he either didn't understand the literary reference to Oshiya's acclaimed mystery writer, or he didn't agree with the comparison of being the designated sidekick.

"Fine, you can be George Fayne." His face remained blank, "Or you can be Bess Marvin," she offered. He set the shirt down on the glass coffee table, waiting for her to explain more.

"Vyolette is someone with important access. She won't give me anything unless I give her something. Showing up at her welcome summer gathering should be enough. You can come as my plus one, or you can play sniper and try not to get caught by her security team. Is that enough information for you? Shirt, now."

He peeled off his navy T-shirt. Kana appreciated the muscles rippling beneath his skin. Under the second line of his abs was a long, pale scar. She was sure that if she were closer, there would be more.

"How do I even?" He held up the shirt, turning it left and right.

"That piece is the neck. It's a halter top, no sleeves."

He grumbled a string of incomprehensible words, some which weren't English. "Are you satisfied?"

She couldn't stop the smile as she drank in his built figure in the delicate, feminine silk. Her silence made him uncomfortable, his face inflamed. She gave him mercy. "Your shoulders look great, and that color is decent. You might be a true winter rather than an autumn."

"I was born in the summer."

She didn't bother explaining that she was referring to his seasonal color palette. The blue was too muted. He looked better in brighter, solid colors. "I set aside other clothes. They'll be in the top drawer. A Carey Grant Riviera look would better fit Vyolette's taste." She waved him off as she picked up the tablet. "Although, you look a little slutty in just those gray sweats. Vyolette would appreciate that look, too."

Spencer's torso became a human thermometer, pink racing across his face, down his neck, and to his chest as he quickly shoved the T-shirt back on. She mentally gave herself a pat on the back for correctly guessing his size.

Kana hummed, "Still slutty." She couldn't stop the shit-eating grin at Spencer's embarrassment.

"How is a T-shirt and sweats slutty?"

"Thirst trap."

He crossed his arms over his chest, not realizing the flex of his biceps, his sharp eyes deliberately dragging over her body. Kana was lounging in an identical outfit, a T-shirt and loose sweatpants.

"I don't make the rules." She shrugged, hiding her teasing smile behind the tablet.

———

A CHERRY-RED BUICK CONVERTIBLE ROLLED TO THE side entrance, and against the earthy and subdued tones, the drop of red reminded Kana of blood against snow. In another time and place, Kana stood in thick rubber snow boots that made her feet look twice as big and clownlike. Blood dribbled out of her nose, the droplets staining the blanket of white. The fluttering of lilac hair broke the memory as the car purred to a stop. "As I live and breathe," Vyolette said, her lips were the color of black currant berries, slick with gloss as she grinned.

Kana smirked, removing her white cat-eyed sunglasses, and walked down the steps, the heels of her shoes gently clacking to meet the older woman who glided toward her as if she were on ice skates. "Ronan said you were back, but you know her little Tweety birds are all gossip with little accuracy," Vyolette said as the two kissed cheeks, as if they were meeting at a boulangerie in France.

"Oh, I miss those maroon eyes," Vyolette said sweetly, her perfectly manicured nail stroking Kana's cheek.

Kana locked every muscle, attuned to Vyolette's talons. She hated when people touched her face. Five years did little to ease the discontent as the older woman saddled into her personal space. Kana stared at her reflection, the red eyeliner appearing black in the dark reflection of Vyolette's sunglasses.

"And who is this?" Vyolette asked, the fabric of her cream slip folding against her frame as the wind blew, highlighting her curved hips and her minuscule waist. "A handsome new friend."

"This is Spencer. He's a nurse," Kana said.

"A nurse," Vyolette said with a lilt of interest, flicking off her sunglasses. Her stunning green eyes latched onto Spencer. The heavy-lashed gaze raked up and down his body.

Kana patted him as if he were a dog. His muscles were coiled under her palm, pressing against the thin cotton striped shirt stretched across his chest. Vyolette certainly had a way with people. "The doctors won't let me out of the hospital unless I have a caretaker."

"He's a catch. A touch gauche, but I suppose he can come." Vyolette returned to the driver's seat. Spencer opened the passenger door for Kana and hopped into the back seat.

Vyolette was the illegitimate daughter of William Oskar, the lovechild of William's supposed soulmate. The media had reveled when they discovered William Oskar's affair with Bella Illon-

Shah. Bella was an astrologer who had made her fortune blending the Western beliefs and her Oshiya roots, her ancestry reflected in her hyphenated name, proving to the world she belonged to one of the southern priestesses' lineages. While William and Bella's illicit affair had gone on, his wife had been withering away in hospice. It was the scalding hot tea which high society lapped at. There were, of course, affairs, but many were sealed, NDAs signed; however, sometimes things slipped and became public. Vyolette was raised by doting parents, catering to her whims and fancy.

"You were in New York? Or was it Montreal?" Vyolette asked, her question snapping Kana back to the present as her tires squeaked with the sharp acceleration out of the complex. The older woman was being generous today, tiptoeing with the facade of politeness as an edge into the recent lake fiasco.

"I left New York City for a little retreat. The city can be stifling."

Vyolette agreed vehemently. "Every year it's like the city gets worse, sinking in its own filth. It's disappointing. How was the retreat?"

Kana cocked her head. Is a "retreat" what they called being held hostage and watching people die now? "I survived."

"You've been the talk of the town," Vyolette said. "I'm surprised you reached out. It's been so long."

Kana restrained a sigh at the sound of Vyolette's exaggeration. So, the other woman recalled their little tiff, and was gauging to see if Kana remembered. "We were at the Clarin's charity exhibition," Kana began, clarifying to Vyolette she did remember their last encounter, but she wasn't going to give in. "And there was that misunderstanding from your fiancé, Maximus."

Vyolette's foot pushed on the brake a little too hard and Kana jerked forward. The seatbelt dug into her stomach. Bitch.

"Misunderstanding," Vyolette laughed, tossing her head back. "You bankrupted his hedge fund. He lost everything."

"Eleven-year-olds handle investments better than he ever did," Kana scoffed.

"Then why did the stocks suddenly dip less than an hour after he spoke to you about his plan to artificially inflate the bundle of stocks?"

"You've taken some economics and investment classes now?" Kana asked, because Vyolette didn't know what she was saying. Maximus's inflated ego and desire to break away from his family's generational investments led him to make idiotic risks, which cost him nearly all his money. Good thing he'd been well fed with a golden spoon, and sat atop a trust fund with more wealth than a hundred strangers would see in their combined lives.

Both women's heads turned to face the other. Sparks could have exploded from the clashing tension. A sharp honk from the car behind Vyolette's caused them both to jerk in their seats.

"He was useless anyway, even more so now that he's penniless." Vyolette faked nonchalance, but there was no hint of letting go. Maximus had made a fool of himself and, by extension, Vyolette.

"You're my surprise guest for the evening." Vyolette grinned, flashing her teeth too white to be natural. she undoubtedly would make a spectacle of Kana appearing at her summer solstice party.

Kana's fingernails tapped against the fine leather of the arm rest.

"Now tell me, how is Mr. Vanhaven? I heard he's still chasing Marianne's skirts. The woman had her second abortion, quite the scandal. You know Ria released a summer single, chart manipulation at its finest. Her sugar-pop song is terrible, but she's been at the number one spot for over a week, and now she's dropped to spot 118 because of a new rule they released in America, and she's saying she's going to sue. Honestly, her song is total trash . . ."

Vyolette talked the rest of the car ride along the coast to her private laguna, shoving fluffy gossip down Kana's throat. Kana wouldn't have thought a woman two years away from thirty would act like a thirteen-year-old, but age was only a number, and Kana mused that Vyolette would regress as she aged, becoming even less patient, with more tantrums, and certainly more demands and toys broken. As they drove around the back driveway between the tall trees, a line of guests stood waiting, their cars parked elsewhere. Men and women in tunics stood beside each guest, each with one arm tucked behind their backs and the other gripping the wooden handle of a large parasol, looking like silk jellyfish tops.

A blaring sound of a deep horn echoed as an elephant stomped along the private road. A woman sat atop, steering the beast and waving to the couples in line. Horses pulling a gilded carriage trotted along a secondary path, carrying another couple. Kana rolled her eyes. At least Vyolette had offered her guests options for travel up to the main event.

"The South Wing is open to freshen up. I'll announce your entrance in twenty." Vyolette swung the car into the underground garage and parked beside half a dozen equally pristine classic cars, all organized by color.

Vyolette blew a kiss as she floated away. Kana wanted the woman's skinny stiletto heels to slip on the polished garage floors, but alas, Vyolette strutted away without tripping, disappearing into the elevator and leaving a stirring of gray, as if a storm had come in her wake. Kana assumed Vyolette would ask for trivial things: a gift of a private jet, or a yacht; she even expected Vyolette to demand scripts of potential films Kana's production company had in the works. But Vyolette didn't hint at anything in particular during the drive, only that Kana was the guest of honor, and that was concerning. Kana didn't like not knowing.

"Kana." Warm fingers touched her shoulder. She'd forgotten Spencer was there, and apparently, he'd exited the car and opened the passenger door without her noticing.

She bypassed the offered hand and stepped out. "She's going to demand something outrageous," Kana said, allowing a sliver of what was on her mind out as she led the way to the other door opposite where Vyolette had exited, passing by four other vintage cars, waxed and glossy, as if they were kept in glass boxes.

"Will she ask for an island?" Spencer speculated, as if that was the most outlandish thing she would demand.

"Edith Queenie asked for a favor, and Vyolette said 'yes,' if she and her partner agreed to attend her 'Let Them Eat Cake' getaway in Croatia. And it was not the baked pastry kind of cake. Edith was Vyolette's favorite actress growing up. Isn't there a saying, 'never meet your heroes?' Well, for Vyolette, it's 'never fuck your heroes.'"

Spencer laughed. "Edith Queenie, the child actor?" he asked in disbelief. The stunning yet odd-looking successful child actor had taken a hiatus before her teenage years and returned to the spotlight as a young woman married to a model.

He stopped laughing, his face twisted. "You're serious."

Kana's silence was her reply.

They left the underground parking garage and entered a slanted hallway that led up to the first floor. The brisk air-conditioned wind left goosebumps along Kana's exposed skin. As she went to push open the door, Spencer touched the inside of her elbow. His rough fingertips never lingered longer than necessary, only exerting enough pressure to grab her attention.

"If she demands anything that makes you uncomfortable, you don't need to say yes."

Kana jerked her arm away, and the large hand dropped back to his side as she leaned into the solid door and removed her sunglasses to stare into Spencer's eyes.

"Didn't you learn anything on that ride?" she sighed, watching the darkening of his face. He wasn't an idiot. He must have observed how Vyolette and Kana spoke to one another, the insuppressible disdain for the other palpable. "It's fun and games to make the other uncomfortable. Vyolette desires the physical things in life." She stepped closer, catching the subtle whiff of one of the colognes she'd purchased. He'd chosen not to wear the heavier scents, but a lighter, citrus tang. It suited him.

"She won't make you do anything without consent." She patted his chest where a red pocket square stuck out.

"Coercing someone to consent isn't consent." He laid his hand over hers, his eyes searching her face. His eyebrows were a little unruly. He would benefit from some trimming or threading, but they were dipped in that concerned way Oliver sometimes had.

She rolled her eyes as she slid her hand out of his. "Vyolette won't be asking for us to join her in an orgy. She wouldn't get pleasure from it," Kana assured him. If Vyolette suspected any hint of a relationship between them, she would gladly have tugged at the frayed edges of the partnership, worming her way between them, but there was nothing to manipulate.

Kana pushed open the door, and Spencer exhaled a low whistle. The sharp sound spiraled upward, scattered off ancient intricate columns over two and a half meters tall, and bounced off the arched ceilings. They entered the South Wing of the Grecian-inspired summer estate. Atop the gleaming white marbled floors were tastefully displayed vases of fresh-cut bouquets surrounded by marble busts and sculptures.

Two maids in identical dark pants and white blouses were dutifully maintaining the space, a cart with cleaning solutions, rags, and a handheld vacuum between them. The oldest of the two noticed Kana first. "Miss Ambrose, may I assist you?" the woman in her forties asked, bending slightly with a gloved hand to her heart.

"South Wing guest room," Kana instructed.

The maid ticked her head to the younger woman, who understood the command and escorted Kana down the long hallway.

"Are these real?" Spencer stopped in front of a painting encased in a glass box. "It says Monnet."

"Yes," Kana said without needing to check whatever piece of art Spencer was referring to. "How many guests are attending?"

"The guest list is totaled at one hundred and one," the maid answered confidently.

"How secure is the property? There were four guards at the side gate."

The maid stopped in front of two floor-to-ceiling double doors.

"Triple. After the shooting incident yesterday afternoon, she's requested more guards."

"What is this?" Spencer bent down to see a shorter open doorway, only about one meter tall. Kana backtracked to stand beside him. Inside was a cinerarium, rich slabs of stone cubbies, with thick glass fronts to see inside. Placed on the farthest back wall was a shrine.

"Those are reliquaries, bones, and other parts of popes and monks. Vyolette likes to think that if she holds their sacred parts, she's somehow closer to being cleansed and closer to holiness."

Spencer straightened, his brows furrowed as he digested her words.

"Don't think about it too hard. She's a collector," Kana said, breezing past Spencer. "I'll be at the main hall in fifteen."

Kana waved the maid away and sealed herself behind the double doors of the guest suite.

Chapter Fifteen

Kana cradled her arms, grasping her elbows as she looked out at the ocean from Vyolette's southern balcony. Black strands danced around the blue of the sky as a gust of wind blew through. All she had to do was agree to Vyolette's terms, smile, nod, listen to the insipid drama at the soiree, and slip away to the observatory. Then she would be free from Vyolette's carefully crafted world that suited Vyolette's needs. Kana had forgotten that Vyolette had redesigned the toilets to be her ideal height, and with Kana's shorter stature, that meant her toes barely touched the ground. A show of Vyolette's wealth, because who else replaced every toilette in her estate as she grew taller?

"Kana." Vyolette had changed into a thin garment that looked as if it were crafted from tendrils of fog. Her diamond body jewelry, worth at least three million alone, was fashioned as a collar that dipped between her breasts to a thin gold chain around her waist, coming back around to her hips, and dripping into streams of raindrop pearls. Vyolette was stunning, with all the confidence of knowing she looked incredible, and she was the one wearing the crown tonight. Kana bit back her tongue and forced her shoulders to curl in, making herself smaller. She had a role to play in the game.

"You are my surprise guest." Vyolette offered her arm as if she were a gentleman. Kana silently accepted the gesture and resigned to being the silent trophy wife in the little show as Vyolette led them through her mansion and to the top of the staircase to the main ballroom. Two doormen bowed at the waist, each man pulled open one of the doors, and the mingling sounds of laughter and chatter floated with the lullaby quartet drawing their bows. A silence fell over the crowd as the two young women approached the railing. Kana held her breath, subtly cracking her neck to the right.

"Friends, lovers, and esteemed patrons, welcome to my solstice festival. I am honored that Kana Ambrose has made a miraculous recovery and has come as my guest."

If any eyes weren't on Kana, they were now. Unlike most people, when faced with a large room of gawkers Kana painstakingly locked eyes with as many people as possible. She moved on when the person she made eye contact with blinked or shifted their gaze; it was a good distraction. As the two young women walked down the steps, an unexpected speck of water caused Kana to wince, until more splashes of fine mist fell from the ceiling, following the curved stairwell. A chorus of *oohs* and *aahs* met them as Vyolette's dress evaporated when the water coated the fabric, bleeding out into smoke until they reached the final step, where Vyolette stood in a gold and emerald two-piece, while Kana stood beside her, damp and cold.

"Enjoy yourselves tonight," Vyolette said with a bow as the audience clapped. A maid approached with a sheer pearlescent robe draped over her left arm, and a silver tray with crystal coupe glasses fizzing with bubbly in the other. "I have a group of exclusive guests," Vyolette began softly as a second maid held open the robe for Vyolette to slide her arms through. Women in their luxurious dresses and men in their dapper suits flowed out of the open wall, a special installation that lifted the wide panels of windows into the roof.

"I expect you to be there," Vyolette said as she lowered her head to Kana's ear. She was a good twelve centimeters taller, plus the additional height of her incredibly high heels. Vyolette tucked a lock of Kana's long bangs behind her ear, an intimate touch, and made another stroke to wipe away the water droplets above Kana's left eyebrow. Kana forced herself to remain relaxed. Vyolette was going to push every button she had tonight.

In the fringe of Kana's periphery, she could see the cluster of people around them, all eyes staring only at them, holding their breath. Kana curled the ends of her lips, planning to get what she wanted well before she met Vyolette's playthings this evening.

"I wouldn't miss it," Kana said, leaning in.

"Kana Ambrose," a voice sliced between the raw breath the women seemed to share as both sets of eyes slid to the person, neither woman turning their heads or their bodies. Vyolette was the first to move, a smile on her face.

"Peter Cullsen, I believe this is the first time you've accepted my invitation." Vyolette made it a point to look down at Kana. "And you choose to ignore your gracious host." She held out her delicate hand.

Peter Cullsen was a man in his late forties, aging like fine wine; the added years only increasing his beauty. He stiffly bent at the waist and placed a peck on the back of her knuckles. The fact that Vyolette had invited him multiple times surprised Kana. Vyolette hated it if someone rejected her; the result meant either they were dead in her eyes or a thing to chase after, rejection making their eventual submission all the sweeter. It seemed Peter was in the latter category, as Vyolette's parties weren't typically for someone like Peter Cullsen, a tech businessman. Vyolette preferred celebrities, idols and artists of the world, the socialites—and above all, the beautiful. Kana eyed Peter's sharp jawline and lifted cheekbones; perhaps he made it onto

Vyolette's radar because he wasn't the typical entrepreneurial tech geek.

"My apologies," he said politely, focusing on Vyolette, but his bright blue eyes, framed against a tanned canvas and black lashes and brows, moved to Kana as if he were about to ask her a question. Kana's left cheek twitched as she tried to rein in her reticence. She didn't like blue eyes. Although she couldn't see the color well anymore, there was the striking memory of blue eyes.

"Your apology is not accepted." Vyolette released Kana's arm. "Walk with me to the pool, then perhaps I will forgive you."

With Vyolette gone, the feeling of being under a microscope magnified. She was used to paparazzi, reporters at events, and not-so-subtle looks in stores or on the streets. The excessively wealthy took the cake for their scrutiny, their eyes flaying Kana's skin and squeezing her insides until her innards spilled out of her orifices. She'd be left with nothing but the pile of organs and blood that made up everyone else, and yet they would still find something wrong, something distasteful about her. Her stomach rolled as the demon of clawing insecurity returned, a vile creature who reveled in her torture, a creature she fought to overcome.

Kana started moving through the dispersing guests, feeling like she was watching a scene from a film, every person interacting as if following a script, moving with a precise grace, a flick of a wrist, the gaze of eyes, a feigned laugh. Everything was too rehearsed, and she was out of place. Kana was about to wave down a waiter, her mouth parched for alcohol, the disjointed feeling too familiar, but as soon as Vyolette was no longer in her orbit, the clucking hens descended.

"How are you getting on?"

"They said you lost a leg."

"Christ, Anne, clearly her legs are fine."

"You look incredible, as always. Have you lost weight?"

"It's like you never gain weight. God, why are Asians so lucky?"

"It has nothing to do with ethnicity, it's called youth," one woman snickered. "Which you lost ten years ago."

"Isn't equating skinniness to beauty standards out now?"

"Oh, Fiona, who knew you had such insightful societal knowledge?" The women laughed, fluttering their hands, bits of gold and gems catching the sunlight. The clouds of perfume clashing against one another were headache inducing.

"Your production company did well this year. There's buzz around that indie film potentially winning at Sundance."

"Oh, yes, that lovely little art film, I found the cinematography just stunning, very Cubric-inspired, but that main actor—"

"I heard you were at the private gallery viewing of that French artist. Didn't you just love the choice of colors and the composition he used?"

Kana sipped down another flute as she slipped into the high-society mingling. It was like sliding on a pair of shoes, worn and familiar, but she hated the way they looked and felt. The inflection in their voices, questions asked using seven syllables, the drag of certain sounds, everything insipid and pointless.

"The Mercurial is back, three by threes." Translation: the Mercurial, an exclusive club, opened its doors only on the third week of the third month.

"Yes, yes, yes." Translation: three yeses meant they were interested in an entrance ticket, two yeses meant they weren't, but knew of a group who might be.

"Fairchild's playing with fireflies." Fairchild, most likely the eldest son, since the second son was only ten, was having an affair with someone significantly underage. Kana supposed they were all groomed to an extent.

The translation was immediate, her brain deciphering the snippets of conversations floating around her in the strange phrasing and words the elite used. While Vyolette had a certain type of person she surrounded herself with, even among them there was elitism, groups forming among each other, the native bloodlines of Oshiya in one corner and the neo-wealthy in another camp, the natural models, the models whose faces were carefully crafted to an ideal perfection. Kana lifted her nose, shutting out the drivel of petty and irrelevant pissing contests.

She caught sight of Spencer's hazy blue shirt, the sleeves rolled up to his elbows. He was speaking to another man; the sharp cheekbones and delicately thin frame, the waist that nearly vanished when he twisted to snag a drink, indicated he could only be a model.

"I heard those people who attacked at the antique fair were Americans."

"Typical, attack only. Does your mother know what they were after?"

Kana tried to push away from the gossiping women and closer to the chief inspector's youngest daughter to listen to their conversation, which seemed to be the only interesting topic.

"Miss Ambrose." A man stepped in her path. Kana was about to brush past him; she had no patience to speak with someone, except that she knew that profile and the elegantly long neck.

"George," Kana said, unable to stop the surprise tinting her tone. "Did you go through another growth spurt?" The last time she saw him was in their second year of secondary school, before her final year abroad. Close to six years had passed since then, and he looked a quarter of a meter taller.

"It's been a while," George commented, grinning. The braces were gone, and the sparkly white bleached teeth were in place. His silk shirt did little to hide his broad, hardened chest and arms. Their paths had often crossed when they were younger. He was the son of the Secretary of Defense, and she was the daughter of the woman supplying A.E. Potentia, but after Kana had fled Oshiya, their forced proximity ended.

Kana waited for him to speak. He'd called her name for a reason, and she wasn't going to engage in any useless small talk.

"I didn't plan on coming this year. You know how it is." He

waved his hand around as if implying all events were the same. "But when Vyolette announced you would be attending, I wanted to see if it was true." He stepped closer, a predatory movement in the glide of his body. He'd certainly changed and picked up those gross habits from the overly confident military influences. Kana planted her feet.

"We all wanted to see the untouchable Kana Ambrose, and it seemed the rumors of your near-death experience were exaggerated, yet again." He was less than an arm's reach away. The weight of cologne was too heavy with amber and wood for her taste.

"How many lives do you have?" he asked softly as his lowered lashes cast a shadow over his toffee eyes. There was a tautness in the line of his body, a tightening string nearing its breaking point, but she couldn't distinguish if the tension was excitement or something more nefarious and predatory.

"More than you'll ever know," she commented. "Last I heard, you went to work for the government, following in your mother's footsteps, since following your father didn't turn out well."

His body twitched, and his right hand tightened into a fist momentarily. His eyes sharpened, and whatever his response would have been was lost as a waiter announced himself with a polite clearing of his throat. "Miss Ambrose," he said, "your presence is requested on the terrace."

Kana controlled her scowl at the thought of Vyolette calling for her to return to her side. The waiter led her through the open glass wall, where some guests were enjoying the massive pool area and the bar. Kana didn't see Vyolette's gathered robe. Instead, Spencer stood near the railing and offered a nod.

What a pleasant surprise. He was useful apart from his muscles. She glided down the stairs along the side of the short cliff to the path toward the observatory. A man and woman holding hands on the same path, heading to the main house, broke apart, parting for Kana, who didn't falter in her step. Spencer apologized on her behalf and trailed after her. Officers on four-wheelers patrolled the beach, and she was certain that more guards were concealed.

"Ask your questions," Kana said. "Your staring is annoying."

"How extensive is the property? It's incredible there's this much open land."

Kana shifted her gaze from the smooth rolling hills to the rocky hillside where the observatory sat. "Her family bought the air."

"What?" Spencer asked in disbelief.

"They bought the land and the air. If they could buy the sea, they would. But that's not the real question you had."

"When did you start attending parties like this?"

"Before I could walk, but I was formally invited without Josephine when I was ten. Vyolette has hosted galas and soirees twice a year since she turned twelve."

"Have you always . . ." He fell silent behind her. Kana had a nagging curiosity about what he observed. Did he see her distaste for the surrounding people, the way she fell into the background? Did he see the plastic smile, the unblinking eyes, just like every other manufactured doll at the party? Kana turned around to face Spencer, curious about his expression, and caught the sad glaze in his eyes, and the slight frown that was more of a concern. She knew that look.

"Don't pity me," she breathed, but the weight of the words were granite blocks. He covered his expression, and she continued her way up the slope.

Kana's bare feet tapped around the linoleum floor as she made rounds, over and over again, in the observatory. She checked the desks, drawers, cabinets, and behind the monitors, but found nothing. She even thought Josephine would have somehow put a message on a computer screensaver, but it was all ordinary. The thunk of a slammed cabinet drawer gave away Kana's agitation.

"Do you need help?" Spencer asked, watching her flit over to the seat of the telescope, eyeing the control panel. Was it possible to put a message in the sky? Josephine had reach and friends in high places, but putting a message literally in outer space was a stretch. Kana hit a button, and the machine hummed to life. Josephine was known for making the impossible possible.

"Unless you know how to use this Goliath of a telescope, I don't need your help." She smashed another button, her nose pointed to the ceiling, but the roof remained stubbornly closed.

With surprising speed and care, Spencer moved her out of the control panel chair and behind his body. A light, bubbly soda sensation popped along the skin of her legs. Kana unknowingly moved closer to the source, nursing what little energy she could snatch. She ran into Spencer's outstretched arm, which kept her from taking another step. The wall with a whiteboard split like soggy single-ply toilet paper as a woman in all black, a baseball hat, and a utility belt emerged out of the disintegrating space. There was one exit and entrance, and the main door was across the room.

"Miss Ambrose, the lady requests your presence in her bunker."

Kana thought she would have more time. It couldn't have been more than an hour since she left the main party.

"Fine," Kana said, but the woman didn't return to her closing portal. "Of course, you'll escort me," Kana commented, and exaggeratedly waved her arm as if saying lead the way. Spencer moved close beside Kana.

"He cannot come." The woman guard pointed to Spencer. Kana couldn't read his face, but the displeasure rolled off of him.

"Naturally, VIPs only," Kana said and stepped around Spencer without a single look back; she followed the guard.

The woman handed Kana a silk eye mask.

"Are you serious?" Kana scoffed.

The woman didn't bat an eyelash.

Kana acquiesced and allowed the officer to tie the blindfold around her eyes. Carefully inhaling and exhaling to keep her composure, Kana allowed herself to be led out of the observatory. This was not going to plan. Vyolette was supposed to be impulsive and demand something outrageous, not bring Kana to an undisclosed location.

Kana had two small knives strapped to the upper junction of her each thigh. They were uniquely crafted blades similar to a scalpel, thin enough to lay flat against the inner part of her thigh and made from polycarbonate so a metal detector did not detect them. But other than those, she had no weapon. The heels of her stilettos could be useful, and logically, she knew the eyes were a vulnerable point to attack. With a churning stomach and a rising tide of anxiety, Kana followed the guard into an elevator.

The storm arrived in full. Kana's lungs filled, her body steeling itself as the elevator ground to its stop. Vyolette was malicious in her way, but also loyal, and abided by their NDA rules. There were limitations to what she could ask for. Kana straightened her posture, counting the steps away from the elevator as the guard led her down a long hallway.

"And here she is." Vyolette clapped as the guard removed the eye mask.

Chapter Sixteen

The entire back wall was an aquatic tank with the shifting, dull cerulean blue peeking at her through her good eye. It was no doubt impressive as the aquarium was at least five hundred square meters, more of a reenactment of a reef than a tank, the bright hues of fish and coral the only pop of color in the minimalist room.

There were five people, including Kana and the woman guard: Vyolette (who had changed from her haute couture robe to an emerald lingerie slip), Ingrid (the daughter of a stock market tycoon and forcibly retired model), and George, whose presence was the most unexpected. The fleeting thought that this could be an orgy request didn't pass by her. But as much as Vyolette liked to intimidate with her feminine wiles, she had no interest in Kana in any sexual way.

"Leave," Vyolette ordered the woman guard.

Kana sucked up the funneled soda pop energy the guard left as she vanished through her portal. Kana's special battery wasn't even a quarter full, and while Dr. Cohen's warning stuck in her thoughts, if she needed it, she had enough stored for a blitz attack. The largest threat was dear old Georgie; the girls, Kana could handle. While Vyolette could set off her panic button to bring fifteen armed guards descending upon the underground aquarium, Kana wasn't worried. Out of her library of dangerous and potentially life-threatening situations, Kana could handle the erratic trio before her.

"Drink? Do you still enjoy scotch on the rocks?" Vyolette moved to the glass and metal-lined wet bar, shaped like a curving worm, and poured a glass of amber liquid.

"I thought you would enjoy your festival. Leaving your adoring guests to hide in this little corner seems unlike you." Kana stepped down the two steps onto the lush carpet. The living space was carved in a semicircle, with the sofas curved to face an electric fireplace stretching at least three of her arm spans.

"I was unaware you two knew each other so well," Kana said to George.

"We've become closer in the past two years," George said, grinning as he leaned back, letting his long arms drape against the back of the sofa. "Bonded over a similar desire."

Kana caught the subtext. Vyolette and George were co-conspirators, and she struggled to understand what they could both want. "Ingrid," Kana said, addressing the youngest in the room in her final teenage year. Ingrid was perched in the armchair, her legs folded neatly at the knees. "It's been so long. How have the runways been these days?"

Ingrid's eyes flashed and her burgundy lips sneered. They all knew about Ingrid's massive scandal that had led to her being unwanted, canceled on every social media site, her exclusive contracts terminated. The kind of scandal that extinguished careers, but not gregarious enough to warrant trials, or future documentary deals for the true crime story. No, Ingrid's scandal was a rightful reflection of her disregard for facts, her loose lips, and the double-edged sword of influence through an electronic screen.

"Always such a pleasure to see you, Kana," Ingrid spat as she stood up, the ridges of her sternum visible through the low V-cut of her sheer dress. "Like you've never made mistakes." She circled Kana. Her bovine eyes, pinched nose, and mouth were exaggerated by her thin frame.

"I'm resourceful enough to cover up my mistakes," Kana goaded.

"I've always wondered if those headlines of your kidnappings and survival stories were ever true," Ingrid chimed. "You certainly seem perfectly healthy to me." Her dark eyes slowly combed over Kana from head to toe, as if trying to see through Kana's slip for the evidence of her wounds.

"My guards mentioned they saw you and your nurse in the Observatory." Vyolette placed Kana's drink at the edge of the tall crystal table behind the couch. "I didn't think much of your little nurse, but it seems Georgie recognized him."

Kana leaned back casually. She hadn't thought of the possibility that George would recognize Spencer, but she didn't expect to see George at all, much less at Vyolette's soiree.

"He's military," George commented.

"Why don't we bring him here?" Vyolette asked, her spider lashes blinking innocently. Kana's mouth twitched.

"Bring the nurse," Vyolette said into her phone. Kana inwardly grinned. Vyolette really was an idiot. Bringing someone she knew was military to an enclosed room was the dumbest move she could make. Kana wouldn't lose another opportunity for a shot of energy, and Spencer could certainly handle three socialites. Vyolette was awfully confident, even if she'd brought a dozen guards for protection.

Ingrid's disdainful gaze matched her voice. "What does the world see in you? You're unremarkable." The curl of Ingrid's large lips and the flick of gold hair over her shoulder said *You're ugly*, as if that were the worst thing to be in this world. "Your mother's name carries everything for you. I heard your little production company is picking up a slasher, ready to use your life experiences as inspo?"

"You think it's a publicity stunt? What about the families? Do you think I placed them there and hired a mass murderer as a PR stunt?" Kana asked, scoffing as if she spoke to children.

Ingrid wanted proof, and Kana was sure she'd demand Kana remove her dress entirely as a way to embarrass her. The small blades would be impossible to conceal, and Kana didn't want to reveal her only weapons unless she had to use them.

Kana tugged the thin strap of her dress until the top pooled around her hips. Everyone's eyes widened, surprised by Kana's bold action as she stood chest bare, her nipples hard exposed to the cool air. The zigzag of medical tape and the raw edges of pinched black flesh held by stitches peeked out. "Do you need a doctor to inspect if these are real and not a makeup artist's work?" Kana asked as she placed one hand on her hip. "Vyolette, you should know how great cosmetic surgeries are these days." All eyes shifted to Vyolette's hard face, her cheeks flushed under the rouge on her cheekbones as she lost control of the situation. "What exactly do you want me for?" Kana asked, her question spoken like a command. The bubbly carbonation returned as a portal opened. Impeccable timing, but the guard still needed to lead Spencer down the hallway, twenty-five strides, give or take.

George was the one to answer, and not in words, but with a 9mm in his hand as he slowly circled the couch.

"We have a bet going. Some people think you're a Sori. How else could a girl survive so many deaths? But judging by those scars, if you could phase through things, you wouldn't have been hurt. It's possible you could rip portals." Vyolette explained, pleased with the turn of events, and sashayed to George's side. Her diamond and emerald garnished nails ran along George's shoulder and loosely touched the top of his arm that wasn't casually holding the weapon.

"I guessed an Active User. Let's see if you can move the bullet," Vyolette said with a curl of her lips.

"And if I'm neither? If I'm just boring like the rest of you?" Kana caught the doubt in Ingrid's gaze, as the skeleton of a girl hugged herself and kept looking at Vyolette and back at Kana. "You're going to risk shooting me to prove that I may or may not be a User?" She held back her laugh. Laughing at them would ensure they pulled trigger, and she needed a few more seconds because, unlike every other Idu who could manipulate objects in motion, Kana couldn't. A bullet fired from a regular gun would be her end. Her power relied on another User.

"You've survived a few bullet wounds." Vyolette shrugged.

"Will shooting me give you satisfaction about Maximus?" Kana dangled the bait. Vyolette, predictably, left George's side, bristling as her expressive features raged.

"Maximus," she said his name as if tossing a cigarette butt. "No, me wanting to see you bleed has very little to do with that waste of a man." The atoms in the air sprang alive, moving between the two of them. In Vyolette's penetrating green gaze, there was old anger, as if Kana was a festering wound, and picking at the scab was unavoidable. Kana couldn't think of any reason for the animosity. Aside from Maximus, Kana was not a threat to Vyolette's beauty, and their levels of wealth were equal. Could Vyolette be so offended by Kana's higher notoriety?

"Are you upset because I'm more popular than you?" She couldn't help herself, and she laughed, seeing the crack in Vyolette's mask. The world in which Vyolette lived was utterly childish. Kana should wait a few more seconds, running the gambit for Spencer's arrival, but the words came out. "I've survived too much to be shot by a boy who couldn't pass the entrance exam for the military academy and a woman who thinks her popularity equates to her worth."

The gun fired, and the crack amplified in the space. Spencer's cooling power grazed her as the bullet whizzed past her knee and lodged itself into the wall behind her. The whiplash of anticipation for the pain and relief was subdued behind her mask of nonchalance. "Are you happy now?" Kana asked, standing unharmed. While she was thankful Spencer proved to be exceptionally skilled—not many people could move an object in motion without being in the same room—a knot of worry was engraved in the back of her mind. How powerful was he?

"Very," Vyolette said. There was a hint of relief in the sag of her shoulders, as if she hadn't been certain Kana would escape unharmed. None of them realized Spencer and the guard were less than two meters away. Everyone assumed Kana was the one who misdirected the bullet.

The sound of shoes tapping on the marble floors became louder. "And our final guest has arrived," Vyolette said, clapping.

Someone came beside her, Spencer, by the smell of the cologne, and lifted the strap at her hip to lift the dress. She'd momentarily forgotten she was topless.

"You're going to get A.E. Potentia," Vyolette said. "A dose for each of us."

There were five other things Kana expected Vyolette to demand; this was a possibility, albeit a very low one, and a bit shocking. She was signing her death warrant.

"You'll die," Spencer said. It seemed she and Spencer could agree on something.

"Come now, isn't that the point of the A.E. Potentia? It improves the survival rate from twenty to eighty percent, and I heard the newer versions were even up to ninety-five percent effective," Vyolette said.

"There's no guarantee you'll be—" Spencer began, his voice dipped with disbelief.

"And if I don't get the doses?" Kana cut Spencer off. "What's stopping me from killing all of you? Or him?" She cocked her head to the side in Spencer's direction.

Kana's threat hung in the air. There was hesitation in

Vyolette's eyes, but she sniffed as if realizing the count: two potential Idus and her single Sori guard, who could only rip portals for herself.

"You don't have the skill," Vyolette said, with not a speck of doubt. "But him . . . I want Mac and Winston here," Vyolette ordered the woman guard. "Imagine the scandal if the son of the head of the Secretary Defense, the daughter of Murad Holdings, and little me were found murdered with the only survivor being Kana Ambrose, again. There's no way even you could escape the shit storm. And then, of course, you're the one that wanted something from me." She grinned.

Truthfully, Kana wasn't sure if Josephine had left a clue somewhere on Vyolette's property. Kana looked at each of them and smiled. "Fine," she agreed. They were self-destructive idiots. They were going to risk it all for more power. Clearly, the trio had been tested for the original parasite, since the synthetic drug was useless if a person wasn't infected. George knew better; he'd failed the final part of the entrance exam that would have admitted him into Oshiya's elite military force. If he'd passed the rigorous tests, he would have been given A.E. Potentia. It wasn't about being mentally sound or having a healthy body; being able to endure the changes they would undergo was imperative.

"Nolan, was it?" George said. "I saw you at the graduation class. My father has a framed picture of the class of twenty sixteen, the most promising students he's ever seen. He didn't fail to mention how I was a disappointment."

Kana rolled her eyes. The chip on George's shoulder may as well be the world. He was such a whiny boy struggling under his father's pressure.

"I will get three doses," Kana said. "You will give me access to all aspects of the estate and allow me and my nurse to walk away."

They all agreed.

It was decided that Spencer would be the carrier of the drugs. They didn't trust Kana to leave, believing she would leave Spencer with them, and they weren't wrong, she'd happily ditch him at a moment's notice. There was also the fact that he could kill them all. It was that they didn't know his rank or the extent of his training. Graduating top of the class didn't mean much to them. George was blinded by his belief that his father's actions were always to spite him, ignorant of the notion that he was mediocre and that there were people more capable and deserving.

This wouldn't be the first time someone took her with the hopes of her having access to the drug. People had broken into the Ambrose estate twice, suspecting that they kept the drug in their home. She supposed people believed there were rooms full of A.E. Potentia like a vaulted bank with boxes full of syringes, but there weren't. The production time was extensive, and the media overshot how much manufacturing time and effort each dose went through. Even Kana wouldn't have direct access, but she had the pull, and Oliver would help deliver the drugs to Spencer.

———

THEY WAITED IN SILENCE. INGRID PACED BACK AND forth, having long ago tossed her heels off. "What were the side effects again?" she asked George.

"The Fever will be the worst of it," George said from where he lay on the couch, his arms folded behind his head as he stared at the ceiling. "And then after the Fever we're fine, and we start being able to do stuff."

Kana stood in front of the aquarium wall, forced to listen to the ridiculous conversation, watching a shark glide along the bottom surface of the tank, unbothered in its watery prison. "Stuff," Kana repeated. "You are sorely underestimating the entire transition process. Your skin will feel like it's been melted. Your veins will feel like they are being peeled out of your body, and you'll wish you were dying a hundred times in only a minute."

"Don't listen to her," Vyolette snapped. "She's making you

doubt. Come, let's have a little fun." Vyolette held out her hand to Ingrid and led the younger woman behind the door where Kana suspected the bedrooms were.

"You despise Vyolette. Why the sudden allegiance?" Kana asked as George claimed the space beside her. Both stared into the expansive blue tank.

"Don't ask stupid questions," George drawled. Kana's left eye twitched. George would love to know he earned a rise from her. "Use or be used, that's the motto."

"And with all your resources, you couldn't get a dose yourself?" Kana asked rhetorically, "Your father has resources, or was it because of your father that they were unwilling to sell it?"

George laughed, a dark, mocking thing. "How I missed you. Always so sharp."

Kana caught his gaze through the reflection and turned so they could face one another.

"What do you plan on doing if you survive the Fever? You failed the last exam, and you are male, which means your statistics of survival are already lower. Your neediness is as obvious as your desperate need for validation." It had been proven, yet again, that women were able to tolerate pain at a significantly higher percentage than their male counterparts. Men still dominated the military because women continued to choose to stay away from it.

"There are other opportunities outside of Oshiya. The Americans are partial to outsourcing their dirty work. And what about you, Kana? You enjoy jabbing at my father complex. How is Josephine these days? You hide and think you want nothing to do with the empire, claiming to be independent from the Ambrose name, but you aren't different from me. You want her acknowledgment just as much as I need my father's."

A white nosed shark the size of a dining table swam by, the shadow moving languidly over George and then Kana. She felt like she had swallowed a rotting fruit, the acrid flavor slipping down her throat. He was right: both of them had crafted a flimsy bond over their larger-than-life parent, and every child clung to that approval. Kana wondered if she would have wanted her father's approval if he was in her life. Approval was not the right word. It was something in the deep shadows behind approval.

Kana hoped George didn't survive. He was too confident. But it was likely that, out of sheer spite, he would survive. "I don't need anything from her," Kana scoffed. "That's what makes us different. You need approval to keep your ego together. I've already proven myself."

George stepped closer. "Oh yes," he said condescendingly as he narrowed the gap between them until they were a hand's width apart. He loved trespassing into personal space, savoring the unease and squirming of this prey. "You certainly have proven yourself. My favorite title was from GQ. 'Venomous Vixen.' You sink your teeth in and let the poison slowly work its way through while you slither away."

"I think I missed that porn film. I certainly hope your taste improves after your transition." Kana grinned; she would be happy to use the scalpel and cut him, just a small nick, nothing to cause serious damage. But that would give away her only weapon, and while George technically hadn't graduated, he still had an intense four years of training and close to thirty-eight kilos on her.

A cold splatter of ice chips sent a chill down her spine as a new guard portaled from the fireplace wall. "Your phone." The unfamiliar Tomi guard said, holding out her device.

"Oliver," Kana answered. "I believe Spencer has informed you of what I need."

No one could call the conversation with Oliver a conversation; it was more of a spoken half-sentence. A final yes, and it was done. George did not approach her a second time as they waited.

It was difficult to tell how much time passed without any real light. There was a knock, and the guard assisted Spencer back into the room. In his hand was a small briefcase; he looked like an attorney on a European summer holiday.

"How do we know she isn't giving us fake shots?" Ingrid asked with a strain in her voice.

"Each unit is tagged with a specific identification code, stored in the master database to confirm its creation and distribution," Kana said. "George has contacts. Confirm these three vials and you'll know that the units were supposed to be shipped to Great Britain."

Spencer locked eyes with Kana. He was trying to communicate something, but Kana wasn't in the mood to decipher his nonverbal cues. She knew what she was doing. She shot him a hard glare—*do not do anything* transmitting like bright subtitles.

Popping the briefcase open, George revealed three needles with clear liquid neatly displayed as the refrigerated control inside exhaled thin wisps of chilled air.

"Are you alright?" Spencer asked. He saddled up beside Kana, who stood behind the three people huddled over the briefcase, whispering among themselves. His eyes lowered to where Kana had her left arm loosely around her torso.

"Just lovely," Kana replied. She'd missed taking her pain meds, and her entire abdomen felt inflamed, constantly shooting pain each time she moved.

"I don't know," Ingrid said louder, moving backward away from the suitcase.

Vyolette's lips curled. "You've been bitching for years about how you wanted to be stronger, how jealous you were of the Yen family for all being able to portal to parties. Now we have the chance, and you're going to back down? I knew I should have invited Cassandra. She knows how to be grateful."

"You go first then," Ingrid wailed.

"I can knock them all out," Spencer said under his breath. The guards shot them a suspicious look.

"They'll come to face the consequences," Kana said. Her voice was ice, but beneath the frozen surface, there was an undercurrent of anticipation. She'd given them fuel. She wondered if they would burn, or burn those around them.

Chapter Seventeen

Kana exhaled the moment the guard disappeared into her portal after leaving her and Spencer at the front doors of the observatory. The slash of salty wind was welcomed, the thumping music from the main house, cascading waves, and the noise of unintelligible voices and laughter contrasting with the isolated silence from the underground room. She hopped down the steps, not looking back at the domed building.

"You didn't give it to them," Spencer stated, so sure she hadn't provided the three idiots with the synthetic drug.

Kana paused long enough to swap her heels into the other hand and tossed a look over her shoulder. "Of course I did."

Spencer's face strained between disbelief and frustration. Kana tilted her head, trying to memorize the tightness in his eyes, the cast shadows across the planes of his cheeks, and the stubble along his jaw.

"They are going to kill themselves."

Kana sighed as she continued down the stone steps. "I don't need a lecture from you."

She could have asked Oliver to swap out the drugs. The serial code tracking was true, but it was easy to bypass. The last time this had happened, Oliver had given a kidnapper a lethal dose of morphine instead. But not this time. As the sun rose, and if none of them succumbed to the Fever, the trio would know she had duped them. And she couldn't kill them. Vyolette was right. Kana already had a scandal involving the killing of prestigious families. Another three winding up dead wouldn't look good, a death by a failed A.E. Potentia transition was acceptable, and not unheard of. It would be covered up, saving face the upmost priority for the families, the headlines stating a tragic OD incident or fatal vehicle accident.

They were insatiable little monsters, wanting more and more power, so fine. She gave them what they wanted. They would survive the Fever, and maybe George would be the only one to actually train and practice enough to utilize whatever enhancement he had. Vyolette, too, could survive, and while she was extremely stubborn, she would tire of the monotony of training. And there was Ingrid, the weakest of the three. If Ingrid survived, she wouldn't train either. She lacked the disposition to do anything herself, which was why she needed an agent to give her a schedule of shows and photoshoots, and why she clung to someone like Vyolette to direct her actions. The rich loved exclusivity, and being a User had appeal.

"Kana," Spencer called, but she ignored him as her feet pushed through the hot sand. She wanted to leave, feeling too wrung out and soulless to do anything else. A waitress with a tray of shots wandered around the beach. Instead of coasters, there were diamond-cut mirrors with lines of coke or ketamine, it was hard to distinguish between the white powders. Kana's mouth dried, and her nostrils tingled with a haunted feeling. Instead, Kana picked up a shot and threw it back. Maneuvering around handfuls of partially nude bodies discarding bikini tops and swim trunks, she knocked back the alcohol. The fleshy pink sunset blended with the licking flames from the massive fire pits. A broken, hazy memory of the sick Synthie, Winter, came to life between the shadows of the bonfires.

"Kana." He touched her arm while plucking the second shot from her hands. "Are you going to let them take the drug?" he asked.

Kana stepped back as a couple ran between them, laughing while they rubbed their hands under their noses, bits of white powder disappearing. One hit. She would stop after one. But there was Bexley, tears and snot smearing against her splotched face, her voice raw with hurt. *I can't watch you kill yourself, this is hurting me. Stop coming to see me.* Kana made eye contact with another server and threw back another shot. Her focus lingered over the curved edge of the glass to meet Spencer's focused eyes.

"Of course, that was the deal," she said.

Spencer's gaze was steady on her, but a tightly restrained tension showed in the rest of his face. "What if they don't make it?" he asked. The roaring laughter and shrieks of people diving into the warm ocean water nearly overpowered his question. Kana's mouth twitched; his concern for them was cute. "You can't give out the drug like it's shots of heroin at a party."

"You've got H?" A boy, maybe nineteen, slurred to Spencer, who glared at the boy.

Kana slipped further into the throngs of people. She didn't want to explain why she did what she did, least of all to someone who wouldn't ever be able to understand. After only two shots, she was starting to feel the alcohol tint the edges of her skin. She hadn't eaten all day, and getting drunk seemed like a fine idea.

"Stop drinking." Spencer reached over her shoulder, his height more prominent with his body against her back. "If you're in pain, the drugs won't mix well with the alcohol."

She frowned, thrusting her sharp elbow back to hit his upper abdomen. It was enough to make him huff, but not enough to make him lose the grip of his hand on her wrist to keep her from the alcohol. Kana turned around, her narrowed eyes fixated on his face.

"If you think they are the only people who have gotten their hands on the drug, you're mistaken," she said in a low voice as she pressed closer to him. "A quarter of the people here are Synthies."

His eyes broke from hers for a moment to consider the people surrounding them on the beach. "You're exaggerating," he concluded. His math wasn't wrong. There were a hundred guests, which meant at least twenty-five had somehow gotten their hands on the drug that only produced a hundred doses a year. But he didn't understand her world.

Kana laughed as she leaned in closer, pushing herself on her tiptoes, letting her words ghost against his lips. "You don't believe me, but they are." She tilted her head to the side, focused on matching Spencer's intensity. "Because it's hard to have a dream if you can have anything you want. Imagine you can make your dreams real, you can buy your way to the best school, buy a Fortune 500 company, buy any house on any continent, buy love, all those silly little goals and desires that normal people spend their entire lives reaching for. It's all already ours with the first gulp of air out of the womb. We must entertain ourselves somehow."

The heat from his breath caressed her lips. "Because you were a good boy and listened to my orders back there, I'll stop after this shot." She patted his chest as she did a twirl, plucked a shot from a different waitress, and happily moved up to the main house.

———

A CHAUFFEUR DROVE THEM HOME. SPENCER OPENED her side of the car door when they pulled up to the apartment, and she didn't hold back the chokehold grip as she used his solid arm to hoist her ragged body out of the car. Kana didn't have the strength to tell Spencer off for leading her through the entrance. Her weight collapsed onto him.

Inside the apartment, her white knuckles gripped the concrete edge of the kitchen countertop, where a tall glass of water and two painkillers were waiting in her line of sight. She swallowed the pills dry, her stomach roiling, threatening to throw the pills back up until she gulped a mouthful of water.

"Don't even think about carrying me to my bed," she threatened once she was sure the room wasn't spinning and the pills weren't going to come back up. "I don't need help."

Spencer remained silent. She couldn't see him as she focused on her breathing, but felt the unnecessary weight of his stare as she collected herself.

"Are we going back to the observatory tomorrow?" he asked.

Kana closed her eyes as she inhaled for a moment and shuffled to the bedroom. "No, Pluto isn't there." Kana reached around her back and unzipped the dress. She removed the thigh straps and tossed the knives away, reaching for a large T-shirt.

"What do you mean, it isn't there?" he asked, with a sharp edge to the end of his question.

Kana blinked as she turned around, surprised he'd followed her into the bedroom. He'd always respected the unsaid boundary, the invisible wall protecting her door. She flipped her hair out from the collar of the shirt.

"According to my calculations, the clue wasn't there. Looks like we have a mystery on our hands," she joked as she dragged her feet to the bathroom.

"When did you come to that conclusion?" Spencer demanded, not amused by her Scooby-Doo reference.

"While we were waiting for you and the special package." She dumped her facial oil into her hands and rubbed at her face, her fingers coated with the waxy residue, ignoring the heated eyes boring into her profile as if trying to dig up her thoughts with the sheer will of his sight.

"I'm trying to understand," he said slowly. The sink faucet gurgled once before hot water gushed into the basin. "You needed to see Vyolette's observatory, and in turn, she made a ridiculous request for A.E. Potentia, and in the time it took for me to get the drug, you figured out you no longer needed to use her observatory. And yet you let her have the drugs?"

Kana patted her face with the freshly fluffed towel, and with the red eyeliner and lipstick gone, a younger version of herself peeked through. "Perfect marks. You can properly summarize," Kana commented as thick clear liquid pumped out of a pink tube and onto her fingertips.

"Where are your morals?" he asked.

Kana laughed, the sound amplified by the spacious stone bathroom. He must have held that question in for a long time. "Rotting in a grave," she sneered.

In the mirror, she caught the storm behind his eyes and the hastily released clenched fists. This was bothering him. "I owe them nothing." She made her way to her bedroom, but Spencer crossed his arms over his chest as he blocked her path.

"You gave them a loaded gun to shoot themselves with." He'd wrangled his expression to a controlled blandness, but his voice was rigid.

"I'm the supplier. I'm not making them pull the trigger. The risk of them reaching any kind of Rabid stage is nonexistent. People who have used their power for decades rarely have Rabid symptoms. Do you think any of them will put in the effort to even properly train?" Kana laughed dryly. "It's shiny and new. They'll tire of it soon."

A.E. Potentia could mimic the Fever, but that was the key difference between a Natural and a Synthetic. A true Fever killed the parasite that infiltrated the host. Being Synthetic was close, but not close enough, and the dormant parasite could be triggered and wreak havoc in the host's body.

"This seems to be a sensitive topic," Kana said. "What is bothering you? The fact that the rich have access to the drug?" No reaction. "Or that I gave them the drug?" That earned a mouth movement.

"Have you seen someone fail the transition with A.E. Potentia?" Spencer asked.

Kana shrugged. "Not as many as you." Her flippant response triggered a blip of anger in the strain of his neck and the sharp tension in his jaw. "Is this why you didn't fight to get reassigned? This has to do with her drug. You're just like everyone else, trying to learn the secrets to A.E. Potentia."

"As you have said so often, I'm nothing more than a mindless soldier. I wonder what you would ask for with a carte blanche? You said the rich don't have dreams, but it seems you want something that money can't buy."

Goosebumps rose on the back of her neck, and her left eye twitched.

"You have a hatred for Josephine and this illustrious lifestyle," he spoke like water rapidly freezing, "but you hold everyone to such a high standard, looking down on the people who live in excess. Your influence has more impact than you can see or care about. You're more like your mother than you realize."

Kana hated that his comment shot straight through her ribs. People made the comparison often, but when he said it, Kana willed her face to remain blank. "You're here to make sure I find Josephine. Don't worry your pretty head about trying to understand me."

―――――

KANA DIDN'T SLEEP WELL. THE PAINKILLERS OFFERED some relief for a few hours, but she woke with the dregs of an absurd dream which faded fast as she pushed aside the damp sweat around her forehead, and her immediate hyperfocus zeroed in on Pluto. She had an unsettling feeling like the cold of winter, causing her muscles to scrunch uncomfortably, because she was wrong about Vyolette and the observatory holding the clue.

After a shower and another pill, she stood outside on the balcony as she mindlessly flipped her phone around in her hands, listening to the soft ringing of the outgoing call, half wondering why she was calling in the first place. But before her thumb could tap on the red button, Bexley's groggy voice answered, "What's wrong?"

"Pluto," Kana said.

There was silence on the other side before Bexley responded. "This isn't a hostage situation with code words, is it? Say yes if it is."

"It's not," Kana said, amused.

A sigh of relief and a rustling of sheets.

"Why are you bringing that summer camp up?"

Kana leaned over the edge of the railing, letting the thin, cold metal press against her chest, staring at the gardens below and the stone terrace leading to a gazebo. "What summer camp?" Strangely, Bexley hadn't assumed she meant the demoted planet.

"The one when you were nine."

"That was before we met," Kana commented. She shuffled through her memory for the summer camp, but everything was meshing together: summer suns, layers of sunscreen, lake shores, beaches—cold ones and hot ones—overly maximalist decorated ballrooms, simple stone and wood spaces.

"You told me about Camp Ridgeview back when we first met."

Camp Ridgeview. Kana straightened up. Most camps were typically in cabins, the exception being if she went abroad like the camp in Italy. Camp Ridgeview in Oshiya was the former. There were wooden cabins littered on tiny islands splattered across the lake, and the camp attendees used rowboats to get to the different locations. Camp Ridgeview catered exclusively to wealthy students and had special teachers to assist with various activities.

Inside a powder blue A-frame building with an orange door, Kana created P.L.U.T.O.

"It's an acronym," Kana exhaled.

"Glad I could help." Bexley yawned. "I know you don't want to talk about it, but I saw the articles—"

Kana nodded and hummed, probably at inappropriate times as Bexley's voice faded to white noise. Kana's thoughts raced over the clue. P.L.U.T.O—Purple, Luminous, Umbrella, Tagging, Operator—her first and only engineered creation, had been crafted from a broken umbrella. She'd created a contraption that sprayed bioluminescent powder from the umbrella tip. The camp counselors in charge of the engineering group had given wide smiles as they examined Kana's purple umbrella.

"You aren't listening," Bexley pointed out. "I'll talk to you later. Call if you need anything else."

Kana ended the call without another word, her fingers typing the camp address. Perfect. It was still in business, and less than four hours away. She was yanking on a pair of shorts when her bedroom door banged open. A staccato shriek broke free while her hands reached for the closest object to throw: the remote, not the best weapon.

"What the hell?" she managed as a duffel bag barreled at her from across the room.

"Shoes," Spencer said.

She felt a trickle of water droplets and shoved her feet into a pair of sneakers. Someone was creating a portal, and by Spencer's steely expression, it wasn't someone he was expecting. But he couldn't sense Users expending power. That was unique to her, and she wanted to ask how he knew someone was coming, because the portal certainly wasn't Oliver and his fine misty power. This was more like thick, hard dollops, rain that was almost hail. Kana didn't have time to observe more of this new expression on Spencer's face. He wasn't panicking, but focused, someone entirely engrossed in the details, his mind probably racing through every scenario.

She jerked as something came over her head. "What the—" she began, but stopped once she realized he had forced a bullet-proof vest over her head.

"The balcony," he ordered, shoving her forward, and fired three rounds behind him. Silhouetted masses rammed through her bedroom doors, the wood smashing against the wall. *Fuck.* Kana ducked as she ran for the balcony. The sound of glass shattering from a bullet, or projectile, was followed by the spraying chunks of glass.

Where else exactly was she supposed to go? She gripped the balcony railing. The thick jagged bits of glass shook on the floor as if an earthquake had rocked the deck. A whirlwind of flavors smashed in her mouth; mint and yeast laid thick like heavy whipping cream. Glass pieces the size of her hand were vibrating in place. There was one unfamiliar Active User, maybe the one with the yeast flavor, attempting to move the glass, and the other Active User with the minty power she associated with Spencer, was pressing the glass down.

"Jump," Spencer grunted, "when I say to." He expertly sliced one of the men's necks.

Kana glared at him. He was fighting off two very large men, and he was handling himself fine. He could dispatch the others. It seemed unnecessary to ask her to jump. It wasn't like they were on the third floor; a tumble off the fifth floor could kill her. She recoiled—the faint, cloying scent of powdered doughnuts barely served as a warning before a third figure, a Sori, emerged, not from the shadows, but through the wall separating her living room from the balcony. The man's body flickered, half there, half not, the air shivering around him as if reality struggled to hold him in place before he attacked.

The Phaser could have shot her. The gun remained shoved into the holster as he tried to grab her. Her back hit the railing with a painful thrust. The man reached for her arm, but she thrashed. His hand yanked at her half-fallen bun of hair, and the skin of her scalp howled. She aimed a solid punch at his throat.

He slammed her into the corner of the balcony with a swing of his arm. The glass quivered from the force. She would have a nice bruise on her face from that back slap.

Bang, bang. Two shots rang, and for half a second Kana wasn't sure where the bullets had ended up until she fell backward. Someone had shot the balcony glass wall, and with a minty push, she flew off the edge. The force wasn't like a shove; if it had been, she could have crashed on the balcony below hers. No, she soared through the air. Wide-eyed, she watched the side of the complex stream by—the tacky fairy lights wrapped along someone's back deck, a jungle of plants growing off another deck—and she braced for the inevitable pain as she splattered on the ground.

A cushion of cool, mint Jell-O enveloped her instead of a sharp final blow of pain. She opened her eyes to see that she had not crashed into the gardens below, but hovered a little over a meter from the ground. Wide-eyed, her heart squeezed and stuttered against her ribcage; she was too afraid to move.

"Oof," she grunted as the lingering tacky, menthol flavor encasing her mouth disappeared, and she flopped onto the grass below.

Chapter Eighteen

Kana rolled onto her feet, catching the outline of a head peeking over the broken balcony. Her hands dug into bits of broken glass as she pushed herself to her feet, snatching the duffel bag that had been thrust off the balcony with her and started running. Compared to being in a pile of contorted, crushed limbs with a halo of blood, she would gladly take superficial cuts from glass. If they survived, she might tell Spencer he was good.

She shoved the garden's iron gate open, and the heavy metal eased closed, automatically locking behind her as sirens echoed in the distance. Police were about to storm the gated neighborhood. Lights inside the other units blinked on, and as Kana ran by, a high-pitched bark startled her. A canine smashed its face against the gated fence, snarling with long nails scraping at the fence door.

The screech of rubber tires ricocheted from around the corner, and Kana expected military personnel on motorcycles with guns blazing. They were incredibly persistent buggers, but she recognized the bulkier shape of the motorcycle and the slim reflective line along the body.

"Get on," Spencer shouted. She ran to him and forced the

spare helmet onto her head. Her arms had just wound around his waist before he sped down the street.

Fucking hell. She gripped Spencer's waist tighter, her thighs straddling his seat as she nearly slipped backward at the abrupt acceleration. The wind whacked against her exposed skin, slicing against the bare cotton of her flimsy clothing. The streets were barren, and any cars were parked on the side streets or tucked in underground parking. He maneuvered deeper into the city's center, the streets condensing as the number of bars and nightclubs increased. Her heart eased to a somewhat normal speed the longer they sped down the streets with no sign of pursuit. After about thirty minutes of being smooshed against Spencer's back, the thick bulletproof vest dug uncomfortably around the front of her neck. He tucked them into a side street and behind a large, tinted van.

The moment she'd gotten back on Oshiyan soil, there had been two attacks within a week of each other. This was unacceptable. Irritation built in her veins as she thought about the president, that smug bastard. He knew more than he was letting on. Josephine had done something, and outside forces wanted that something.

A gloved hand touched her iron fisted grip still around Spencer's waist. She released her hold but her hunched neck and shoulders remained stiff as she silently considered the complicated situation. A tap on the helmet's shield jerked her back. Spencer was already off the bike, his helmet tucked under his arm. "Are you hurt?"

"No," she said, removing her helmet, but cringing as strands of hair were twisted. Her thoughts ping-ponged between the brief conversation with the president and what she needed from Oliver, because if the president was going to be an ass, Oliver would find the essential information she was missing.

"I believe now would be a good time to explain some things." She scowled and adjusted the grip of the helmet, trying to reach for her hair that was knotted like a tangled necklace chain.

Spencer set his helmet on the handlebars and reached to help. Kana shrank away for a breath, long enough for Spencer to pause before untangling her hair, leveraging the helmet in one hand to keep the pressure off her scalp.

"I know as much as you," he replied, working skillfully to free the strands of hair. Kana's suspicious eyes stared at Spencer's focused expression. She imagined him with his younger sister, helping untangle a piece of gum that had accidentally fallen into her hair.

"You're lying."

The side street had enough illumination from the main street, and the occasional hanging lamp over the side doors offered contrasting warm and cool glows. His facial muscles weren't ticking and his eyes were focused on her hair, which helped maintain the indifference. With the adrenaline fading, the smell from nearby garbage bins and dank, decades-old buildings infested with mold became more prominent.

"Fine," Kana said as her hair was released from the helmet's grip. "As we wait for a Special Assault Team to descend upon us" —his mouth tilted into an almost dry smile—"I need to go here." She reflexively reached for her phone in her back pocket, but realized she didn't have pockets in her tiny running shorts. Her phone was stuck in the wrinkles of her bedsheets. Fantastic.

"Phone." She held out her hand, expecting Spencer to offer his device.

"We're going to the safe house," he said with finality.

Kana raised her brows. "You must have taken a hit to the head. You," she pointed at him and then back at her, "follow me. The sooner I can find Josephine, the faster I can get out of here."

"Your hands," Spencer said, his eyes narrowing in on her hand. There was dried blood from the small cuts in her palms and along parts of her forearm from the glass.

"Superficial." She waved it off.

He gestured for her to stand up, which she begrudgingly obeyed and swung off the bike. His gaze ran up and down her body, lingering on her torso. The white shirt would show if she'd pulled a stitch. Satisfied, he lifted the seat compartment and pulled out a compact medical kit.

"I need to contact Oliver." She tried a different request.

"Hand," Spencer said, and she offered her right hand.

"Phone," she countered.

They stared at one another, but he relented and removed a small, old model burner phone, judging by the sheer bulk and thick bezels, and tapped five times before offering the device to her. As Spencer pressed an alcohol wipe against her palm, Kana typed an SOS to Oliver with her left hand. Oliver needed to wipe the phone and tablet left in her apartment to ensure no one hacked into the devices.

The peals of laughter and music from around the corner of the main street sounded muffled. She felt the moisture of the alcohol wipe on her palm, but the stinging was so faint. His hands were rougher, calloused, and far warmer than her icy hands. She'd been told on more than one occasion that people were surprised she had any warmth, that any amount of heat must have to go to her heart to keep it pumping.

"Satisfied?" Kana asked as she tugged her hand away and twisted to show that the shallow cuts had stopped bleeding.

"Left hand."

He was being dramatic, but she gave him her other hand and finished searching for the summer camp, checking the directions and noting the estimated drive time of three and a half hours from their current location.

"We need supplies," Spencer said. He placed a bandage on her inner wrist where the largest nick was.

"Oliver can deliver us supplies," Kana dismissed.

"It's best if no one knows our location. Your whereabouts

were supposed to be a secret. We put out false rumors that you were staying at other properties, and somehow, they broke into your apartment."

Kana's thumb stopped on the screen, and she looked up. The implication of his words was an icy blade sliding up her ribs. In the low light, his eyes were nearly black, prepared for the backlash because he knew what he'd said, and he meant it.

"You believe Oliver is feeding information to someone." Having to say the words felt as outrageous as saying the world was flat.

"Let's discuss this in a private area," he offered, and checked his watch. "We've been here for too long." Spencer drew a single key fob out of his pocket, and the van, which he had tucked them behind, responded to the click and cast a flash of orange from the rear lights. It seemed he had safe houses and random getaway cars prepared.

She remained unmoving as he opened the back doors and unfolded a ramp to load the motorcycle into the back. Her eyes glared at Spencer, his accusation at the forefront of her mind. His suspicion of Oliver didn't make sense. What would Oliver's motive even be?

"You're angry," Spencer said as the back doors clicked back in place.

"Didn't your sisters ever tell you? Never tell a woman she's angry."

At the mention of his siblings, his eyes narrowed, and she saw a single spark of anger. It was a low blow. "The next best move is to resupply and keep moving. We don't know how they located you."

"I'm less concerned with how they found me. The who and why are more important. Tell me who is after me. An attack every year is my average; being attacked twice is out of norm. That will dictate whether I go to the safe house with you or not."

"Why is everything a negotiation?" he asked. His gloved

knuckle rubbed at his nose in irritation. "It's best to not stay in the same spot for more than fifteen minutes."

Kana adjusted the duffle to her back and began walking out of the narrow alley to the main street.

"A rumor has started," Spencer began, reaching to hold Kana's arm as she moved past him.

She twisted away. "And what is this rumor?"

Barking laughter from a group of men passed by. Spencer's body moved forward, his gaze sliding the fractional space from the potential threats and back to her. He had proven to be a good soldier and the most competent bodyguard. This only added to her concern that the president truly sent his best, so he needed her alive long enough to actually find Josephine.

She took another two steps forward before Spencer placed himself between her and the alley entrance. Kana scoffed dryly. "You're going to toss me into the back of the van?"

"I will."

Kana refrained from rolling her eyes and chose to stare him down as if he were a riled up dog she was battling for dominance. "You wouldn't dare."

"I'm trying to keep you safe, and you constantly make it as difficult as possible," he commented, and lunged. She didn't expect him to try to snatch her. He lifted her off the ground and she suspected he would have thrown her over his shoulder, but she was quick enough to thrust her fist up to his face.

His stumble lasted a fraction of a second before he scooped her up. The plane of hard muscles in his back rippled as he draped her over his right shoulder. He maneuvered her carefully; she'd been thrown over different shoulders before, but he was at least mindful of her abdomen.

"This is unnecessary," she huffed, trying to wiggle around, pressing her palms against his back as she tried to keep herself upright. She considered just screaming like a banshee, but she wouldn't stoop so low as to have a tantrum. He set her down by the passenger door, as if proving that he could lift and carry her was enough.

"Because I wouldn't put it past you to scream," he said as he reached around her left side to pull on the passenger door handle. "There's a rumor that started over a month ago, close to seven weeks now."

Kana should have moved two steps to her right to allow space for the door to open, but she resolutely remained in place. The door opened enough that it bumped against her, the cool metal pressed into the back of her naked thighs.

"And what did this rumor say?" she asked.

"I'll tell you in the car."

She didn't want to get in the car, but given her situation, stuck between a car and someone who could easily overpower her, she leveraged what she could. "You prepared an escape van thirty minutes away and you don't have a prepared go-bag of supplies in here?"

Spencer leaned back. "Your persuasion is formidable," he said, humor softening his voice. "I do have a small bag with a single weapon, but not nearly an arsenal, or cash and other items that could be useful. And before you ask, that duffle only has clothes, shoes, and two knives."

She briskly walked around him, in front of the hood of the car, and entered the driver's seat. A tiny, disbelieving smile touched his face before he acquiesced to claim the passenger seat.

"If the rumor is good, worth my while, I'll drive us to the safe house. If it's not, I'm going to the camp." She laid out her negotiation, angling her body to rest on the side of the seat and door frame so her unblinking gaze could pin Spencer.

He similarly moved his body, but let his right arm prop against the interior of the car door, his eyes thoughtful. "They say that Dr. Ambrose successfully formulated a serum to counteract the Rabid side effects. A cure. There is trouble among the Synthetic Users. A new illness."

Silence condensed in the cold car as Kana considered the two bits of information. Josephine concocting a cure was preposterous. That was her initial disbelief, but this was the woman who created A.E. Potentia. Maybe when the president said her work consisted of a new version, it was an evolved form without the side effects. Then, the second part about a new illness. The team that attacked her at the lakeshore wasn't random. They wanted to speak with Josephine. Their teammate Winter was a Rabid Synthie, one that was deranged and mutated. Was that the future for all Synthetic Users afflicted with the new disease?

Spencer was intently watching her face for any reaction.

"Isn't that the beauty of a rumor?" Kana finally spoke, breaking her gaze to look out the front windshield. She counted the barely visible rises and falls of his chest. He had good lung capacity. He'd only taken two breaths since she'd started keeping track. "It's appealing to those desperate enough to believe them. That's why the retired military team found me at the lake house. They believed she could help their Rabid teammate." She laughed dryly. "So what, I'm on every hit list because no one can locate the elusive Josephine Ambrose, and I'm the next best option? And for what? Maybe finding a supposed cure? Hope is the worst poison."

A woman searching her purse for her keys walked to the car parked at the mouth of the alley on the other side of the street.

"Was the information worth your while?" he asked, knowing the answer was yes. She wasn't sure what she expected, but the answer seemed obvious, and that worried her. Rarely did things fit together neatly.

"Where did you hear this rumor?" she asked, watching brake lights cast a red and orange glow to the slant of shadows along the sides of the building and road. Spencer remained silent, as if he struggled to find the correct words. She turned her head a fraction.

"Don't tell me, the military has some dark web chat room and some idiot went on posting conspiratorial bullshit."

He laughed. The unexpected reaction surprised her. The sound was like a single ray of golden hour sunlight in a space of gray. His posture relaxed further into the seat; his arm reached for the seatbelt. "You were sarcastic, but you aren't wrong," he admitted.

Kana clipped her seatbelt into place and started the van. "Haven't you learned by now? I'm rarely wrong."

"I'm beginning to see that," he said softly. "The origin of the rumor isn't known, but it's spread rapidly through different channels around the world. So, do you see why I need to resupply?"

"I'll give you fifteen minutes." Kana conceded, because she would also like to be armed and ready. "But—"

She could feel his desire to heave a heavy sigh. "Always a 'but.'"

"If the president knows that every ex- or current military person from every country was descending upon Oshiya, hunting for this fabled cure, why only assign you as a bodyguard? Why not a team or multiple teams?"

Spencer's expression closed up and Kana smiled smugly. It seemed he'd considered the same question. "I can't speak on behalf of the president's intentions or reasoning."

"Diplomatic response," Kana muttered as she pulled out of the alley. "Give me the address."

Chapter Nineteen

The safe house was not in the middle of a forest or on the beach. The last two safe houses Kana had visited were in both those locations: a stereotypical cabin in the woods facing a wide open field, and the other a rickety shack angled against a cliffside. Unpleasant memories from the locked attic where she had been banished made Kana doubt her ability to handle a safe house in any location that fit those memories.

"Miss Ambrose, we need to get you to the safe house. There's been a break-in on the estate, everyone's being evacuated," the head of the security team had informed twelve-year-old Kana as she was ushered into an unmarked sedan the instant the bell signaled the end of the school day. The back seat had her designer carry-on bag and her favorite headphones. She didn't question him as she buckled in and silently listened to her playlist.

Young Kana didn't think anything of the additional three men in the safe house. They all looked like the head of her security: bald military men. She was shoved into a room no bigger than her closet back home, the air thick and stale, pressed in by windowless walls. Behind her, metal ground against metal—one lock, then another, then a third—the first red flag. There had been no threat and no evacuation of the Ambrose estate, Oliver would inform her, after she was rescued.

Spencer's safe house was in the borough of Alyesa, an industrial part of Oshiya, and now she knew why Spencer had picked this car. The nondescript fleet vehicle blended in with the other construction and industrial vans. Some had ladders on the top of the vans, others had cement rotators attached to a trailer.

Kana parked in front of a short cluster of business offices standing in a uniform line parallel to the main street. Cheap plastic blinds covered the dark windows, and fading white paint, the color of baked sand, trimmed the doors and windows. Three smoke lines drifted into the sky further down the street where a steel plant was chugging.

"Fifteen minutes," Kana said stiffly. There were three vans and six cars parked in the same lot, all facing the identical, bland offices. She zeroed in on the insides. All the vehicles seemed empty, no suspicious person behind any wheels, which barely offered ease in her clenched shoulders.

"I can't leave you in the car alone," Spencer said. He reached behind the driver's seat and pulled out a baseball cap.

"Then you better get back fast," Kana quipped.

"A safe house isn't labeled a safe house. If it's compromised, I'd know," Spencer said, his careful gaze roaming her face. The location might be secure, but Kana didn't trust that the inside was safe. "Did something happen, because—" he began, and Kana snatched the baseball hat off his head and shoved it over her mess of hair. The unseen grime of paranoia and the souring of fear cracked her composure.

"Let's get this over with." She shoved the car door open and came around the back of the van.

"Put this on." Spencer offered a worn denim jacket.

Kana supposed her braless state in a thin T-shirt and shorts wasn't an incognito style. With nimble fingers, she buttoned up the jacket. The inside was lined, warmer than she expected, and the smell was nonexistent, the clothing purchased and never worn. Spencer went first, but took her hand. The unexpected touch caused her to tense. His long fingers wrapped delicately over her fisted hand.

"I'm not going to run away." Kana scoffed at his ridiculous action.

"If there's an advanced Idu, they could pull you away." Spencer explained using the formal terms, unlike Kana who preferred the simplistic descriptors of Pusher or Active User.

Kana supposed it wouldn't be impossible for a highly trained Active User lurking about to drag her away when she was walking. With Spencer adding his weight to hers, he ensured an Active User would have difficulty moving them both. It was extremely rare for an Active User to be able to move mass over thirty-seven kilos, and yet . . . her eyes fixated on the back of Spencer's head, at the junction of his hairline. He was one of those highly advanced Users. He'd stopped her plummet from the fifth floor.

She ducked her head as they went through the front doors and into a hallway, just in case there were cameras around. Each door had a drilled plaque with the business name. Spencer stopped at the last door, closest to the back exit. He reached into his pocket and tapped a badge against the small, black electronic reader. With a gentle push, the door swung open. Kana's hand gripped Spencer's harder, and her eyes flitted around the small space. In the entranceway, there was only a faded carpet, the kind that used to be an off-shade of white but with age had turned ashen. Most importantly, there wasn't anyone waiting for them. She eyed the walls, which bore yellowed outlines of long-removed picture frames, that led to a secondary room. Someone could be waiting in there. Her body locked up even as her mind tried to reason that she'd been in rooms without knowing who might be inside a million times; this was no different.

Spencer didn't rush in and pull her along. He entered first, until their arms stretched across the doorway as he waited for

Kana to follow. Her weakness was showing in her hesitation. Kana slowly released a hot, quivering breath, hating her ineptitude, and entered the safe room, shutting the door firmly behind her. Her head felt airy while her sense of balance tilted.

"Well, get to it," she snapped, letting the door bear her weight. With her safely inside, he rushed through the vacant office.

The previous tenant had left a short oval coffee table and a lamp near the front, with a layer of dust permanently staining the fixtures. She moved to the back of the room, where Spencer had disappeared behind the second door. The flick of a light switch and the tap of his shoes signaled his movement through the room.

"When did you set this up?" Kana asked as she leaned against the open doorframe. It was just as bare as the entryway, with a single metal desk and a carpet stain where two chairs had probably sat for a decade.

Spencer rummaged through a giant desk, removed a drawer, and reached into the empty space to withdraw three guns and an ammo can. "A month ago." He assembled the guns and tossed them in a duffel that lay deflated onto the desk. A month ago, she was in New York City. "I didn't know about the case until you were injured at the lake. It's good to prepare safe houses. You can never be too careful."

That quelled a portion of Kana's paranoia. "Did you set it up yourself or did you use one off the list?"

He paused, a second, smaller drawer in his hands.

"There's obviously a list of safe houses the government has, that's common knowledge. All those high-profile cases," she pointed to herself, "eyewitnesses for cases, transfer of criminals making their way to unknown locations, you know how it goes."

"I didn't use the list." He dumped bands of banknotes into a duffel bag.

"Good," Kana said. It would be stupid if he used one of the official safe houses. If the military were on their tails, they would have access to the list and may have already raided locations, or been monitoring them at the very least. "I want a gun."

She raised her eyebrows at three objects that looked suspiciously like small grenades.

"Nine millimeter? Or smaller." He opened a metal file cabinet.

At least he didn't say no with some bullshit about how dangerous guns were. Oliver might have told him that she had adequate training to handle a gun properly. She wouldn't ever be a sharpshooter, but she could hit her target and kill if needed.

"I'll take a nine."

He flipped the gun in his hands and offered it to her, then stashed a few other items and a plastic bag of cheap T-shirts and shorts.

"I'm starving," she announced as Spencer led them out the back door to a tinted windowed CRV. The duffle across his shoulders landed with a heavy thunk in the back seat as he claimed the driver's spot.

"Take a left right off the Three. There's a Korean restaurant that sells the best *Yukhoe*." She yawned as she settled into the passenger seat and sank deeper into the jacket. There was something about the gentle motion of a car ride that lulled her to sleep. Her eyes peeled open occasionally to peek out the window. They were on the familiar drive to the restaurant. Spencer could have ignored her request and taken her anywhere, but he kept his word. The car came to a full stop, and before Spencer could coax her awake, she was unbuckling herself.

"We aren't dining in," he said. Kana rolled her eyes and slid on thick hot-pink framed glasses.

She quickly ordered from the sweet old lady punching in the food request. "Not many like *Gopchang* and *Yukhoe*. Are you Korean?" she asked in Korean.

"No," she responded.

The lady smiled. "Lovely couple. You teach him how to eat

well." Her entire body twisted as she waved at Spencer through the streaky window. He was parked directly in front of the store, caught by surprise, he offered a polite smile and a hesitant wave back from the driver's seat.

Kana cracked a smile. "He's a vegetarian."

The lady shook her head and grinned wider at Kana. "Extra kimchi, and rice just for you," she said, handing Kana the large plastic bag.

"What did she say?" Spencer asked once she was back in the car.

The plastic rustled loudly as she adjusted herself to sit criss-crossed. "She liked that I ate real food. Why? Don't worry, we weren't making fun of you too much."

"You were smiling," he commented.

Kana snapped the wooden chopsticks apart. "I smile," Kana said.

Spencer pulled out of the parking spot, their eyes meeting briefly. She could see the words he wanted to say: *not a genuine smile, only that strained smile you use in front of society or the fake saccharine smile to the cameras.*

"I hope you like kimchi. The car is going to smell for the rest of the trip."

She happily ate her meal. Spencer looked discontented as he glanced at the meat. "Is that raw?"

"Is that judgment I hear in your voice?" Kana asked as she stuffed rice into her mouth. "It's safe. It's difficult to get the right cut of meat, and fresh enough. It's no different from pate."

"What about parasites?"

"You're a Natural." Kana stuffed hot rice and meat into her mouth. "You've already beaten arguably the strongest parasite."

Moon Dust, as they used to call it back in the ancient days. Various cultures across the world all had similar origin stories: gods' tears, drops of the sky's blood. They were, in fact, asteroids. Bits of space rock, the potential impact of which recent studies had narrowed down to around present-day Mongolia. The unknown life form had mutated and the parasite infected people for centuries, bestowing the survivors with gifts. It was in the turn of the nineteenth century that people began to hone in and explore the capabilities of Natural Users.

The drive to the camp was uncomfortable. The radio did little to mitigate the unease, and the more Kana dwelled on why she couldn't ignore Spencer as she easily as did —everyone else, the more uncomfortable she felt. She shouldn't have mentioned parasites and the Natural User status.

"I didn't realize what was happening when the Fever started," Spencer said. Kana cracked her left eye open with a slitted gaze. Under normal circumstances, she would have told him to stop for so many reasons—he was talking about the Fever, he was launching into a narrative—but she didn't tell him to stop. He paused, eyes landing on her before continuing, understanding her silence meant to continue. His voice was like playing a favorite film to fill a silent home.

"I remember the day because it was my best friend's thirteenth birthday. The first year of being a teenager. Chris's voice finally decided to crack on the *ah* vowels. There's an age when you stop going to a pizza parlor, beach parties, or drive to the amusement park."

Kana frowned. A few hours at the beach for a birthday didn't sound like a birthday-worthy event. She supposed that's what regular people did for birthdays. She was pretty sure she was on a yacht somewhere around the Maldives while Spencer was at his party, but that could have been a month before her twelfth birthday. Spencer continued.

"Chris hosted at his house. I couldn't stomach the pizza. A kid who couldn't eat pizza meant there was something definitely wrong." There were shades of amusement in the last sentence, an inside joke only he knew.

"My mom would tell me later that she tried to manage the

Fever at home, but I was taken to the hospital that night once I broke forty-two Celsius. After that, well, it's as everyone describes. I realized why adults and books always called it The Fever, because it was a fever to end all fevers.

"The Fever keeps your mind clear, and that's probably why you wish for death a thousand times over. The awareness of every cell in your body, every centimeter of tissue burning constantly and there was nothing anyone could do. Any pain medication they attempt to give me, a balm for my skin, medication through an IV, crushed pills, hell, I'm sure they had me try to snort powder —and nothing works to counteract the impossible temperatures of the Fever. After the first day, I thought sleep would be the only safe haven, but sleep was impossible too. It pushed my body in ways that I've never felt before.

"I scared my parents. The screaming, the begging for death. And when you feel that final moment, when your single thread of life is about to be snipped, it all stops. I thought I had died. The fire, the aches, and pain, all ceased. I was finally able to sleep, and that's only because I was in an induced coma for four days, to give my body a break."

For a brief moment, Kana attempted to imagine people two hundred years ago, unable to get a reprieve from an induced medical coma. The recovery process for the survivors must have been debilitating.

"When I did open my eyes, my parents were there. Their eyes," he was forced to pause as the words clogged in the long column of his neck and his Adam's apple bobbed. "I'd never seen my parents cry at that point, so to see them completely broken by emotion—" he stopped short, as if clipping the words he wanted to say. "It was okay because I survived." He had a soothing voice and a way of retelling his past narratively, better than anyone she'd ever met.

Kana feigned disinterest, defiantly curled against the side of the passenger seat to glare out the window. How could he speak

so easily about his experiences? There was a gaping hole she struggled to bridge when it came to speaking about experiences that
mattered.

"What about you?" Spencer asked out of politeness.

That's what people did; they shared their stories and expected
you to share your experience to compare notes. He fell quiet,
leaving space for her to speak; a more breathable silence fell
between them over the soft hum of a radio song.

Kana's Fever story was not like Spencer's, another tick on the
list of things that were unusual. For most people who tested positive for the parasite, puberty was the trigger for the Fever, the
hormonal levels being the main cause. Girls statistically experienced the Fever earlier, closer to ten years of age, while boys typically started around thirteen. The parasite was sometimes
triggered later in life, but it was a rare occurrence and many hosts
lived their lives with the dormant parasite. Spencer was correct in
describing a sharp awareness during the entire process, but time
heals all wounds, as they say, and the distance between the Fever
and the present was nearly eighteen years for her. That experience
whittled from a prickly spikey ridge to a smooth sanded form; she
rarely thought of that time. Her Fever started when she was four.

Chapter Twenty

What about you? An uncontrollable reflex snapped her mouth shut. The head rush overwhelmed her as the need to keep her secret consumed her and smothered any inclination of wanting to share. The pale flesh like the white marbled fat in meat permanently affixed to the top of her left thigh itched. The scar had healed well, barely noticeable unless you knew what you were looking for, fainter than the stretch marks that it was easily mistaken for, but it was a bite that triggered her Fever. Josephine had instilled the warning: *do not discuss the topic of the transition.* It wasn't unheard of for a bite from a User to trigger the Fever, it was unheard of for someone so young, the first of Kana's attacks and one that Josephine wanted to keep away from the spotlight. If Kana remembered correctly, that was the same year as the announcement for the drug to officially be incorporated in the military process.

"You made it all sound dramatic. My experience was quickly forgotten after a handful of near-death experiences. You quickly forget a painful experience when a fresh one takes its place." Her response was blasé.

They rounded the mountain and entered the sloping valley

where a collection of native trees grew, unusual trees with thick trunks and skinny, sparse branches, almost cartoon-like, as if a child had slashed a pencil to create tree branches.

"This is Camp Ridgeview," Spencer commented as the paved road became a single dirt path winding through the trees, until the road evened out and the dark body of water was visible through the gaps. The lake was made by some old-money family from Europe who enjoyed the mountainous landscape and the foreign trees, but wanted to step out and admire a lake. And when someone had enough money to last ten generations and all other vices became mundane, tackling projects was a source of entertainment and the patriarch created his own lake.

Kana slammed the door shut, causing two ducks near the shore to flap their wings and lift into the sky. "We'll need to take a boat to get to the main island in the lake's center." The campground was vast, its scattered islands home to the communal spaces: the dining hall, activity buildings, and several lodging areas. As the camp grew, it spilled into the surrounding land, adding cabins beyond its original bounds.

Spencer parked at the lake's edge, where a pier stretched out and three shallow rowboats were tied to posts.

The air was different here. As if they were transported to a different country, the sweltering heat simmered away. The trees lacked a fresh pine scent, instead giving softer notes with a floral aroma. Kana stood on the large rocky shore, staring off into the distance where four small islands stood before making her way to the pier. The late afternoon light bounced against the window. In two months' time, the shores would be lively with laughter and water splashing.

A vague memory surfaced. One of Ambrose's chauffeurs dropped her off, and the sleek black Rolls Royce parked among the equally expensive black cars. "Miss Ambrose." The man had her duffle on his shoulder as the camp owners greeted all the students. He'd checked her attendance on the tablet and smiled too sweetly at her.

"You came here often?"

Kana blinked to find that Spencer had already loaded the small rowboat with one of the duffel bags. "Only for one summer," Kana answered as she stepped into the boat, not bothering to pick up the oars. She cupped her chin with her palms and stared off into the tree line while Spencer worked to release the boat and stepped in, sitting on the middle plank, leaving one bench between them. His knees were crammed up to his chest as he started rowing.

"Good memories?" he asked as he rowed the boat.

In the absence of her response, Spencer received more of an answer than if she had spoken. She had very few fond memories. Only those on the list were invited to make a reservation for their children, meaning it was the same orbit of children Kana often associated with. One of her many therapists mentioned her holey, Swiss cheese memory could be a defense mechanism—therapists always seemed to have some metaphoric explanation, and then a blanket answer of how complex the human mind was, especially in child developmental stages. Kana chalked it up to the normal passage of time, or that the events had had such little impact on her.

The boat lazily rocked along the lake, the stroke of the oars mirroring the ebb of Kana's attempt at digging in her memories for her time at the camp. Her gaze fixated on nothing in particular, ignoring Spencer's sharp eyes on her profile.

"Want to tell me what we are looking for?" Spencer asked. The boat drifted closer to the pier leading to the largest island.

"I don't know," Kana admitted. P.L.U.T.O. wasn't here. She'd tossed her invention in the garbage before returning to the estate. Even now, the profound disappointment in Josephine's expression burned in her mind. Kana would have tossed P.L.U.T.O. into a bonfire if she could.

If this were the right spot, Josephine would have left a clue. She stepped out of the boat, ignoring Spencer's hand, too focused on a lingering heat fanning to life. What was the point of all of this? The last time she and Josephine spoke in person was four years ago, and the conversation had lasted less than five minutes. Neither of them could endure an exchange any longer than that.

Eighteen-year-old Kana had stumbled into her apartment, kicking off her extravagantly high stilettos, the arches in her feet cramping at the abrupt change to the flat floor. The softened haze of the alcohol kept her in a jittery buzz; she'd sniffed, wiping at her nose, the last hit fading, but the particles of powder left a tickling in her nasal cavity.

"Why were you at the Rotherham facility?" The sharp question had echoed and rebounded unnaturally in the shadowed crevices of her entryway. Kana fumbled with the switch knife she kept in her purse while her free hand slapped for the light switch. The blade popped out as she aimed it at the figure seated on the sofa.

"Put that down before you hurt yourself," Josephine said in that concise, authoritative voice, never yelling or raising her voice. Her presence alone commanded attention.

Kana's sluggish mind had listened, and she would wake up hating that she obediently folded the knife. She'd kept it in her clenched fist, her fingers digging into the hard metal of the handle.

"I don't like repeating myself," Josephine said with a finite power that could shake the ground. It took all of Kana's self-control to not quiver, because anger was easy, and it overpowered her insecurities and the smallness she felt when confronting Josephine.

"Why would I be at one of your facilities?" Kana spat. Earlier that afternoon, Kana had set her plan in motion, all to prove that her hunch was right.

Josephine's frigid eyes stared at Kana. The dim lighting from the contemporary chandelier above hadn't offered enough light, and Kana was glad. She'd suddenly felt seven years old, small and powerless, being told she wasn't good enough.

"Don't lie to me."

"Where is it?" Kana asked, changing the subject and the trajectory of the conversation. Fuck it. Kana had originally planned to confront Josephine after her return trip from the States. Kana had wanted the medical exam with hard proof, but her veins burned under her flesh with Josephine's unexpected appearance and accusation.

Josephine remained silent, allowing the distinct agitation in the space between them to enlarge. Kana wanted to bait Josephine a little more. She reached over and increased the chandelier light, saturating the living space.

"How could you know I was at Rotherham? I made sure to lose my tails, change my clothes, transportation, everything. I even made sure there wasn't any satellite footage for twenty minutes. I didn't step foot in the facility. The cameras didn't get a chance to see me entering the building, so how could you know I was at Rotherham?" Kana had felt a rush. For once in her life, she had the upper hand. Josephine's eyes lurked beneath the heavy shadows cast by her pronounced brow, the hollows beneath her sharp, jutting cheekbones carving her face into something skeletal.

"I don't like repeating myself," Kana mocked. "Where did you implant the tracker?"

In hindsight, Kana could argue the usefulness of a tracker, but Josephine never asked for permission. She always took, including Kana's ability to make choices for herself. She closed her eyes, forcing the memory out with the darkness behind her lids. How easy it was to slip into the past, to the times she didn't want to remember.

A pudgy sepia colored bird flitted onto the first step of the imposing structure that looked akin to a church, all it was missing was the religious iconography. Kana shoved the door to the dining hall open. There was nothing that stood out. The room, while large, was bare, a rustic haven with wooden beams and walls dressed in natural hues of earthy browns and greens. The afternoon sunlight slanted through the vaulted ceiling, casting gold beams of light atop the two rows of long communal tables crafted from sturdy timber on either side of the room as she walked through the aisle. She shoved the swinging kitchen door with her hip.

The broad kitchen was still. The nicked and worn countertops were bare, the industrial refrigerators were silent, and the pots, pans, and kitchen appliances were all stored away. The space, much like the rest of the camp, looked eerie and ghost-like without occupants.

She left the main dining hall and sped toward the cluster of cabins that were more like tiny homes. A mixture of glass and repurposed wood made up a dozen forty-five-square-meter narrow, rectangular cabins. The small kitchenette and living space had a sofa draped with a cloth to keep the gathering dust off the rich leather. Her sneakers creaked over the wood floors as she moved further into the cabin. On the right side of the next room were two single beds, stripped of sheets, topped only by a mattress cover.

She was an agitated pendulum, swinging back and forth as she stormed through each cabin. The slamming of the doors rose in volume. This had to be the spot, but each building was empty. At the fifth cabin, she shoved one mattress off the bed and even checked under the bed frame. A thin layer of dust with a tiny bunch of dust balls stared back at her. There was no symbol etched into wood or a doodle on a Post-it note. Josephine wouldn't pull the same trick a second time. The doubt wormed around. Maybe this wasn't the location and she'd interpreted the clue incorrectly, again. She gave up on the cabins.

"The other island," she ordered as she stalked past Spencer, who waited patiently on the front porch of the cabin. He looked at peace. The hard lines of his back softened with his hands tucked in the pockets of his jacket.

"Fond memories?" she tossed out sarcastically.

"It reminds me of a place I wish I could have experienced when I was a kid."

Kana couldn't understand his sentiment. The campground was nothing special. She was a knotted ball of agitation. If Spencer had any questions, he rightfully kept his mouth shut as he rowed them to the second smaller island, where two buildings occupied the cramped space. In Kana's hazy memory, one was designated for engineering and sciences, the other arts and crafts.

The exterior of the first building had a nearly panoramic view of the back part of the lake, with the exterior wall nearly all windows. The door was locked. And that was a good sign. Every other building had unlocked doors. Kana frowned as she jiggled the lock again, but the steel handle refused to budge.

"I'll open the door," Spencer said, climbing the three steps.

She gestured for him to go ahead. A murmur of a cooling mint lingered in her mouth for less than two seconds as Spencer picked up a pebble and tossed it at the door. A thunderous crack split the quiet and the door handle from the speed and force of the pebble.

Kana's greedy body craved more of the lingering, minty energy. She was still so low on her reserves, rising up to a quarter tank. The swathe of residual energy he'd used to keep her from smashing onto the garden grounds earlier that morning had charged her more than she realized. She licked her lips, not realizing she was shifting closer to Spencer until he looked over at her, feeling her encroaching on his space. She blinked, blaming her lack of sleep for the unusual desire to be closer to someone, and sped past him to reach the front door.

The building was for the arts, with tables coated in layers of dried acrylic and oil paint, and the pungent scent of turpentine created a resinous note. There were built-in cabinets stacked full of canvases of different sizes and jars with paintbrushes. She was about to move to the next building, her hand on the door handle —after all, her goal was the engineering designated space where she created P.L.U.T.O.—but the air held a kiss of dampness. A bright red warning sign.

Kana ducked inside and moved away from any windows, glancing over her shoulder to see Spencer standing without concern, because he couldn't sense a portal ripping open. Each person had a different signature, and this portal creator was not from the same group that had been in her apartment. An unknown User. But seeing her startled reaction, he rushed in and closed the door behind them.

Chapter Twenty-One

A Tomi's power was distinct. Was it due to the sheer amount of energy needed to rip a wormhole in space and time, or because Kana was attuned to the kinds of Users who ripped portals since Oliver was a constant in her life? She didn't care to understand. What she knew was that the change in pressure against her skin was not strong enough to distinguish the kind of water, Tomi's always felt wet in some way, and that in itself was painting a cautionary yellow across Kana's vision. The User was close, maybe an island away. The chances of a Tomi User on their own were slim to none, especially given the past few weeks. *Tick, tick, tick.* The clock was counting down faster. "Someone's here," she said in a low voice as she crossed to the back wall where tarps covered canvases. There was one painting, separated from all the others, propped against the wall beside a drying rack. The painting was the length of her arm and stylized similarly to Degas's swirling, delicate colors and light atmosphere. The landscape depicted a spot in the Azores, which could be Faial Island.

"Did you see someone?" Spencer asked, gun removed from his holster. His body maneuvered to cover her as she tucked against the far corner of the room, away from windows and doors.

Kana ignored his question as she moved the canvas, checking the back. The texture wasn't rough, not like hemp or linen stretched across the wooden board. She ran her fingers over the painting, finding it was a printed picture in a frame.

"Kana."

She waved her hand at him, not bothering to speak or look in his direction. Was this a clue? Her pulse kicked up a notch to match her shortened breath. It had to be. Every other space was vacated, and this was the only canvas facing the door, as if purposefully displayed; all the other canvases had their wooden backing exposed. God damn Josephine, only she would make it something so convoluted. It was probably something philosophical and deep in meaning, a painting that wasn't a painting.

"The hollow tree," she whispered to herself. And the dots connected.

During one of the warm summer nights at camp, a counselor had spun a tale about the hollow tree. The proverbial tree grew around a well. If found, you could flip open the top and jump down, and inside were supposedly dozens of bones from campers centuries ago. It was one of those camp stories a counselor made up years before to spook the children. A tall tale around a campfire and, for those brave enough, a treasure hunt to find the hollow tree. Strips of light bounced off the forest floor as groups of kids went hunting, their glow in the dark vests like fireflies.

A painting that wasn't a painting and a tree that wasn't a tree. Was the clue in the hollow tree? She could run with this bare thread of logic, even though there had to be more. But how was she supposed to find a tree stump while a team of Synthies was trampling around the campgrounds?

"What do you see?" She tugged Spencer's arm. The relaxed version of him was nowhere to be found. Spencer was alert, his entire frame coiled and ready to spring. His eyes swept the same area, checking each window, wall, and door. If he could get imaging from a satellite, she was sure he would be beeping like a thermal reading.

"Relax," Kana muttered as she tugged at his arm, the bands of his muscles immobile.

"You spotted a threat," he said with a pinch of doubt. He kept his firearm fully loaded, his finger poised on the trigger.

"I didn't really see anyone." She corrected his statement. "It doesn't matter. What do you see?" She pointed to the painting. Bexley had supplied the memory of Camp Ridgeview; Spencer might be useful, too. An outside perspective and all.

"It's a painted landscape of an island."

Kana scowled. He was useless.

"It's the Azores," she corrected him. Her momentary lapse of judgment proved incorrect; a second opinion wouldn't help. Josephine had made this ridiculous scavenger hunt for her and her alone.

"Which island?" he asked somewhere over her shoulder.

"Faial," Honestly, she should just take a picture and think about it later.

"Why is there an additional island?"

Kana almost missed Spencer's comment, too distracted by forming plans to search the campgrounds. "What?"

"In the right-hand corner."

Kana assumed the blob was a darkened cloud near the horizon line, but as she squinted, she thought perhaps the form was another island. The image of the clustered islands was much like the Bahamas and her brief vacation in Malaysia; her memories coalesced, and she didn't realize the island was even out of place.

Her fingers ran over the fabric until her nail dug under the surface and the island peeled right off, leaving behind an unblemished white absence of space. She turned the piece of dried paint that was the length of her pinky. Kana shook her head in silent disbelief. On the other side of the peeled dried acrylic paint were tiny dots arranged in braille.

"Any chance we can get off this island?" Kana asked, tucking the plastic paint strip into her front pocket while her other hand skimmed across the canvas, searching for any additional strips of thick paint.

"We can't go in the boat. Too risky and isolated." He objected.

"You want to swim?" She shook her head. That seemed like a worse idea.

"How do you know someone is here?"

Kana sighed hot, irritable air, unable to restrain herself. She seemed to be letting a lot of her little emotional bursts bubble out. There was an uncomfortable familiarity with Spencer, like finding a nostalgic toy buried in a closet. She chalked it up to him acting as an Oliver 2.0 for the time being. "How about I go in the boat? They won't shoot me. They know someone must be here. The rowboat near the pier is a dead giveaway, don't you think?"

Spencer was silent.

Kana's hands checked the knife in her back pocket and another in the jacket pocket. "This isn't my first time being bait."

The plan was awful, they both knew it, but the choice was out of their hands. A waft of honeysuckle triggered the silent alarm in her mind as a body ran through the wall, passing through the canvases and shelves of paints. Kana's mind registered the attacker, and then Spencer was firing his gun, his body planted in front of hers, and he shoved her to the door with a single word passing his lips. "Boat."

She burst out of the cabin, securing one knife in her hand, ready for anyone looming by the door. *Be quick, jab and yank*, the words of a long-ago trainer echoed. She'd gutted and stabbed before, and she would do it again. While she could logically repeat these steps to herself, her hand around the knife trembled. Her frantic eyes swept over the landscape for immediate danger. There was only one boat docked.

A crash startled her down the steps, and she shoved the boat off the inclined shore.

She checked over her shoulder, her hands blindly gripping the thick oar. Spencer wasn't running after her. No one was. There was a jerk, as if an invisible tether attached to the front of the boat had yanked. The unexpected movement flung her backward, her ass plunking on the bottom of the boat. The oar slipped out of her grasp and bounced out, the plank of wood floating uselessly along the surface of the rippling lake.

The compact boat wasn't jet skiing through the water, but moving faster than when Spencer rowed. Kana shuffled to the front of the boat, keeping as low as possible, and lifted her head to see a woman standing ankle-deep in the lake, with awful cartoonish lines of concentration in her frown and throbbing temple veins. The Idu was impressive. She'd manipulated the ebb and flow of the water until she'd created turbulent waves. Kana crouched low, bracing her left knee against the boat's floor to anchor herself. She drew her gun, both hands gripping it, muscles straining against its weight. She drew in a breath, let it out slow, and squeezed the trigger—*bang!*

At that distance and from the moving boat, Kana didn't have any hope of hitting the woman. An unidentifiable taste of a powder, like flour or pancake mix, coated her mouth, and Kana knew someone else had moved the trajectory of her bullet. Either the woman was good enough to simultaneously keep the rippling momentum while deflecting a bullet, or, more likely, a second Active User was covering their partner.

Kana wouldn't waste the precious opportunity to siphon energy. Three flavors: mint, powder, and a nutty base battled in her mouth. Should she take a chance and slip into the lake? Would she have a better chance at swimming? The metallic sounds of bullets sounded off, forcing her to flatten into the boat, unsure of who was shooting. The boat's momentum stopped, leaving it swaying at a natural pace.

She chanced a look over the rocking boat to where she first saw the woman. Spencer was blocking and dodging before ruthlessly tackling the woman. How on earth had he reached the main island so fast? The waves beneath her bucked and slowed, like a car jolting under a rookie driver's heavy foot on the brakes. She lurched right, and there it was, a powerboat cutting across the water, the answer to her question. It was almost comical how smoothly he moved, as if the unfolding events were on a movie set and these other people were all stunt men and women.

Kana lowered herself back to the bottom of the boat. Spencer had it handled. Her sag of relief was short-lived as the air condensed, and she sat up, eyes wide and transfixed on the space one meter above the rocking boat. A thirty-centimeter sphere of air warped, as if there were an iridescent bubble pushing out. No way was a Tomi trying to get on the boat through the air. From Oliver's previous babbling, ripping wormholes usually required an anchor; she'd never seen or heard of anyone attempting a portal in midair.

Her eyes narrowed as she aimed the gun, ready for whoever might step out. The portal didn't open fully, and she knew something was very wrong. The wet sensation she associated with Tomis was vastly different for this User. This felt like thick, sloppy sand. Portals had to be big enough to fit the entire body. Users who couldn't accurately bend the space to the correct size were still in the early learning stages, they couldn't step through a wormhole that couldn't fit their entire body. The splitting space was like a thin paint bubble growing larger, until only a head pushed through. Kana's eyes widened. The person's left eye wasn't visible. In the pocket of the eyelid grew a ribbed mushroom, while smaller, unidentifiable sprouts shot out from the top lid, and the thin flesh beneath the eye was rigid as the veins bulged with tiny fungi trying to break the surface, like the suckers on starfish limbs.

The man's skull was split, oozing chunky matter as fleshy fungi bubbled out. The smell of rancid puss floated closer as he forced more of his body through the hole. The thin paint texture of the portal tore, leaving a crude crescent shape of ripped space. A Rabid Tomi User. She'd heard it was possible, but had never seen one before now.

Kana aimed the barrel of the gun and fired. The first two hit, and the screech emanating from the mouth—how it could still even make noise was beyond her, with the mouth cavity overflowing with fungi—was a high-pitched wail akin to radio static, as if the invasive fungi had stretched around the vocal cords.

What she didn't account for was the User falling out of the hole and smashing onto the edge of the boat before flopping into the dark depths of the lake. Her hands wrenched out to grip the boat's edge as it thrashed under the weight, nearly tipping onto its side.

She grappled for the other oar and paddled two strokes before a hand shot up from the water, gripping onto the side of the boat for purchase. By the time she scrambled to find the gun which had fallen halfway under the seat bench, the Rabid Synthie had already hoisted itself up. The lake water sloshed around them as the rowboat's nose pointed straight to the sky. Kana pushed her feet to the side of the boat, her arms struggling to keep herself from sliding right into the Rabid Synthie.

The man—honestly, Kana couldn't tell if it was a man—had an unidentifiable face and an even more deformed body. He reached toward her, his palm split in half as a Venus flytrap mouth emerged. The vermillion plant had human-shaped teeth, but thin and more pointed, like icicles.

Fuck that.

Kana unloaded the gun, five more rounds, and the person's hand was minced meat. Each bullet caused a flinch, but the Synthie held onto the boat as if they couldn't feel their flesh being shredded. The mutilated Tomi shifted their weight just enough, at just the right angle, and the boat tipped over.

The cool lake water stunned her for a moment. *Swim,* she yelled at herself as she kicked through the murky depths to get away from the bobbing boat. The dark lake water lacked clarity, hindering her visibility of the Rabid Synthie. Her head broke the surface, her gaze frantically grazing across the A-frame windows of the camp building, denoting the main island and the nearest source of land. With strong strokes through the cool water, something grabbed her calf, and she was dragged down.

A shrill scream escaped her as air bubbles blocked her vision. It must be a hand, or the remains of the Synthie's hand, biting into her flesh like a small anchor tethering itself around her leg. The water's surface rose higher as she sank. She twisted, and through the haze of color and form, there was the disturbing mass of bloated fungi, umbrella caps bulging like water-filled balloons. She thrashed, trying to kick with her other leg as the Rabid Synthie dragged her closer to its body. The shredded fungi on its other arm resembled jellyfish tentacles and hung limp at its side. Her hands grappled for the knife in the jacket pocket as her lungs ached, and she sawed through the hand that had skewered her calf. The Rabid Synthie screeched, the sloppy weight of wet sand grating against her skin.

The Rabid Synthie was trying to make a portal. She didn't have enough brain power to consider why the hell it was attempting a portal, but she was in luck. Dr. Cohen had said not to use her power, but his vague warning didn't matter now. As the Rabid Tomi moved its other arm, she snatched the fluid energy. Unlike moving Idu energy, portal Users' power was slippery and difficult for her to catch, like wrangling an octopus; regardless, she shoved the redirected energy at the exact moment she stabbed the blade into the appendage gripping her calf. The Synthie's deformed arm was torn from the rest of the body, snapping at the elbow, and blown like a torpedo deeper into the watery depths.

Kana sputtered to the surface. The lake water slipped into her mouth as she kicked to keep herself afloat. With her head tilted at the sky, she pawed blindly at her calf where the severed hand's fingers dug in. The squishy, smooth tops of the mushrooms split between her fingers, but it was the crunch of cartilage that made her shiver. This was wrong. Passive Users didn't manifest flesh and bone, not like Rabid Active Users. She ripped it out of her leg. Black spots burst like a single firework across her vision. She cried in pain, hacking as lake water sloshed into her mouth.

The image of the swollen creature slithering through the water kept her moving to the shore of the nearest island. Her leg pulsated with each kick, and an age-old warning—*don't let them touch you*—repeated on loop in her mind. Well, failing Josephine was the least of her worries; the Rabid Synthies could have a contagious disease. Her stomach knotted at the image of her flesh tearing apart, mushrooms and clumps of calcified tumorous bone and cartilage gurgling out.

The tip of her shoe scraped against the side of the island as she crawled out of the lake. She tossed the sopping jacket on the reedy bank, and it fell with a waterlogged slap. Her gaze went across the water, but she couldn't see Spencer. Two bodies lay on the lakeshore, the water circling their thick shoes and ankles, but they were dressed in all black, not in jeans and a black top. That was a good sign. Spencer wasn't dead.

To look down at her leg or not? She imagined the flesh peeling off, a portion of her calf eaten, or the black necrotic flesh crawling up her leg. Luckily, her imagination was hyperactive, and when she looked, she faced an irregular set of penetrating scratches on her quivering calf, almost like an animal's claws, but not consistent enough to be teeth. She'd survive.

She groaned, equal parts distressed and annoyed, as the air moistened in that sludgy way of the infected Passive user. She staggered away from the short shoreline, further away from the open space, and toward the nearest building. Her water-logged sneakers made squishing sounds as she stomped further into the island.

For a moment, déjà vu washed over her. Here she was again at a lake and a Rabid Synthie, so far gone she wouldn't call them human anymore, was chasing her. Oliver would lose all his hair if she landed back in the hospital for rounds of more surgeries. Her stomach ached in protest as she ducked down into the cafeteria for a moment to catch her breath. Her hand touched her torso. The area felt hot against her pruned fingertips. Kana lifted her shirt and cursed.

Through the thin, bloated bandages, the skin was furiously enflamed. One of the large bandages on the lower right quadrant had peeled back to reveal black splotches more prominent than they had been this morning, as if physical strain or the use of her power had flared the unknown disease. Either way, she was screwed. Using her power was triggering an unknown reaction to her wound, and she wouldn't survive if she couldn't use her trump card. Not that she had much left. Her tank was nearly empty.

The doorknob jiggled. She sucked in a breath and shuffled further into the space, past the long lunch bench. The thick, grainy, wet sand feeling lingered as the residual energy rolled off the Rabid Synthie at the dining hall door.

She tentatively reached out and took a morsel of the radiating power. The incredible euphoric rush was instantaneous, and it sent her spiraling back to the disaster at the lake a few weeks earlier. She should stop. But it was so addicting, flooding her taste buds, clouding her nostrils, creating a clashing symphony incoherently off-key in her ears. And through Kana's delirious haze, the Rabid Synthie was closing in. The sound of tables and bench legs scraping against the hardwood floors warned her that the deformed Rabid Synthie was stuttering in their steps. There was no rescue team this time. But that didn't matter, she would protect herself.

With more effort than she would like to admit, she stopped guzzling the energy and, with a semblance of coherency, redirected it. A force stronger than a car hitting her sent her hurtling through the opposite wall. Correction, this was worse than the time she was hit by a car; this felt like the car was on top of her, but the pain lasted for less than two seconds, since her head smacked into the hardwood wall with a loud, echoing crack. She thought she saw Spencer outside the corner window. Before her body crumpled to the floor, her vision blacked out.

The dining hall was at a slanted angle when her vision refocused. The pale wooden leg of one of the lunch benches was the sole subject of her vision. There was a scratching sound as if a dog's nails were clawing at a door.

"Are you serious?" she groaned and blinked to stop the double vision, partially in disbelief at the thing dragging half its body toward her. It would be humorous if it wasn't truly disgusting. The body was a fusing glob of flesh and fungi, like soggy, chunky oatmeal. She didn't know how it was even alive. Kana couldn't tell where its head was, if it still had one. Even in her concussed state, she knew this was so far beyond what a Rabid Synthie usually looked like. Synthies understandably wanted a cure; if this was what she would be reduced to, she would want a cure too. The lurch of raw nausea left tears in her eyes and wet bile lifting in her throat.

The zombie hunk of flesh continued to crawl closer, using the length of what used to be an arm to drag itself to her. Somehow, even without eyes or any discernible parts, it knew where she was.

Kana scooted away, not wanting it to touch her, part of her searching for a weapon, another part wanting to escape. Her eyes drew to the window where she thought she saw Spencer, but there was no one.

A cry escaped her lips as her skull throbbed. If she had a clear mind, she would laugh at how pathetic this moment was; she was backing away as a blob of flesh moved like a snail toward her. She hauled herself to her feet, stumbling into the back kitchen, where she found cooking oil and matches. Black spots with tiny bits of stardust clouded her vision, a warning before she came to a stop.

"Fuck," she cursed. This was unacceptable. Kana slapped her

palms against her cheeks. She needed to light the bitch and be done.

By sheer stubbornness, she momentarily watched a second pile of inhuman flesh crawl to her. A slithering serpentine arm reached out to drag itself. This was the type of shit Josephine lived for, an unknown organism that needed to be studied. Kana sneered at the thought and lit the thing on fire.

There was no sound for the first precious seconds until the flames grew, stretching over the wood floorboards, crackling with laughter as it grabbed onto the wooden legs of the nearest bench. She should move, but her body wouldn't listen. Queasiness unexpectedly plundered her insides, and she doubled over and puked. The bile splattered on the floor as Kana's eyes spilled tears from the pain. She wheezed from the thickening smoke and another building crest of nausea.

Through the suffocating smoke, she tasted mint as firm hands pulled her far enough from the major fire to lift her. One slid under her knees, the other balancing her weight as she was lifted bridal style. Spencer didn't carry her far, depositing her on a patch of grass.

"Asshole," the word slurred out as her cheek rested against his arm. "Did I pass?"

"What?" Spencer asked, his face flushed from exertion. So he was human after all. The team on the lakeshore had proved to be a challenge for him. She responded with another cough, the sound racking through her lungs. Her torso muscles tensed and retracted, sending painful jolts to the rest of her body.

"Ugh," she groaned, the sound from the back of her throat. She was never going to a lake again.

Chapter Twenty-Two

Spencer was rightfully concerned about her concussion, but that didn't lessen her desire to punt him to the next town, especially as cold water flicked at her face. A scowl dragged across her lips as she jerked awake. The slight movement sent a hammering nail from the back of her skull through her left eye.

"I'm going to punch you," Kana groaned as her thin eyelids lifted half open. "If you didn't want me falling asleep, why am I lying on a bed?" The plush mass under her prone form told her where she was.

She pushed herself up and instantly regretted the decision as she rolled over and retched, the stomach bile splashing inside a bucket that was lifted from the ground and held under her. After she'd dry heaved twice with nothing left to expel, the bucket was lowered.

"Is this the camp?" she groaned, observing the dark room. The layout was unfamiliar, with bulky shutters over the windows and a thick curtain haphazardly taped to the kitchenette window. She couldn't remember anything after setting fire to the dining hall, and as she tried to recall more details, it was like trying to buffer a video over dial-up that stuck every few seconds.

"Found a cabin not too far away." Spencer's voice blared, as if his voice had a direct microphone into her head. Kana cringed, her hands flying to her ears. He whispered an apology and let her know he was setting a water bottle beside her hip. Between the pulsating ache in her head and the high-pitched ringing in her left ear, it took her quite some time to gather herself. She focused on the sounds of Spencer's movement, the brush of fabric as he walked, the squeak of a faucet turning on, and the whoosh of water as the plastic container was cleaned before she opened her eyes.

"Oliver," she managed to say, cracking open her eyes enough to sip the warm water that tasted like melted plastic.

"Not a good idea," he said, elbowing the faucet off, and turned to face her.

Kana's anger flared. She had a raw need to contact Oliver. He was her paddle. He was the only constant in her life she could count on. "You're the one who was watching me and didn't help." She managed to force more water down her throat, taking careful deep breaths. *Your power is your secret. If one person knows, only death ensures their secrecy.* Josephine's voice wriggled out from the depths of the locked parts of her mind. Kana couldn't stop her body from tensing, because Spencer saw her. As far as Kana knew, only Bexley had ever witnessed her using her power. Everyone else was in graves.

"I saw you watching me. You might not be ordered to kill me," she began, shifting to prop herself against the creaky headboard and noticed she wore a mysterious, large, red flannel shirt. Fearful heat stirred slowly in the depths of her stomach. She pinned him with her stare as she mentally felt for any abnormal aches.

"Your injuries needed to be redressed, that is all," he said, perfectly clinical.

She lifted the hem of the flannel to reveal fresh bandages neatly placed over the black and ridged healing flesh. There were two new bandages on her right arm, and one around her calf. The memory of the diseased Rabid under the murky water returned. Her fingers gripped her calf.

"It wasn't a bite," Spencer said, "The puncture marks were from sharp nails or very large thorns."

Relief was short-lived. Her body attempted to relax, but on her left shoulder blade, the sticky adhesive from a medical patch pulled tight across her skin. An ache in the back of her head sent her fingers to ghost over gauze, and she found thin strips of bandages wrapped around her forehead.

"You are doing more than being a bodyguard," she said, turning the conversation back to Spencer. Even in the muted monochromatic darkness, his gaze penetrated, managing to hold her own even though she was tucked in the darkest part of the small cabin.

"I'm going to call Oliver. I need a reason not to."

She fought to maintain her gaze on Spencer's as another wave of nausea hit her with a touch of vertigo. He set the rinsed bucket by the bedside, retreating to lean against the kitchenette counter, maintaining a respectable distance.

"Access to your apartment was compromised, plus the antique market and the camp, and he is familiar with all three locations."

"If that's your only reason, that's weak." Technically, that was all true, but loads of other people knew her favored apartment in the city, and the antique market was a public place. The camp location was more obscure and out of the way, but anyone could have been tailing them from the safe house.

She should keep her mouth shut. If she were smart, she would wait it out and find a way to escape. Stop showing her disdain for Spencer, who could easily overpower her and had many opportunities to do so. He didn't have to flick water at her to keep her awake. He could let her fall asleep. Hell, he could have slit her throat when he changed her clothes or just let her die in the fire. Was he truly so bound to his honor and duty to the president?

The rumor made more sense now. If they reached a Rabid stage, Synthies were morphing into something exceptionally gruesome. Kana frowned while rubbing her temple, her head cradled in her hand as she thought of the Passive User. Typically, Active Users were more likely to reach the Rabid stage. Passive Users' symptoms were different. The plants bloomed out of veins. At some point, bloodletting wasn't enough, and their organs shut down as the disease turned the ripe, nutritious, squishy bits into a little ecological paradise. Never outwardly deforming the host, not to the extent of the Portal User.

Why was she here again? She should be lounging at a resort, stretched out on the beach, and enjoying a three-star Michelin restaurant. Josephine had transformed into Dr. Frankenstein and concocted something in her labs, and everyone thought Kana would know where the mad scientist had vanished to. Kana wanted to laugh. It wasn't like she'd implanted a tracker in the woman. Only Josephine would tag someone like a dog. After the confrontation, Kana had the implant removed and swiftly started her hotel-hopping lifestyle. Kana hadn't seen anything in her medical records after the recent surgery from the lake attack. She made sure Josephine couldn't track her again.

"You're talking out loud," he said, and what on earth was that soft voice for? Pity because she'd just blabbed about her mother placing a tracking chip in her daughter. He cleared his throat. There was a dip in the mattress as he sat on the edge of the bed.

"You're still talking."

Kana snapped her mouth closed. Her concussion was impairing her brain-to-mouth filter. "Good," she said, keeping her eyes closed. "I hope you feel uncomfortable."

A dry bemused laugh. "You do enjoy making people uncomfortable."

She fell silent, letting herself be dragged with the crashing waves of annoyance.

The mattress lifted. "Don't fall asleep. This is your fourth concussion." Kana shrugged off the warmth of his hand as he touched the top of her arm. Her fourth concussion? Admittedly, she didn't track the bouts of trauma her body endured, especially a hit to the head; there were more life-threatening attacks that left more permanent damage.

"I'm glad you familiarized yourself with my medical history."

"Another two hours, then you can sleep."

Two hours, two days, two years. A gentle pressure on her upper arm was enough to earn a hum, but her eyes remained closed as she listened to the soft shuffling and plastic crinkling. "It's apple juice."

She peeled open her eyes to find a small green and white box with a white straw in front of her.

"You were right," he said as he stepped further from her bedside. "I have separate orders, but they aren't as nefarious as you think."

Her ears perked, more alert now. It took effort to bring the small box to her mouth, but she sucked up the juice. The sugary liquid tasted better than her cavernous, stale mouth. She could go for a good toothbrush and mouthwash.

"Aside from keeping you alive, I needed to make sure you were trying to find Dr. Ambrose, or determine if you were going to cover up on her behalf." His planted stance was formal. She wanted to better interpret his reactions, but the sensory overload frenzied her attention.

"And," Kana said, because there had to be more.

"The best scenario is that you cooperated, and the animosity against your mother was real. We would find Dr. Ambrose, who would be hunkered down in a lab somewhere in the middle of nowhere."

Her stomach rolled with the next sip of juice, threatening to throw it back up if she drank any more. Spencer carefully took the juice box from her outstretched hand and deposited it on the counter's edge.

"And the worst scenario: you knew where Dr. Ambrose was and would help her escape."

Kana's laugh squeezed out and, like a can of soda, cracked open, the carbonation hissing angrily. "Don't make me laugh," she tried to bite out, but it came out far weaker and almost like a sob. She closed her eyes, counting ten breaths.

"The most probable?" she eventually asked.

"Hm?" Spencer hummed as he returned to her side, a half-empty water bottle in his hand. His shirt was rumpled, and fatigue screamed in the lines of his downturned lips and sloped shoulders.

"You said the best-case scenario and the worst, but what about the most likely scenario?" Kana clarified.

"You wouldn't know how to find her."

Kana scoffed. Wasn't that the truth? "I'm going to sleep, two hours my ass."

Spencer didn't let her fall asleep. She stopped reacting to the flick of water against her face, and when a small electric shock zapped her forearm, she flailed, kicking out her leg, pleased when she hit something solid, followed by a grunted *oomf*. That's what he got for shocking her.

"I'm not going to let a minor concussion be the cause of your death," Spencer said.

"Dying in my sleep is looking awfully appealing," she argued, with her eyes firmly shut. A sharp gasp, and her eyes blew wide open as she was hoisted off the bed. Her arms flailed, her right hand smacked against a sharp jaw and found the junction of Spencer's neck and shoulder.

"Warn a girl," she muttered. She didn't like being manhandled, but any further protest was bulldozed by nausea. "You have no one to blame if I puke on you."

A cold draft caressed her exposed skin as she squirmed away from the open door. She wasn't able to move that much. He had her in a tight grip against his chest, setting her back on her feet beside a fading blue hatchback.

"We can't go far," she said yanking open the car door. "The trunk that isn't a trunk, like an island that isn't an island." She was here to do a job.

The leather scent was a stark contrast to the musky cabin. She wrinkled her nose and cracked her eyes open at the sound of the passenger door closing. He really had found a random cabin in the woods. Near abandonment, the decrepit cabin had one of its front windows boarded up with thick wooden panels. She couldn't tell how far away from the camp they were.

"Are you sure it's here?" Spencer asked as he jabbed the keys into the ignition, the crystal pink heart and palm tree on the keychain clinking against each other.

Kana stared at the tree line, her resolve wavering. There were troves of people trying to snatch her, and a bounty on her head, and moving around or trying to escape the country was becoming less feasible. Would finding Josephine stop the hunt she was trapped in? There was also the minor issue of the US wanting to interrogate her for the lake slaughter. She'd forgotten about that unfortunate fiasco. She didn't know what was happening in that regard, and without access to information, she needed to see Oliver. Spencer continued to refuse contact, but he had a burner phone on him. She just needed to find it.

"Kana." Spencer's voice broke her thoughts and her glaring at the hideous air freshener dangling from the rearview mirror.

"Find another cabin," she ordered. "The clue is somewhere at the campsite."

The accommodation he'd already found was abandoned and looked like a set from a cabin horror film. There was no reason to leave it now. Kana could only surmise Spencer was antsy about staying in one place for too long. She needed time to contact Oliver and slip away from the watchdog.

The fading light still bothered her sensitive eyes, her face crumpling in distaste when Spencer offered sunglasses as he threw the car in reverse. She gratefully shoved them onto her face. The urge to sleep was a siren song, ruined whenever Spencer would pinch the skin on her biceps.

He found another cabin quickly. The small boxy wooden structure had peeling paint and an unfinished deck that read, "UNINHABITED." He tucked the car by a dry patch of dead grass halfway behind a tree, and entered the building first, reappearing less than a minute later from around the back, one hand still with a gun, the other opening the passenger door.

"I'm not an invalid. I have two arms and two legs," Kana hissed and smacked away his hands that were attempting to steady her. He'd better not try to lift her bridal style again. Spencer had parked the stolen car out of sight by the time she reached the front door, and then he set to rearranging the limited furniture: pushing a questionably stained futon against the wall out of sight from the windows, and unfolding the two collapsible camping chairs from the car trunk. The unexpected movement in the abandoned cabin stirred up dust and plumes of dirt, making the small space hazy. She spotted the bathroom directly across from the front door.

"Are you going to follow me into the bathroom?" she asked with a lifted eyebrow, her body half in the bathroom doorway. He said nothing but took another step in her direction.

"Fine." She kept the door open as she shoved her shorts and panties down.

Spencer's cheeks reddened while his eyes landed on the vinyl floor. He stepped in enough to grip the doorknob as the steady stream of her pee began. Her scoff was muffled by the door clicking shut. He acted as if he hadn't done covert assignments and hadn't had to pee and shit with his teammates in worse conditions.

An airplane bathroom was larger than this minuscule space. She splashed cold water on her face as she devised a plan. The first step was to find the burner phone. She'd watched Spencer toss the old one in the trash when they exited the safe house, but he would have another phone in his go-bag.

When she demanded food, he excused himself to return to the car, having mentioned there was some food in the trunk. The phone was suspiciously easy to find. She didn't dwell on the fact that he left it in his coat pocket, which he happened to leave on the back of the blue camping chair.

She stared at the small, old iPhone in her hand. The device didn't have a passcode set up either. It was too easy. The suspicion that this was a test returned, but what did she have to lose? With an SOS to Oliver, using the campsite as the last known location, she wiped the message and slid the phone back in place as the creaking floorboard warned her of Spencer's return. She sat innocently on the futon.

"It's not much, but it's food," he said as he dropped a wrinkled brown paper bag on the coffee table. Inside were three packs of instant oatmeal, four energy drinks, a small jar of peanut butter, and granola bars. That was it.

Spencer laughed, the sound sudden. He bit his lip to stop himself. "You couldn't look more offended."

"You aren't hiding a steak or a burger?" The thought of a juicy slab of steak had her mouth watering, even though she would undoubtedly throw up the rich meat.

"Unfortunately, I can't create portals and pop into the nearest steakhouse."

Kana grunted in agreement. It was truly unfortunate. Portal Users were useful.

"You're unusual," he said, rinsing a teakettle to start boiling water for the oatmeal.

"You're just realizing that now." She sighed, wiggling on the couch and stretching out her legs.

"You're an Idu, but you didn't try to move the bullet."

Kana was momentarily lost. "You must forgive my concussed

brain. Which bullet?" She'd been shot at numerous times in the last few days that she couldn't remember which incident he was referring to.

"Your . . ." He paused, trying to find the right word. "Acquaintance that wanted a trade for A.E. Potentia." He was referring to the little tiff with Vyolette and George.

"You may have forgotten, but most people don't do extensive training, and it's hard to move objects that move that fast," she said, as if the flimsy excuse of her not practicing was enough to explain why she wasn't going to stop George's bullet. But he saw how she'd pushed the infected Portal User in the cafeteria—she still didn't have the brain power to dissect how that was possible —and assumed she was like him, telekinetic to some degree. He was poking to see if she would take the bait. Did he think she would become a pile of mush because he'd saved her life? That she would just answer all his questions? Correction, she saved herself. He was a bystander. She wouldn't forgive that minor fact.

"The president wasn't full of shit. You can take on full teams and come out without a scratch. Any tips you want to share?" Her deflection was painfully obvious with the forceful focus to skirt the conversation back to Spencer.

"What is your weapon of choice?"

Kana blinked, sent off kilter with the question. "Words."

Spencer laughed, a pleasantly warm sound, as he ran a hand through his hair. He had a barely noticeable dimple in the lower part of his left cheek. "If it's you against another person, what weapon can you handle best?"

"A gun, longer distance, but my trainer said I was better with a knife." Kana rubbed the pad of her pointer finger over the dry skin of her thumb cuticle. "But I don't like being too close." She didn't like holding a weapon, especially a blade. Flesh split easier than she'd realized. Her small, thirteen-year-old hands had gripped the handle of a kitchen knife longer than her forearm. She belatedly realized how the last comment sounded more like a deeper admittance.

"Guns are more effective and offer a better chance at running away," Spencer said. "You favor your right side when you fire, it's messing with your trajectory."

"If I survive this nightmare, I'll be sure to go back to training." Kana rolled her eyes and eased her sore body into the lumpy sofa, as she formulated the best way to slip away from Spencer's vigilant watch. She must have dozed off, because she awoke to a beam of sunlight hitting her face from the crack of a curtain near the fireplace window.

She peeked over the edge of the sofa arm. Spencer was slumped in the kitchen corner, his arms crossed over his chest, his neck tucked down. Centimeter by centimeter, she crawled off the futon. Thankfully, her sneakers were mostly dry by now, and there was no obvious squishing sound.

By some miracle, the floorboards didn't creak, keeping her approach to the front door silent, until the pressure of her tiptoes caused a faint sound, as if a mouse were shouting, but Spencer remained still, eyes closed. He'd had to stay up equally as long as she did, and hopefully his exhaustion would smother him for a few hours.

So far, she was lucky. She leaped off the deck and landed with a padded thud onto the moist soil from the morning dew. She needed to find her way back to the camp. The braille word *chouette* was French, a homograph meaning "owl" and "cool," and that told her where to go. The thing was, Kana couldn't deny that Mr. President was right; Josephine was playing a game, leaving random clues just for Kana, and that made her feel sick all over again. Because Josephine didn't play games. The waste of energy and time was something Josephine didn't appreciate, so the smoke and mirrors were worrisome. The tiny day birds Kana had seen at a national reserve in Portugal inhabited pastel painted birdhouses in a seemingly endless field. Even if someone could connect those two ideas, they couldn't know how it related to the campground. The answer was in the back of the camp, the wood-shop graveyard, where a collection of birdhouses that kids had made had been flooded shortly after the camp opened, transforming that area of the campgrounds into a slushy swamp. Now, birds found refuge in dozens of terrible arts and crafts projects.

It wasn't as hard as she thought to retrace the short drive. She cataloged the path Spencer had taken, her eyes thankfully shielded by the sunglasses. For the most part, Spencer had driven straight down the road, making two lefts and one right turn. The sun still hung low in the east, resting on her shoulders. She had plenty of time.

She was terrible at gauging the distance. It felt like she'd walked eight kilometers, but in reality, it could have been two. A car approached at a leisurely pace, the rubbery tires crunching off in the distance, and Kana flattened herself behind sparse bushes. The car drove far too slowly to be someone passing through the grounds, but she didn't dare check to see if it was the blue car Spencer had stolen.

The air thickened with the rising humidity and temperature as another two hours dragged by. Kana licked her dry lips, wishing she had taken a water bottle.

"Finally," she exhaled. The long paneled, dried blood-colored planks of wood and rectangular stained glass window told her she had found a cabin. She crouched down, resting for a minute, rubbing her palms over her face before letting her head hang over her folded forearms. The exhaustion pooled to the soles of her feet, shackling her to the ground. Just a brief break.

Like a startled animal, her head rose in the air. Faint but lingering in the air was the familiar fine mist, a sensation she could pinpoint with her eyes closed. Oliver had come.

Knowing he was somewhere close gave her the last burst of energy. It really did suck that Portal creators couldn't bring anyone with them. Oliver could have whisked her away. She moved around the first building, trying to see through the gaps in the trees and identify what part of the campground she was in.

There were clusters of narrow cabins. She couldn't spot the lake or the smaller islands. Maybe she was on the far eastern side. The hint of Oliver's presence was long gone. She carefully crept down, maintaining a generous distance from the buildings, which would be the first place Oliver would check, but she couldn't risk exposing herself. She didn't know how people were locating her, but they knew where she was, and she didn't want another surprise.

The corner of the camp was unfamiliar, and she gave up after ten minutes and walked further north. She would book a spa week in Dubai, then a week at a hot spring in Jordan. She sighed dreamily as she thought of the recovery she'd need from this nightmare.

A black bird flew low to the ground, startling her. If phantom tears welled in her eyes because she was so happy, she would vehemently deny that fact as she spotted the orange, wooden roof of a half-built birdhouse.

Chapter Twenty-Three

Karma, the moon goddess, or the holy universe was on Kana's side. With a clap of her hands, and a gracious thank you, the relief was enough to make her momentarily forget her bone-sinking exhaustion. She didn't know how she would have survived if she had to keep walking for another few hours. She'd give up and fall asleep in one of the cabins. But she found the place, a round of applause.

The rotting primary-colored birdhouses were faded and chipped. Some birdhouses managed to stay on poles, while others piled on the ground in stacks of square wood. A finch poked its head out of a small hole before flying off.

Now what?

She was trying to find Oliver but stumbled onto the birdhouse graveyard, which seemed stuck in a vast pool of mud. A small, raised part of land was untouched by the muddy trench. If there was a hidden passage, she'd have to step through the slush and move the birdhouses around to find the opening. Her face scrunched, not pleased with that prospect.

After another inspection of the fringe of the marshland yielded nothing, she didn't have any other choice. One step forward and her foot sank as if she had stepped on a waterbed, eventually swallowing her entire sneaker and ankle. She slugged across the muddy landscape, shoving piles of birdhouses, collapsing into heaps of roofs and broken walls.

A half-formed yelp escaped the back of her throat; her eyes caught a snake slithering out from under a small stack of roofless birdhouses. The snake's bright yellow coloring was enough to make Kana skitter away as fast as her mud-logged feet could take her. She muttered incomplete curses and complaints. This was exactly why she never went backpacking. Another bird, startled by her rattling of a nearby birdhouse, flew at her face, frightening Kana. Her feet were stuck, and she nearly toppled entirely into the mud. She flailed, and her left hand gripped a half wooden post from a broken tree house, and like the gearshift of a car, it easily bent back and abruptly stopped as if it had been blocked from going further.

Kana gripped the pole as leverage to haul herself out of the mud. The birdhouse post was too heavy to be made just of wood. She yanked the pole forward, and it locked back in place at a forty-degree angle. The ground didn't slide from under her like a metal trap door. She moved the lever back and forth, but nothing around the landscape appeared different. Beads of sweat rolled down her neck and soaked into the hem of the shirt. With renewed focus, her hands ran over the birdhouse, wrenching the roof off, checking the inside wooden box and finding two puffs of molted gray feathers. She bent down into a deep squat and squinted up at the bottom plank of wood and came across an engraving, not on the birdhouse but deeply set in the wooden post. A single vertical line like the slash of a tally mark.

She dipped her hand in the mud and smeared a circle on the front of the beige birdhouse, resigned to the notion that she had to check all the birdhouses. It would be too easy if there was only one lever; any kid at camp or even a large animal could push the pole by accident. The minutes stretched like fresh taffy, and as more time passed, her short temper increased. Gone were the soft tugs. Wood crashed to the ground, her concern for potential attackers long forgotten. On the opposite end of the swamp was a broken pole, its tip slanted at an angle like a stake that could pierce a vampire's heart. Her heart quivered as she felt the adrenaline rush and shoved forward and back. The stake didn't move as she intended, but it shifted left and right and like the first wooden post, this had three vertical etchings into the wood; the first one hadn't been an accident.

She moved directly to the left, circling the perimeter until she found a third lever. A blooming cloud of serotonin, and a smile crept on her lips. Not even the drying mud and mosquito bites could dampen her triumph. Of the three levers discovered, two moved forward and back, and one only moved left and right. That was only eight combinations, but there was a possibility she'd missed a lever or two, which made the number of combinations even more. The mud was thickening as the midday heat rose. She could Sherlock Holmes this. She'd gotten this far. "Owl" was a three-letter word, but the levers didn't spell anything. If anyone else found the hints, wouldn't "owl" be the first thing they would try? Kana was exhausted and starving. Her body hurt, her hearing intermittently decided to screech a banshee song, and she was tired of schlepping through wood crafts and mud. She shoved the back levers forward and the other lever to the left. Nothing. It was hopeful thinking that she could nail it on the first try.

She yanked her feet out of the mud pit, but her right sneaker stuck. As she reached down, a figure with familiar gray hair caught her eye through the gaps of packed trees.

"Oliver!" The name was almost reverent as relief overwhelmed her. The figure of a man pushed through the tall bushes. Oliver was in an odd mix of clothes: finely pressed suit pants, the collar of his deep green button-down laying awkwardly under a bullet-proof vest, probably the only item he could grab after reading her *come and get me* text. The sleeves of his dark blue windbreaker with vibrant lime green stripes down the arms made a crinkling sound as he reached for her.

"Kana." Oliver ran over to her, his eyes sweeping over the drying mud on her skin, pausing carefully at each visible bandage. Oliver released a sigh of relief, as if realizing her dirty body was a significant improvement over the other times he'd come to her rescue. "What happened? Where's Spencer?" He looked around as if expecting to see him close by. Kana nearly collapsed, overwhelmed by the familiar smell of his favored cologne and aftershave. She could care less about Spencer. Her escape was within reach.

"You don't happen to have food in your pockets? I could go for a double-double," she said seriously.

Oliver shrugged off his windbreaker and slung it over her shoulders, revealing long bandages wrapped tightly over his forearms, which did little to hide the tiny mushroom heads poking out from the edges like overgrown weeds breaking out of the cracks in the sidewalk. Her eyes narrowed at the bulky vest, imagining the lines slit across his body to release the growing flora. He opened his mouth to say something, but an invisible force dragged his body back two meters as a mint flavor gushed onto her tongue. Oliver's eyes flared wide and his hand shot out for Kana's, but she was beyond his grasp. The cool flavor told her exactly who had just joined them.

"Unnecessary," Kana growled and whipped around, her eyes latched onto Spencer's frame, a familiar sight now as he stalked over. His expression was empty, but his muscles were tense, agitated in that controlled way of his.

"Why did she call for my help?" Oliver demanded, facing the younger man. "Why is one cabin burned, with two abandoned cars but no bodies?"

Kana raised her eyebrows. She'd forgotten about the fire in the dining hall. There should have been fire trucks swarming the place. A fire in a forest was never good. But she had seen no smoke or anyone else around.

"Kana and I are leaving," Oliver continued, taking a step toward Kana. He was immediately pushed back. Spencer's eyes were dark. The muscle in his jaw ticked and Oliver was pushed another meter further for good measure, as if to prove how easy it was for him, like flicking a bug off his hand.

"What's wrong with you?" Kana demanded. She moved closer to Oliver, but Spencer tugged her back with less force, more of a gentle push, as if a friend had pulled at the loose fabric of her shirt.

"*What happened?*" Oliver asked, his hands moving fluidly and efficiently in sign language. "*What did the president want?*"

"*Josephine's disappeared. It's always about her,*" Kana responded, her fingers faltering between the words as she tried to recall the signs.

"*He asked for your presence in the White Room to help find Josephine? That's it?*" Oliver's hands and arm movements were harder, punctuating the question with a sharp flick of his wrist, more aggressive.

Kana scowled. Good, Oliver agreed that the president's request seemed ridiculous. "*Do we have a way out of here? He can throw you through a tree.*" Kana wasn't sure if she signed her sentiment accurately, but Oliver received the gist.

"*I can break his neck faster than I can throw him,*" Spencer signed perfectly. His file didn't say he could use sign language; French and Arabic were the only other languages listed.

"You wouldn't dare," Kana hissed. "Did you put out the fire and get rid of the bodies?"

"I smothered the fire. The smoke would have alerted too many people to our location, but I didn't do anything with the bodies. Why did you call him?" Spencer said, a lilted edge to his question.

"You didn't give me a good reason not to. Sorry not sorry, but you are the one isolating me, and that makes you more suspicious," Kana fired back.

"Ask him where he's been for the past few days," Spencer said, coolly. His gaze leveled on Oliver's. Kana rolled her eyes but humored Spencer.

"Where have you been? Visiting UN offices in the Middle East or Asia?" Kana asked with a sarcastic tone, because Oliver was always in another country, passing along Josephine's messages or helping a board member of the company. The bandages from his wrists up to his elbows did little to hide the thick, lifted wrinkles and the mushroom tops squeezing their way out of the bandage edges. He'd been traveling a lot, and not on a commercial or private jet. He hadn't had a chance to bloodlet.

"Bouncing between Canada and America, actually," Oliver replied.

"Dr. Ambrose has been officially missing for at least three months," Spencer said. "The person delivering her orders has been Oliver for the past six."

Kana sighed, moving a step closer to Oliver. Spencer tugged her back. It was gentle and quick, the initial rocking of an elevator, the chilled mint barely on her tongue as she glared at him. "Stop moving me," she snapped and jabbed a finger over her shoulder to where Oliver stood. "Oliver's doing his job. He goes around and checks the different labs, governments, and companies on her behalf."

"An American Ex-Marine team was spotted near Long Beach Peninsula in Washington on April eighth," Spencer said.

Kana faltered, her lips parted but no words formed because she understood Spencer's implication. Oliver had sent her the itinerary for the beach on that exact day. How could they know she was supposed to be there, unless someone had told them? Her eyes flitted to Oliver, a silent demand for an explanation etched on her hardened face.

"Are you implying I sent the team to harm Kana?" Oliver demanded. His entire body tensed, his eyes narrowed at Spencer.

"Ask him where he was when you were taken hostage on the lakeshore."

Kana chose not to ask, because the answer implied that Oliver hadn't been abroad, but did Oliver's location matter? If he was actually at the lake, why would he be there and not help her? She didn't realize she'd taken a step back from both men until Oliver reached for her.

"Kana, stop." Oliver shook his head in disbelief. "He's lying. He doesn't want you to trust me."

"How long were you out of contact with her?" Kana asked.

"A month," he answered without hesitation, knowing she meant Josephine. The thing was, Kana remembered the brief conversation in the dressing room after the failed photoshoot in New York City. He'd said her last order had to do with a Title action lawsuit in Switzerland or some other European country. He'd lied to her.

Oliver knew her too well. He must have seen something in her expression, because he tried to approach her. But the seed of doubt had been planted, and she glowered at Spencer. He was a bastard.

"If anyone shouldn't be trusted, it's you," Oliver said darkly, turning to Spencer. "I've seen your file. You are the least trustworthy person here. If you think either of us believes the president ordered you to be her bodyguard," he laughed dryly, becoming more expressive with each word, "then you are sorely mistaken. The incident in Ireland, not even ten months ago, is enough proof that you'll only follow orders."

Spencer's face crumbled for the first time. The dark bags under his eyes sunk further as his chest cringed inward.

"Killing your entire team, even the poor coordinator," Oliver said in a mocking tone as he clicked his tongue. "But that's what you do best. Eliminating your friends. I know the president created data dumps, making it seem like Kana planned on staying at the lake, false emails between the Ambrose company and the pharmaceutical COO." Oliver turned to Kana. "You can't trust him. The president is framing you to keep you here, fabricating the American threat."

Kana raised her eyebrows, lips parting at the ticking muscle in Spencer's jaw and his furrowed brows. She let out a bone-dry laugh. "It doesn't matter," Kana concluded, ending whatever goading Oliver could throw at Spencer. They were like little boys on the playground, digging into one another, trying to get a rise and prove they were better.

"You're both assholes," Kana said, shaking her head more to herself. Those walls she'd built weren't strong enough, and the fact that she felt hurt meant she had trusted them both, to an extent. Oliver more so, but that cynical part of her was gloating, telling her how naïve she had been to think Oliver wasn't as conniving as everyone else in her life. As much as she wanted to flip them both off and run away, she was in a tricky predicament with Rabid Synthies targeting her, believing she could help them get to Josephine, making it harder to disappear. She needed Oliver's help.

"I'm hungry," Kana repeated. "I'm tired. I'm going with Oliver," she said succinctly, as if addressing a toddler. Oliver puffed up in the corner of her eye. He shouldn't gloat just yet. "Spencer is coming with us. Since neither of you trusts the other, you can keep watch on each other," Kana explained. Her gaze ended on Oliver.

There had been a time, two years before Kana confronted Josephine about the tracking device, when she found a think tank. Only the second one she would ever discover. Hundreds of colorful Post-it notes in a small windowless room. Without the Post-its covered in scratched notes and illegible formulas, the space could have served as a solitary confinement room with white walls, floor, and ceiling. The room appeared to have been air dropped into the half-demolished apartment complex.

"Get out." Josephine's impatient words cracked down like a ruler. The scribbling scrape of the pen against paper didn't stutter. The woman was leaning over a thick text, one finger gliding down the lines of words, her dark hair had grown past her chin and was yanked back by a clip.

Kana was torn between scavenging around the room for any information and blowing herself up to confront Josephine. Although the prospect of being in the room, breathing the same air as Josephine was not the plan, she didn't exactly have a plan. Finding the think tank was the end goal, if anything, to irritate Josephine, the woman who thought her secret work location was the Holy Grail.

"You can't understand what's in front of you. You're wasting your time." Josephine continued, flicking her wrist as she straightened her posture.

She was right. Kana had attempted to read the nearest document on the wall that wasn't equations or diagrams, but found even the written notes were coded in short hand.

"I'll ask Oliver what M.A.A.M is then." Kana goaded, latching onto the only phrase she could spot and read.

Josephine's lip twitched into contention as she set her pen down and faced Kana. "You'll never tell anyone of this." She spoke and Kana's eyes lowered as her head bowed. How could she explain this power Josephine had, how easily she supplicated?

"I see the defiance in your eyes, Oliver is useful but not indispensable." Her thinly veiled threat was her last words as Kana left.

Kana never asked Oliver about the think tank, in fact, the next day it was demolished along with the rest of the apartment. Now she had one question. "What's the research for M.A.A.M?"

Oliver's reaction was priceless, because he tried so hard to cover up his shock. She'd known this man as long as she'd been alive. His lips opened and closed twice. "Kana," he began, pausing to try buy time.

Oliver had known Josephine before Kana was born. He wasn't smart by Josephine's standards, but he was useful enough to keep him close. Josephine never spoke about her projects. She was a secretive artist, never wanting to tell anyone about her work until it was finished and perfected, and when it was ready, she didn't just tell one person. No, the world was her stage. But it seemed Oliver knew about whatever M.A.A.M was even though it was a project Josephine told Kana to never tell him about.

"Kana," he tried again. Whatever else he wanted to say, whatever obscured version of the truth he wanted to spout, all died as a mass running on all fours lunged from the sparse trees, ripping through a tree trunk. She didn't have time to scream or react at all; her breath was knocked out of her chest as Spencer shoved her hard. She sailed through the air, nearly to the edge of the soggy mud.

In the middle of the day, the deformities of the hungry Rabid were obscene. The creature's right hand had a second hand growing out of the side, with additional fingers jutting from the mass. A terrifying scream caused the remaining birds to flee into the sky. It was like watching someone take apart a chicken leg, but it was an arm, and then it was a hand. Sprays of dark mist exploded. A gun fired, and the loud bang repeated as bullets sailed through the air.

CHAPTER TWENTY-FOUR

THE CONCUSSION DID something to her brain. The world was off-kilter, like a car driving the wrong direction on an open road; everything around her was normal, but felt wrong. The air vibrated with the sheer amount of power like fireworks of exploding energy. A mixture of flavors caked her mouth and throat, and traces of honey clogged her nasal cavities. A reverberating snarl like a lion's roar ripped through the space, startling her to a semblance of sense. Her hands squished the mud between her fingers as she lifted herself up, staying slightly crouched below a short stack of birdhouses.

Based on the immense layers of energy, she expected to be surrounded by a team of eight, but there were only Spencer and two others. As her eyes lowered away from the moving forms, it felt like trying to walk on a moving platform, her mind fracturing. A third body lay on the ground, the torso cracked open like a smashed pumpkin, strips of a thick vest torn apart, the familiar shirt blackened by the sheer amount of viscera. The view of the body was covered as Spencer slipped like water around the Rabid Synthie and pivoted around the partner, sharp sounds of pinging metal smashing against one another at speeds too quick to catch with a passing glance. Sparks shuttered like paparazzi cameras. No one noticed as she trekked through the marsh and ducked behind trees; she didn't feel her body moving until she collapsed behind a bush.

Kana was a melted candle, her head and shoulders curled like a burnt wick. Her mind flipped back to the last few minutes, the past not feeling like an irreversible event. Oliver was about to give her a lame-ass excuse for how he'd somehow gotten to know beyond-secret information and explain how apparently he'd secretly been running Josephine's company under the guise of her orders. His shocked expression looked guilty. Or did she imagine the dry swallow as his throat bobbed, and the glossy eyes? Then the Rabid Synthie—it ripped through Oliver—split him like soft bread. Oliver, who'd laughed as he handed her an ice cream cone, dressed in a linen suit, dribbles of sweet cream melting down the cone and splashing on his leather shoes. She was six at the time, and didn't understand the odd looks the other people at the beach were giving Oliver as he set her down on the soft shore, having escaped from an overwhelming gala. Oliver, standing at her elementary school graduation with a wheelbarrow of freshly cut roses. She clenched her fists, her vision blurring as moisture built in her eyes. She blinked them furiously away—no, crying was unacceptable. She was stronger than this.

There was still a commotion ahead; silence would signal when someone won. With enough resolve to continue moving, she pressed her hand against a nearby tree base, steadying her teetering knees. Her palm ran over an etching cut into the wooden trunk. She leaned closer and found a crude arrow, pointed downwards, with the number three as the tip. Another rush, this one less terrifying, because it was a hint. That's what the three slashes in the bar meant: lever three was supposed to be pulled down. As she searched for another tree trunk with an engraving, the violent noise ceased. No more snarling or crunching noises. The other flavors and burnt-honey scent were gone, all except the mint. She felt him approaching, even though she didn't hear him, his footsteps and movements silent.

"Don't speak to me." Kana didn't want to look at him. Spencer, thankfully, kept his mouth shut. They should give him the code name Terminator. If she listened carefully, she could hear his short breaths. She circled the trees, eyes focused on the bases until she spotted another trunk.

Hunger tackled her out of the blue, sending sharp pains through her body; she would kill for a lamb burger. If she found this bunker, she would gladly lead Spencer straight to Josephine and let him deal with the doctor. Kana's part of the deal would be done, and she could skip merrily away.

She marched back to the birdhouses. She had two of the hints. That was good enough. The third one left had only two options. Even at a distance, she could see two mangled heaps of bodies, one looking like a squashed spider, an elongated arm bent backward, limbs snapped and broken at irregular angles. The other body was unrecognizable. The grass concealed the smashed head, but the rest of the body had been pulverized into organ and bone pea soup.

"Don't—" Spencer's voice behind her began to warn her, but she snatched a discarded gun, with speed and swiftness she didn't think she possessed, and aimed it at Spencer. Her action cut him off abruptly.

"I said, don't talk." She didn't know if it was loaded, and she didn't care that shooting at an Idu was the worst idea, but Kana wanted to unload the gun. Spencer, for his part, looked older, worn out, a twisted and knotted rag. The weariness of someone who'd reached their limit three days ago. *He should suffer*, the vicious voice inside her spat. If he had listened to her and allowed her to contact Oliver when she had been targeted at the apartment, this wouldn't have happened.

Her cheek twitched as the smell of carnage strangled her nostrils, but there was nothing left in her stomach to regurgitate.

One corpse was further from the other two, a man in his fifties with holes in his body from where small projections had turned him into a cheese grater. She focused on the lever with the missing engraved instructions, pushed the base of the marigold-colored birdhouse, and waited.

The ground didn't quake, and there was no sound of gears turning. She looked around, her gaze defiantly overlooking Spencer. This was supposed to be the answer. She wanted to scream and drive her fist into a wall. An emotional wave smashed down on her, the oppressive weight crushing her. Her face felt warm, and she squeezed her eyes shut, feeling tears swell, and her throat bobbed.

"Over there." Spencer spoke, unfazed, as if this ordeal were a leisurely afternoon through the park. Rage lifted Kana's hand, and she pulled the trigger. Her hands shook, but it wasn't like she was aiming for him, only in his general direction. The *click, click, click* of an empty Glock filled the quiet space. Kana's face crumbled, her head shook sharply to the right, banishing the incoming memory of Oliver's face and she tossed the useless gun and forced her eyes to look behind her to where Spencer gestured.

A few meters ahead, away from the thick mud, there was a spot of land, raised like a patch of uneven grass, utterly normal. She wanted to argue, her tongue ready to crack like a whip, but she swallowed her doubts as she marched over to inspect the ground first. Spencer wouldn't have pointed it out if he hadn't spotted something. A square patch close to one and a half meters long was raised, and under tall fake grass and dirt was the thick metal frame of a trap door. Her hands curled under the slightly raised top and shoved it up. The reflective sheen of silvery walls caught the light, reminding her of a trash chute.

She found a stick that was thicker than her wrist and half as long as her thigh and tossed it into the waiting black throat of darkness. The stick banged against the chrome wall. It wasn't a vertical shot down, then, and based on the scraping sound, it could be slide-like. Kana bent down, her ears strained as the wood scraped along the metal, but then nothing. She waited, trying to listen for any signal that the branch had reached the bottom. But after two minutes of bending over the dark mouth, she sat down, tossing her legs over the edge until the chilled metal pressed against the flaking mud on her skin.

"I should go—" Spencer began, but she pushed herself through the black tunnel before he could finish. Should she worry about where exactly this old laundry chute might lead? Absolutely, but she didn't care enough. It was like being inside a water park slide, the space narrow but smooth, until she was spat out on a cushioned surface. Her right leg spasmed, the muscles kicking out as if a doctor was testing her knee reflex. Her leg flopped uncontrollably as she reached down to clasp her hands around her calf, her fingers digging into the muddied bandage. Thankfully, there was no pain, and the uncontrollable spasms ceased after another three breaths.

She ignored Spencer's distorted voice echoing down as she stared at the space. An underground bunker was either a futuristic sci-fi basement or it was a doomsday hole. Since Josephine was a diligent doctor, Kana had expected the first, a space with a sterile look, but she found herself half seated on an old mattress in a plain room that could be an unfinished basement. A single overhead light set an amber glow against the incomplete walls, with insulation fluff leaking out. The room had a pile of fading cardboard boxes stacked in the corner beside a single door. The echoed thunk and the sound of a weighted mass coming down told her to move as Spencer fell out of the chute.

She pushed off the mattress as he landed with a heavy thump and dust sputtered into the air. The ceiling was lower than she expected. Anyone over 185 centimeters would have to bend their chin to their chest. The plain wood of the door stared blankly at her as she hesitated. There was that terrible, tiny drop of hope inside her; what if this was it? Kana could envision it perfectly:

when she opened the door, Josephine would be bent over, a white lab coat tossed on a metal stool, and aside from the scratching of a pen as she scribbled notes and the relentless drone of machines analyzing and breaking down samples, the room would be silent. Josephine wouldn't acknowledge Kana's presence, not until she finished her work, and even then, she'd barely lift her eyes to send Kana a perfectly tailored and disdainful look.

Kana's curled hand over the doorknob was immobile. The insurmountable shadow of seeing Josephine, having to face the woman, was regressing Kana to her haunted childhood self. The jumbled mess of memories and reactions tangled inside of her. The words she had to choke back, the expressions she had to force. Kana had learned quickly that avoidance was the answer, but how could she escape when Josephine was somehow both absent and as constant as the air she breathed? The shifting specks of light, the blurring halo, a telltale sign gave little warning to the sharp pain that blew through her head, sudden, and painful enough that the headache snapped her back to reality. All she had to do was open the door. The action was simple, and with a twist of her wrist, the wooden door eased open with a sigh.

One step through the threshold, and the overhead lights flickered on, triggered by the motion. The interior of this section was renovated, a stark contrast to the first bare room. The flooring was reflective linoleum, and there was a scent of plastic and faint chemicals. She didn't hear the door close, but felt Spencer's presence behind her. There were two lab tables, two carts with nothing on the shelves, and a three-shelf unit with glass equipment, bottles, and jugs of chemicals and solvents. Kana stared directly across the space, through the large waist-high windows into a second room that, from the fume hood, must be a clean room. The noticeable absence of Josephine was a knife carving through her ribs and skewering her heart. Her blood pressure spiked as she stared at the unused and spotless area. This couldn't be happening. Her body moved the instant her eyes caught a closed door immediately to her right, and she crashed through the space.

A single room with a bed and an old desk with a metal folding chair greeted her. The bedsheet was tucked tight and unwrinkled over the twin-sized mattress. She swung open the final pocket door, shoving it into the wall frame. The door bounced back out from the force and slowly closed halfway behind her as she stood in a shoebox of a makeshift bathroom, with a toilet, sink, and a shower head installed in the corner, and a short wire shelf with a box of generic soap, toilet paper, and two hand towels. That was all. Not even a mirror.

The sound of white noise dulled her hearing. She lost all feeling, her body propped against the bathroom wall, her knees tucked to her chin. Her hand blindly pushed the rest of the door closed. There was a war in her mind, half-formed thoughts battling about what to do next, and she felt like the world was slipping away into the shadows. Her hand rubbed her forehead, catching the frayed edges of the bandages still secured around her skull. Hope was terrible, because the disappointment hurt more than she could have anticipated. This was supposed to be the answer. Her mind prowled around the same question: now what? But she couldn't plan, not now. She wanted to fall into a hole and vanish.

Her eyes peeked over her knees and stared at the tips of her mud-caked sneakers and the thick, cracked mud along the front of her shins. The shower worked, and even more surprisingly, the water was warm. If tears mingled with the water hitting her face, she didn't notice. Kana hated failing. Failing implied there wasn't a contact she could use, there wasn't anything else she had to offer or bribe or extort, and crying meant she had reached her end. Kana scrubbed her face, slapping her cheeks. She cringed as she dragged the sweaty and muddy clothes back on. Having to flip her underwear inside-out was a new low. The bed had a set of folded scrubs laid on it. *Thoughtful bastard,* she cursed through the closed bedroom door as she pulled on the starchy scrubs and fell on the bed.

———

There were distant sounds: a door opening, a muffled thud as something landed on a hard surface. She thought she felt a presence over her for a second time; normally, she would have lashed out, but her body, exhausted from the day, was unable to react. Still, there was the lingering taste of mint, somehow weighing down her body as she drifted back into sleep.

Waking up was the worst part. She rolled over, burrowing deeper under the thin blanket. She rubbed her eyes, dislodging the crystallized eye guck. There was a tray on the desk: a bag of chips, a granola bar, and a small bowl of something that smelled like tomatoes. The crack of the plastic cap broke the silence as she chugged the water. Her eyes were drawn to the bleak, blank wall, the space of stillness unable to calm her mental gears as they cranked with more speed.

If no one was here, then that meant there was another clue, and Kana felt a new headache forming in the forefront of her brain. She ripped open the chip bag and flung the door open. Spencer's legs spasmed as he stood to attention, his eyes bulging open.

"You can shower, take a shit, whatever," Kana said. Her voice cracked twice. He looked lousy: the stubble around his jaw was more prominent, the deep coloring under his eyes was forming saggy bags, and he smelled of sweat and blood. The odor sent too many broken memories to her fatigued mind. She dragged one of the stools out from under the lab counter and crunched on a stale chip.

"I'm not going anywhere," she said, guessing the wary look and the dip of his brows was about her escaping. He stretched his arms, the jacket lifting up and revealing the shirt underneath and the brown, dried blood. Judging by his wince, he was injured somewhere, but he sent one guarded look at her before disappearing into the bedroom, leaving the door open.

He always seemed to find her, and she didn't have the energy to check where an exit might be. The way they came in was down a steel chute. There had to be an accessible way to escape somewhere.

Her tongue poked out to lick at the lingering salt in the corner of her mouth as she bent down, opening the drawers and cabinets. A white and red medical kit was under one of the sinks. She tossed it into the bedroom, and the tin box flopped on the rumpled blanket atop the bed.

The clean room was the only other space she hadn't explored yet. The space was an echo of the other research facilities, but on a smaller scale. There was only one fume hood, which was strange; most lab spaces had at least two. A sink with a shower spray attachment on the nozzle served as a makeshift eyewash station. The left wall had a small desk with stacks of vials and tubes. She found herself looking back at the sink. Something about it was familiar.

A vague grasp of déjà vu whispered in her mind. Like a word on the tip of her tongue, she couldn't place why this space was familiar. Her hand ran along the edge of the center table as she slowly circled the room. She'd been to maybe a dozen clean rooms, especially when she was younger and had run around the company headquarters. There had been two basement levels. A vague memory surfaced. There was a political gala, and attendance was required for both Josephine and Kana. Kana had spent a good portion of the day with stylists, her short eight-year-old legs kicking back and forth in the salon chair. The stylists had painted her tiny nails a pretty pinky-rose color with tiny heart gems.

She'd managed to escape the boring conference room where she was supposed to be waiting for Josephine and took the elevator down to the first basement level. She'd peeked around the corners of the long hallways, seeing a few adults in long lab coats. They smiled kindly at her, a few waving, but most of them ignored her. One lady with massive, clear goggles atop her frizzy hair had approached her and led her to where Josephine was working. Kana frowned. That wasn't the right memory. Those labs were massive, with state-of-the-art machines.

She leaned over the glass window of the fume hood. Her fingers found the switch, and with a satisfying click, the hood light flashed on. The noisy vroom of the machine was a guttural groan as the air was sucked out. Was there something inside the fume hood?

She closed her eyes and listened to the hum of the machinery, slipping into a semi-meditative state. The only other memory she could dig up was the Christmas when she'd entered her first year of secondary school. After the Italy sensation, she'd ended up in a slump. Kana didn't consider the Ambrose Estate her home, so her therapist concluded that Kana had to settle and rediscover a safe place she could label "home." There was a metaphor about her trauma and a window—there was always a new metaphor with that therapist. Kana had refused the invitation to a holiday retreat in the skiing lodge. If it resembled a cabin, she found an excuse to not go. She'd spent Christmas in New Zealand, in a quaint city large enough that it didn't leave her feeling isolated. What she didn't expect was an emergency. Code *Gone with the Wind* had gone into effect. Whoever had made that code had a sense of humor; it meant Josephine was MIA. Josephine was supposed to make an appearance at the luxurious spa and ski lodge, but had never boarded the private jet. Ironically, it was Kana who'd returned from her trip and decided to visit her dead grandparents' home, only to find Josephine in the garage.

Kana's eyes opened. Josephine's childhood home was located in northern Oshiya, in the coastal town of Pradstong. That's why this layout looked familiar. There was a picture, one of the rarest moments captured of Josephine, not yet thirteen, in her parents' garage that had been remodeled to imitate a downsized science lab after Josephine won a huge contest. That's why the sink looked like a child's attempt at engineering, because Josephine had created it as a makeshift eyewash station.

Why would Josephine recreate a clean room from her childhood home? The president had surely sent someone to raid all the obvious locations as soon as Josephine went *Gone with the Wind*, and her childhood home would have been thoroughly searched. There was something here that Kana was missing.

Kana pinched the bridge of her nose. There was little she could control right now, and having a damn cup of coffee would be a godsend. She would brew tea if she had to. "Thank Jesus," she said as she left the clean room and met a robust earthiness in the air, and saw a small pot half full. Ask and you shall receive! Spencer offered a thick beaker filled with precious black liquid toward her. The shower had treated him well and brought pink back to his face. Spencer looked away first, pouring his coffee into an identical beaker.

With an absence of things to keep him busy, he defaulted to the silent shadow role, of not having to say anything. His posture was placid, his eyes somehow lowered enough to not stare at her but seeing everything in the room; meanwhile, Kana couldn't stop her fingers from picking at the starched collar of the scrub top, eyes roving like a bee in a flower garden. Bitterness was as easy to feel as the coffee burning down her throat.

Kana perched on the stool. "I hope you're happy," she said, her fingers tracing the side of the beaker idly. He was dressed in the same blue scrub set as her. The top was tight across his wider shoulders. Someone other than Josephine had used the lab if there was more than one scrub size. Spencer leaned forward, resting his forearms on the tall lab table erected between them. He set his face in a motionless mask. If he understood where she was taking the conversation, he didn't show it.

"If Oliver was giving someone information, he won't be doing that anytime soon," Kana said coolly, and by a miracle, her voice didn't reflect her hesitation in speaking Oliver's name. Spencer frowned as he straightened back to his full height, unable to meet Kana's eyes.

"That was unexpected," he said, taken aback by Oliver's name, yet unapologetic.

"Where did you put it?" Kana asked, changing the subject.

He delicately sipped his beaker of coffee, "Put what?" he asked.

"The tracker. I doubt you had time to conduct a brief surgery and stick something inside of me, but maybe I'm underestimating your skills. Or maybe you are an expert tracker or part blood-hound and found me trekking through the campsite."

He, at least, looked guilty now. "Your shoe," he admitted. Kana flexed her bare foot, which rested on the stool's footrest. Not a bad spot to hide a tracker. She imagined him with a small razor cutting into the rubber soles and sliding in a GPS tracking chip the size of her thumbnail before super-gluing the sole back. She took another gulp of coffee before announcing her decision.

"If we find Josephine, you can eliminate her."

Chapter Twenty-Five

Spencer met her unwavering gaze, while his eyebrows flattened from their curve of confusion; the lower part of his face was still, showing a conscious decision to keep his lips and jaw stiff. "She must have fucked up big time if the president has ordered her to be assassinated," Kana continued. She cupped her chin in the palm of her hand, resting her elbow on the icy surface of the lab table, a small smile on her face. "I just now realized your secondary role. Team killer."

There was a spark behind his eyes, and his cheeks twitched as if trying to pull an expression; his control was admirable.

"And I suppose if you thought I was helping Josephine, we would both be killed. You don't need to answer me. I just want you to know there won't be hard feelings. It's a wonder the president hasn't ordered anyone to kill her yet."

"How can you speak about her like that?" He paused. "With such dismissal? She's your mother."

Air pushed through her teeth in a strained laugh. "She's always been Josephine Ambrose, the doctor and researcher above all else. Mother . . ." The word was sacrilegious as far as Kana was concerned. She'd received more affection from her tiny hamster,

Neo, who'd only lived for a year. "Mother is a label, a title given to women with a role to play, to provide a home—" Kana's jaw tensed and locked. Josephine was never a home, rather the shadows of one who built a cage. She couldn't remember ever using the word *Mom*. No, Josephine disapproved of that title greatly, and had corrected her for as long as Kana could remember.

Kana wondered how people measured their value. Who they'd been in the past, the way they lived in the present, and how their actions affected the future? Was their value increased based on the people they affected, the ones who wrote history? The woman had proved her capability, and Kana feared what else in the future Josephine would influence.

"Oliver may have been going behind Josephine's back and running things, but telling a group of marines I was going to a Washington lake house? I don't believe it. Why would Oliver hire people to kill me? He certainly thought you had some motive."

"They weren't ordered to kill you."

Between the panicked and chaotic hostage situation, being shot, and then stabbed, Kana had forgotten that Average Joe's original order was to reach Josephine. Josephine, who according to Spencer, had been missing for half a year. But Kana didn't believe Spencer wasn't piecing together something. He seemed like the kind of person who wouldn't share information until he had the facts to build a coherent picture.

"How are your stitches?" Spencer asked.

Kana glanced down at her torso. She'd momentarily forgotten about that. The lighting in the bathroom was piss-poor, and while she rubbed the slick soap between her hands to scrape the dirt and grime, she hadn't been focused on the state of her wounds. "Shit," she exhaled and lifted the scrub top, and he was around the table's edge before she had time to yank her top down.

"It's fine," she said, slapping his hand away before he reached for the shirt's hem. "I will break this beaker and stab you with the glass. Don't touch me."

Spencer may have held back the deep sigh, but his nose flared. "Do you need bandages? I don't see blood, I can stitch—"

Kana rolled her eyes as she stood and lifted her shirt. "It's not the stitches."

His eyes widened. His hand lifted from his side as if he wanted to touch her, but he paused, and his hand fell back. She looked down, the locks of her black hair sliding over her shoulder.

"The doctors said it wasn't flesh-eating," Kana said, eyeing the black, veiny structure that stretched out from the stitched flesh. The black roots extended much further, creeping up the planes of her stomach and growing their arms around her lower ribs. "But it doesn't look great."

"Does it hurt?"

Surprisingly, her torso didn't hurt. "No, my leg hurts more." The rough scrub top dropped back in place. She peeled back the edge of the lifting bandage around her calf. The claw wound was fine. *Fine* as in it didn't look like a strange, black, flesh infestation or an oozing pus, just broken skin, puckered and red.

"If I ask a question, will you answer honestly?" Spencer asked.

Kana laughed, ignoring the smothered hurt in his soft gaze. "Will I get the same courtesy?"

"Yes."

Kana's eyebrows rose. Why did this feel like a countdown before a group of friends all jumped into a pool, and everyone stepped back while one person jumped in? "Bullshit," she announced. "Now you decide to start telling the truth?"

"I'll go first, and you can decide if I'm being honest."

She pursed her lips and scrutinized him, trying to understand what he wanted from her. She'd been (mostly) honest, more honest than he'd been. Spencer was interesting in the unsettling way a painting is, when turned upside down and reveals a truth you hadn't noticed before. On paper, he was a good soldier. There was no question about his skill in combat, especially after handling the Rabid Synthies. His emotions and reactions were well-guarded behind a comfortable facade. He didn't voice any complaints and was executing his task, and yet there had to be more.

"Fine," she said with a shrug. She had nothing to lose. "This'll be good."

"You get five questions."

"Well, I won those five questions at the Western steakhouse, but are there other rules to this little truth game?" she asked sarcastically.

He shook his head and waited for her to ask the first question. She wanted to take a seat. Her limbs were too sore to be standing, but she didn't like being any smaller in stature than she was, especially if she was addressing someone. One of the reasons she didn't particularly like tall men was that it was hard to assert dominance if she wasn't close to their eye level.

Spencer retreated to his spot across from the table. He settled for leaning against the wall with his arms crossed.

"What were all the president's orders when you were assigned to this little fun adventure?" she asked, lowering back to the stool.

He didn't hesitate; it was probably a question he knew she would ask. "The initial assignment was to guard and make sure you were staying on task. If you found Josephine, I needed to bring her in immediately. If you found her . . ." He paused. ". . . Not in good condition, I had to report my findings and her location, and if you ended up trying to help each other leave, you both needed to be handled."

The president had considered the possibility that she might try to help Josephine. She supposed he'd needed to cover the basics. "There were secondary orders," Spencer continued.

Her ears perked.

"I was required to report any suspicious behavior you might

exhibit." A vague request from the president. "He was particularly interested in your designation—Idu, Tomi, or Sori—and your skill level."

Kana stopped herself from tapping her fingers on the table and controlled the telltale itch of her foot dancing nervously. He didn't have to keep answering her question. Technically, he'd answered everything in the first few sentences, but he was waving a white flag as if saying, *See, you can trust me, I'm telling the truth by offering more information.*

"Tell me everything you've reported to him."

"Was that a question?"

"What have you reported to him?"

"You're an unskilled Idu." Kana crossed her left leg over her right. He wasn't wrong, and she was certain the president knew at least that much. "And the likelihood of you secretly communicating with Dr. Ambrose is almost zero. I expressed my doubts that you had anything to do with Dr. Ambrose's disappearance. Multiple people did background checks to see if either of you had communicated with the other in the past two years, and not so much as a 'Hello' was on the radar."

"The president wants Josephine because he believes the rumors about a cure." Kana changed the subject, as the conversation was in dangerous territory of her secondary status as an Idu. "Because that's the catch with Synthies." The fear that if they went overboard, the Hunger could destroy them, or the fungi disease would spread and their organs would fail. The limit that applied depended on the person, but it kept people from overexerting themselves, and governments didn't want their investments to expire prematurely. "Imagine a world where the governments' manufactured soldiers didn't have to worry about repercussions."

"The president seems to believe Josephine has something of value. If that's a cure, there is no proof," he said. His mouth tilted downward in tandem with his eyes moving towards the table. "Is it a coincidence that a rumor of this nature started around the time Dr. Ambrose disappeared? There are rarely coincidences. You said yourself that Dr. Ambrose is a very secretive woman, and not many people knew what she was working on. Did someone leak the rumor? But for what purpose?"

Kana ran her tongue along the back of her teeth while her body sank into the stool. A supposed cure for Rabid Synthies would be a monumental benefit, but was the president desperate enough to pull Kana back to Oshiya and lock her here? There was more: he wanted the cure just as badly as the deranged Rabid Synthies chasing them.

Assuming Josephine had created something, it warranted her disappearance. As far as Kana knew, Josephine had been secretive as she formulated A.E. Potentia, but never went off the grid. Plus, Josephine had gone to great lengths to create a bread trail. The sheer amount of time it had to have taken her to prep everything —were these clues laid out years ago or recently? And how sure Josephine had to have been that Kana would continue the treasure hunt was more astonishing. The questions were piling and branching out into a tangled knot without a reasonable answer. Her legs vibrated, as her hands uncontrollably went from pressing against her temples to digging into her palms.

"What do you think we'll find?" Spencer's abrupt question was a paper cutter, slicing through her thin mind.

"What do *you* think we'll find?" She sent the question back as she scrambled for a response.

"A lab, similar to the research facility at South Beach."

Kana fought back a smile. She knew the facility he referred to. "You know that's a gimmick, it's all about aesthetics. Universities do more substantial research than that facility. Six films and two TV shows used that site for filming purposes."

"That's why it looked familiar," he said, rubbing his chin as his eyes tilted up and to the left, deep in thought. "Was it in that movie *Chronos Shadow*?"

Kana bit the inside of her cheek to halt the smile. "*Chrono-*

code. They blew the budget on the film locations." She hadn't pegged him for a low-budget movie enjoyer.

"You can laugh," he said.

She exhaled a puff of air.

"It's surprising how many low-budget films are available across borders," he commented.

Kana imagined faceless men and women hunkered in the middle of a nowhere jungle, with only *Sharknado*, *Killer Squirrel*, and *Chrono-code* as a form of entertainment. She pumped the brakes on her thoughts. This wasn't the time to get to know one another. "I suppose I thought she would be here," Kana said, answering the original question. The reality of the vacant lab plummeted the room temperature.

"You have one more question," Spencer reminded her.

"What do you get out of this? I'm sure the president didn't want you to spill the beans about your secondary task. You were given orders, and isn't the first rule 'Don't go against your orders?'"

He didn't point out that those were two questions. "It wasn't explicit to keep the other tasks a secret."

Kana didn't hide her soft scoff. Well, it certainly was implied.

"I have no plans to go against my orders. I want to know more. Control of information is maybe the most dangerous thing. There have been problems with Synthetic Users."

"Problems only you have noticed, or problems the government is tossing under the rug?"

He didn't answer her question; instead, he moved through his story. "After I reported on your reluctance to solve the painted box, the president had an attack staged."

It was like she'd eaten a head of bitter lettuce; her stomach was unsettled. "I knew it," she hissed as she thought back to the prone form, the color of the blood, and Spencer blocking the body from her view. She reared back, her hair standing on end. Was everything planned out? Spencer had blamed Oliver for planning something nefarious in the state of Washington, and yet the president had sent a fake group to attack and scare her at a public fair. If peacocks did not surround her, it was snakes. "And the apartment?" she demanded. She'd been attacked there too.

"Only the first attack was planned. After two weeks of nothing to report to him, he didn't feel you had any sense of urgency," Spencer added as he moved away from the wall to sit at the stool across from her. He hunched his shoulders forward, making himself smaller, as if that would make her more comfortable.

"And the campsite?" Her question burned like the edges of paper curling from flames.

"Not staged," Spencer said with finality, as if somehow he knew the president hadn't hired the other groups.

Kana laughed dryly. "As far as you know."

"He wouldn't want me to mistakenly kill his men."

Kana held back a grunt in agreement. "I commend you for your sense of justice," Kana began. "Your commanding officer gives you orders, but you are suspicious of his motive and you search for your own answers."

"What do you think is at the end of the clues?"

She contemplated the question. Josephine was the obvious answer, but there was something more than just a person. "Chaos," she said, and she knew that whatever was discovered would amount to pandemonium.

Spencer laughed, his shoulders shaking at the short bark. "Of course. You aren't a normal Idu. You seemed to know when the group arrived on the island and pushed the Rabid portal User." His gaze softened. "I knew someone, a Sori, who was supposed to be able to alter their physical form, but he was different. He couldn't alter his body mass, but could alter things around him."

Kana stilled, counting her inhales and exhales. *Do not let anyone know how your power works*—that was what she'd been taught before she could do simple math. She knew where this was leading: he thought, because he knew someone a bit abnormal, that a little anecdote would make her open up.

She wasn't at all interested in how the Passive User came to find they weren't normal, or whether the Passive User was a Natural or a Synthie.

"And from what I've seen, your physics manipulation is different."

Kana didn't blink. She wouldn't gratify him with any response, but her silence would still be an answer. "Do you have a question?"

"Why the secrecy?"

Kana scoffed. "A few days ago, you didn't believe me when I said Vyolette's guests were Synthies, and you're asking why I haven't disclosed my designation? Because, as you said, knowledge is power. Letting people think they know you, letting them build their assumptions, is the easiest way to hide. Keeping my Active status a secret has helped me survive. The rich get bored very easily. They say the key to happiness is wanting less, but we always want."

"You're smarter than people give you credit for."

A dry laugh escaped her lips. "It doesn't take a genius to regurgitate clips of motivational speeches or poorly summarize words from wiser women and men. Your expectations of me must be low." She knew what people said about her: the racist comments, the sick, submissive fan art, the explicit fan fictions, and the pornos made with poor women, some barely of age, who looked similar enough to her, so trash human beings could wank off to their fantasies about her. As she aged, the media had faded, and she knew how it was for women. Men grew more attractive with age, but in a few years, the media wouldn't sexualize the white T-shirts she wore. There was a strange phenomenon that happened when she reached "legal" age, as if the difference between eighteen and nineteen was a stoplight, and green meant "go." Lurid remarks and prying comments were more acceptable because it was legal. As soon as she entered her twenties, there was a significant decrease in the public's interest in her. She was still young, but not young enough to warrant any accomplishment as truly remarkable. Achievements as an adult were expected. And thirty, well, those two digits were a lifetime away, and while she could envision her self-assuredness crystallizing, society would discard her if she hadn't met certain milestones. God forbid she reach fifty childless and husbandless. Even with more wealth than any person would see in two lifetimes, she was no exception to the rigid societal expectations.

"My opinion was low," Spencer commented.

Kana smirked. "My charm has rubbed off on you? Was it the motorcycle, or was it me shooting you?"

Spencer didn't dignify a response, but she caught his faint smile.

"The Rabid Tomi, they weren't reacting normally," he said carefully. It seemed he was done with the banter and led them back to the serious discussion. His gaze, even though he was looking right at her, went distant as though trying to recall what he'd seen, and Kana wasn't sure how much he'd caught.

"You mean when his body became a pile of mush like some zombified guck and still tried to come after me?" Kana said. "That was a recent development."

"How much interaction have you had with Rabids?"

"Only once before the lake incident, and that wasn't an interaction. I saw her from a distance, not as bad as any of this new breed of Rabids."

He fell silent. His face was stern in deep concentration, and she could smell the rubber of his mind. "Don't fry your brain," Kana commented.

"You haven't tried contacting Oliver before?"

"No."

"And Dr. Ambrose has inserted a body tracker before. Is it possible that another was implanted?"

"I told you, I checked my X-rays." She caught the hint of doubt in his face. "I'm not an idiot. I can tell my X-rays from someone else's. Don't think I haven't thought how easy it is to swap records."

She knew the instant he understood what she was saying, that she'd purposefully implanted something inside of her body that no one knew about, so if someone showed her X-ray pictures, she would know if they were fake or not.

"I hate pity," she said. He had that forlorn puppy look.

"If you're sure no one can track you, it's concerning how quickly they can find you."

"Another mystery for another day. I can only handle one at a time."

Spencer removed the coffeepot from the warmer and leaned over to refill her beaker. "Why do you think Dr. Ambrose laid out the clues for you?"

And wasn't that the golden ticket question? The more Kana tried to reason out what Josephine wanted her to find the answer to, a mystery she didn't know she was following, the fewer explanations there were. What made the elusive answer so classified that Josephine didn't want to step on her pedestal and brag to the world? "I don't know. It's a wonder I was able to get this far."

"What are the clues, exactly? The painting of the Azores. You peeled off the island from the canvas. I thought there were coordinates on the back of the paint, but it was braille."

Kana raised her eyebrows. There was only one way he'd found the painted island. "Nice to know you rifle through a girl's clothes while she's unconscious."

"You happily showed me the clue, speaking in French about owls."

Kana held back a hum. Now that he mentioned it, there was a foggy memory of her waving her hand around, showing the wrinkled paint strip.

"I'm curious how you connected the picture of the Azores to

a braille French word meaning owl to a mosh pit of birdhouses. It seemed random and convoluted."

"Is that a question?"

It was difficult. "The painting wasn't a painting," Kana said. "That island wasn't an island, and beneath the fake land was the clue. I once took a trip to Portugal, and there was a small park where day owls would nest in trees. I wanted to make a birdhouse after the trip."

"That's extremely specific. And I can only guess a clue at the antique fair led you to this campsite."

"She's lucky that I even remember enough of this," Kana muttered, her eyes lowered. If she thought of her childhood, it was filled with sparkly lights and beautiful sights, but a bleak blackness, a dark void, existed that she chose to ignore.

"Was there something here?"

"Maybe," she replied, because she wasn't sure if she wanted to tell Spencer, or anyone, the answers. If she was supposed to be the only one to solve the puzzle, she wasn't about to let loose lips be the end of it all.

"What are the chances you'll let me slip onto a small private jet and get out of here?" she asked sweetly, peering at him.

"None. I still have orders."

Kana shrugged as she slid off the stool and chugged the last of the coffee. "Worth a shot."

Chapter Twenty-Six

After Kana finished ransacking the lab, she unfortunately came up empty-handed. There was nothing unusual; it was a regular lab with the standard equipment. She crushed her third water bottle and tossed the plastic into the trash, rubbing at her hairline, plucking at the fine hairs.

Spencer was silent the entire time she turned the space inside out. He tried replacing the items after she blew through. Desperate, she suggested he search a drawer for a trapdoor or compartment, since hidden passages seemed a likely possibility as they were standing in a literal underground lab beneath a kid's summer campground. She wasn't paying attention to his presence, not realizing he had left to sleep in the small bedroom.

Kana glared at the clean room, her shoulders and back hunched as she willed the four walls to give her an answer, because Josephine's childhood home wasn't the location for X marks the spot. Anyone could take a picture of the lab layout, drop it into an online image finder, and find a matching newspaper image. If it was supposed to be just for Kana, there was something she was missing.

When he emerged, she took over the bed. The mattress and

blanket were still warm from Spencer's body heat. She turned over so her eyes stared at the concrete wall.

She awoke feeling displaced, her mind having fought through the incoherent hodgepodge of images that made sense in her unconscious state. She rubbed her eyes as she tried to focus. Heat radiated off her skin, and she pressed the back of her hand to the clammy flesh of her forehead. Her stomach was cramped and her intestines felt hot, almost as if she'd eaten a block of fresh feta and her body was rejecting the lactose with a vengeance.

She pulled up the scrub top. All her symptoms suggested infection, but the black lines on her torso stayed raised like poisoned veins, with no inflamed flesh or pus.

"I feel worse," Kana complained with a forceful yank to open the door. "Is the car parked nearby?" The painkillers were rather appealing now. A perfect cocktail of fatigue and pain kept her from standing for more than a few minutes. She sagged onto the nearest stool. It wasn't just her stomach; her leg throbbed, and her skin felt itchy and warm.

"If we leave, the likelihood of someone locating you is significant," Spencer warned.

Kana knew the risk. Even if a Sori knew of the underground location, they needed to know the exact location of the trapdoor to slip through.

"Good thing I have the best bodyguard around. I assume you know where the exit is, so less talking and more walking."

He led them out of the lab room entirely and to the hallway that separated the lab from the small room with the trash chute entrance. He stopped at the midway point between both doors and pressed his hands against the wall. The lines of his muscles grew taut and bulged as the wall gave in about seven centimeters, revealing enough space to slide it into the rest of the wall. A stairway appeared. Huh. She imagined Spencer scaling every wall and doorway to figure out the secret passage.

"I'm going to do a perimeter check first," he said.

"How long will that take?"

"Twenty minutes and I'll be back."

"Bring shoes," Kana said as he took the first step. The staircase seemed to have shrunk with Spencer's frame, providing a scale he could barely fit. "Don't think I didn't notice how the shoes are missing."

A faint laugh ghosted in the hollow stairwell.

Kana returned to the clean room and yanked out the 70s-style roller chair to twirl mindlessly in the seat. As the room lazily spun, the walls of Josephine's recreated piece of childhood blended into an infinite circle of walls. Kana closed her eyes, trying to envision a thirteen-year-old Josephine, a girl who compared herself to the older teens and women with their shiny halos of hair, their painted faces, their clouds of sweet perfume. A girl who had to swipe her hands against the back of her jeans as she stood up on days of her periods because it felt like she'd gushed blood and leaked through her thin shorts, a teenage girl who dreamed of being older, confident, a girl who knew what to say to boys, a girl who was anything but herself. Kana laughed. No, Josephine was never like that; that's how Kana was. Josephine was never like normal girls with those normal worries. The Josephine of her youth was just like the one now.

She exhaled as her eyes opened. Break time was over. She cracked her neck to the right, then the left, and started another search. At a table, there were small stacks of plastic trays assembled on top of one another with small vials of chemicals. Inside one of the cabinets, in the bottom drawer, was a disarray of solid metals. That was unusual because it defeated the purpose of a clean room if items could contaminate the space. She slid off the table's edge and crouched down for better access to the jumbled mess. It was organized, to an extent, appearing like a rock collection, with the small bits of crystals inside a labeled case. She pushed things aside, looking for one assortment in particular.

"Aha," she said and hefted the metal collection onto the top of the cabinets beside the sink.

In the left corner, there was a piece of metal smaller than her pinky nail with a white label: Toxic-*Silence of the Lamb*. That wasn't so weird, because all the items had labels with movie names, but what made this one stand out was the fact that it was the winner of the 64th Academy Award for Best Picture. No other film labeled on the rock collection was an Academy Award winner. She was an idiot. This was a clue. There was no reason to label a rock collection with Hollywood films. Josephine did not indulge in brain-rotting entertainment like films or music. Josephine tolerated classical music but worked in silence, generated white noise, or whale calls.

Kana searched for her phone, her fingers itching to type her questions in the search engine for an immediate answer. The periodic table and the number sixty-four were connected. Her eyes were wide, and her body thrummed as if she had caffeine jitters. She ran to the other side of the room with the trays of chemicals. Sulfuric acid and saline solution were in giant jugs against the wall. But lined in front were the chemical vials, each one with regular labels. There was no quirky movie title reference.

She ran to the file cabinet and pulled open the top drawer. The metal edges scraped against one another. Inside were old rolled blueprints and posters.

The door opened, and before Spencer could ask what she was doing, she spoke first. "Do you have a phone with internet?"

"I could have been someone with a gun, and shot you before you had a chance to look up," Spencer said, unimpressed. Kana didn't dignify that with an answer. One of the many reasons she didn't like spending too much time around Naturals or Synthies: she became sensitive. His subdued winter mint lingered on her tongue even when he wasn't pushing around energy. Spencer set the pill bottle on the counter.

"Internet, now." Kana's pain was forgotten.

"What do you need to search for?"

"I need the picture of Josephine winning the district science fair back when she was in her first year of secondary school. It was the headliner for Pradstong Chronicle."

With a few taps and the scroll of this thumb, his eyebrows rose. He looked up from the phone to gaze at the room, then back to the phone.

"Well, are you going to show me?" she asked, a deep sigh in the meat of her question.

"You were able to recognize this room as the same setup from a picture decades ago?" Spencer said, not disguising his impressed tone as he held out the small phone.

"You already said I was brilliant," she commented as she stared at the picture, pinching the screen to enlarge the image to better scan over the walls and items.

"I didn't exactly say that," he said with gentle lightness.

A poster of an atom was in the corner of the photographed room, but it was missing from the underground room she and Spencer stood in. "Atom poster," Kana said as she pointed to the file.

Spencer looked through the posters. She couldn't stop her eyes from glancing at Spencer's face. He didn't look displeased, which was a bit shocking. Most people resented being ordered around, even indirectly. She was used to snarky responses: *I don't hear a please. Why can't you get it? Was that a request or a statement?* Few people understood and accepted her lack of niceties. Oliver never complained, too used to her lack of please-and-thank-yous. Oliver—the three syllables sent three sharp aches into her chest. She popped open the bottle and dry swallowed two pills.

A soft hum distracted her from the pain. "The coloring is a bit strange," he said as he held up a poster. Kana eyed the laminated graphic. It looked correct to her. She stopped herself from closing one eye. A brittle sensation made her squirm. Even though

Oliver had most likely told Spencer about her damaged eye, it was different than seeing the person and their flaw.

"See if there's more," she said as she placed the poster and set it on the lab table. While he crossed the room and opened the second drawer, she turned her back and closed her bad eye. The coloring was slightly off, almost like there was a pink glow or haze around the diagrams. They'd take the poster, and she could examine it later.

She turned back to the phone, zooming in, trying to see the grainy details. In the bottom corner near the edge of the table were trays. She walked over and looked back and forth between the picture and the trays in front of her.

"What are you looking at?" he asked, so close that she could sense his body and smell the hint of bland soap from his shower yesterday.

"Are you good at hidden picture?" she asked.

"Hidden picture?" he repeated, the question mark dangling off the word *picture*. "Is that an app?"

Kana lowered the phone and lifted her brows. "How old are you? Hidden picture is the game on the back of kids menus, where you find the items that don't belong or spot the difference. There's been something in each section of the room." Josephine was weird about that. She always used each wall to organize her thoughts, and Kana slapped on an OCD label to explain Josephine's quirk.

"May I see?"

She tossed him the phone. Her eyes were starting to hurt from squinting at the screen anyway. It was impossible to read the labels.

"The vials are different."

Kana swiftly moved to Spencer's side as he lowered the phone for them to examine.

"Something less obvious than that," Kana corrected. The small bottles in the newspaper image were tall, skinny test tubes with small plastic caps. The vials in the clean room were roughly five centimeters and stout bottles with standard silver caps.

"The caps," they both said at the same time.

"What do you see?" Kana asked first.

"The pictures are in black and white, so the caps look dark in the picture." He picked up one of the vials and brought it closer to his eyes. "But the caps have a notch to twist and release. They are all twisted to the left, except one."

Soft clinking sounds echoed in the quiet space as Kana found the one vial that had the unsealed cap twisted to the right. "Fluorine." Another chemical. Two clues led to chemicals, but that left the poster of the atom, which, as far as Kana knew, was not on the periodic table. She flinched as her stomach cramped. She not-so-subtly folded forward, as if adding pressure would relieve the pain.

"We need to go," Spencer announced. "Someone is combing the area, closer to the campsite islands and smaller cabins surrounding the lake. They haven't come this far back yet."

"I just need a minute," Kana groaned. "Four walls, four pieces to the puzzle."

The last wall was the shortest one, where the door was embedded. There was nothing much except a squat bookcase. Because of the angle of the newspaper image, she could only see the side of the bookcase, not what was inside the shelves.

She collapsed on the ground, sitting cross-legged as she picked out the first book and mindlessly shook the pages to see if there was a note or scribbled piece of paper.

"What are we looking for?" Spencer asked as he claimed a spot beside her, his knee almost touching hers.

"If we're lucky, an obvious clue." But Kana had doubts. She felt like it might end up being an obscure clue like everything else.

"There are half a dozen books. Let's take the poster, books, chemical vial, and whatever else you might need," Spencer suggested.

Kana considered his offer. She was doing okay, ignoring the

fact that her intestines didn't know if they were being shocked or if they were being stretched slowly. The painkillers would kick in soon.

"Let's get food. There was a diner thirty minutes down the road, it looked like they specialized in steaks and shakes."

"Why didn't you speak up sooner?" She dumped the books into one of the cardboard boxes from the entrance chute. She didn't know how far away Spencer had parked, but he had enough muscles to heft the goods around. With the rolled poster tucked under her arm, she marched behind Spencer and out of the bunker.

Chapter Twenty-Seven

"I'll take the rarest steak you can make, and water." According to the large sticker name tag, Kana had ordered from the waitress Maud. A commonplace name, much like meeting Mohammads in India or spotting a Ji-Young in a department store in Korea or ordering espresso from a Miguel in Brazil. Maud was pushing fifty, and used a cheap box of red hair dye, the color of rust, with spots of her blonde hair peeking through uneven patches. "Sparkling water."

"I'll have the fish and chips with a blue corn shake, please," Spencer said with a megawatt smile. Kana's expression changed to shock at Spencer's order—blue corn was neither the color blue nor corn, but the ridiculous name had stuck after some American explorer discovered the berry. Kana was also taken aback by the waitress's blush beneath her pink rouge.

"A man—" Kana began, her upper lip curled, but Spencer nudged her foot with his own under the table. Kana kicked him back with an affronted glare. She wanted to say, "A man offers a polite smile and that warrants a swoon," and didn't appreciate being cut off.

"Let me know if you need anything else," Maud said, her eyes toggling between Kana and Spencer as if trying to understand their relationship, before she wandered behind the counter to relay the orders.

"Please try not to draw attention to yourself," Spencer whispered. His eyes swept over the compact cabin diner. Maud dropped off two cups of water and left with a saccharine smile only for Spencer. Kana didn't get a second glance.

"I wasn't going to say anything rude." Kana ripped the plastic straw out of the paper casing and stabbed the large ice cubes, listening to the *shclick* as they bounced against the red plastic. "I was just going to make a simple observation."

He leaned back into the hard plastic of the booth. His sharp gaze under the rim of the baseball hat was unyielding, but the fan of thick lashes couldn't hide the sparkle of humor.

She mindlessly stirred the straw, eyes fixated through the window at the layers of dark greens from the trees, thinking back to the clean room. She suspected the periodic table was the key, at least for some of the clues. The terrible nagging returned. Why, after all this time, did Josephine decide to go AWOL? And Oliver —Her brain screeched as she tried to stop the onslaught of images: his body under the Rabid's carnivorous wrath, the cracked-open chest like a broken egg, the soft, squishy insides slipping out. The dull ache in her jaw told her she was clenching it. But Christ, would she stop remembering his last moment before being ripped apart? Would this be the last core memory she archived of him? Oliver had taught her the importance of remembering people.

"I understand you don't like these events." Oliver had claimed the chair beside nine-year-old Kana, who was sulking at the round table with a centerpiece vase made of bejeweled raindrops and a massive floral arrangement of white and blue flowers with pearls floating like little treasures in the water, concealing her and most of Oliver from the identical men in suits and women in sweeping gowns. "But it's important to try to remember the people you meet. It may be useful."

Kana scowled at Oliver, flicking the gold flecks off the pastry on her plate. "I don't care about them."

"You don't need to remember everything about them. Like that woman who spoke to you, that was Laurel Monroseum. She's the better half of the Monroseum lineage, and not by much, but her husband will leave her everything. I find it best to reduce people to distinct interactions or associations."

"She looked like sweet corn with the husk," Kana said, glaring at the woman who'd attempted to speak to her. The woman's pale hair stood out even more against her emerald green dress with an extravagant collar.

Oliver grinned. "She does, doesn't she? And this," he gestured between him and Kana, "will probably form a core memory you'll associate with her. You'll remember Laurel from the event because she looked like sweet corn with the husk, and that will remind you she's the inheritor of the Monroseum fortune."

Kana turned to Oliver with a deadpan expression. "You want me to remember everyone I meet and make up three memories?"

"Such seriousness for someone so young. No, not everyone will be worth your time, but I want you to try and not toss out everyone and everything that people say with an exhale."

"What are you thinking about?" Spencer's voice was a life buoy back to the present.

Kana forced her hand around the straw to unclench. "When the next assassination team is going to bust through," she drawled. Without moving she looked at Spencer.

His gaze on her was heavy, as if calling out her bullshit, but she didn't feel like a staring contest right now. "And you?" Kana asked. "I imagine you're thinking about all the places you'd rather be than here."

Spencer's eyes drifted off into the distance for a moment, as if debating whether his response was a good idea. "You're good at that."

"At what?"

"You answered honestly enough and diverted the question back to me. You do that often. Hide what's important. I can only imagine how many times you've been betrayed."

Kana's mouth tilted into a frown as she met his sharp eyes, more upset that it rang true.

"Here's your shake, sweetheart." Maud appeared with a wide cup, the jagged edges of ice shavings piled with polka dots of blue from the berries. On the tray was a ceramic bowl with the sweetened heavy cream to dissolve into the shake. Spencer got a "sweetheart" and a fluttering of lashes, pretty privilege at its finest.

"I'd like coffee. A fresh pot," Kana said with a forced smile, "would be great."

Maud's pointy chin did a single shift down as she acknowledged the request and turned, but stopped. "You look familiar." Maud tapped the cap of her pen against her apron as her eyes roamed over Kana's face.

"Ah," Kana said with a hand wave, "I get that a lot. I look like Kana Ambrose, don't I!" Kana's voice ticked up in pitch as her face was cupped by dry hands, crafting a *V* shape to frame her facial features. She knew how terrible she looked. The car mirror hadn't pulled any punches. Maud probably assumed Kana was recovering from a serious illness. Kana's skin was sallow, the baseball hat covered her slick, greasy roots, and her lips, without a tint of lipstick, were pale with a touch of blue even though it was nearing thirty degrees Celsius outside. She didn't look like the glamorous heiress, so it was always fun to make the comparison. People flustered and puttered when she toyed with the fact that most folks generally had racial blindness, and it was fun teasing because no one had the gall to say she looked like Kana Ambrose for fear of stereotyping.

Maud's bright fuchsia lips parted in a dry laugh that she covered with a cough. "Never mind, I'll get that coffee for you."

"No 'sweetheart?'" Kana couldn't help herself. "I'm younger than him and very sweet, so I suppose a sweet nickname like 'honey' will do."

Maud smirked. "You got sass, kid."

Kana grinned as Maud shuffled around the high-top diner bar, where she dumped the stale pot of sludge they called coffee and started a fresh brew. Kana guzzled down the water through the clear straw. Her eyes lifted to meet Spencer's gaze under the brim of her hat. He was using the large spoon to mix the cream into the bowl of ice, the shards melting and the snowy white shifting to a cornflower blue.

"You look like an aggressively overbearing boyfriend if you stare at me like that while I drink water," Kana commented with another long slurp, until the straw made a rasping cackle at the last drop.

There was a family on the other side of the diner, but the parents were too occupied with the children to take any real notice of them. Spencer's large knuckles were bruised and flushed red as his hand lifted the spoon to his lips and sipped the thick shake. He had nice fingernail beds, but the cuticles needed severe trimming and more moisturizer for the cracked calluses.

"What's on your mind?" Kana repeated his question back to him. Spencer lowered his head, the hat hiding his eyes.

"Trying to figure out who is leaking information. I checked the main campsite island. The bodies are gone." Just as Oliver had said: the cabin was in flames with empty cars, but no bodies.

"Anything you want to share with the class? I'm guessing you tossed the tracker in the shoe, unless you lied about giving the president information."

"Nothing concrete, like you. I have theories."

Kana's eyes landed on the thick plastic cup, following the swirl of darker blue streaks in Spencer's sweet treat. Oliver would be useful right about now. His absence was noticeable. The way walls would crumble when he portaged into a room, the fine mist against her skin. She wouldn't ever feel that again. Bastard. If Oliver had known Josephine was MIA, why didn't he say anything? Kana laughed at herself because, naturally, she wouldn't have listened. She didn't like anyone bringing up Josephine. If Oliver even uttered the *Jo* sound, she shut him down. How could he have come to her with news that Josephine had vanished? If anything, Kana would have celebrated.

Maud breezed by, managing to fill Kana's empty ceramic mug with piping hot coffee in a fluid movement as she shouted to the kitchen.

"Would you like some?" Spencer asked, assuming she was interested in his sweet milk because of her fixated gaze.

Kana lifted the ceramic mug to her mouth and sipped the coffee. "Lactose sensitive. Unless you want to survive the next few hours with my gassy body, it's best if I don't."

Spencer smiled. It was still quite a sight. He had one of those broody faces, but a smile changed him entirely. She imagined he had a lovely girl back home, or a boy, but Oliver's research did not annotate his dating history.

"You are surprisingly very honest about some things, and silent about important things."

Kana hummed, "Astute observation," she said as Maud came up with a plate in each hand.

"Bloody steak for you, buttercup, and fish and chips for you, sweetheart."

The urge to use her straw and suck at the collection of rusty juice pooling beneath the meat nearly overwhelmed her. She didn't cave to such a ridiculous impulse; instead, she sliced a single line and was greeted with fleshy, bright pink meat. Perfect.

Spencer said a polite "thank you" to their waitress while Kana stuffed her mouth.

The hunk of meat was not close to her normal expectations,

but it was good enough that she didn't spit it out. She was famished.

"Do you eat a lot of meat?" Spencer asked.

Kana slowed halfway through the hunk of the cow and decided to eat one of the broccoli stalks. Random question, but she supposed he'd only seen her eat meat these past few days.

"I'm partial to proteins," she said, "especially every month, when my vagina becomes a gushing, bloody jellyfish." Kana tried to hold back her grin at Spencer's micro-shift of discomfort at the mention of menstruation. She continued as she sucked on a slice of meat. "Not even the greatest drugs can curb all hormonal things. Farm-to-table is the best. My body can't stand all the fake shit in a lot of mass-produced foods. Having a chef from a Michelin-starred restaurant cooking baby mush before I had teeth left me with a certain palette."

The tinkering of the bell, and another family squeezed in, following Maud to one of the three barbecue grilling tables.

"We should head out in about five, restock supplies, and head back down," Spencer said, checking his watch. "Police will be here shortly."

"And you know this how?"

"I'm going to leave an anonymous tip." Ah. He wanted to piggyback on the information from the police. That wasn't a bad idea.

They didn't get a chance to go to the grocery store or retreat to the bunker after their meal. Kana's hand was reaching for the passenger door handle when a warm dampness tickled the roots of her hair. A portal split open near enough for her to sense it, indicating that whoever it was had to be close. She flung open the door and dove in. Seeing her abrupt reaction, Spencer moved into the driver's seat.

"We need to go," she said as she sank low into the passenger seat, until her knees bumped against the underbelly of the dashboard.

"Your Spidey senses are tingling?"

Kana rolled her eyes. "Har-har-har." But she didn't deny it. Her skin felt tight, like when she used a mud mask and it cemented over her face, but under the taut skin there was an unfamiliar electrical current that eventually faded.

Spencer didn't push for other answers and yanked the car out of the dirt parking lot.

"Guess burrowing back underground isn't an option," Kana sighed. Maybe that was for the best.

Spencer merged onto the main highway, and three hours later, he stopped in front of a roadside lodge. The flat, neutral-colored rectangle of a building blended with the barren landscape, which was filled only with a few pockets of dry shrubs and skinny trees that looked like they were screaming for water. There were beaten-down trucks and cars with sun-bleached and faded tops. The lodge catered to the laborers and nomadic folk who couldn't afford to dish out two hundred a night for a mediocre hotel.

Parked in the corner of the lot, diagonal from the front office, they argued over who should go and pay. He didn't want her to be alone, even if she was in the car. She told him that if people were looking for them, someone might report if they saw a couple, the female partner of Asian descent, the male counterpart white, because realistically they would generalize both their physical appearances. If he booked it alone, it would be less suspicious.

"We could be inside the room by now," Kana complained. "I'll lie down and no one will see me."

"Fine."

Kana crawled into the back and lay on the faded and suspiciously stained seats while Spencer ordered a room for one night.

Chapter Twenty-Eight

Inside the room, she lunged on the bed; the bedsprings squeaked under her ass. "Bedsprings, really?" She peeled back the blanket and eyed the white bedcover with distrust. "What are the chances we get ravaged by bed bugs?" she asked from her claimed twin bed.

Kana had never been inside a roadside lodge or anything less than a five-star hotel. It was exactly as television portrayed it to be: a grungy space that smelled of the cotton breeze artificial fragrance from the plug-in diffuser, as if that would cover the cigarette and marijuana scent absorbed into the walls. Her nose scrunched as she spotted a sticky ring on the chipped end table separating the beds. She settled a textbook from the bunker onto her lap and flipped through the pages, because she still needed to figure out the rest of the clues.

It got boring really fast. She rubbed her eyes and held back a yawn as she turned another page. The TV played in the background, a jumbled drone of boring news. She groaned and flopped on the bed. There was a drag in her body, the heavy sensation of being unable to keep her eyelids open.

"The sixty-fourth chemical on the periodic table is gadolinium, abbreviated 'G-d.'" Spencer's voice exploded in clarity, thrusting Kana's mind back to focus. She blinked, trying to reorient her vision on the popcorn ceiling that looked like a napkin stained with coffee.

"'G-d,'" Kana repeated, her mind back on track. She blindly reached for the poster, her hand smacking against the plastic-coated, cheap wood end table until Spencer placed the thin, rolled paper into her extended palm. He retreated to his side of the room as she held up the poster, eyes nearly crossed as she scrutinized the atom, but her mind zeroed in on the periodic table. Fluorine was F. Why give them only two chemicals if the periodic table was the key?

"How many abbreviated vowels are in the periodic table?" she asked.

"Single letter or with two letters? Oxygen is 'O,' osmium is abbreviated to 'O-s.'"

Kana didn't know, and asked for a list of all the vowels. Spencer always seemed to remain in her line of sight as he stood off to the far right of the room, leaning against the wall in vantage of the space.

There were twenty chemicals abbreviated with vowels. Spencer caught on quickly and listed Scrabble words. The list didn't look promising. There weren't many words you could create with *F* and *G*, even with a mix of vowels.

"Use just 'E,'" Kana concluded. She unraveled the poster, her fingers tracing the faint pink rings that connected the electrons.

Spencer tapped away on the phone. "There aren't four-letter words with the letters 'F,' 'G,' and 'E.'"

"What about 'A' instead of 'E?'" Maybe the hint wasn't an electron, but an atom in general.

"Flag, Fang, Fray," he read off the list.

Her face scrunched. That couldn't be it. She needed to find the fourth letter in the books. After Kana tossed the third book across the room, she hung her head off the foot of the bed, staring at the TV upside down. The Gd clue could be wrong. Maybe it wasn't the sixty-fourth element. The 64th Academy Awards took place in 1992.

"What's the ninety-second element?"

Silence was her answer. She twisted her head and looked around at an empty motel. The TV was turned off, and she was under the covers. She must have fallen asleep, and Spencer had left at some point. He wouldn't have gone far, possibly mapping exit routes. He didn't seem as concerned about potential attackers. Maybe now that Oliver was out of the picture, he felt like the rat was no longer a threat. That still didn't sit well with Kana. Oliver could be selfish, and it wasn't a terrible stretch that he would edge his way to the front of Ambrose Inc., but to betray her? Kana's throat lodged around an invisible pill that she couldn't swallow.

She looked up at the sound of the motel door unlocking. Spencer covered his surprise as he turned his body to set a convenience store plastic bag on the edge of the console table. "I want to test something," he announced.

"Do I get the luxury of knowing what this test is?" Kana asked, forcing herself out of bed. He, of course, refused to elaborate and tossed her a baseball cap from the plastic bag.

"I want to test a theory regarding the Rabid Synthetics," he repeated in more detail.

"What do I get from this?" She fixed the cap on her head. She didn't have anything else to do, and being trapped in the motel was making her feel like a crusty barnacle. The bunker seemed more sanitary than this place.

"Possibly some answers." Spencer slung their two duffels on each of his shoulders. She frowned. When did he have time to repack their go-bags?

"I could go for some fresh air and real food." Kana pointed accusingly at the trash full of wrappers, empty chip bags, and crumpled takeout bags. "It will be too soon before I ever eat another cheap burger made with questionable meat."

Spencer drove them three blocks from the motel and parked behind a dusty black car.

"You couldn't find a better car?" Kana teased, catching onto the fact that they were doing a car swap.

"The Audi was too obvious," he replied.

"At least this one has AC." Kana sighed blissfully as she got in and was hit with a blast of cold air. The ride was silent, the buildings becoming more frequent until they drove for close to an hour. The tall apartment complexes and office buildings gave way to fewer, one-level, flat businesses, with the occasional gas station becoming the norm. Eventually, Spencer pulled into a warehouse.

"This feels suspiciously like I'm being taken to my own murder location."

He parked the car in the back by a loading dock and turned to Kana.

"I won't ask how exactly your Active ability works, but I do think there's something that connects you and the Rabid Synthetics." Kana quietly digested his far-fetched theory. "I chose this location because the warehouse is under construction, blocked off, and separated from the main road that's undergoing work. Here." He handed her a knife and a gun. Kana accepted the weapons. The buzzing anxiety under her skin calmed with the metal in her hands.

She eyed the two chunky rectangular cameras aimed at the parking lot. "No cameras," Kana said. There was no way in hell she trusted Spencer to not have placed cameras inside the warehouse.

"They've been jammed."

"Prove it."

He reached into the backpack behind Kana's seat and removed a block of technology that was reminiscent of an old 80s walkie talkie. A device she'd seen before, it was a laser jammer. She flicked the switch on the side and the tiny green light signal died. With another flick, the neon green light returned.

"Alright," she said, "either you are very prepared for a ruse, or this is a real jammer."

"Is that your only objection?" he asked, surprised.

"I want a second gun." She didn't need another gun, but it didn't hurt to have more. He reached behind the driver's seat and handed her a second 9mm. Her fingers locked the safety in place. "And I want to know the plan. The unnecessary secrecy isn't needed."

Spencer ran a hand down the side of his mouth and jaw, and his eyes leveled on the large garage door of the loading bay. "There's a Rabid Synthetic User in the warehouse." Kana sucked in her lips and glared at Spencer, who quickly added, "They are secured and can't hurt us. We will enter to the right." His finger pointed to the side of the building. "It will take less than ten minutes. I have a simple idea I'd like to test. Then we will leave and relocate to a different motel."

As he'd described, the warehouse was mostly blocked off for construction. There was nothing inside, and the windows were boarded with thick, wooden planks. As far as she could tell, there weren't cameras in the vacant space. A razor-sharp stab slid between her ribs. She would be inside a windowless space, with one door. If he wanted to, the betrayal would be easy. Spencer could leave, close the door behind her, and keep her locked here as food for whoever was stuck in the corner of the space. But he could have hurt her long ago. She couldn't stop her finger tapping against the gun. Spencer's eyes lowered to watch her nervous tick and she inhaled slowly. "Let's get this over with."

———

THE WAREHOUSE SPACE WAS SMALLER THAN SHE expected. Cement walls sliced the open area, carving off a quarter behind a thick barrier. Kana's nose scrunched as the air stewed with molding wet clothes, bitten by dust. Kana stayed close to the door. Cardboard boxes, half crushed, half soggy and crumbling apart, were scattered around the open space. The left wall had six empty glass bottles lined up in a neat row. Crushed cans and bottle caps were scattered around a forgotten sleeping bag thinner than the sheet at the roadside lodge. And there was the person, across the room diagonally from Kana, by the only other door. Their back faced her; their form was hidden in massive clothes. Large chains wrapped around their chest, the metal links pressing into their body, thick rolls and irregular lumps straining against the binding.

"What am I supposed to do, exactly?" she hissed, keeping one hand on the doorknob. "Wave my hand around and 'Bibbidi-Bobbidi-Boo?' I'd rather not prod the predator."

Spencer crossed in front of her to stand to her left, allowing space for her to flee out the door instead of blocking it. "Don't do anything to him." He walked across the wide space, his thick soles mute as he picked up a can of soda that stood innocently on the concrete flooring. "Move the can and we'll see what happens." His voice bounced around the cavernous space, and Kana's eyes flew to the Rabid Synthie; her hand tightened around the gun, ready for the roar and attack, but the creature remained motionless, unbothered by Spencer's voice.

She exhaled slowly. Move the can, he said. They were knee-deep in dangerous territory. He'd claimed he wouldn't ask about her abnormality, but he was smart. If she asked him to move it first, would he take that small hint and conclude she used other Users' energy? Her abilities had limits, and one of them was that inertia manipulation worked best if another User initiated the push. She could use the blanket excuse of her lack of training and energy to have him push first. But Spencer presented an opportunity; this was the best controlled environment she'd get, and a chance to know why the Rabids were hyperfixating on her was too good to pass up. "You think I send out some sort of signal?"

"Yes."

The Rabid Synthie didn't respond to either of their voices. She wouldn't know the person was alive if it wasn't for the croaking breath. Kana thought back. She only pushed when she had to. The infected Synthies were already attacking when they came to her, so she could see his logic.

"How did you find him?" Kana asked, pointing with her chin at the unmoving, slumped form.

"He was lurking around the campsite."

Bullshit. Kana squinted at Spencer. Did he think she was dumb? "You were able to locate a Rabid User, rendering them unconscious enough to bring them to this warehouse in less than eight hours? Just admit you're still the president's bitch and you called for a delivery."

He did not comment on her accusation; he looked contemplative. A low grumble of hissing sounded in her mind; it sounded a lot like *Don't tell anyone*. Josephine's warning clawed out of the back of her mind. She slammed that voice down.

"Toss the can to me, not with your hand. Push it," Kana said as she stepped to the other corner of the space.

He pitched the can in the air. It paused just before gravity took control, and it drifted down millimeter by millimeter, so slowly it still looked like it was levitating. Kana sucked at Spencer's fresh energy, her mouth full of rich mint ice cream. "Ready?" he asked.

Not really. She felt this was a very bad decision, but he was pushing the can through the air, a quarter of the speed it would normally fly if someone with his strength threw the can. It came within arm's reach, and she redirected it, being careful to scrape the surface of her depleted energy, using the thinnest amount she could. The chains rattled as the Rabid Synthie moved.

Kana turned her attention to the Synthie, another Active User based on the lack of fungi busting out of the thin flesh. Even more menacing were the deformed, displaced body parts. At least the person still had their face, mostly intact, with the curve of the nose split open as if someone had sculpted their wet face and plucked and peeled back the skin from the nose to the cheekbone. There were sacs beneath the flesh like fifteen freshly laid fish eggs. The spherical sacs rolled, and half-formed eyes with crooked irises looked at her.

"Poor bastard," Kana whispered.

The chains straitjacketing the person clinked as they tried to move, but their pasty ankles were bent at irregular angles, the knee joints pressed crudely against the thin cotton of the pants. That was sick. She didn't know if they had been injured before, or if Spencer was ruthless enough to break their legs to keep them immobile. A shiver started at the base of her neck at the thought of Spencer stomping on a person's joints.

A motion from the corner of her eye caught her attention, as Spencer pointed from her to the opposite corner of the room. She silently obeyed his signal, and walked across the space to be directly across from the Rabid Synthie. Spencer's power was still a mouthful of cool mint spritzed in her throat as the soda can rose, suspended between them. Her attention was on the Synthie. It remained a lumpy boulder, unreactive to Spencer's power. The Synthie remained unbothered by both of them moving in the space or speaking, as if it couldn't hear. Her hand on the gun was a sort of comfort, but proved unnecessary as the Rabid User didn't follow Kana.

Again, Spencer mouthed as he tossed the levitating can back to Kana. She used even less of her energy to redirect the can. It barely looked like it changed its projection, but the Rabid Synthie's reaction was immediate. It fell forward and tried to drag its body to her. She knew that, unchained, they would have army crawled, but it seemed like a mutated snail painfully dragging itself across the concrete floor. Spencer seemed to be right. Two instances didn't make him correct just yet, but it was awfully coincidental that the Rabid Synthie only reacted when Kana pushed.

A second flavor, a potent stinging scent like freshly chopped onions, hung in the air as a residual cloud lingered. Kana consciously stopped herself from reaching out. It was familiar, like the time at the lake. *Don't absorb their energy.* The Rabid Synthies probably had polluted energy, and she'd been gobbling it up. Maybe that was the cause for the black flesh. She was poisoning herself without realizing it. But it felt so good. She got a taste at both lakes, and it was incredible. Better than incredible. Her memory made it impossible to truly recall the intense, blissful feeling. She moved along the wall to the door, realizing the thing had made decent progress across the space. Now that the Rabid Synthie was closer, she could see the tattered clothing stretched against the chains and the holes, hundreds of them, the size of blown pupils all along his neck and down his shoulder where dark yellow pus dribbled out.

"You proved your point," Kana said, exiting the warehouse, but caught Spencer aiming his gun, and the loud bang of three rounds ricocheted in the steel and concrete building.

Kana crossed her arms, pulling the jacket across her chest, the gun heavy in her hand as she leaned against the warehouse wall. She didn't like the idea of the inexplicable draw the Synthies had to her. Her jaw ached as Josephine's warnings bubbled to the surface. Was this the reason she didn't want Kana using any of her power?

The warehouse door creaked open behind her, and Spencer's intense gaze was back on her body. "I'm hungry," she muttered. Her stomach was twisted in knots. Maybe it was hunger, maybe it was an ulcer forming from the amount of stress these past few days had put on her. If a Rabid Synthie was near, at least she knew what not to do.

Chapter Twenty-Nine

Spencer drove them to a different, equally dingy roadside lodge two hours away. She at least got a nice pork chop and learned the ninety-second element was uranium on the way. The new temporary lodge attempted to lure its prospective customers with an animatronic palm tree that looked like Disneyland's ugly cousin, the branches chugging around like a windmill. She shoved into the room, noting the owners stayed true to the tropical theme: tacky palm tree-printed bed throws, coconut-shaped bedside lamps, and plastic bamboo-looking bed frames. It was certainly a choice. She dumped her small backpack onto the bed while Spencer hefted the duffel bags through the door.

"Why did you go through all the trouble to set up that little stunt?" she asked.

"Do you know what day it is?" Spencer asked slowly, unable to meet Kana's gaze as he moved through the condensed room, checking the bathroom, and pushed the closet doors to inspect the empty storage space.

"Knowing what day it is isn't exactly top of my priority list," Kana commented. Spencer's lips thinned as he turned to face her, keeping his posture purposefully at ease, but the skittering hesitation was unusual for him.

"Earlier, you were suspicious of how long it took me to find a car and locate a Rabid Synthetic while managing to get them to the warehouse."

Kana nodded slowly. Yes, that was what she'd said.

"It's been almost two days." He looked at his watch. "Nearing forty-one hours." Kana blinked, and the back of her legs slowly lowered onto the bed.

"That . . ." She stopped, because that wasn't possible. She hadn't fallen asleep, hadn't dozed off for a short nap. She had been flipping through those boring textbooks and would know if more than a day passed. "You're lying," she concluded.

Spencer remained standing a little to her right. His face wasn't set in a sharp mask like she expected. He almost looked forlorn, and a film of sadness blinked away in his eyes. "How much do you know about Synthetic Users?" The question was innocent enough. He'd asked that question before, but there was something hidden in his tone, like a candle he'd snuffed out.

They stared at each other. Kana was trying to understand the question he was really asking her. She knew the basics of Synthies. They were like Naturals, except the parasite still lived inside of them.

"Passive Synthetic Users experience the flora and fungi that need to be removed through bloodletting, while Active Users become hungry for meat." Spencer said.

Kana's jaw was wired shut with strained tension.

There was no way he was implying what she thought he wanted to say. The danger for Active Synthies was meat consumption. At some point, the Hunger phase couldn't be quenched by animal products. As soon as they ate another person, they were too far gone, and the floodgates opened. A line crossed. It was not only the taboo of cannibalism; the Synthie's biology altered to that of an obligate carnivore. Their entire anatomy mutated, which was why the Rabid Users looked like a walking tumor, gaining appendages from the poor suckers they ate.

"You wouldn't dare," Kana said slowly. She couldn't finish the sentence. It was ridiculous. "Because I eat meat, you—" Her words died in her mouth.

"Both Passive and Active Synthetic Users occasionally experience a blackout period. They don't realize they experienced the blackout. They are in a catatonic state," Spencer said with clear precision, as if he were reading a textbook.

"Stop." Kana's voice rolled like a crashing wave. She'd heard of a blackout stage, the body's natural warning from overusing energy, a symptom that irreversible changes were happening to the body. "Your mouth is moving, you are saying words to me and it's the most absurd thing I've ever heard," Kana said through her teeth as she moved to the door, throwing the hood of the cheap sweatshirt over her mess of hair. She needed to get away.

"Please, don't. I didn't mean to upset you. It wasn't an accusation."

"You didn't mean to upset me?" she echoed. "You have the audacity to accuse me of being a Synthie based on two very loose instances." Her voice rose, and her face was hot. If he had done his research, he would know her medical records showed hospitalization at the age of four for the Fever recovery. So she liked meat that wasn't cooked into oblivion. She had one instance of a blackout, which wasn't even proven yet! If anyone else were being dragged around the country with trained killers after them, and seeing people being eaten alive, they'd have a minor blackout, too. Given the sheer number of life-threatening situations she'd endured, any sane person would have had multiple mental breakdowns. She wasn't a Synthie. She'd never taken the drug. She'd done every other drug, but would never stoop low enough to take the drug that made her familial name renowned; it would have killed her. No doubt about that, idiots before had tried, because the next question after the success of A.E. Potentia was easy:

could someone create an even stronger person with a double dose or by boosting a Natural with A.E. Potentia, like a steroid? The answer was no. Death was assured, and a gruesome one.

Spencer exhaled, which almost sounded like a sigh as his fingers grazed his bottom lip. "You're going to hate this, but I knew you wouldn't believe me." He reached into his pocket and removed a new phone. All his previous phones had been black; this one was white.

He didn't have to hit the play button as he faced the phone screen in her direction. She saw the still frame. It was her, lying prone on the previous motel bed. Her eyes were half open. Dark lashes blinked once to prove she was alive, and the textbook rested limply in her lap. The sight of herself on a phone recording split her mind like spidering glass. An icy chill exploded as she remembered being in an unfamiliar room with another man holding his phone. A mask had obscured his face, blue eyes shadowed by the overhanging light, but she saw the pleased grin through the open mouth hole as he turned to Kana and replayed her ransom video. The smell of the tobacco clinging to the polyester of his sweatshirt.

Her chest ached and her lungs burned. She couldn't be here. Her hand twisted the doorknob and pulled. The door snapped shut as soon as the force from her movement registered. The mint in the back of her throat was pissing her off.

"You asshole," she hissed, yanking open the door with both hands. The hot air snapped like a whipped towel as the door slammed shut. Kana turned around and picked up the gun from the side table and aimed it at the Active User.

"You are not keeping me hostage." She would not be held against her will. Her voice was stable, even if she cringed at the shrill tone. He could move the bullets, but the gun didn't have a silencer. The sound would attract attention, and she was being stupid and risking their location. He tossed the white phone onto the nearest bed and held up his hands, his face at least pinched in an apology.

"Get out," she barked. If she couldn't leave, he sure as hell could. She didn't want to look at his dumb face any longer.

He wordlessly left, the door clicking shut behind him.

Kana wanted to scream, but opted for punching the pillow on the bed. The notion of escaping resurfaced. She could figure it out, find a woman and beg to be hidden away. There was still a hefty wad of cash in the bag. She could try and hide, but goddamn it, Spencer was too skilled. How long could she be on the run from him, the president, and god knew who else? She glared at the grimy, thick, painted door. He was probably planted on the other side.

She flopped back and rubbed her face. God, her skin felt like drywall. She would kill for a deep moisturizer. Her fingers traced the raised ridges of her skin along her belly button. It felt like the pleats of clothing. Gross skin pleats.

Her fingertips continued to mindlessly trace the strange skin pattern. The stitches from the surgery, which felt like a decade ago, were untouched. She still had smaller bandages over those wounds.

There was a strange fascination with whatever was happening, an intriguing puzzle in front of her. She remembered being a kid and hating math word problems until her tutor broke it down like a riddle, a puzzle, and she was the detective. She hated to admit it, but there seemed to be an unknown connection between her and the Rabid Synthies, and Josephine had been warning her for years to conceal her ability. For a split moment, she saw a glimpse of what Josephine must have experienced—the addictive allure of being on the tip of something big, and that hint of revelation splintered something inside of her. For the first time, she truly acknowledged a tiny kernel of understanding. She could almost relate to Josephine. Never in a billion years, not even if the sun extinguished, did she expect she would have come to understand Josephine.

When Kana looked at Josephine or thought of the woman, there was so much distance. She was untouchable, completely unapproachable. She might as well be an AI projection, a hologram.

Kana was too young to fully remember the Fever. What she did recall was being told to never push things. There was a brief summer when Josephine hired different instructors. There were flashing moments of running on the beach, and a pink beach house she visited during her Bluette phase. Bluette was akin to the famous Malibu Barbie, a little collection of overly idealistic plastic dolls that altered children's image of what a beautiful woman should look like. She couldn't remember any of the tutor's physical features, or if it was a man or woman—there was more of an impression of a powerful presence guiding her. She didn't want to assume a male figure, but her mind filled in the space, and a silhouette of a man sliding a dog plushie at the other end of the room came to mind. He was showing her magic, and she was amazed.

From the bright streetlights and overhanging fluorescent lights outside the motel, the cheap, thin curtains failed to hide the shadow of someone walking by. Her heart skidded a beat before her taste told her who the distorted silhouette belonged to.

He couldn't leave her alone for more than ten minutes. The digital clock, citing two hours passed, told a different story, which she defiantly ignored. She'd simply been lost in thought; she didn't black out. Kana rolled off the bed, snatching the small backpack, a pillow, and a textbook, and locked herself in the bathroom.

The bathroom, thankfully, was cleaner than the previous motel. There weren't suspicious tiny pubic hairs behind the toilet seat cover and a ring of residual dirt in the bathtub.

She tossed towels in the bathtub and settled the pillow behind her back. The back cover of the textbook elicited a plastic crack as she turned it to examine the graphic of the periodic table. There were other things she needed to focus on: *F. E. U.* There was only one four-letter word with those three letters—*fuel*. That was so vague that Kana thought she missed another clue; at least P.L.U.T.O. was specific to a time and place in her past.

The nagging returned—what if this was her life now, on the run like a fugitive, chasing obscure and meaningless clues? What a terrible life that would be, to experience the past few weeks on repeat, with no ending in sight. Absolutely not. If there was one thing Kana was sure about, it was her drive. If she didn't want something to happen, it wasn't going to happen. The defeatist thoughts were unhelpful; what she could do was find Josephine. *Fuel* couldn't be an acronym, Josephine wouldn't use the same structure twice. She sighed, resigned to playing word association for its significance.

Fuel was like gas for vehicles. The train of thought brought her to her first car, a 1964 Ferrari, a truly gorgeous maraschino cherry-red car, but fuel could also be for any of the other cars she owned. Or fuel for airplanes, which made a little more sense since the clues were bits and pieces from different countries around the world. Airplane. They had their private jet hangar. Was there something there? Or did fuel refer to traveling? There were too many other words attached, spindling outward.

A quick knock on the bathroom door broke her spiraling thoughts. "You can piss in a bush." Kana glared at the bathroom door.

"We need to move." The door was wafer-thin and acted as an amplifier, his voice echoed in the minuscule bathroom.

"Why, are there people raiding rooms?" She rolled her eyes.

"Only the rooms with guests."

That didn't seem right. She would feel if an Active or Passive User was expelling energy. "I don't believe you," she said, not moving from her spot.

"You're behaving like a child." His frustration leaked between his words.

Anger resurfaced, a small trail of gasoline that took a single match to burn. "I'd rather take my chances with—" She yelped as the door flew open, the wood smashing into the wall with a loud bang, causing the cheap hinges to snap off, as it caved under Spencer's kick.

"What the hell!" He didn't push or add extra oomph to move the door, and if it weren't for the explosion of sounds outside the thin motel door, the neighbors would have heard the door breaking open.

"I'm going," Kana snapped and jumped out of the bathtub before Spencer could jerk her out.

Spencer went through the front door first, and his shoulder smacked into another man who ran out of the room to their left. A flurry of chilled water tickled the back of her neck. A Tomi was coming. He muttered a curse as they ran straight for his car. Other people were wiggling around out of the grips of men and women in standard-issue clunky vests belonging to the Oshiya police force. She didn't realize how full the motel was until random people spilled into the parking lot like ants frantically running around flecks of water. Some attempted to dive into their cars and others opted to sprint down the street.

They were halfway to the car when a woman shouted. "You two!"

Kana yanked open the door and dove inside. The car started before she could shut the door behind her. She instinctively sank low in the back seat, ready for bullets to fly through the air.

How they got through the other fleeing cars and police barricade, Kana didn't know. She smacked her head against the door at a sudden sharp left turn. Her body slid around the back like a penguin on its belly. The rubber tires screeching drowned her painful yelp. She shot her arms out to keep herself from tumbling to the floor of the car.

"Are we in a car chase?" Kana shouted before her leg slipped and her knee smashed into the center console. She managed to pull herself upright and a look behind the back window confirmed the flashing blue and white lights from a police car.

"Seat belt," Spencer ordered, his narrowed eyes looking down at her from the rearview mirror. "They'll have to give up in less than ten."

Kana wasn't sure where that confident statement came from. Did the military train for evading and escaping in a car chase as part of the curriculum? She fumbled with the safety belt as she jerked right, following the car's momentum, but successfully clicked the seat belt in place after another sharp U-turn, and the car blasted through a red light. The startling shift from run-down roadside lodges to industrial warehouses and cranes made their location recognizable.

"You aren't going on the Mishya Bridge?" she screeched as the bascule bridge came into sight.

The bridge was lifting as the morning cargo ships drifted into the harbor. The barrier to keep traffic from crossing was already in place. Her hands shot out in panic, her nails dug into the fading leather as she braced herself. He couldn't be crazy enough to think the car could make it across a bridge that was literally breaking in half.

He didn't plow through the barricade. Instead, he made a last-second sharp right turn. The gushing mint told her he'd cushioned the car so it didn't flip on its side and once the vehicle landed on four wheels, he sped straight into the tunnel carved into the side of a rocky hill. The police cars came to a screeching halt. The crash of metal told her one of the cars rear-ended another.

The tunnel was short, and once they were through, Spencer decreased their speed, casually stopping in a side street. Kana's heart was still thundering in her ears as she tried to calm herself down.

"We need to change cars," Spencer said as he leaned back in

the driver's seat, his body unwinding. "We'll need to figure out where to stay and pay someone else to purchase the room."

"You've been paying in cash. The attendants don't even see me," Kana said. "How did the police know we were there?"

"Wrong place, wrong time, seemed like a standard bust for petty crimes," Spencer said, mostly confident.

Kana snorted. "That's a big fat coincidence."

"Or someone is monitoring my face as well. Facial recognition in the cameras."

"Big Brother at work? So now we're both flagged." Kana flexed her bare toes. She needed to be like Spencer and wear shoes constantly, even to sleep.

"There's a beach house," Kana said slowly. "We are close to the Kikum coast. I haven't been to the Bluette House since I was five or six."

"They have people watching all the Ambrose properties and affiliated locations." He dismissed her suggestion.

"It's not mine or my family's. It's a bungalow a nanny used to have."

"Are you sure it's still there?"

"It's a few kilometers away." Her voice became distant as she dug deep into the flipping memories.

"Is it inconspicuous?" Spencer asked, one hundred percent doubting Kana's idea of a beach house.

"It's fit for lowly peasants," she replied.

Spencer found a car, a minivan of all things, but it worked. There was even a pair of flip-flops inside.

Kana grinned. "Search Kikum Beach. It's somewhere along there. There'll be a line of bright houses." She slid on a pair of sunglasses someone had probably purchased from a grocery store, the bands a cheap, bright pink plastic that scratched the junction of her ears and temples.

"Ooh," she exclaimed, spotting snack bags piled into a canvas tote. She ripped open a candy bag, and crunched a crystallized shell between her teeth. Josephine had a lot of answering to do. If only she could have escaped the woman's grasp years ago. When she was fifteen, a boy named Luo Yun Xi, but to everyone known as Grayson, asked if she wanted to run away, but would that have helped? She couldn't leave Oshiya for long, but she could slink off, withdraw stacks of cash, and live a quiet life in a town with a thousand people. But that mundane, unseen lifestyle was not for her. She would find Josephine, hold the president to his promise, and start her legacy.

CHAPTER THIRTY

"My Fevermark faded when I was fourteen." Spencer said. Kana's slitted side-eye spoke of her judgment. The abruptness of the personal statement caught her off guard.

"You could just say Stamp, like everyone else," Kana muttered as she closed her eyes. The official term was Thermal Dermatosis, commonly referred to as a Fevermark, which later turned into the term Hot Stamp, now shortened to Stamp. The blue skin slowly faded over time, splotching away in vitiligo patterns, until it faded completely. When that happened, the host was fully healed, and their ability would manifest.

"I've asked others, their experiences at the academies for Stamped kids," his eyes moved to Kana, offering a natural pause to open the conversation to her. "I didn't particularly care for the after-school academy but one of the teachers pulled me aside and connected me with Idria." Spencer paused, the name of his seemingly important person weighted in the syllables of Idria's name, spoken with warmth and pride.

"He praised me, saying I was quick to learn, with an innate understanding, a true raw talent. I wasn't great at anything; I was passable at most things, but no one had ever said I was talented.

To have someone who was the best in their field, someone who complimented very little, and was not shy of voicing their expectations, say you are special, well, that was one of the happiest moments of my life."

A gut punch, was it the reverence that floated between the spaces of his words or the jealousy that reminded her no one had sincerely complimented her to such an extent?

"If I entered the military academy, there would still be three years more of training before any decisions were made; three years was a long time, I would still be in my teens with my entire life far off on the horizon, and the answer seemed simple in the moment. And I said I would do it."A twinge of an ache coiled in her gut. "Someone says you're special and you decide to make a life-altering decision for them?" Kana said, the curl in her lip echoed in her words.

"Coming from an adult, someone you admire? Being told you are special? Isn't that what you wanted from your mom?"

Kana resolutely said nothing to the rhetorical question. It was a cheap shot. Of course she wanted validation. Everyone wanted that from their parent, even as much as Kana rejected Josephine's title of "mother."

"There were other factors. My parents wanted me to enlist, and if everyone else seemed to believe in me, doing good and helping people with something I could excel at, I could at least try."

Kana licked the top line of her teeth—how honorable of him. She scrutinized Spencer. "It sounds like you regret it."

"No, not at all. Idria is a close mentor, someone I couldn't regret meeting. He's an inspiration, and he helped me throughout the academy, even when I graduated and was assigned my first team. And to this day, he's just a call away." Spencer gave a low chuckle. "He's a recluse, extremely paranoid, so by 'call' I mean 'carrier pigeons.'"

Kana crossed her arms over her chest, digging her fingers into the loose fabric. There was an unsettling knot weaving in and around her stomach, like burning acid stinging her heart. The way in which Spencer admired this mentor, the pure respect, was nothing like the adoration from fans. She was jealous.

"I don't want to hear any more about your idolization," she muttered, curling to press more of her body to the car door, and focused on the speeding landscape.

A lot had changed since the last time she was in this district. If it weren't for a few of the houses that hadn't been remodeled into boutique storefronts to attract tourists, the area would be almost unrecognizable. For a brief moment, she wondered if she'd remembered correctly. The narrow roads and tall reedy grass were familiar, but it also looked identical to most of Oshiya's coast.

"There it is: the Bluette Dream House." Kana leaned forward and pointed between the seats. The collection of run-down bungalows was further back from the main tourist pier. The once-vibrant fuchsia pink was almost white from the years of sun and ocean wind.

Bluette Dream House was comically small; her memory of the house could not represent its compact size. Even as a kid, it was tiny in comparison to the extensive estate she called home.

"No one's home," Spencer confirmed as he returned to the car, tucking his gun into the back waistband of his pants. She adjusted the canvas bag of snacks over her shoulder as she followed him to the deck. The rush of the ocean waves down the slope and the taste of the briny air were calming. Despite the lack of cars near the pink house, a beaten Honda sat in the neighboring green bungalow's driveway.

The Dream House was long and narrow, and in order to leave space for a person to move around, everything was pressed against the left wall; a collapsible kitchen table was screwed in between a sunken sofa and the kitchenette. A fine layer of sand crunched under the soles of her flip-flops and compacted into the twine of the thickly woven entryway rug. The air smelled like old wood and salt. It felt familiar, like her mind was trying to draw memories from the depths of the well, and she was stuck in a déjà vu loop. Her feet carried her to the front right corner of the room, where the ashen floral wallpaper and the window frame met. Spencer continued down the hall and pushed the half-open door to the next room.

Her left hand traced over the print, and her eyes found the baseboard where a corner was peeling up. She shuffled closer and bent down to tear back the wallpaper. A memory of herself drawing a pink house on the peeled decorative paper overcame her, but there was nothing but the crusted gunk adhesive.

As she straightened up, she was startled to catch sight of Spencer on the front porch. His back was to her as he faced the horizon. He turned around, blinking once at her as if feeling her gaze on his back.

She leaned over and strained to pull the window open. The rush of salty wind blew against her skin.

"Neighbors?" she asked, knowing he had checked to see if people were around.

"No one."

Kana hummed.

"One night. We shouldn't stay any longer than that," he said, more to himself, and faced the ocean. She gave a half nod and drifted deeper into the sectioned house. She remembered there being stairs, but it clearly wasn't a multilevel house. This only added to her shit memory. The kitchenette was minuscule. She opened the fridge to find it empty and not cold. She reached over and tried to flick the light switch. The hollow click of the light without a bright flicker confirmed the power was out.

"There's no power," Kana shouted, her voice carrying easily through the small space, and walked into the second room.

The bedroom was stripped bare, but at least the queen

mattress was present. Another wave of intense déjà vu hit, her neurons firing, trying to make connections in her mind. This was the place she remembered, but it wasn't at the same time. The room she'd stayed in as a young child had an explosion of pinks. Maybe it was the same bedroom, but someone had repainted the walls, no longer having to cater to the whims of a spoiled child who had a fixation with the color pink.

The second door in the room was an empty closet. There wasn't a single hanger, extra pillow, or blanket stored inside. She was happy to leave the large spider in the right-hand corner in peace, but after a second look at the closet floor, she noticed it was wood. And not regular wood panels—they were much shorter strips of rectangular boards.

She saw herself: tiny Kana with silk bows mixing with her black hair as she crouched in this closet, her pudgy hands roaming over the corners of the wood, sliding the panels around as if moving a puzzle. Kana bit her lip as she bent down and ran her fingers over a strip of wood and tried to move it. The wood remained firmly in place. A warm puff of air was exhaled as she scolded herself. There was no way the floorboard was some complex Rubik's Cube that would magically open up if she moved the bottom-right square sixth from the corner, but without much thought, her hands moved on their own. Her muscle memory proved stronger than her episodic memories, and the slim wood panel bent in and shifted. The single block of wood dipped into a cubbyhole, like a secret pocket, allowing the rest of the rectangular pieces to move around.

She closed her eyes, holding her breath, a part of her afraid. She stuffed the fear down. Fuck it and let her hands move.

"Well, shit," Kana breathed as the last strip of wood fell in place with an audible click. She opened her eyes. The closet floor popped up, as if all the pieces in place triggered the panel below to lift, and at the far back wall, a glint of metal was visible. She shuffled around until she could reach and grip the handle. With a shove, she pushed the wooden floorboard into the closet wall until only the handle was left poking out.

She didn't remember the Bluette hut having a secret passageway, and she definitely didn't recall the creepy metal staircase descending into a black hole.

With a flashlight in hand from under the kitchenette sink, Kana stood in the closet doorway, shining the beam down the cavern. The stream of light revealed nothing else, just a staircase. She aimed the flashlight at the walls, but the light bounced right back as if there was a mirror.

"Spencer," Kana called out. Any courage she had to go down by herself, which wasn't much, vanished quickly.

"How did you find this?" Spencer asked, eyeing the dark, hidden stairwell.

"I remembered something," Kana answered vaguely.

"Do you know what's down there?"

Kana shook her head. "I think more rooms, but it's creepy as hell, so," she patted his chest muscles, "off you go." Honestly, Kana wasn't sure if Spencer would fit. The length of the space didn't look like it would allow anyone over 168 centimeters, but he somehow maneuvered his body down.

"Make sure to shout if you get attacked by a vampire," Kana joked, but in all seriousness, she didn't discount the fact he could be walking straight into a creepy lair. At least the underground lab at the campsite had proper lighting and ample space.

His footsteps became faint as Kana waited, her flashlight aimed where she'd last seen Spencer's back. She tapped her fingernail against the edge of the plastic flashlight. It took a long time to go down some steps.

"There's a switch," is what Spencer must have said, but she only heard a mumble of "*Sasitch*" before the lights blinked to life. "All clear." His voice was closer, probably at the base of the staircase.

Kana awkwardly extended her hand to the edge of the

rectangular hole and lowered herself down the stairs. After she passed the first six steps and bowed her head at a nearly ninety-degree angle, the space opened up. It was not a dingy basement that could be used for a serial killer's kill room. It was a fully furnished space done in a Nordic minimalist style, with a simple woven cream sofa and a shaggy white rug over hardwood floorboards. An artistically uneven wooden built-in with toys and books stood along one wall.

"Not what I was expecting," she admitted, as she bent at the waist and picked up a wool alpaca. Her eyes landed on a far back door.

"I checked. It looks like a girl's room. There's no one inside."

Kana's back went rigid as she set the stuffed animal down and pushed open the door. Three of the walls were in alternating shades of pink, starting from a vibrant orchid, to a flamingo, and a watermelon red. The carpet was the faintest splash of pink sherbert. Kana couldn't remember if there had ever been a bed in the space. But she felt like there had been a table and a chair, and the smell of coloring pens and waxy crayons. She walked the perimeter, her hand ghosting over where a bookcase used to be. There had been a window, or at least she thought there was one.

There were still hooks where a curtain road could hang and a perfectly square sunset picture glued to the wall with black strips of tape creating a cross, a child's crude drawing of a window frame. She swallowed, recalling a time when she had looked out a window to catch the sunset over the ocean. But there was no window because they were underground, and someone had created the image with curtains.

She sat crisscrossed in the center of the room, staring at the opposite wall, the only wall not coated in a pink hue. This wall had blocks of pink in shades from reds to purples. The frame around the wall made the large paint swatches seem like a giant cubist painting.

Bits of her childhood memory told her there was a window

inside a pink room, but reality was providing different evidence. No one had kidnapped her, but it wasn't impossible. Not all kidnappers were evil men in masks. Maybe a nanny or tutor had taken her, and she didn't realize where she had gone. But how did that explain the wooden puzzle board that opened the stairwell? She knew the pattern to unlock the code.

Kana's stomach churned again. She'd played in this room, and it felt and smelled the same, even though years had passed. With her eyes closed, she plucked at a memory. She could see herself walking down the staircase, calling a name: Sean, Sam, Sebastian, Simon. It started with an *S*. She reached for a hand, much larger than her own, and pulled the person to her room. The pink room had a large Victorian dollhouse under the window. There were pink and purple beanbags and plush toys.

"Kana," Spencer's voice was suppressed by a pillow over her ears.

Kana blinked, and he was kneeling in front of her. "There's something you should see," he said softly, as if providing a soothing balm of preparation.

"Is it some sort of lab full of babies in tanks, or a torture chamber?" Kana joked because she was one breath away from a mental breakdown.

"There's another room you should see. It's not as bad as anything you just suggested, but it's concerning." His tone was even and didn't give away anything.

She accepted his offered hand, strangling his as they both stood. He didn't say anything about her iron hold or question why she didn't release his hand as he led her to another door, this one crammed into the last available space on the wall of the first room. It looked odd, almost like there shouldn't be a door at all. The room was a little larger than a closet, narrow, and could fit two adults max, and even then, the lines of her and Spencer's bodies were pressed against one another.

From the ceiling to her waist was a two-way mirror looking

into the pink room. The view wasn't super clear—there was a film, almost like rose-tinted sunglasses—but it was certainly clear enough to see the people in the room, and it was even more obvious that when she was inside the pink room, she'd have had no idea the wall was a two-way mirror.

Chapter Thirty-One

There was an overwhelming rush, a heady brain fog that clogged her senses like churning butter as it thickened. She may have said something to Spencer, and then her eyes fixated on the V-thong of the red flip-flops as her feet left the closet space. *One, two, three*, she counted the stairs. Thirty-four steps.

She paced through the bungalow's cozy living room, and with each step, her anxiety slid through the slush of her brain. Her fingers itched for a cigarette, her throat burned for alcohol. She'd be happy with anything to take the edge off. Unfortunately, the house was empty. With the stolen bag of sweet treats offering the only indulgence, she tore through the first chocolate bar. Her teeth barely chewed before she swallowed, nearly choking twice as she went for a second and third bar, gorging until her stomach flipped, causing her to gag.

The crashing waves intermittently softened the edges of the thunder in her head; the old wooden bones of the house groaned with a strong gust, grounding her back in her sad reality. She inhaled a large gulp of the salty air as she slouched in defeat on the front steps that led down to the beach trail.

It could be worse. The room she'd played in for a brief

summer had a secret two-way mirror. Was it so different from a house bugged with tiny hidden cameras? The pink room was like a therapy room, where children interacted or spoke with a counselor. At the same time, the therapist observed and politely regaled the diagnosis and everything abnormal to the parents in the other room, about how the uncle was touching the child, how stuttering could stem from cruel classmates, how this child drew in dark colors but the mother was colored red—such roundabout and polite ways to say, *All in all, you are failing as parents, congratulations.*

Regardless of whether it was hidden video cameras or a two-way-mirrored room, Kana was hyperaware of her fleshy form: the layers of dirt and grime, the identical rough patches on her elbows with patchy flakes of dead skin.

She couldn't remember her time here, and that was what disturbed her the most. God, she was six, of course she didn't remember much. Even with the barest fragments she'd picked up, she couldn't trust the accuracy of those memories. She was sure there had been a window in the pink room. In her mind, she could feel a breeze (which in hindsight could have easily been the AC or a stationary fan), but the remnants of the jarring reality painted a different picture. Her knees bounced, and the plastic soles of the flip-flops slapped on the wooden step. It was fine, that was all in the past. This was just more proof of her deeply unstable childhood. She had been happy in the pink room. That was better than the alternative; there were certainly worse situations she'd been in. And there she went, over-rationalizing the situation.

The weight of a gaze sank into her hunched shoulders. The pinch of mint told her whose gaze was locked on her. Kana shoved the flimsy plastic wrappers into the bag before returning inside the bungalow. "What else was inside?"

Spencer was predictably standing near the front window, where he could watch her. "It's been a long day," he deflected.

"You're right, it has been a long day. The longest week of my life, actually, so I'd rather get this over with. What else was in the basement?"

Spencer was quiet as his eyes roamed over her expression. "Tunnels. If I were to guess, I'd say all of these bungalows connect."

Kana turned to look out the kitchen window at the blue home to their right. So much for one nanny owning the Bluette hut. Josephine must own the property if there was an underground network connecting the bungalows. "Any labs?"

"I didn't check thoroughly."

"It looks like an underground bunker for human trafficking," she muttered.

Spencer coughed a strangled sound, as if he'd choked on his spit.

"There have to be other rooms," Kana concluded.

"Do you remember what happened when you were here?" There was hesitation in his question as he tiptoed around it, wanting to know more, but wary of what might trigger a memory.

Kana crossed her arms over her chest and looked at the discolored stain on one of the sofa seat cushions. "No, I was here maybe one summer when I was in my first year at primary school. The most I remember was the pink room, and that wasn't—" Her voice gave up. She opened her mouth because she wanted to say, *That's not what I remember it being like* or, *There was a playroom and the nanny was nice*, but she couldn't speak. And what was wrong with her vision? Spencer was a blob of blacks and beiges.

She blinked as warm, wet tears fell out of her eyes. "Wh—" she blubbered. Kana never sobbed. Her voice sometimes shook, but even that was a rarity. Never again would she stand in front of adults and their scrutiny, their minds made up about who she was and how much she could fail. She snapped her mouth shut, and her hands flew to her face as she drowned. She wished she had blacked out. But no, she was painfully conscious of the uncontrollable tears flooding out of her eyes. Stringy snot collected in her prominent Cupid's bow, and her body shook like the last autumn leaf clinging for dear life on a branch. This was embarrassing, not because she was bawling in front of someone, but because she couldn't control her body.

A heavy material landed around her shoulders, and one hand against her lower back, and another around her shoulders led her to the sofa where she rolled into the back cushions and cocooned herself in the blanket Spencer had offered. At least she shut up and cried silently, rubbing her face in the extra fabric.

———

THE SMELL OF MEAT COAXED HER BACK TO THE LAND OF the living. With the tips of her fingers, she pushed the blanket down just in time to see a pair of long legs walking over to the wicker coffee table to set a mug and plate down.

"Is that goulash?" Kana croaked, squinting at the bowl of slosh. The ringlets of noodles poked out from the grayish hunks of meat. Thank god she'd regained control over her voice and her eyes.

"There were limited ingredients," Spencer said.

"Where did you even get ground beef?" she asked while sitting up and reaching for the steaming mug.

"A can."

Kana sipped the chamomile tea. "They don't have burger meat in a can."

She raised her swollen eyes to Spencer, just in time to catch a faint smile as he left to return to the kitchenette and returned with a can.

"You learn something new every day," Kana muttered, reading the label.

"They also have chicken in a can."

Kana rolled her eyes in response. From the absent natural sunlight, Kana guessed she had been asleep for at least six hours. She gulped down the remaining tea, ignoring Spencer, who sat on the floor. The sound of paper turning told her what he was doing, even though she couldn't see the book in his lap over the coffee table.

"You get to deal with me if this induces explosive diarrhea," she warned as she slid off the couch, clutching the blanket around her like a protective cape, and settled in front of the bowl. The gray, soggy, noodle mush wasn't as bad as she'd thought. The fact that she was willingly eating a burger from a can was a massive turnoff and almost made her lose her appetite, but she didn't have other options. It seemed even her stomach found the meat better than nothing.

The silence was unpleasant. Kana's clenched body was anticipating the moment when he would mention her breakdown. He was rather straightforward with her, so she expected him to bring up the dreaded topic, but as the silence stretched she supposed he was also respectful. He'd been concerned when she was topless in Vyolette's underground bunker, and there was a massive pile of shit in her background Oliver gave him, so maybe he wouldn't bring anything up.

"I—"

"What—"

They both began, with a momentary pause as they cut the other off.

"What else did you find?" Kana asked, not waiting for him to be polite and offer for her to continue. "Any video cameras or footage lying around?" It would be a hundred times easier if there was a backlog of film and she could hit a rewind button to see what happened.

"There were two other units. Each had two rooms the size of the living space here, and there was a smaller closet space with two-way mirrors. There wasn't anything else. The floors and walls all seemed to be made of concrete, and no other colorful rooms."

Kana forced down one more bite of the warm meal before letting the spoon clatter into the bowl and standing up.

"Where are you going?" Spencer asked when she didn't make her way to the kitchenette, but instead went back to the bedroom closet.

"Going to see for myself," she said and tightened the blanket around her shoulders. Soft thumps of a second pair of steps with longer strides became louder as she pushed open the closet door, and a warm hand touched the back of her arm.

"I don't think that's a good idea. Not today." His voice shouldered the concern, and she didn't need that; she shook off his hand.

"Didn't you say we were only staying for one night?"

It was hard to see his expression. The only source of light came from the single bulb from a standing lamp in the far corner of the bedroom. She continued down the steps, Spencer quietly following behind her. "Are there any cameras?"

"None," Spencer confirmed. "The jammer would have picked up a frequency."

Kana purposefully didn't look at the door that led to the pink room, instead whirling around, the long-haired fur of the carpet tickling the sides of her feet. "Where's the connecting hallway?"

Spencer led the way to the back wall of the space behind the staircase and pushed. She hummed in the back of her throat as the wall pivoted, only allowing enough space for one person to walk through at a time. Spencer went first, Kana clutching the thin blanket around her shoulders, feeling like a child following after an older friend in the dark, unfamiliar hallway.

"No dead bodies or captives?" she asked and attempted to see through the shadowed hallway.

"Nothing like that," he said as he stepped through, and the motion sensor lights blinked. The hallway was a narrow tunnel, the ceiling curved above them, and at the end was a flat white wall. The wall didn't have a handle, but it easily pivoted open to reveal the additional room. The space was about the size of a small living room, with cheap vinyl flooring; there were no other doors or furniture.

Circling the perimeter, Kana asked, "You checked the walls?"

"There's a door here." He pointed to the far-right wall, which he'd slid open to reveal a door with an electric keycode lock.

"Don't tell me you can hack into these things too?" Kana asked with a smirk, because she wouldn't be surprised if he had hacking skills. She would find something he couldn't do, eventually.

He twisted the doorknob. "It wasn't locked."

The room was similar to the hidden closet adjacent to the pink room. The wall revealed a two-way mirror.

"Look at this," he said, leaving the tiny room and opening a second door. This one was without a lock, but it also had a two-way mirror in the closet. It was an *Inception* of rooms, each wall a window into the other room. The first room was a blanket of white in the open space, the walls, floor, and ceiling, while the second room had a keypad lock—the only door with a lock. The third space they occupied had a desk shoved against the window with a clear view of the other two rooms. She leaned her weight on the desk, the oils of her fingertips blurring with a thick layer of dust.

Kana frowned as she returned to the first room, which felt like a vacant museum. She closed her eyes and inhaled. Her tutor had carefully placed stuffed animals into a single line against the white wall. There was a red panda, a koala, and a sea otter. Their heads were disproportionately large above their compact bodies. *Copy the tutor.* An order from a disembodied voice resurfaced.

"I think," Kana said more to herself as she opened her eyes, "I was in this room." She didn't remember ever practicing in the pink room, and when the tutor asked her to copy him, it had been in a space of white walls.

"Did something happen?" Spencer asked.

"No, it was boring." Kana didn't know if that was accurate. She had a vague outline of boredom that summer, compared to the summers when she bounced from the Disney parks in Tokyo and Paris and Florida, or the summer in the Maldives, or the one spent boating around the Greek islands. This summer had felt too similar to school.

Kana left the room. With more time, she could find the list of everyone hired to assist her when she was younger. The tutor's name had to be recorded on someone's payroll. Was it worth investigating and learning about what had happened down here? Time was precious. "Maybe Josephine's big plan was to build an underground science utopia," Kana joked as they climbed out of the closet floor. It seemed the doctor had a penchant for underground bunkers. Once Spencer managed to get his taller form out, she moved the wooden floorboards around and sealed the passageway.

———

She rested curled against the corner of the poor excuse of a sofa, her shoulders downturned with a hefty weight. Spencer preferred to keep any lights off, and while the bungalows may have been vacant, it was best not to alert anyone that they were squatting. They sat in darkness. Spencer had found a reading light clip tucked between the back row seats of the minivan. She glimpsed the cover of his book, an empty dark road stretching into the darkness with bold red text stamped on top. It seemed he'd found a beach-read thriller in the minivan.

She'd been sidetracked. She wasn't supposed to find a secret passageway to a spot from her childhood. *Fuel*. A headache formed after she repeated the word for the hundredth time in her head. She was really starting to hate that four-letter word.

"What is fuel?"

The soft pages shut as he closed the book. "It's material like coal or gasoline," Spencer said slowly, as if trying to discern whether this was a trick question.

"Let's try this again. When I say 'fuel,' you tell me the first things that come to mind. Fuel."

"Gas, exhaust, cars, highways, driving in the desert." His eyes moved away from her. The lines of his profile shifted as he looked out the window to the dark ocean off in the distance. "Mum driving to pick up fried chicken after a sports game. What did you think of when you think of fuel?"

"I thought of my first car, the private jet. Maybe it's not a bad idea to check out the hanger." She ran a hand through her oily hair. "The average person spends about forty-eight hours in the sky throughout their lifetime. You know I beat that record by the time I was two days old?"

Spencer, as usual, was quiet, with a pleasant stillness that told her he was listening. She hated that she was finding that rare ability to truly listen a bit too endearing. "Josephine went into labor on her way from Singapore to New York, but can you believe the worst snowstorm of the winter hit New York, and they rerouted the flight? I was born stuck in the air over the border of Canada and the US, after nearly twenty-two hours of labor. Josephine wanted to put the exact coordinates on my birth certificate for the location of my birth about 11,000 meters in the air, but that wasn't allowed."

"You don't think 'fuel' is hinting at an airplane or a specific spot?"

"Too obvious."

"The clues are specific to a memory or something in your childhood. What about a restaurant or a place you visited together?"

Kana laughed. "We didn't do bonding family dinners. In general, we were never celebratory. No extended family, since her parents died before I was born, and no siblings—" Kana stopped.

The newspaper. The lab was fashioned to be identical to Josephine's childhood home, the grandparents Kana had never met, and the word *fuel* connected with a spiderweb-thin string, weaving the bits of information together in a tentative hold.

Kana never had a chance to enter the house where Josephine grew up, which was sold immediately after Josephine's parents died. Kana's grandmother was the old-fashioned type and had neatly labeled photo books in chronological order, most of the pictures centered around the kitchen, pictures of grandma's culinary conquests and experiments. There was a collection of photos spanning a few years of Josephine's childhood, from when she was four to about seven. In one, young Josephine wore a red apron matching her mom's, with messy kitchen bowls piled high in the sink behind them, as freshly baked pies cooled on the kitchen island.

Kana was sixteen and had just gotten her license. One afternoon, after another short yet swift encounter with Josephine that left Kana boiling, she borrowed a friend's car and mindlessly drove. She didn't remember if she had visited her grandparents' home when she was younger. For some reason, she was on that side of town and decided to swing through the neighborhood. She forced the convertible to park along the sidewalk across the street. Under the brim of her baseball cap, she saw that the modest Victorian home had minor updates: a fresh coat of paint and a garden landscape. She ended up eating at a diner, enjoying a double-patty burger and a slice of cherry pie, or three slices of pie.

Stomach painfully full, she arrived home. The perfectly neat and swollen notes were a slap to Kana's face as she opened her front door. Kana wanted to turn on her heel and leave. She'd assumed Josephine would be in a lab, but she was tired of being the one to run. She sucked in a lungful of air and marched through the long hallway. Josephine, midway through a complex classical piano piece, probably Vivaldi, Bach, or another old master, stopped, the abrupt silence jarring as the last resounding note died a swift death. She turned and said, "You smell."

Kana ignored Josephine's comment. The grand piano was the centerpiece of the front room, and she was already up half the staircase when she heard the second comment.

"I hate cherry pie."

Naturally, Kana ordered a charity ball banquet centered around cherry pie as the theme. A photographer captured Josephine and Kana side-by-side, each with a forkful of pie. The entire night, Kana reveled in seeing Josephine's discomfort; the woman shook for the first time, her hands curled into fists. Who knew a little cherry pie was able to crack the all-powerful Josephine Ambrose?

Chapter Thirty-Two

"Cherry pie," Kana said, tasting the words. The more she mulled the idea over, the less confident she became. Josephine hated many things, from small, inconsequential things like time left on the microwave or blinds slanted in the wrong direction—according to her, there was a right way to close blinds—to people being incompetent and the blatant misogyny in nearly every industry. But what else connected Josephine's childhood home to the word *fuel*? She was now forty percent confident in her initial guess.

"You need sleep," she stated. Spencer was, by some miracle, still standing on two feet, guarding the bedroom door. Aside from her maybe-blackouts, he didn't seem to rest, and how was he supposed to be any use as a bodyguard if he didn't get the minimal amount of sleep?

She moved off the bed. "We'll leave in a few hours. Is there hot water?"

He gestured to the closet. "Downstairs, there's a half bathroom. The generator has been working well enough."

"I'll shower."

She didn't wait for Spencer to respond and clomped down

the staircase to the bathroom. By the time she returned, he'd curled his long legs up on the couch to keep them from dangling off the end. She laid out a blanket on the floor—god knew what was embedded in the carpet fibers—as she tried to conjure any other potential location with the image of syrupy cherries and golden-brown crust imprinted behind her eyelids.

———

"I'm driving," Kana said, "you can chill in the back or be a good silent passenger." She jabbed her thumb over her shoulder. The drive was calming—Kana tapped along to the bubble gum summer pop songs. Spencer wouldn't let her roll down the windows, so she was stuck with the air blowing through the dusty car vents.

"You eat counterclockwise," he pointed out.

Kana paused mid-chew, her left cheek puffed with soggy bread. "And?" she asked, taken aback by the abrupt comment. Only one other person had pointed out that habit.

Spencer shrugged. "An observation."

"If I drove us to a pier, would you let me get on a boat and sail away?" she asked.

"You know the answer," was Spencer's response. She hummed and pushed the cheap sunglasses back in place as they slid down her nose. Spencer allowed her space to enjoy the brief time, but necessity forced her to crawl into the back and sit on the car floor when they needed gas, fearing the security cameras.

"This isn't the end," Kana said as she poked her head between the driver and passenger seats. They left the coastal city and wound further inland, the roads leveling out along with the land-scape of flattened fields.

"She doesn't own the diner, but she continues to prove me wrong. I didn't think she owned the pink bungalow, but that turned out to be incorrect, and she even made a nice renovation.

But a diner, that doesn't seem like her," Kana ended flatly. Josephine would leave her final message permanently in the sky if she could. Something obscene and grandiose was her style.

Yesterday—or had it been two days ago?—when Spencer had asked what she thought would be at the end of all this, Kana knew deep down that she was expecting to find a body. Supposedly, Josephine had been gone for over eight months. The woman had connections, and a grand adventure revealed posthumously seemed like the perfect last game to drag Kana back into her orbit.

"It's still around," Kana commented in surprise as the brakes squealed to a stop. Spencer parked directly across from the diner, at a run-down bank with their key logo out front splattered with old soda residue. An overgrown bush partially hid the cardboard cut-out "Open" sign in the front window, but an even larger sign in the next window clearly advertised the special: "FUEL YOUR-SELF WITH A SLICE OF PIE. BUY 1 GET 1 FREE." Kana laughed as she fixed the hat on her head. If that wasn't an obvious sign, she didn't know what was. With her hands shoved into the windbreaker, she crossed the street with Spencer.

Spencer, after peeking inside, held open the door for her. The run-down space was inhabited by seven customers, regulars of the establishment, judging by their relaxed postures. Four teenage boys with matching red jerseys were engrossed in an elaborate conversation at the farthest table, the tallest boy howling with laughter, the one beside him shoving at his thin arm, while ceramic mugs plopped onto the countertop with clipped sounds as two men in their seventies sat beside one another, mumbling about the papers in their hands.

"Take a seat anywhere," a man behind the counter said over his shoulder as he carried two large plates with chicken and waffles over to the boy's table.

"That looks good." Kana stood on her tiptoes, trying to get a better look at the steaming, crispy chicken.

"Come." Spencer grazed the inside of her arm, but didn't

touch her any further as he led her to a table. While she was admiring the chicken, he'd probably cataloged each person in the diner, and the windows and doors.

"Good morning, my name—" the young teenage waitress started introducing herself. A bit of pink lip tint was stuck to her upper tooth.

"How long has that sign been up? The buy one, get one pie?" Kana dove straight into her question.

"Er—" The girl fiddled with the mini spiral notebook in her hand. "It's always been there. I mean, I just started a month ago, and it was there."

"May we please have a soufflé pancake, coffee," Spencer ordered, and paused, looking at Kana.

"Slice of cherry pie."

"Will that be all?" The new waitress carefully wrote out the order.

"Yes, thank you," Spencer answered politely.

Kana moved to slide out of the booth, but Spencer stuck out his leg, their limbs knocking against one another.

"Am I not allowed to go to the bathroom?" Kana asked.

"You are going to do more than that," he said. "I'll come with you."

"It'll look more suspicious if we both go to the bathroom," Kana hissed as she shoved her leg against his, knocking it away and stepping out. "So overprotective," she said louder, petting his hand mockingly.

She went down the narrow hallway and found the single door with a rectangular sign marked with two metal triangle-shaped people. She did have to use the bathroom, and if she meandered around the diner, then sue her, because apparently it was common for Josephine to build hidden rooms. The diner was completely unremarkable and forgettable. Her face twisted at the sight of the grimy bathroom. There were streaks on the walls where it looked like someone had attempted to clean, but rust covered the edges of the mirror, and its cheap glass warped her reflection. She left as soon as she entered, the soles of her shoes gripping to the floor by a sticky substance.

"They don't have cherry pie," Spencer announced as she plopped back down.

Kana got back up and went to the counter. The squeak of the plastic cushion moving told her Spencer was right behind her.

Kana knocked on the counter as she leaned forward, watching the teenage waitress crouching behind the refrigerator display of baked desserts, shoving a key lime pie beside a bright yellow custard one.

"I really want a piece of cherry pie," Kana explained.

"Sorry, we don't sell that," the waitress said, sliding the display door closed.

"Is it a seasonal option?" Kana pressed.

"Um," the waitress faltered. "I don't think the diner does seasonal specials."

"You don't think," Kana echoed, and she felt a gentle hand on her back, a warning. Kana glared at Spencer.

"Let me ask the manager. He's been here longer," she squeaked and scurried into the back kitchen.

"You got your hands full with that one," a voice said, the words frayed at the edges.

Kana immediately turned to the old man who'd spoken. He sipped his coffee, smiling at her and Spencer, but clearly addressing Spencer.

"Excuse me," Kana said slowly. He wasn't smiling in a mocking way, so she was going to give him the benefit of the doubt.

"I meant no offense," he said, "my wife was demanding, always knew what she wanted, and wouldn't take no for an answer, but as soon as we were in public, she was docile. You should have seen her when she was pregnant. She had the strangest cravings: pickles and peanut butter. It's good to see girls these days taking charge, being more vocal outside."

"Sir," Spencer began before Kana had the chance to snap at the old fart. Had he somehow implied she was pregnant while praising her for not taking no for an answer about pie?

"It's nice that we remind you of your wife. It sounds like she's passed, given you are speaking of her in the past tense, but I would refrain from commenting on the status of strangers' relationships and generalizing women." Spencer continued politely.

The man chuckled. "Ah, yes, of course. I'm a feminist. My niece is a lesbian."

"Commenting on how girls like me express our opinions doesn't make you a feminist, and neither does commenting on your token niece, you old fu—"

"Excuse me," the waitress cut in, "the manager would like to speak to you?"

"She's cute when she's angry," the second geezer commented, grinning.

Kana took a step toward the old man, a verbal lashing on the tip of her tongue. Spencer slid his arm through hers and tugged her away.

"Spit in their coffee," Kana spat at the waitress as she held open the swinging kitchen door.

The waitress's head cocked in a questioning manner, but her words died as the door closed and a gruff voice asked, "You the one asking about cherry pie?"

Kana shoved Spencer's arm off her shoulder. The manager was a man in his early sixties, with a receding hairline that was erasing chunks of thin hair from the temples first. He motioned for them to follow him into a small office space, where he collapsed into a rickety chair, the seat cushion worn and concave to hold the manager's ass in a perfect hug.

"I had cherry pie here," Kana said. "I know you sell it."

"Hate to break it to you, kid, but we haven't sold cherry pie in years."

"What do you want?" Kana asked. "You don't bring customers in the back because they are asking about a product you apparently don't sell."

He stroked his jaw; the rough skin held divots of old acne scars. "When did you have cherry pie?"

"Is this some secret code?" Kana asked with a raised brow.

The man shrugged.

"Autumn twenty thirteen."

"Full date, kid."

Kana scowled, not appreciating the degrading nickname, as if the age gap between them made her a lesser person. She tried to narrow down the month when a chill ran down her spine, and cold, wet flurries splashed against her.

"Fuck," she cursed. "Portal," she said to Spencer, who was out the door, gun in hand, without a moment of hesitation. "Shit is about to go down at this diner. What do you have?" Kana demanded.

A muffled scream and shouts followed closely behind Kana's question. The manager's eyes widened as he jumped out of the office chair and moved to rush out of the tight office space.

Kana whipped out her gun and blocked his path. "She hated cherry pie," Kana said. "What did she leave with you?"

He lunged. To be fair, Kana was half his weight, and he must have thought he could take her or that she wouldn't shoot. He was mistaken as the expelled bullet sent a sharp crack, and he bent forward as the bullet pierced through his leg.

He cried in pain before the rants and half-curses spewed.

"I will shoot you again," Kana said.

"The fire extinguisher. It's by the back door," he growled.

She swiftly left the office. There wasn't anyone in the kitchen, but the swinging door told her someone had just left. Through the opening where food sat on the warming counter, she saw

Spencer move through the diner, vanishing from her sight, but she caught a flurry of people escaping out of a broken window, the sharp sound of metal hitting objects. The heady taste of mint told her he was holding his own. She ran for the back door, her eyes locked on the red fire extinguisher, when someone stepped out of the wall to her right. A woman, dressed casually in jeans and an old jean jacket—not like an assassin or ex-military—aimed a hefty, very illegal, automatic gun at Kana. Automatic weapons were prohibited, and while by no means was it impossible to locate one, it confirmed she was not in any official sector of the government.

"That seems unnecessary," Kana commented as she held her hands up, finger clearly off the trigger.

The woman cracked a smile. "Can't take chances. Toss the gun." She gestured with her weapon to the floor. Kana slid the gun onto the floor and kicked it to the older woman.

"Move," was the next command.

Kana didn't have a choice. The woman could make her tenderized steak with that massive gun. Even if Kana could have miraculously shot her gun, she had to be a hell of a shot and ensure, without a doubt, that one bullet was enough.

"Two," the woman said, holding up two fingers. "One."

Kana clicked her tongue, resigned to start walking. She pointedly avoided looking anywhere but straight ahead, not wanting to clue anyone in to the reason she was there. She had two knives, one in her back pocket, the other a flat razor tucked in the underwire of her bra.

A sedan waited only a meter away from the back door. Sirens whooping in the distance spurred the woman to dig the butt of the weapon into Kana's back to urge her faster into the awaiting vehicle. Whoever this team was, they hadn't shot and asked questions later. That was always a good sign. The door opened and someone was waiting—not a burly man with another gun, but a familiar face.

"George," Kana said in surprise.

George wore a thin navy sweater, the extra fabric hanging loose on his lithe frame. He must have lost sixteen kilograms since she saw him. He didn't look good, almost like he was still experiencing the Fever. His glowing sun-worshiped skin was gone, and instead his flesh was sallow and gray with splotches of flushed pink, lacking any shade of blue. He was not Stamped, which irked her. The Fever should be over.

His body leaned heavily against the door, angled to face her as soon as the door was opened. The pressure of the barrel of the gun against her shoulder blade told Kana she needed to get in the car.

"Enjoying your new status?" Kana asked, the door slamming shut behind her. She eyed George's gloved hands that were neatly folded in his lap.

"What did you give us?" His voice was unrecognizable, coarse and muffled, as if he'd screamed all night.

"Exactly what you asked for," she said.

In under three seconds, his hand reached between the seat and the car door, whipped out a gun, and fired. Hot pain exploded in her right arm. She gasped as her left hand went to clutch her right bicep. The woman and driver didn't flinch as the bullet lodged itself in the car frame. The additional nozzle stifled the gun's firing. How considerate for all their ears.

"Fucker," she hissed, blinking through the gathering wetness in her eyes. "You'd know I'm telling the truth if you bothered to cross-check the vials and serial numbers."

His ashen face twisted in anger. "You forged the records. You and your butler did something. The drug is wrong."

Oh. Kana had forgotten about Oliver. He was the one who'd supplied the drugs during Vyolette's soiree, but she was certain Oliver hadn't done anything to the drugs. She doubted Spencer had bothered to tamper with them.

"You knew the risk," Kana said.

He hissed at her, more animal than human as anger stormed through his expression. "The Rabid side effect only happens when you overuse your power."

Kana stilled, and the pounding of her blood in her arm felt like a beating drum. "You can't be Rabid," Kana said, struggling to comprehend George's claim. It was impossible. George had passed through the Stamped stage, and his designation had already surfaced. All of that in less than a week? Even if his ability had manifested by now, there was no way he'd used enough to even to come close to entering a Rabid state. Her eyes narrowed as she looked for any other exposed bit of skin; his hands were gloved, and it seemed only George's face and neck were visible. Not a speck of blue.

"I almost believe that confused look," he said in a low voice.

"Maybe you're confusing the end of the Fever stage," Kana replied. It hadn't been a week yet; any semblance of consciousness wasn't being drowned in agony or warped by delusions.

"Does this look like the Fever?" he growled as he pushed up the cashmere sleeve.

The flesh of his forearm shifted as if made from soft gelatin. There were irregular translucent splotches where the veins, shifting muscles, and tendons were visible. Kana blanched as thousands of tiny worm-like organisms moved beneath the flesh. A shiver sent spindles of pain from her wounded arm to the rest of her body.

"I've never seen"—Kana tore her eyes away from his arm to look at his face—"that happen to anyone." What an understatement. His arm was ghastly. She wondered if George could feel them moving.

"You have the cure."

Kana frowned. "I don't have any cure. Whatever bullshit is being spread, I don't know about a cure for Synthies."

"If you don't have it, Josephine does, or she has the capability to make one."

Kana wanted to roll her eyes, but held back. She didn't want to get shot a second time. "Josephine has been missing for months."

George's face darkened, the veins in his neck protruded as he coiled his anger. She could taste the desperation, and Kana wasn't sure if she could locate Josephine, but she was confident; this delusion that Josephine would have a cure was a useless hope. Shadows consumed the entirety of the car as the sedan drove under an overpass and through a tunnel. As light filtered back, she looked beyond George at the heavily tinted surroundings. She couldn't recognize anything besides the line of trees.

"Good thing I have her daughter, then," George said.

Kana didn't say anything. He would find out soon enough that she wasn't a bargaining chip.

"You haven't asked about the others," George commented.

"Don't care," Kana replied, and she really didn't.

"Ingrid pussied out, and if she had left instead of trying to care for Vyolette, she might have lived. Vyolette is . . ." He grinned. "Well, you'll see shortly."

Kana could do without the ominous warning and the maniacal smirk.

Chapter Thirty-Three

The house was an overly modern design. The right half of the main building was a blank slate of concrete, from roof to walls, without even a square hole for a window; the other half was the complete opposite, a massive single paned window came together with a cleverly crafted clear beam to connect the roof of glass. Young Japanese maples symmetrically lined the curved garden hedges; in autumn, their leaves would be streaks of blood.

The driver stepped out of the car first. The chunks of rock crunched loudly under his thick boots, and as he opened George's door, the woman opened Kana's side and manhandled her out of the car, gun discouraging Kana to make any sudden movement.

"Strip her," George ordered as the driver lowered George into a wheelchair. Kana pointedly stared at George's legs, wondering if they were completely useless. "We'll be waiting in the study." The driver pushed George along the line of Japanese maple trees.

The woman motioned with her gun. "You heard him."

Kana sighed as she struggled to pull off the sweatshirt, shirt, and bra. Her arm felt like it was on fire as wet blood leaked out of the hole and down her wrist, into the palm of her hand. The woman didn't reveal any surprise at the hidden blade and razor as she tossed them into the open trunk of the car. After a quick and clinical assessment that Kana wasn't concealing anything, "Underwear too,"

Kana sighed. "What, does he want you to finger me to make sure I don't have a tracker up my vagina, or maybe squat and cough?" She slid off her underwear, and the woman threw her a package of boxers and a black shirt.

"Let's go," the woman said the moment Kana had struggled into the massive cotton shirt with her injured arm, the waistband of the boxers barely hanging onto her slim hips.

Kana tightened her hair in the scrunchie. "Can I wear those shoes, or do I get a new pair?" She pointed to the discarded sneakers beside her bundle of rumpled clothes.

The woman quirked her brow and cocked her gun. "Move."

The rocks dug into Kana's fleshy soles as she headed up the driveway. A short man, close to Kana's height, scuttled out from the side of the house, keeping his head tucked down. He slammed the trunk down and drove the car around the side of the property. Kana was weaponless and laughably outnumbered. She needed to stall for time and figure out how the hell she would wiggle out of this trap.

The front door had a waterfall feature with a portion of thick glass that sealed the water cascading down. The woman let out a low whistle, impressed—evidently, this was also her first time entering the home. Kana pushed the door to let it swing half open. Without a doubt, this reeked of George's family's bourgeois taste. Inside, a second water feature curved diagonally across the open space like the arcs of a rolling valley, water flowing down and vanishing into the concrete ground.

"Do I get a tour?" Kana asked.

"We don't have all day." The woman nudged Kana further into the estate, where two guards were stationed by a set of French double doors. Across their chests were guns larger than the woman's torso. The weight of the weapons alone looked uncomfortable.

"Boys," Kana said. The man on the right opened the door, and the smell stunned Kana; she had to lean back. She'd smelled a lot of death in her life. There was that unfortunate time when she'd been in a room with a dead woman for half a day. But this was not the stench of old blood, it was acrid pus and rot that had been souring for days, and an immediate gag punched through her. At least she had the sense not to curse out loud.

Vyolette. It could only be her, but if George hadn't mentioned that she would be here, Kana wouldn't have recognized her. Vyolette's body was bloated, as if she had eaten ten of herself and been submerged in water for years. The slippery skin was blistering like large air pockets on pizzas, and like George, she lacked any hint of blue. She wasn't Stamped either, and worse, her Rabid state was plain on her face. Her skull had reformed, her forehead protruding as if a softball had been forced beneath the skin, obscuring Vyolette's facial features, aside from a glimpse of her bottom lip and chin. There was a wheezing sound, like the hiss of a machine.

"She wants you to come closer," George stated as he wheeled away from the window and approached the edge of the large carpet, between Kana and Vyolette.

Kana didn't move.

George grinned as he snapped his fingers, and a man built like a professional heavyweight champion stepped into view. The lower half of his face was covered by a large mask as he lumbered behind the sofa and pushed. Jean Royère was rolling in his grave at the installed wheels on his iconic polar bear sofa, but apparently a necessary adjustment to guide the sofa across the space.

"Look at her, and tell me the drug you gave us wasn't tampered with," George hissed.

The smell was nauseating. Kana stopped the airflow from her nostrils and tried to breathe through her mouth, but even then, the air particles were saturated. The couch stopped in the center of the room, and Kana finally caught sight of the origin of the stench.

Vyolette's body was laid out on a tarp. She was perched near the edge of the sofa because her head was split in the back, letting bits of brain matter dribble down into a pool of liquid building in the folds of the plastic, while the large trapezius muscle and flesh had torn open, revealing a half-formed ribcage ripping through. Rotting, tumorous flesh clumped together and slid around the black tarp, bits spilling over the edges and soaking into the carpet.

"If Oliver gave you a faulty drug, that's not my problem," Kana managed.

"Get your butler then," George said.

"I hope you have a Ouija board or a priestess on hand, because that's the only way we can speak to him. He's dead."

"Tell me I'm beautiful." Vyolette's voice barely escaped her mouth.

Kana ignored Vyolette's question. "How many did you eat?"

Vyolette's rolls jiggled like a mountain of Jell-O, as if she were laughing.

"Four," George answered. "Poor Ingrid."

"You didn't try to stop her? You know Rabid Hunger gets worse as they eat people." Kana glared at George; it was easier to look at him than Vyolette.

George clicked his tongue. "We want the cure."

Kana leveled her gaze on George, who pushed his wheelchair closer to her; they were both pointedly ignoring Vyolette, the girl's breathing the low rumble of a truck engine.

"I don't have a cure. I don't have contact with Josephine. No one does."

"Vyolette's hungry. Why don't we give her a little snack. Five little rice cakes?"

Kana swallowed as she stepped back—this was not good. Two guards were standing outside the door behind her, two across from her, one man stationed in front of the door in the right corner, and the other massive one with the strength to move Vyolette circled the room. Her back bumped into a solid chest, and the heavyweight champion snatched her injured arm. She shrieked at the pain zinging up and down.

"My answer is not going to change. I don't know where she is, but I'm looking for her," Kana said, trying to subdue the panic in her voice. "When I find her, I'll gladly turn her over, but I need time."

"And you thought your mother was taking a break in a run-down diner?" George asked sarcastically. He lifted his chin, eyes commanding the sumo wrestler behind her, and she was forced two steps forward.

"I'm not fully human. She can't digest me," Kana argued, trying to lean all her weight against the man, even though she knew it was futile.

"We'll give you time, but Vyolette is hungry and has acquired a taste for Naturals. Says they taste like fresh lamb." George grinned, and the overly macho man dragged Kana to Vyolette.

Kana flailed, trying to twist her body away. She managed a kick at his groin, but he didn't flinch as he moved her closer to Vyolette, whose mouth opened, the bare animal instinct to eat seemed to be the only thing she was capable of. Rabid Synthies inflicted with hunger only ate people, people who, notably, were not infected. George wasn't teasing her to scare her; Vyolette was eating other Users. Was that why the Rabid Synthie had attacked Oliver?

Vyolette shifted. Her eyes still weren't visible under the sagging skin, but her stretched nostrils flared as if smelling ripe flesh.

"It'll only hurt a little. The fingers snap easily," George taunted. Kana could see him scooting his wheelchair closer. The fucking bastard wanted a front-row seat. "Then maybe she'll go up your arm slowly, or ask for your skin to be sliced like prosciutto, or fried into a chip."

Kana was panicking, a part of her denying her situation, the other, rational part telling her this was not like staring at the barrel of a gun aimed at her face or a bomb strapped to her chest. This was the promise of a painful, slow, sadistic array of pain. Begging wouldn't do much; George would derive too much enjoyment from watching her grovel and would draw it out even more. *Shit.* Kana thrashed harder. She tried kicking, but it was difficult when the man was behind her.

He forced her arm forward to the unhinged jaw that opened wide. The cavernous hot breath exhaled against Kana's trembling fingers as she struggled to yank her hand away. There weren't any Users around for her to piggyback off. The gaping mouth was the depths of a leviathan, a massive chasm with rings of teeth, and it snapped closed. She threw out all her stored energy. A foreign sensation, the thrumming of a hummingbird's wings, rippled through her chest and shot down her arm and out of her hand.

It was a surprise when her fingers didn't snap off; instead, a gurgling scream tore loose as the couch wheels screeched backward, jolting as though a car had rammed it head-on. The acrid breath and glinting teeth were gone. Kana took advantage of the distraction and smashed her foot on the guard's boot and managed to slip out of his grip.

Kana ran, her eyes honing on a porcelain vase. She tried to move her right arm, but it was useless. Unable to feel her limb, she had to visually confirm it was still attached to her body. With her left hand, she smashed the vase and gripped a large shard while swinging her body around the wheelchair-bound George.

"Don't move!" she warned the guards, who had guns aimed at her. The scene in front of her peaked into a static fuzz as the guards bled to black. Now was not the time to black out. Her grip on the chunk of porcelain tightened; she didn't realize she had dug the pointed shard into George's neck.

She shrieked as a slippery, sweaty, see-through hand grabbed her and teeth sank into her forearm. A scream ripped through her, and she did the only thing she could. She smashed her head down to collide with the crown of George's head. A loud crack stunned both of them, giving her enough leeway to rip her arm free while stabbing the broken ceramic into him a second time. The shard met little resistance as it pushed into the supple flesh and muscles of his neck.

Bullets weren't pounding through her body. She stumbled back, her right arm limp and useless against her side as she pressed her left forearm to her ribs to staunch the little bleeding. A splat and a slopping sound like heavy, wet towels flopping on the ground made her turn to her right. Vyolette slid off the couch, attempting to crawl to Kana. The two guards were trying to keep Vyolette's body together. The back of the sofa hid most of the grotesque body parts erupting out of the back of her head and spine, black, bloody masses that looked like liquid-filled trash bags, as if her organs were displaced and ballooning and ready to spew at any moment.

One guard shouted for help as he crouched down to use the plastic tarp to keep the internal organs from spilling out further. Vyolette roared. The sound didn't come from her mouth but from behind her, and the guard screamed. Crunching noises and slurping sounds rattled through the room.

Where the hell was Spencer? The tracker in the hair scrunchie had been transmitting her location. Now would be a great time for him to swoop in, guns a-blazing, and lean into the white knight role.

George gripped his neck while the other hand feebly tried to wheel himself closer to her. His eyes quivered, bouncing around like olives in a jar, as if he couldn't see properly. Drool leaked out of his mouth as his tongue, twice as long as it should be, snaked out and lapped around his lips, the tip curling at the bottom of his chin and slinging up to his upturned nose.

A cold, sickening sensation gripped her body as she looked down at her left arm. Sharp teeth marks marred the inner flesh of her forearm. Only a small collection of blood pooled around two of the deepest marks. He broke her skin. Kana started to hyperventilate. *Never, ever, let an infected person contaminate you.* She was going to be sick. The tiny worm creatures swimming under his flesh could be inside her now. Microorganisms multiplying and wiggling around her bloodstream, sliding through her tendons, and infesting her organs. Bile made its way up her throat. Her skin would slowly fade until all that was left was a plastic wrap, barely containing her atrophying muscles and those disgusting little worms feeding off of her.

Kana swallowed hastily as she ran to the nearest door. The sweet scent of leather offered a welcome relief from the foul pus cloud she'd been trapped in; she sensed someone about to move through a door or wall, but the familiar, overpowering mint signaled the person she was waiting for.

"Took you long enough!" Kana shouted as Spencer threw open the door. She barely discerned a waft of darkening cherries over Vyolette's decaying stench. A second person phased through the wall to her right. It was the woman who'd led her to George's car and up to the house, but she was not attacking Kana or Spencer. Instead, the woman swiped a bead of sweat along her hairline, her face flushed with exertion, her body poised and prepared to strike.

Kana opened her mouth to speak, but the cloud of mint lashed out like a whip, yanking her forward just as George propelled himself from his wheelchair and into the space where she had been standing. The woman fired rounds, not at Kana or Spencer, but at George, who flopped on the ground as the bullets blasted through him. Good, the woman was on their side.

"Are you alright?" Spencer asked in a single breath. His eyes moved swiftly, cataloging the injuries. He zoned in on her left arm, to the blood that stained her skin where George's teeth had sunk in, and then her right. His nostrils flared, as if he could tell it was paralyzed and useless.

"Through and through," Kana commented. She couldn't feel the pain from the bullet wound anymore, because she couldn't feel anything. Her first assumption was that the energy from pushing Vyolette's body back had somehow exited from her hand. That was something she'd have to visit at a later date if she managed to survive this ordeal.

"What the fuck is that?" The woman looked over at Vyolette, who wiggled around the bodyguard like a snake, her mouth unnaturally large, the jawbone distending out of place and chewing through the man's torso.

"We need to move," Spencer said while moving further into the room and unloading his gun through Vyolette's head. "Burn them and do it fast," Spencer added as Kana rested her weight against the door.

"Infection control," she commented, wiping her forehead with the back of her left hand. The room felt ten degrees warmer. Was she coming down from the adrenaline high, or was she infected by George's bite? "If I got rabies . . ." Kana muttered.

"We're leaving. Handle the bodies, code silence," Spencer said to the woman and turned to Kana, who was trying to tamp the hurdling anxiety about potential infection. "Can you walk?"

Kana nodded, and they hurried through the house, passing by fallen bodies. There were no pools of blood. A nondescript sedan with its engine running was parked by the side garden.

"There's something very wrong with the drug. That was George and Vyolette," Kana said as she shoved herself into the passenger seat while Spencer ripped open a medical kit he had in the glove compartment.

"I know."

A harsh, dry laugh cut through her throat. "Great, glad you have a secret network. I'm guessing the woman back there is an old teammate?"

"What's wrong with your arm?" he asked, ignoring her question.

Kana couldn't feel his hands twisting her arm. At first, she thought he meant her left arm with the bite, but he lifted her right one, the paralyzed one, which also had a gunshot wound.

"Vyolette was going to snack on my hand," Kana said. His face darkened at the implication. Vyolette would have eaten more than just her hand. "I had to push, and as you know, I'm abnormal. My arm is useless for now."

"To answer your earlier question, Maud owed me a favor. I needed someone to watch the three you gave the drugs to. She's been doing independent contracting work for years now."

Maud, very much not the waitress, was not good at her job and Kana loudly voiced her failing performance review of Spencer's friend.

"She wouldn't have let you get hurt too much. There were complications and more guards to handle." Spencer finished dressing her bullet wound and drove them away from the property.

Kana looked in the side mirror as the cabin estate became smaller and smaller in the distance. "I think Mr. President knows about the faulty drugs."

Spencer's silence was his response.

"I don't know if Josephine purposefully altered the version, or maybe Oliver began to cut corners and tailored something in the drug's makeup. Who knows. But the president knows, and he wants the cure."

"You don't think Oliver swapped the real drug and gave your acquaintances a bad dose?"

That was possible, but it implied Oliver carried around both a lousy and a proper version.

"We need evidence," Spencer continued.

Kana rolled her eyes. "Break into a lab and snatch up some of the drugs then, and while you're at it, we can find some people to test it on, too."

"You are making a massive allegation against the president. If he is knowingly allowing bad formulations to be circulated . . ." Spencer drifted off, unable to complete the implication. Deals were made across borders; this wasn't about dosing their own militia. The ramifications would blow up their agreements with fellow countries.

"Fine. Let's assume Oliver is the evil mastermind and that only a small amount of the drug is bad enough to make people go straight to a Rabid state after the Fever breaks. George was different. His symptoms weren't like the others; there wasn't any fungi, and he wasn't hankering to eat anyone. Did you see his skin?"

"We need to find Dr. Ambrose."

Yeah, no shit. What did he think they were doing these past few days? But it was more than that now. Any thoughts about the president hijacking and toying with her barreled through the metaphorical wall. Josephine was playing a larger game, tampering with the compound of A.E. Potentia, and Kana wanted to know why.

"We have to go back and get the fire extinguisher."

CHAPTER THIRTY-FOUR

KANA COULDN'T FOCUS on the drive. One minute, they were winding down the valley hills, and then they were parked on a side street half a block away from the diner. The commotion had caused every officer from the nearest two districts to descend upon the rundown restaurant, which drew the nosy townsfolk, who clumped around the barred street, trying to see what was happening.

"Let me," Spencer said, retrieving the mini bottle of antibacterial solution out of Kana's left hand. Her paralyzed right arm was no longer her paramount concern—any sensation from her shoulder down was nonexistent—it was her left arm she was scared of.

Spencer drowned her forearm in an antibacterial solution. The minor tears in her arm fizzled and stung as white froth hid the dried blood. He tore a packet of gauze and nimbly wrapped her arm, concealing the bite from her sight.

"I have some clothes and shoes," was the last coherent sentence she heard. She awoke with her skin feeling crispy and hot, as if she were recovering from an awful sunburn or laser treatment. Groaning, she moved, shoveling through the sludge of fatigue quicksand. Her cheek rubbed against the rough material of a denim jacket that was draped over her front like a blanket. They were not in her grandparent's hometown. Spencer, sensing her return from the land of dreams, cleared his throat.

"We are a little over two hours west. Apparently, the owner of the restaurant is now the local hero, wounded in the midst of an attempted robbery."

Kana snorted. Well, she didn't have to do damage control for the diner. The owner wouldn't be keen on divulging to the police that Kana Ambrose had shot him. "And here we are." The car rolled onto a plot of a gravel drive-up in front of a collection of boxy units, which looked like someone had enlarged cardboard delivery boxes, and plopped them on a plot of land, cheap, rentable, single cubes. Before Kana could gather her words to reprimand Spencer, he threw his thumb over his shoulder. "I have the fire extinguisher in the back."

Kana's lips parted to ask if he'd snag the right one. The restaurant had to have more than one fire extinguisher; it was the one—

"Specifically, the one in the hallway, closest to the bathrooms. You gave me instructions earlier."

Kana sniffed as she shrugged the oversized denim jacket over her shoulders while Spencer disappeared into the rectangular trailer that acted as the concierge and popped back out in less than five minutes, a room key in hand. He drove to the farthest box.

"If I start to lose my shit, just kill me fast," Kana said as Spencer opened the brown door with a tarnished, crooked "08."

She didn't wait for him to sweep the room, instead collapsing onto the nearest twin bed. The smell of stale cigarettes and citrus disinfectant caused her to sneeze.

"Do you care so little about your life?" Spencer asked, locking the door behind him while setting the duffel bag at the foot of the unclaimed bed.

Kana's lips curled. "If I'm reduced to anything like Vyolette, or George, that isn't living."

"What are your symptoms?" Spencer asked as he crossed the narrow walkway into the bathroom.

Kana rolled onto her back, her left arm clutching her invalid one, her nails digging into the skin. "I'm not feeling a ravenous hunger for meat, so don't worry. George had something inside of him, and I'm guessing you don't have contact with any leading doctors in infectious diseases. Unfortunately, my go-to man is halfway digested in a corpse."

Memories were cruel; the image of a bleeding Oliver transformed into a younger version of him, without a strand of silver hair, with the barest hint of a worry line starting to crease in his forehead, waiting for her at the estate. Black velvet mouse ears were obscenely out of place on his head. He'd whisked her to Disney World for her ninth birthday when Josephine forgot the day. Kana closed her eyes, fighting the swell in her throat.

Spencer was silent. Not that she expected an answer to her commentary. "Here."

She opened one eye to see a thermometer extended to her. "If it'll make you feel better," she muttered, even though they both knew it was for her benefit. A standard thirty-six point five degrees Celsius blinked into existence, nothing to be worried about just yet. Kana could reach out to Dr. Khan, a doctor specializing in infectious diseases. He was retired now, but served as a leading specialist for the CDC. Dr. Murphy, known for her microbiome research, was another option. Another uncomfortable roll of wooziness wormed through her. The distinct possibility that she could become a skin-drooping, gelatinous creature, who may or may not have a worm-like infestation, was frightening. Kana knew fear. Fear was the unlikable cousin who came around to visit too often and at the least opportune times. She'd survived this long and knew when her life was on the line; there was terror, a slow, creeping, crawling shadow drawing longer with every second, but there was also a primal instinct that somehow ripped itself free when faced with a life-and-death situation, and when it came down to it, she would fight and fight to the death. Then there was a final level of white noise, a tightrope of reprieve from the oscillating fear, terror, and wildfire of adrenaline, the final stroke of near acceptance.

But whether the new mutated form of the Rabid disease was an evolution or a fluke, it didn't matter. Her end would be agonizing, and the clawing desperation from the previous Rabid Synthies was beginning to reflect in her. Josephine stood at the end of the endless tunnel, the fading light silhouetting her frame as the darkness grew and the light shrank. She needed Josephine.

A touch on the back of her hand, near her pinky knuckle, was as comforting as a warm mug. She hummed as if being coaxed out of a drug-induced sleep. The ceiling had strips of peeling paint, like curling, wilted flowers. She frowned at the light hanging between the two beds. It stuttered and flickered. She moved, but the sheets tucked around her kept her in a cotton cocoon. She didn't remember falling asleep.

"I'm fine," she grumbled as she rolled over so her back was facing Spencer. Even half-present, trying to shove out the last of the haze, she was not fine, but she didn't need him to say she'd blacked out.

With a silent exhale, she sat up and tried to stealthily gauge how much time passed. There was no light coming through the sheer curtains beside the bed.

"Let's use the bathroom for the fire extinguisher." Spencer stood, and his body softly cracked as if he had been stationary by her bedside for a day.

Kana had almost forgotten about the fire extinguisher. They stood side-by-side in front of the shower stall, the plastic curtain pushed back.

"Do you think there's something inside?" Spencer asked what they were both considering. Kana rolled the compact fire extinguisher in her hands. The label looked standard enough, and it was heavy, close to two and a half kilos. She handed it back to Spencer and gestured at the shower.

"Go ahead."

He raised his eyebrows. "You don't know how to use a fire extinguisher?"

Kana lifted her chin a fraction, her eyes narrowed.

Spencer continued. "It expired eight years ago. I doubt it'll work well. It's a simple acronym: P.A.S.S—"

"I don't need you to explain. I know how to pull, aim, squeeze, and sweep." She cut him off. "I've never done it before and this seems like a one-shot deal, so I'd rather not fuck it up."

Spencer maneuvered the fire extinguisher in his hands, the small pin clinking against the side of the metal container, and pulled the lever. It released not a frothy liquid, but a chalky cloud of powder that almost instantly dissolved into ribbons of smoke.

His reaction was immediate. He set the fire extinguisher on top of the closed toilet while his other arm shot around Kana's waist, and he pulled them out of the room before Kana even realized that wasn't what fire extinguisher residue was supposed to look like.

"Wait," Kana said as he closed the door.

"We don't know what that fume was."

She smacked him with her good arm. "That might have been the clue, and we just missed it."

"Or it was a diversion, and we could have inhaled a poisonous gas."

"You go in then," Kana said with a shooing motion. "And if you pass out, then I'll know it was bogus."

He didn't argue and went inside the bathroom, closing the door behind him. She didn't hear a heavy thunk of his body hitting the floor, and she counted to sixty before tapping with the back of her knuckles against the wood. "Did you die?"

"It's safe," he said, opening the door, "but there's a smell."

Kana had a bathroom comment, but it died when the faint

scent became prominent. "What is that?" Kana moved further into the bathroom, inhaling deeply as she poked her head into the shower. The scent was a mixture of things; initially, chamomile, but closer to the source she detected a different scent, too faded to pin down.

"Spray again," she demanded.

He obliged and aimed the nozzle at the drain of the shower. A second cloud of finely milled flour blew out. Kana closed her eyes and inhaled.

She was inside a bookstore, holding the glossy pages of a magazine, and the faintest hint of patchouli perfume folded over the paper. The congestion of bustling people around her, the sound of heavy machinery clunking away in the brutal Indian summer heat. A new scent wafted over, and she walked to a cliff between the oak moss and eucalyptus trees. Someone was speaking. She couldn't parse the words, but she felt a woman's presence. A figure beside her pointed into the distance.

Kana gripped the memory, trying to figure out where she was. The harder she tried to cling to the memory, the faster it faded. She wasn't on the cliff, and as hard as she tried to imagine what the person was pointing at, all her mind created was the line delineating the sky and land.

"Is that it?" she asked, trying to control her frustration.

"There might be enough for one last try."

Kana frowned. "No, let's not waste it. Let me think." She fell back on the bed, mulling over the bits of different memories.

"What did you smell?" she asked.

"Initially, I thought of paper, and then herbs?" he responded, with a tilted question, as if he wasn't sure.

Kana hugged the pillow to her chest, comforted by the validation that they had smelled similar scents. "Did you think of anything?"

He was quiet as he gathered his thoughts. "Not particularly. The scents were fleeting. At first, I thought of my biology lab: the paper, and the green smell. My secondary school biology teacher was famous for her plants."

Spencer was quiet. She heard the rustle of fabric as he sat on the bed beside hers. "It's quite clever to use scent," he commented.

"She wouldn't have it any other way," Kana added, but didn't share anything else. The unsaid questions he wanted to ask were clogging up the musky room, but she wouldn't share her memories, not when they were too vague for her to understand.

She abruptly sat up, thrusting both arms against the mattress, forgetting her useless arm.

"Where are you going?" Spencer asked. He was resting his back against the headboard, his legs angled off the side of the bed so his hefty shoes weren't touching the duvet.

"The concierge for a magazine."

He was off the bed. "Let's go together. You'll wait in the car."

She grumbled, but he didn't have to explain that he didn't want her alone in the hotel room, and he didn't want both of them to pop into the reception area, too many eyes.

She lay out in the back seat. The rich leather smell of a new car was unmistakable. Spencer tapped on the tinted window, startling her awake. They returned to the hotel room.

"You need to wait here," Kana said as she took the magazine from his hands.

"Why?"

"You're tainting the smell."

Spencer stretched at the collar of the shirt and took a sniff. His eyebrows dipped together, his mouth tilted into a confused line. "Do I smell bad?"

Kana ignored his question. He wouldn't understand. The crisp mint might as well be a subtle cologne around him, and it wasn't so much that she could smell the mint, more that the taste was distracting her from the other scents. "Go stand over there." She waved her hand at the corner of the room by the motel door.

Her hands split open the magazine, and she inhaled the smell. It was far stronger and more notable, and she was right. The first layered scent was paper.

Opening the bathroom door released the last of the odor into the open space. A subtle, juicy aroma; a citrus fruit, maybe, but not a common citrus fragrance like orange or lemon.

She closed the bathroom door again and set the fire extinguisher inside the shower. Her hand hesitated on the lever. This was her last chance. One inhale and one exhale to calm her jittering hand, and she squeezed.

The final puff of misty cloud coughed out, significantly smaller than the other two attempts. The paper scent was more prominent. She inhaled deeply and was back in a store.

She wasn't in a bookstore—probably a convenience store, or a gas station—but she felt cramped, as if everything was squeezed into a tiny room. The window reflected the neon red numbers of a foreign lottery. Her fingers leafed through a magazine, pausing for half a second when she saw a girl dressed in a dress matching her mother's, a pink fascinator made with tulle and pearls, and dainty white gloves. They were at an event in Great Britain. The magazine snapped shut, and she was at a massive factory, with machinery chugging along as sheets of paper pushed through. She'd forgotten about the three day trips to the monstrous paper factory, outings that had stained her springs for three years.

The second coiling scent of eucalyptus, native to Oshiya, sent Kana to a different memory, one where she didn't see anything aside from the sky. At first, she attributed the emptiness as a failure of her memory to bring back the full picture but on the frame of her memories was a blanket of condensed fog. Josephine was there. The outline of the woman was unmistakable as she turned, her regal nose and sharp cheekbones in profile, and the ever-present tight frown. One hand gripped the strap of the backpack on Josephine's shoulders while the other gestured ahead. Her lips moved as if she were talking.

A tiny drop of panic bled through Kana. She needed to see what Josephine had pointed to. She focused back on the smell of the damp eucalyptus.

Her mind swirled through the memory. She'd forgotten about these moments. On rare occasions, Josephine had a moment of weakness and brought Kana along for something unrelated to a public appearance or her work: excursions. A hike through a region of Oshiya, or a random long weekend trip to Zimbabwe. The clean, earthy odor faded, and took Kana's memory.

She waited as the final scent edged in slowly, like a sneaky surprise. The smell was extremely potent, as if someone had left a fresh citrus rind on the counter. She returned to the cliff, staring at the tops of leafy trees losing their green color in return for dull oranges and finally rich reds. A few people poked at the tree canopies with long sticks, and red blobs fell into nets below. The voice beside her remained a muffled mix of syllables and vowels she couldn't understand. A hand, darkened to a leathery brown with rough calluses along almost every finger, gestured to the land ahead, out to the sea of pomegranate trees.

Chapter Thirty-Five

Kana didn't want to wait. They were so close, and this, *this*, could be the end. In all the other memories, Josephine hadn't been directly present in either the location or her memory. The woman plagued every association, but this one was an exception, and Josephine stood as the subject of the memory.

Spencer turned his head to the side in refusal. "Let's wait until your arm is better," he argued, crossing his arms across his chest, and resolutely positioned himself in front of the door.

Kana sighed dramatically. "Most orchards are on the other side of the country. It'll take half a week if we drive. Unless you want to take the bullet train?"

His body shrank backward minutely while his mouth pursed. Kana grinned. The high-speed rail would be the worst idea, with no way to escape if unwanted people boarded. "MIDNIGHT TRAIN MASSACRE." Kana could see the catchy headlines in all caps that would be all across newspapers and articles the next day.

"Let's take our time. Think about our options and make sure you're better." His gaze returned to her limp arm. "How are the other injuries?"

Kana chose not to respond to his question, mentally running

through the catalog of injuries: her abdomen was no longer the source of her worry, the minor head injury was low on the list of concerns, the clawed puncture wounds in her calf were minimal, and the latest bullet wound was of no concern because any acute shocks traveling up to her neck and down to her fingernails were numbed when she moved her arm. All in all, she was fine.

"What pomegranate orchard is near eucalyptus trees? It might not be on the other side of the country."

Spencer's thumbs moved across the screen of the burner phone. "They are all located in agricultural counties, mainly concentrated in the southern and eastern parts of the country," he said.

Kana groaned as she flopped back on the bed. That wasn't right. She'd only visited that side of the country once when her class voyaged to farms to experience the agricultural working class to help enrich their privileged minds. "That area doesn't get fog. The western coast gets the rolling waves of fog. It has to be on this side."

Spencer looked at her with a hint of doubt.

"Keep searching," she snapped.

The news played on a boxy television set that looked like an early 2000s prop. The world hadn't gone to shit yet; there was no breaking news about Synthies running rampant at the antique fair, the campsite, or anywhere else.

"In other news, an insider reports that Ambrose Inc. has issued an abrupt hold—"

Kana perked up and snatched the remote off the sticky end table to raise the volume. A woman newscaster stood in front of the freshly built Ambrose Inc. headquarters, all sleek, white stone and glass windows.

"While the research facilities continue to work, sources say all production of military drugs has ceased. Dr. Josephine Ambrose's whereabouts remain elusive." An image of Josephine Ambrose wearing a custom indigo suit at a conference, a small microphone in front of her, appeared in a panel beside the newscaster. "And her only daughter, Kana Ambrose, has been recovering privately from the gruesome attack in the United States earlier this month."

Kana frowned. "That's the picture they decided to use?" She huffed at the image of her at an independent film festival. It wasn't a terrible picture. The lustrous beaded gown was stunning, significantly more impressive in person; the still shot did little to capture the diamondesque refractions of light. Her signature red eyeliner and red lips were flawless, as expected for a public appearance, but it was like looking at herself in a fishbowl. Kana Ambrose on the screen felt like an entirely different person. The life she wanted was close to her grasp. She could apply for citizenship elsewhere, focus on her production company, and never be called back to Oshiya.

"There have been no comments made from anyone on the board of directors. The CFO was last seen in the United States for a conference with the president, and the company has released no further statement."

Highly Suspicious, with a capital *H* and *S*. She looked over at Spencer. He was the one who doubted her accusation against the president for continuing to release A.E. Potentia, and now there was a chokehold order? She quirked her brows as if silently saying, *See*.

"We don't have evidence," he repeated. "Let's see if we can find Dr. Ambrose or see where this orchard leads us."

The broadcast droned on about the latest crime, a family murder-suicide, a group of workers on strike for unfair labor and wages, a royal family member spotted at the grand opening of some public space, and an update about a recent trial. The same old news.

Kana lowered the volume, staring numbly at the flickering images. Josephine hadn't layered three scents without a reason. The pomegranate orchard and the eucalyptus helped narrow down which agricultural plot it might be, but what about the first scent? The paper smell was less obvious, but it had to serve a purpose. With closed eyes, she shuffled through her deck of memories. Back when Kana was obedient and followed instructions, Josephine sometimes took them on a tour through Northern India, to meet the Dhali Lama, or to see some technological manufacturer. The obscure locations Josephine led her to were random farms, ancient caves, and a man-made island created for the sole purpose of being a landfill. There was that trip to that backward city in Canada with the funny name: Flin Flon. Behind her closed lids, she caught the fleeting image of younger Kana in a ridiculous pink hat.

"Search 'Ambrose visit to Buckingham Palace,'" Kana ordered. The room was dark, and she was alone. She had missed the hours when the golden coin sun dipped into the velvet night. A surmounting dread closed in at the realization that the time was lost, and she could not account for the transition from where she was to the present at all. Her clarity of thought was distinct, but not enough to fill three hours. She turned on the faded cream lamp at the bedside and stared at her immobilized arm.

Spencer moved away from the worn arm chair beside the TV console. He removed a water bottle from a grocery bag that hung from his wrist, the thin plastic bag stretching with his haul. The beverage was clouded with condensation, cold in her hand as she accepted the offered drink, eyebrows pushed together as she tried to remember when he had left the motel room.

She cracked the plastic cap, and the carbonation fizzled. He'd remembered her preference for sparkling water. The echo of an ache in her chest faded as quickly as it came.

"What am I looking for?" Spencer asked as he set the bag down and pulled out a narrow foil-wrapped food item. It smelled like salted meat. She grinned as she unwrapped the shiny gift to find a sausage bun. Although the bread was soggy and pillowy, the sausage was charred and leaked salty juices.

"I need a year," she said.

He tossed the hot ketchup packs to her without asking if she wanted them; he'd remembered she liked ketchup, too.

"Three years ago, you made the most headlines for leaving Christopher Kent's estate in the early hours," Spencer said with the barest hint of a tease.

She scoffed around the large bite and swallowed before responding. "It would have been when I was younger. A publicity stunt, some sort of mother and daughter outing, maybe when I was eleven."

The low jingle of a toothpaste commercial played in the background. Spencer removed a cup of stew from the microwave. Based on the spices and golden yellow color, it looked like a traditional bouillon-iro.

"Someone saw you and Dr. Ambrose at the Ascot racecourse ten years ago," Spencer said.

"Cross-check for a pomegranate orchard, near eucalyptus trees."

Kana looked away from the television, observing Spencer's illuminated face as his thumb scrolled through the search engine.

His lips stretched into a smile. "Well, I'll be damned."

Kana grinned. Oh, how she loved it when she was right.

Spencer's gaze lowered to the bottom of her face, and he tapped the side of his. Kana ran the pad of her pointer finger against the corner of her mouth, catching a smudge of sauce.

"You know, you only smile like that when you win."

"Is it wrong to be happy when you're right?" She smirked and ended her question with a lick of her finger. Spencer was focused on her. Strangely, not in a creepy way, almost like Oliver. Respectful but with a glow of fondness. Her chest ached as she remembered the older man standing near a wall, eyes always trained on her: watching her curse, kick, and scream, standing poised beside her as dozens of flashing lights blinded her, or catching her as she stumbled into a room, giggling with people far older than her.

"You're sad."

Kana blinked as a breeze of mint tickled the back of her tongue, and Spencer pulled the crushed foil paper from her hand and sent it into the bin. There was a torn-up look in his eyes, less intense, softer, but in a guilty way, as if he knew exactly who she was thinking about. The dark part of her roared, pointing her claw-like hand at him. He should feel guilty. Oliver was dead.

She cleared her throat. "The orchards," she said, struggling to find the string of conversation they were having before her distraction.

Spencer returned to sit on the edge of his bed. "There were some orchards close to Mount Lassen, but the land was bought after a fire five years ago," he said, easily guiding her back to the prior conversation.

"How far away is Mount Lassen?"

"Less than eight hours."

"Rest up," Kana said, smiling again.

———

THE DRIVE WAS UNEVENTFUL, WITH ONLY A FEW MINOR hiccups, one being that Spencer proved to be popular. As they stopped for gas, Kana sat in the back, keeping her head down. Most of the drive, Spencer wouldn't allow her to sit in the passenger seat, saying that he preferred her to be laid out in the back seat. That earned a teasing comment and a smirk, which he responded to with a half-grin, muttering how he'd walked into that one.

Spencer casually leaned against the car door, blocking Kana from sight, waiting for the gas to finish.

He removed his hands from his pockets. One hand went casually behind his back, where a gun was in the holster. Kana leaned forward to try to see around Spencer and spotted the gas station worker. The woman's little vest, decorated with tiny pink heart stickers, showed the station's logo and her name, 'Maud.'

Maud-the-gas-station-employee grinned as she offered a cup of coffee and a bag. Spencer's sharp shoulder line relaxed as he accepted the items and said a few words.

"Did you get free coffee?" Kana asked as he closed the driver's door and pulled out of the gas station. Kana poked her head through the driver and passenger seat gap to get a better look at Spencer's face.

"I accidentally left it. She was being nice and brought it out. It's actually for you."

Kana took a sip. "Maud left you her number." She turned the cup to show the silver script with her digits and a smiley face. "It seems every Maud has a soft spot for you."

Spencer's ears reddened. She snickered behind the coffee and prepared to tease him more.

"Your arm," Spencer said as his eyes left the road to meet her gaze in the rearview mirror.

"It's fine, and by fine, I mean I can twitch my fingers." She wasn't lying. Her arm was slowly gaining sensation, and the muscle spasms had become less frequent. Unfortunately, she felt the thin threads that Spencer had tied to knot her skin together.

"Was it a tranquilizing injection? Or damage from an external wound?"

"Yes," Kana said, not at all answering his question.

"Should I be worried that other parts of your body will suddenly lose all feeling and become paralyzed?"

"Nope," Kana said, popping the *P* sound. She had zero plans for using more of her power and being bitten by anyone or anything.

Finally, after much arguing and complaining on her part, Kana drove a stretch of the awfully boring road trip, but after a police car drove past them on the two-lane road, Spencer demanded they switch.

"Are you still contacting the president with updates?" Kana asked, leaning closer to the window and exhaling hot air against the glass to draw a cloud with her finger.

"No, I stopped after we arrived at the camp."

Kana hummed as she tried wiggling her left big toe without moving the other four toes, for no other reason than the drive was very boring. "Why?"

Spencer was quiet for some time. "I am hesitant to tell you the truth."

Kana quirked her brows and leaned forward, resting her left arm on the center console to scrutinize his expression better. "The honesty is appreciated, but don't leave me hanging."

Spencer offered a smile, but his eyes were resolute; his secrets were his own for now.

God, she was tired of looking at Oshiya's landscape. She'd heard of people vacationing via long road trips because driving for hours on end was somehow fun. She'd never thought she'd enjoy a road trip, and she was right. Even if she didn't have people chasing after her, the idea of being stuck in a car for hours was unappealing. Her ass went numb on more than one occasion.

"I've been thinking about the bungalow," he said abruptly as Kana was midway through contorting her legs beneath her for a different position on the uncomfortable leather seat. "The locked room between the other two rooms was soundproof."

Kana hadn't noticed that little fact.

"When you were in the bungalow before, what did you do? You said it was boring." He asked it carefully, as if each word spoken might set her off. She propped herself up straighter, her immediate response ready on the tip of her tongue. Anything other than the truth was her default, but three heartbeats later, she conceded to be honest. "I was vacationing in a pink beach bungalow during the peak of summer. It may be shocking, but I spent the summer playing, building sandcastles, swimming, and eating too many milk snow bowls." The incredibly light shaved ice that melted like cotton candy on the tongue was an Oshiya staple. He glanced over at her, mutely inclining his head as a gesture to go on.

"I had a tutor. They moved some toys around, and I copied them," Kana said seriously.

"And you practiced in that white room, not the pink room?"

"I was like six or seven at the time. Forgive my poor memory. There were stuffed animals lined up against a white wall. That's all I remember."

Spencer took his time to consider his response. His free hand, which wasn't steady on the wheel, brushed against his top lip, a tick he was doing more often.

"I think there was a Synthetic User in that smaller room," he said. "While you were pushing the stuffed animals, the Synthie could see you. There were vents along the top to hear and smell, and the third room was an observation room to watch the Synthetic's reaction. I wondered what the purpose of the third room could be. It was the only space that had a view into the other two rooms, and must be important."

Kana opened her mouth, then snapped it shut. She could see it, everything he explained. Little Kana listened to her tutor, trying to figure out what the funny taste was in her mouth and how to tug at that pool of energy and make Mr. Bunny with the pink floppy ears move to his friend, Mr. Sea Otter, just thirty centimeters away. A soundproofed room was just behind her, where the screams and the body slams of a Synthie couldn't be heard, and the third and final room, where Josephine observed it all.

"How long were you in the bungalow?"

Kana's blood felt hot under her skin.

"Kana?"

"I'm silently seething over here." The insuppressible icy heat of anger reached every corner. "I never went back to that bungalow until, obviously, a few days ago." The playful summer song from the radio couldn't thaw the frigid atmosphere. Instead of picking up the nonverbal cues to keep his mouth shut, Spencer started talking.

"You asked me why I haven't been in communication with the president." Her curiosity silenced the growl for him to shut his trap; of all the things he could bring up now, he'd chosen a topic of keen interest.

"One of my more recent assignments was shocking. I was dispatched to observe a military unit from Russia. That alone was unusual, but not rare. I'd noticed an uptick of assignments requiring observation of foreign countries' Synthetic Users, more than ours." He paused, enough to force his shoulders from lifting any higher with tension. "That was the first time I'd seen a Rabid Synthetic act differently, compared to others I'd encountered. The observation task turned into immediate intervention. The Russian team member I'd been assigned to had killed his team and I subdued him. After witnessing what he did, I was most interest in my assignment's autopsy. He had eaten his team. Rabid Idu Users don't consume people infected by the parasite, but the rules dictated that anyone infected with the parasite was to be cremated. Two more assignments and a pattern was emerging, something was happening to the Synthetic Users."

Chapter Thirty-Six

"We're here." Those two words broke the silent stasis and brought Kana back to reality. He'd parked at the base of a hiking trail. Her eyes moved to the time on the car dashboard. Four hours had piteously slipped by without her notice, but her body certainly felt it with each knee cracking as she stepped out of the car, and her hip made a loud *pop*.

"There's nothing," she stated, accepting a backpack Spencer offered her. They stood beside each other looking like they were ready for a hike with matching backpacks. Her statement wasn't quite true. There were trees, freshly planted, their trunks not yet the span of her hand and two heads taller than Spencer.

She turned around, and about two meters away in the distance was a mountain edge. There were tall trees with distinct peeling bark. She could envision Josephine and her lanky teenage self on the edge, Josephine explaining something in clipped sentences.

"You said someone bought the land," Kana said. She'd expected buildings or some form of infrastructure.

"The government. Records say this became an agricultural testing ground."

She clicked her tongue while her eyes roamed over the fresh orchard. Government records didn't mean shit. Josephine could have easily paid someone to purchase it as a third-party representative.

"We know she loves underground spaces." Much like the underground lab at the campsite, Josephine would have layered a nonmetal foundation just below the dirt and some sort of padding or insulation to shield from metal and heat detectors or imaging.

"Any thoughts on how we find it?" Spencer asked.

"Not a clue, but she left something here." Kana started walking down the dirt path. She reached over and pushed the nearest tree with her good arm, hoping that by a miracle, Josephine had been lazy and tried to repeat the same trick with the birdhouses. But alas, the tree was only a tree, and didn't budge.

"Just look for anything out of the ordinary," Kana said. "It could be a mark on the tree, something about the rock formations around the roots, or how the trees are planted." She stepped away from the tree and stood in the clear row. The trees were all planted in even, equidistant lines.

She silently walked down the path, and then the next, and the next. Spencer combed through the other side of the growing orchard. There was no obvious sign of anything out of the ordinary. The trees were all the same height, with nothing marked on them or around them. She rubbed a hand down her face as the sun lowered in the sky. They weren't getting anywhere. She reached for a branch and snapped the flimsy wood. How long would it take to figure out the cryptic puzzle Josephine had left this time? Spencer may have been hesitant about the president's hand in the new drug variance, but Kana wasn't fooled. There were about a hundred doses of A.E. Potentia produced annually. What if that number had doubled or tripled in the past few months? There could be upwards of three hundred Rabid Synthies running rampant. She ripped at a lower branch, this one thicker. Her bitten arm was finally mobile enough to be useful. She could close and open her hand again and snap the branch by leveraging the wood on the top of her thigh.

"Break time," Spencer announced, crossing into her row of planted trees. Kana half-heartedly muttered under her breath, but followed Spencer's lead to the car.

"The cliff," Kana said as she stopped to shield her eyes from the sun's rays and look past Spencer's frame.

Spencer lifted his arm to block the sun. The rivers of sunlight slanted at the perfect angle. If she were a painter, she'd want to bring this moment into permanence, his silhouette against the honeying light, his skin set aglow. He turned to face her, and she caught the luminosity in his gaze; there was no hard mask, no containment of any kind. When had he stopped concealing his emotions? This abrupt softness was jarring, given their circumstance. A subtle shift in his flickering gaze, and he bottled up the warmth she'd caught sight of. She rubbed her eyes. The weariness was kneading amicability into her.

"The road isn't large enough for a car," he said. "We will have to hike."

Kana grunted as she pushed past him.

"Will you be okay?"

Her eyes narrowed into slits. "I may not be a professional hiker, but I am capable of walking up a steep hill."

The edges of Spencer's lips lifted. "I meant your injuries." His eyes dragged to her leg, the cotton material from the sweatpants covering the wrapped calf.

"I'll manage."

She didn't question how Spencer produced a map as he led them to the start of the trail. Her thoughts fluctuated between muttering curses at her entire situation and feeling the stinging in her leg, with the soreness in her abdomen intermittently flaring as if waving a hand and shouting, *Remember me*!

Kana paused, closing her eyes as she inhaled deeply. The overhanging trees and the thin, wobbly, dirt trail looked more like an outline for a rollercoaster, yanking at her different memories. There was the trail in Sweden, filled with far more lush, green hues, and the Zhangjiajie National Forest, but the air was far too humid and compact.

"We're about two kilometers in. Let's break," Spencer said, touching her good arm, steadying her swaying body.

She held up her hand, her eyes still closed. "I'm thinking."

"You look pale." *You look like you're about to pass out*, was what he meant.

Kana shushed him and wiggled away from his hand, shoveling through her memories. "We need to get to the top while there's still daylight."

Spencer silently returned to leading. If he dragged his pace to match her slow shuffle, neither acknowledged it.

"The land was bought five years ago?" Kana asked breathlessly, her fists curled at her sides.

"It was."

"And the trees were imported when?" Kana braced her hands on her hips, her chest heaving while the shadows from the trees stretched longer across the ground, the sun slipping further down. Spencer commented that they wouldn't be able to make it and offered to turn back, rest in the car, and start early in the morning. Kana threw a stick at him.

The longer they walked the trail, the denser the trees became and the more strongly the eucalyptus smell permeated the air. She blinked, stopping to breathe and allow the lightheadedness around the edges of her mind to settle as a memory clawed through the locked coffin in her graveyard of memories.

A conversation with Josephine was usually short, not more than a handful of words, like a guillotine. On rare occasions, however, the interaction was professorial, a dissertation with words and jargon. That was far worse and mind-numbing. Kana closed her eyes and filled her nose with the smell.

Josephine's distant voice surfaced, and the memory sharpened into view. Not the details, of course, but the feeling of being lectured. Kana stood further back, placing distance between them, but Josephine turned her head and snapped like a whip near a sled dog.

"This is an important day. While you were hopeless at the tournament today, they say you show potential of a strategic mind. But, and there's always a but, you—"

Kana didn't listen to the rest. Her gaze found the shape of the eucalyptus leaves, like delicate pieces of origami paper.

"Get over here." The command was sharp, clinical, leaving no room for anything but obedience.

Kana's legs carried her to stand closer to Josephine; the imposing woman stood a meter away from the jagged cliff edge. Josephine's slender back faced Kana, and with each step closer to the spot that overlooked the flat hectares, Kana envisioned it: a push, no more than a playful shove and the statuesque woman would fall. The singular, delicate thought came on a butterfly wing, and Kana's stomach wretched, her body viscerally rejecting the horrific idea, the preposterous notion of doing that.

"What do you see?" Josephine demanded, without a glance at Kana.

"Land," Kana said softly, a snail curling into herself. The obvious answer was never the answer Josephine wanted. She braced herself.

Josephine exhaled sharply through her nostrils. "Potential, just like the chess board this morning. You fail to see the true game. The vantage point at the highest location lends you the best perspective. You always want to be in a higher position than those around you to understand the limits of the game."

As much as Kana pretended not to listen, her traitorous ears hung onto each word, echoing and carving into her mind.

"Kana." Josephine said her name like it was a chore. "You will be better."

"Kana."

The two syllables of her name seemed to vibrate against her chest, through the hard planes of whatever she was resting against. She moved her chin, and the small bone knocked against a hard shoulder. She attempted to shift, but realized that Spencer had wrapped her legs around his waist and was tightly gripping her thighs.

Kana groaned as she forced her hand to unclench around Spencer's shoulder. A piggyback ride was unexpected. "You can let me down."

Spencer wordlessly crouched to the ground. The trail was almost nonexistent around them, the trees packed around them like the walls and roof of a house. A chill ran down her spine. The sporadic blackouts were happening more often.

"It was only for a few minutes," Spencer said, as if answering her unvoiced question. He shifted the backpack from his chest to its place on his back.

Kana frowned, trying to ignore his flushed face and the line of sweat gathered at the collar of his white shirt. A few minutes her ass. Something stirred low in her stomach, an uneasiness. He didn't have to give her a piggyback ride.

"We're here."

They made it before sunset, the golden hour bathing the world in a dreamy ambient glow. This high up, it was obvious what she'd missed below. While an entire hectare of land was planted with trees, there were some trees trimmed so their upper foliage and branches were shorter, thus crafting a dimensional image of a neat square, an eight-by-eight of trees different from the rest, for a total of sixty-four trees.

"Do you know what has sixty-four squares?" Kana asked rhetorically as she scanned the rest of the land. Most of it was cleared but still unused, and natural forestry overtook the rest.

"A chessboard," Spencer answered. Kana glanced to her side, surprised by his quick response.

"I played when I was a kid," Spencer explained. "Up here, the fruit trees that look sunken into the ground make a chessboard."

Kana nodded. One of her many tutors was a chess master who'd shown Kana the game and had her memorize different plays. "Josephine played white. She would always have a slight advantage that put her one step ahead."

"Who was your teacher?"

"Callum Dwighton."

Spencer sputtered. "He was almost a grandmaster seven years ago." He sounded genuinely impressed. "How was he as a teacher?"

"Just because you are the best doesn't mean you have any skill in mentorship, and I didn't have the patience or interest in chess. He caught onto that rather quickly." Kana waved dismissively and stepped closer to the cliff's edge, overlapping with the memory of where Josephine had stood.

"Her favorite play was the Vienna Game," Kana whispered as she lost herself in black and white squares, the letter and number sequence of the boxes, but it was futile. She didn't remember enough. "You can push a tree, right?" Kana asked, her mind three steps ahead.

"Which side is white and which side is black?" Spencer asked, breaking Kana from her plan of returning to the car to find some internet connection for an image of the play setup.

Kana tilted her head and appraised Spencer's thoughtful gaze. "You know the opening play?"

Spencer hummed. "Black counters their king's pawn to e5 after White's e4 opening, and White develops the queen's knight to Nc3." He rubbed his knuckles along his jaw in thought as he regarded the sixty-four trees. He followed her thoughts and leaped to the same conclusion. If the trees represented the board, then the game had to be set. Kana was sure Josephine would have used her favorite play, but Spencer's question was valid. Which side was white, the side Josephine would start from? If Josephine stood at this cliff facing the board, the sun rising in the west would be white, but that was the obvious answer. The player's colors were usually determined by a coin flip or a pawn picked from a fisted hand.

"I played white and was seated on the right." Kana crossed her arms over her chest, her face scrunched in doubt. It was a gamble to use the last game Kana ever played, but she had a fifty-fifty shot. "Knock down the trees, set the board for the Vienna Game."

Mentally snapping trees was not as easy as it looked, and Kana appreciated Spencer's skill to make it appear effortless. He had to wait for movement from a tree, which was relatively easy when he fired a gun into the air to startle the birds and other creatures away. From there, he used the momentum of the tree canopy to force a branch to snap, and used that momentum to blow through a tree trunk. One by one, like lined dominos, the trees fell.

With the trees broken in half or blown away, it was becoming more difficult to see their chess game. As the sky's last harsh line of red and pink faded into black, Spencer wiped his forehead with the hem of his shirt, exposing the lines of muscles and a thick scar, starting from the lower right side, curving over to where his pancreas was. It was obscenely long. "That's it." He exhaled, the shirt falling back, hiding the scar from view.

Kana chewed the inside of her cheek as she faced the shadowed mess of broken trees below. "Tomorrow morning, we will see if anything's changed."

Spencer handed her a flashlight, another secured in his hand, and twin beams swept across the forest floor.

———

"I'M IMPRESSED," SPENCER SAID. KANA HELD HER tongue as she aimed her flashlight at the raised building. At least a third of the orchard had lifted three meters high to reveal an entire first floor of concrete. They were right, the Vienna Game was the answer.

At some point, as they trekked back down, the hidden structure had slowly risen from beneath the ground. The property looked like an angled ramp, lifted to the sky, angled at a forty-degree slant, with the remaining building stuck beneath the surface. They slowly circled the odd concrete building, checking for points of entry.

"There's a door over here," Kana called out from the other side. Her flashlight shone on the single entrance at the mouth of the tallest point of the building. There was no handle, but it was the only area not made of concrete. Kana pushed against the metal wall, but it remained resolutely in place. Spencer's beam of light swept up and down, left and right, before landing on a keypad beside the sealed wall.

Kana stared at the metallic buttons. An engraved message on a small plaque below the keypad read, *I chart the way, helping sailors navigate night and day.*

"The North Star?" Spencer offered.

Kana shook her head. No, while it was a note about coordinates, longitude and latitude, the answer was obvious to her. Her fingers glided over each of the numbers, symbols, and letters before she punched in the only set of coordinates she knew by heart: the coordinates Josephine had wanted printed on her birth certificate.

A hollow clunk—then the low grind of gears. Spencer and Kana exchanged a glance. Even in the dead of night, that awful, aching hope stirred in her chest and flickered back at her through Spencer's eyes. He gave a quiet smile and tipped his head, leaving the first step to her as the metal door groaned open into darkness.

Chapter Thirty-Seven

Kana lied to herself when she said she was ready. She lied to herself when she said it was fine if Josephine wasn't hiding here. Her heart tripled in size, expanding with each strain to pump blood, sending a constant painful ache in her chest cavity as they descended the staircase. The slitted, dull lights implanted along the base of the icy walls illuminated each parallel line of the stairs until both their feet left the last step. A light overhead flickered on to reveal a hallway where a pair of thick, frosted glass doors stood a few meters ahead. Kana eyed the thin tablet no larger than her palm beside the only entrance. It wasn't a keypad to unlock the doors; the frosted glass split apart with a soft whoosh.

She was faced with another iteration of gray laboratory countertops in the center of the space, with more counters along the farthest right wall, bland vinyl flooring, and in each corner, a next-generation sequencing machine. There was a deafening silence. No sounds of footsteps, machines at work, or even the AC units. She felt the disappointment sink its fangs into her neck and suck her dry until she was a leathered corpse.

Kana wanted a massive screen TV with a recording of Josephine, like a poor James Bond villain, revealing her master plan. Hell, Kana would take a body over a ghost town of a lab because this had to be Josephine's main location. Everything was updated in terms of technology and design with state-of-the-art lab tables. There were tablets on the walls with temperature, oxygen, and radiation readings.

Kana's soul left her body as she frantically ran around like a chicken without its head. Reaching the farthest wall, she triggered a line of lights in the ceiling that showcased a wall made from over a hundred wooden blocks, similar to the floorboards in the bungalow—a Japanese puzzle box. Another clue. Another goddamn-mother-fucking-clue.

Sensation in her legs was gone, and the sound of the stool crashing into its partner was muffled as she stumbled backward. "I need a minute." She wasn't sure if she spoke out loud. The repeating and confounding notion that this wasn't the end, just an Ouroboros. The lab or a section of the stairwell had lifted itself out of the ground. If anyone were here, they would hear the structure moving and would have been ready to greet the unknown guests or run away through a secondary door. No one was here.

"Kana," Spencer touched her shoulder. "You should see this."

"Is it Josephine?" Her question and tone betrayed the hope in her voice.

"No,"

Kana moved away from his warm hand and plopped onto the nearest stool. "I don't care." She was petulant because she deserved to wallow in hopelessness for another hour; did he not understand the gravity of their predicament?

"She was researching your abnormality," Spencer explained. She perked from her curled clam posture atop the stool. Kana ran both her hands through her hair, closing her eyes as she gathered the building blocks of her broken self. She wouldn't let this be the end.

His arm hovered behind her back, not touching, instead a presence as he led her to a second frosted door that slid into the wall once the motion detector picked up their approach. The space wasn't any larger than a hundred-square-meter space. Fish tanks divided the middle space, five back-to-back for ten in all. Newspaper articles, tiny printed research documents, and headlines covered the walls. The X-ray and MRI results stood out from the collection of words. Kana went to the first document at eye level.

It detailed glucose, sodium, potassium, and other levels checked with a standard blood test. A paper above the blood test included EKG readings, vitamin levels, and other medical test results from when she was one year old. The next cluster of documents, half-tacked on top of one another, were the same tests, but from when she was two years old, the sequential pattern continuing to display a timeline of Kana's health. The papers went around the far back wall and stopped when she was nineteen. Her skin felt too tight, as an invisible weight started compressing against her sternum. Legally, Josephine had the right to view and maintain copies of Kana's medical records when she was underage. She turned away from the last record obtained after the Christmas shooting incident, a sinister coalition of emotions bubbling in the pit of her stomach. She balked at the tank that illuminated once it caught her movement. If only it were a normal fish tank with a family of happy clownfish and sea anemones.

Instead, she faced a suspiciously dick-shaped thing. The creature was floating in the water. The skin around the balls was translucent, like George's splotchy arms, but growing inside was a rolled tongue muscle with ridged taste buds. The head of the phallic creature split apart like a cuttlefish, spindly bone spider-leg tentacles reaching against the glass. Its mouth aimed at a small dome stuck to the top of the tank out of the water. Inside the small dome was a clear solution with unidentifiable tufts of detritus. Kana leaned back to examine the label below the tank: *J. Doe#19, K.A BxLiver-09.*

Her feet carried her one tank over, and the eerie blue light flickered on. A foot torn at the ankle rested in a waterless tank. Tall, weaving sprouts of fungi shot out from the gaping area of severance, twisting like ivy vines as they stretched upward. The fungi tops were gray while the underbelly was a plum purple. Instead of a half-dome glued to the top of the tank, this had a single tube dangling from the top. Kana bent closer, the tip of her nose almost touching the glass as she scrutinized the threads to confirm, yes, the stems were rippling like worms as they coiled around the glass tube with a dark brown liquid. The plastic plaque with a label inserted read: *J.Doe#22, K.A.Bld-22.*

Her brain couldn't form words in her consciousness, let alone move her mouth to speak, as she looked at each tank with a disfigured body part, the Rabid disease somehow keeping the mass of tissue alive, and at the top of each tank was a sample of something.

K.A. CSF-06

K.A. WBCs-11

K.A. LeftM3-19

Kana calmly walked over to the origin of a faint high-pitched humming noise. A gust of chilled wind sent goosebumps up her bare arms as she strangled the metal handle of the refrigerator. There were three shelves. The top level had five vials of blood, and the middle shelf had even fewer sealed, unidentifiable samples that were flat in airtight bags. The bottom shelf had a small cylinder with three tiny baby teeth.

Kana reached for one of the bags and read the label: *K.A. Biopsy of R Quadricep-03/06/06.*

K.A, her initials. The answer was obvious, but denial was easier than the truth. She didn't need to reference the medical records on the timeline plastered along the walls like grotesque propaganda. She knew what happened on June 3, 2006.

Her vision inverted and twisted into an abstract painting as the sterile white ceiling light shone above her like a lifeless sun. The buzzing, static noise silenced the sloshing blood, roaring like angry ocean waves as her grip on reality slipped. Before she could have even fully stopped in her step, someone with large hands had grabbed her and inserted a needle into her arm. They hurled her into the trunk of a car; the tires screamed for her before she was flung into something even smaller. The cramped space prevented her from turning; she could only bend her head forward to touch the smooth box she was trapped in. A dank smell of water and seaweed crept through, and she cried, thinking they were going to toss the coffin box into the ocean. Instead, she was thrown into a dark room, answers demanded from her, voices she had never recognized, choking on water, strong arms pressing around her. Escape. People were monsters; they thought Rabids were the monsters. No, people were far worse, capable of something more evil than ripping into another person and feasting on them because of hunger.

"Kana."

Mint and warm patchouli, the surrounding arms weren't as large, and ironclad; they weren't squeezing to harm her. She recognized those forest floor colored eyes. The left iris had a black dot, a unique trait she only now realized. The dilated pupil reminded her of an eclipsed sun, the additional black dot simply a lonely planet. Her skin felt sticky as she attempted to take a step back. He was too warm, too solid. She needed space; she needed to be alone. Spencer didn't let her get far. His hold lessened enough for her to put space between their chests. She just needed to tell him she was fine. He shook his head no. A quiet storm of concern clouded the softness of his gaze.

The world muted, and the edges dissolved away as his mouth moved, as the dimensional forms silhouetted, structure became unfamiliar lines, the taste of mint vanished, the pressure of a second physical form against her lessened as if the numbness from her arm infected her nervous system, and she felt nothing. She was fading, her mind shutting down like the final credits of a film. A pair of long fingers snapped in front of her. "Come back to me."

Chapter Thirty-Eight

The snap propelled her out of the depths of her mind; she was thrust back with clarity, and a singular, malicious thought blared in her mind: *I'm going to kill her.* The explosive rage carved those five words while her mind ran with how she would do it. She wouldn't make it painful—she wasn't sadistic—one bullet was all she needed. Because she knew it: there was something wrong with her. After years of trying to escape, to peel away any memories connected to Josephine and toss them to the bottom of the ocean, these past few weeks had forced her to face them. Was she even Josephine's daughter? Maybe she was a Petri dish baby, a one hundred percent lab-grown fetus, one of a kind. Josephine could have been like any other mother and deposited her in the farthest boarding school, because it seemed like Kana's presence was worse than a nuisance. Why did Josephine keep her close? Here was the answer: Kana was interesting because she was different, a puzzle, and Josephine would push and tear apart a subject to understand its inner workings.

A sickening, feverish stretch pulled her further away. She didn't feel Spencer moving her out of the horror lab and back into the primary lab space. Nor did she feel him prop her against a wall and lay a shock blanket over her.

Her return to her body was murky at best. She wasn't in shock, not anymore. The shock and disbelief were long gone because she suffocated those emotions and focused on the facts: Josephine kept Kana's biopsied body parts and samples of her blood, and she maintained all of Kana's medical history. Had she discovered why Kana was special? Her eyes were transfixed on the wooden wall puzzle, counting each square twice.

Spencer returned three times, or maybe this was the fourth time. He moved silently, but his presence hovered before he collapsed in front of her, and two arms wrapped around her. It was an awkward position—he angled most of her torso into his left side, her chin smashed into the top of his shoulder. He was saying things to her, words of comfort most likely, but the syllables flew in one ear and out the other. The wood design on the opposite wall was reminiscent of the flooring she'd seen before; it was the same, but the colors were inverted.

A small corner of Kana's mind questioned why Josephine had used the same puzzle design. It was possible Josephine didn't believe Kana would recall the floorboards in the Bluette closet, but the prominent part of Kana couldn't give a rat's ass. "Move."

Spencer released her. His stiff body relaxed, as if hearing her voice was a reprieve. Her fingertips traced the wooden puzzle on the opposite wall until she pressed into the cube. The solid wood square sunk in a thumb's length with an audible click, before it popped out. She could do this, funnel all her mental bandwidth to solving the problem beneath her fingertips.

"Kana," Spencer coaxed her name, as her hands flew over the board, moving the pieces around. "Let's step outside and get some fresh air." His touch was a graze, the rough pads of his fingers pressing enough on her arm to stop her movements.

"Don't touch me!" Kana shouted. Some people said they saw red when they were overcome with anger. They were wrong.

There was only white. The explosion felt like a volcano bursting out of her chest. She wanted him gone. She wanted peace. But that was no longer an option, not when she had more questions, was potentially infected by a mutating Synthetic, and everything led back to Josephine. *JosephineJosephineJosephine*—that's what the president hired him for, so why couldn't he just shut the fuck up and let her finish this? She didn't need him to care; she wanted to stomp her feet and punch a hole in a wall.

Spencer stepped back, his mouth snapped shut, his face hard, but not his eyes. She hated how sad they looked. Beneath her skin and the intricate highway network of veins, there was a faint vibration. Her left arm trembled uncontrollably, the right arm thankfully functional, cradling her forearm, covering the bandage where the bite marred her flesh.

"I'm solving this now."

Spencer remained silent as she messed with the wooden pieces. The last piece went in, the entire wall sank backward one full stride, a mechanical crane clicked, and the wall moved into the concrete gap, leaving enough space for a person to walk through.

Kana stared at the black gap. Spencer murmured something about checking it first, but he didn't stop her from edging closer to the void. Kana stared into the darkness, unable to tell if there was a room beyond or just one meter of unbroken concrete.

She walked through. At this point, a three-headed person could be lying in the mysterious dungeon, ready to rip her apart and slurp her insides like noodles, but she would at least have an ending. The lights were automatic, like every other research space they'd stumbled upon in the past few days. One by one, they blinked on, not the awful fluorescent lights like in most labs, but a soft amber to add to the ethereal nature of the sole subject of the wide space. It centered the room like an overly extravagant art piece. A raised glass capsule.

Kana didn't step closer. From her odd-angled spot in the left-hand corner, she had a distorted image of a leg and the wrinkly sole of a pale foot. There was someone inside the glass coffin. Should she dare believe who was inside? She felt each of her muscles and tendons as she raised her leg to plant one foot in front of the other. Every step took more effort, as if the ground were endless mounds of sand, slowing her movements.

She closed her eyes, the ongoing signs of a panic attack obvious even in her muddled brain. The air felt too thin, and each erratic heart beat sent pain through her chest. She inhaled and exhaled, but each drag was more difficult, and it took an embarrassingly long amount of time for her rational thoughts to scream, *There's air, breathe*. When she opened her eyes, she was a meter away, and there was no longer a distortion in the glass as she faced the capsule. Josephine lay on the black silk. Her hands were crossed over her stomach, dressed in what looked like a black cashmere turtleneck, black fitted slacks, and, of course, her crisp white lab coat. Even in death, the woman wore her lab coat.

Kana glanced at the face, but her eyes couldn't linger for more than a second, only long enough to confirm she knew those overly large, deep-set eyelids, the fan of lashes, a nose shaped like a small elf boot with the tip curved upward, the thin lips with the corners permanently downturned in stern disapproval, the three small moles: one above the arch of the left eyebrow, the second close to the right temple, and the last dark speckle on her chin. It was her. Kana knew those features, but she couldn't believe what her eyes were seeing.

Kana didn't know how she left the room. When she opened her eyes, she lay on the vinyl floor, the blanket tucked around her again. "It's her," she said eventually.

In her periphery, she saw Spencer's body move to lie by her side.

"It is."

The searing anger cooled to an indefinable feeling resting heavily on her chest. She couldn't get up if she wanted to, and right now, she didn't want to do anything. Instead, Kana lay on the icy surface. Sometimes she would open her eyes, sometimes she would close them. If only she could just slip into the ground. If there were a god, Kana was placing her request to be reborn as a rock in the next life. Her mind battled it out in the trenches, listing off every accident and injury she'd sustained. Had Josephine stooped so low that she'd set up the kidnappings so the surgeons cutting Kana open could take samples? The anger was overwhelming, layered with other emotions, eclipsed by the rage. Kana's eyes snapped open, and she stormed into the second lab. Her hands ripped off the medical notes, tossing shreds of paper into the air.

"Kana," Spencer said, his voice firm, and she wasn't sure what she would do if he sounded soft.

"You got what you wanted," Kana shouted. "Go back and tell the president to fuck off! She's dead and she can rot in hell." She faced the first tank, her eyes frantically looking for something to smash the glass.

"We don't know what she was testing or why. Why do all of this?" Spencer reasoned as he positioned himself between her and the tank, blocking the grotesque stomach bobbing in the water.

Kana punched him, her fist cracking along his jaw. "Christ." She cradled her throbbing hand, flexing her fingers to make sure she could still move the bones. The pain felt good.

"We have time," Spencer said, lowering his hand from his jaw. He could have said a million other things: *I know you're angry, you were wronged in so many ways. We need to look at the evidence. Stop being so angry.* But he said none of those things. He was right. They had time. The bastard knew exactly what to say. She wanted to punch him again. She was the overly rational one in situations. She sucked in her cheeks, gnawing on the scar tissue, not wanting to look at his forlorn and worried puppy expression.

She stormed out and went back to the death room. The chilled lingering mint remained, but the further she moved into the room, the more she could pretend he wasn't watching from the doorway.

Kana walked straight up to the glass coffin. The body was preserved, without a hint of decomposition. She eyed the glass structure. It didn't appear special, and no pipes or drains emerged from the back or bottom.

For the first time, Kana realized there was a handle in the center, a slim bar to lift the top. The coffin was supposed to be opened at some point. She walked around the room to the only other item aside from the walls and flooring, a single, long, rolling cabinet made of chrome. Inside were sharp metal surgical tools: the handle of a sternal saw, a row of reciprocating blades in various sizes, and scalpels, all neatly laid out on a white cloth as if displaying a tasting menu.

Kana shoved the drawer closed.

As Spencer said, they had time. She ended up seated, with her back propped against the wall, eyes unfocused on the coffin. Josephine was dead. Unless the form was an exceptionally realistic mannequin or a perfect hologram, she was dead. How didn't matter. Kana would bet good money the woman had committed suicide, a beautiful, poetic death. But why? Why would Josephine end her life? And what was the purpose of laying out all those clues for Kana? A vintage box leading her to the antique fair, a beaded doorway with the Pluto symbol, a fake painting at a summer camp she'd visited once, scents locked away in a fire extinguisher in a retro diner—it was a convoluted plan. There had to be more, something in the order of the clues that had led her to this final resting place. Because Josephine had left everything here: the timeline with Kana's medical records, the tanks with the experiments. And if Kana could succeed and find Josephine's resting place, then Josephine had to know Kana would learn about everything. So why lead her here? If the only purpose was for Kana to get to this bunker, why not leave one clue to the final destination? Why four?

Let it burn. The viperous anger tangled around her heart and squeezed. How easy would it be to forget about Josephine and her intentions? Spencer could run back to the president with the news. She could get the first flight out and never look back. But what about the newly evolved Rabid Synthies? If George was infected, she might be too. Josephine was the only one capable of formulating a cure. The tiny wiggling worm broke through the surface of her thoughts: she would be reduced to George or Vyolette. But she stomped it down.

Sometimes she found herself seated, staring at a wall, sometimes standing in front of the shelving units with jugs of solvent solutions, sometimes it was beside the refrigerator where there was a miniature steel box shaped like a fume hood with a chimney for the ventilation, but the materials were an odd choice. After the third time of staring at the object, she finally flipped the switch, located on the side of the hood. The clear window vanished with a swoosh as a steel shield dropped with a harsh click, followed by three beeps before the machinery whined.

On one occasion, she was planted in front of her timeline, rough twine twirling between her fingertips as she stroked the only piece of yarn in her timeline. The white string was tacked vertically, close to her fifth birthday, splitting her timeline. She knew that date, the old scar on her left thigh flared. Kana played with the corners of the documents tacked on the wall of the smaller room. Other times, she faced the walls in the main lab. The thin wallpaper was a terrible choice. Why bother pasting decor the color of sweat stains on a white shirt? She picked at the paper and found stainless steel beneath. The wallpaper tore with a brittle sound like dry leaves cracking under shoes until she confirmed the entire bunker was walled with stainless steel.

At one point, she found herself lying on the ache-inducing floor, staring at the ceiling, counting the overhead air vents while her mind rolled over the same questions without landing close to an answer. Spencer was an ever-present figure, hovering in each room she floated into.

"There must be more," Kana announced as she sat up, blinking away the thick haze. She began her search again, combing through each room until she was in the hallway right before the frosted doors opened. She tapped the sturdy display that felt like the touchscreen of a tablet or phone, but it remained resolutely black.

"Hello?" she said to the small rectangle. A single white line, like a heart monitor ECG, dashed across the screen with two peaks. "Kana Ambrose," Kana said. The line appeared again, lasting two seconds longer before disappearing. It was voice-activated. She called Spencer over, but his voice did nothing, so it was only registering her voice. But she was missing the activation code, and she really didn't want to search for any more clues.

She shrugged and went back to the main laboratory space. Spencer had piled the ripped pieces of paper on the counter, and there was a bowl of soup and salted crackers laid on a plate.

Her stomach twisted in retaliation, hungry, but not for the tart puree of tomatoes. "Cameras, audio, a thumb drive, a Moleskine journal, anything," she went on as she opened the cabinets.

"Was she known for keeping notes?"

"No, she wasn't. She didn't leave a sappy video message, a suicide note, anything?" Kana slammed a cabinet shut. The glass beakers rattled from the force.

"You believe it was suicide."

"I can't think of a single person that she would trust to set this up. She didn't trust anyone with her research; there's no way she'd trust someone to help her with her death plans. And once the deed was done, only then would she have contacted Oliver, unless she crawled into the coffin and gassed herself. There's something here. Don't just stand there," Kana snapped.

They couldn't find anything useful. The only documents were inside the second room, plastered on the walls. The tanks of experimentation were useless without Josephine's notes to understand what she was attempting to study.

"There aren't any Wi-Fi or internet signals?" Kana demanded. "Maybe she sent something to the cloud or an Ambrose Inc. satellite. There are one or two in orbit. Are there any secret rooms?"

"One makeshift bedroom with a small adjoining bathroom, like the lab at the campsite." At least there was a space to sleep and shit.

Kana surveyed the open lab space, the open drawers, and the cabinets. There was one spot she hadn't thoroughly checked. She faltered at the edge of darkness, the stark black line of the rectangular hole, before marching into the death room.

The bones in her knuckles pressed against her thin skin as she gripped the handle and lifted. The coffin top was heavy. It lifted ten centimeters, and suspicious smoke leaked out, frigid air caressing the tops of her thighs, but the top slammed closed, too heavy for her to lift. "Spencer!" Kana shouted.

The man came in as if he'd lingered in the doorway, ready for her call.

"Help me open this."

He paused in his stride. "Is that a good idea?"

Kana glared at him, and his pace quickened. With a shove, they lifted the coffin top; streams of smoke, like dry ice, leaked out and tumbled over the edge of the coffin. She expected the smell of death, but there was only a distinct disinfectant scent.

Josephine was rather pale in real life. Being trapped inside labs kept her from enjoying the sun, but death left a waxy quality with a gray and unnatural green cast. She was gaunter—Josephine had always been underweight—and the low percentage of body fat was evident in her face. Kana could trace a right angle starting from the woman's temple over the curvature of her cheekbones and down the sides of her mouth. And while Josephine was obsessed with her work, Josephine ate. She was not the sort to forget to eat; if anything, Kana suspected she gorged then purged because the woman could never sustain a healthy weight or muscle tone.

"What are you looking for?" Spencer asked under his breath, a blurred timidity shading his tone, a tone a little too soft, a tone Kana had never heard from him before.

"She's dead," Kana said loudly, "you don't need to whisper." And with all the false bravado she could muster, she reached out to touch Josephine's hand, her throat bobbing. "There are medical tools over in the drawer, bone saws, and only one body," Kana explained. She tugged at the sleeve of Josephine's right wrist, hesitant to touch her dead skin. It didn't take a genius to put the hints together. In the far corners of her sight, Spencer went over and inspected the drawer. Who would Josephine trust enough to handle her body and keep the secret? Oliver was the obvious choice, and maybe he'd taken control over the production because he knew she was dead.

A warm hand touched her shoulder, but lifted as soon as the pressure registered. "You don't need to do this. What she did is wrong. What she wants you to do is wrong."

"We finally agree on something."

"Kana," Spencer said sharply, his voice raised at the last moment as if he'd tried to cover his shock. "You think she left her body for you to cut into?" he asked in disbelief.

"Obviously." She gestured to the cadaver. "Do you see any other bodies hiding anywhere?" Kana gripped her false courage and wrapped her fingers around Josephine's wrist. A chill ran down her spine as she came into contact with the corpse's flesh. It was nothing like she expected, a dichotomy of emotions. On one hand, the body was cold, lacking the natural warmth from a living person, but certainly not the chill of an ice cube. "Which tool is used to open a chest cavity?" Kana asked.

Spencer's short inhale was so faint that Kana wasn't sure she heard it. "Why?"

Kana let the rigid hand drop back, and the lifeless appendage tilted to the side, not falling back in place. The red curve of a drawn heart on the corpse's palm peeked out. "There's a heart in the palm of her hand," Kana said.

Spencer returned to her side, his gait more hesitant. He paused longer than she did before lifting Josephine's left hand to inspect the drawn heart. "I'll do it." Spencer gently set the hand back over the other hand, understanding Kana's conclusion.

Kana shook her head as she spun on her heels and walked to the cabinet of tools. "No, I need to do it."

"Stop trying to be strong." He must have seen her recoiled expression. "If you think there's something in her chest . . ." His voice lost strength at the last three words. "I'll do it."

The cabinet of tools with its handy wheels glided across the space and to the side of the coffin. Her lips curled as she touched the tools and picked up the bone saw. With her free hand, she opened the top drawer. Inside were a single pair of goggles, a mask, and a red apron with white text across the front.

"I don't need your help. You can go," she said, holding up the apron. It was heavy, made of a thick PVC material, *Jr. Chef* was stamped large across the chest, and as she unfolded the apron, a quote was engraved: *Food is the passport into different cultures, get away from your home country and taste to experience the larger world out there. – Chef Rossi-Yoon*. Kana scoffed. What a bitch, even in death.

"I won't let you do this to yourself," Spencer said with resolution. She didn't need to see him to guess the pillar stature his body had morphed into.

She didn't know what he thought her reasons were, and frankly didn't care; he didn't understand. She couldn't let anyone see what was inside Josephine's chest. If she let him see, then he gained knowledge. At least if she saw it first, it was her choice to give up the information. Kana refused to let anyone take any more of her power, and with Josephine dead, she needed to be more cautious with what the woman left behind.

"Please, just leave." Kana didn't want to fight, argue, or try to force him out. She even used the *P*-word, the word she despised, never understanding the false pleasantry before asking what she wanted.

They stared at one another, and Kana caught the ache in his eyes, as if he understood the tragedy unfolding before him. He couldn't fix it. His shoulders drooped in concession, his eyes lowered; there was a moment of hesitation, as if he wanted to say something, but instead left. Kana pulled on the apron and faced Josephine's body, scissors ready to cut the clothes off.

This was fine.

Chapter Thirty-Nine

The weight of the trauma shears in her hand may as well have been a solid brick of gold. They were scissors, a simple tool to cut fabric—god knew more than one trauma surgeon had snipped away at Kana's clothes. She had to clasp the tool with both hands, the hunk of metal shaking. Her heart was an overheated engine, growling against her rib cage while her bones felt like they were concaving under the weight of her mortality. She closed her eyes. The black curtain behind her eyelids offered her a reprieve.

This wasn't Josephine, it was just a body; a scaffolding of bones and sacks of organs encased in flesh. She'd dissected multiple animals, and she'd seen more dead bodies than she could count on both hands. The first step was to cut away the fabric on the body. Simple. She didn't need to touch a scalpel or a bone saw yet. But her hands wouldn't move, and her body kept sweating, no matter how many rational mantras she repeated. The shears landed with a thunk on the metal top of the rolling cart. Her hot breath smacked right back into her face behind the surgical mask. The overeager disposition had jumped ship too quickly. With a swipe at her forehead and twenty inhales and exhales, she secured the mask back in place. Just do it. The mental command was easy enough to force her hand to pick up the scissors again and she snipped until the knitted fabric parted.

Funny how it always seemed like there was either never enough time or too much time, and right now, in this singular moment, time stood still. The last thread of conscious thought slipped away as the body's chest settled in full focus. The precise Y-shaped incision was not unexpected; the crude cartoon heart had indicated something inside the chest cavity, so someone before Kana had put it there. She noticed additional incisions spreading outward and beyond the standard autopsy *Y* form; those were not normal. Kana quickly cut away at the sleeve fabric to reveal identical incisions on the inner section of the biceps, like a highway down to the body's inner wrist. Thin staples had been used to keep the delicate flesh together.

There was no reason for the body to have that kind of incision. When she attempted to reopen it, with the scalpel firmly in her grip, Kana's trembling hand missed. The pointed tip of the blade sank into the body's pliable flesh like a spoon sinking into flan. She waited for the red to spill, but it never came, only adding to the strange feeling that the form in front of her was less than human.

Kana didn't realize she'd closed her eyes until she saw only the blackness behind her lids. By the dull ache in her knees and the warm throb of her shoulders, she'd been hunched like the letter *C* over the coffin. With a held breath, she tried again. She zeroed in on one section of skin and plucked at the staples until, with the help of tweezers, she pulled apart the flaps of skin and stared into the vermilion depths and the network of purpling veins.

The color gave her pause. She remembered someone telling her about gravity and blood pooling which explained the purpling, but the veins would have embalming chemicals. She removed more staples, reopening the entire incision along the right arm. The thickest vein was a bleeding watercolor of indigo and violet hues. Her head dipped closer to the corpse. The circulatory system was a disaster, a tangled mass of a porous sponge laid out in the baking sun, the largest vein bisected and hollowed like a drying pumpkin carcass.

The surrounding air was leaking out, and a gathering pressure against her skin grew stronger as the room became smaller. This was the vein of a Passive Synthetic User, clogged with roots.

Kana stumbled away until cold steel hit her back. The world cracked into focus. The short exhale stuttering out of her mouth sounded like a wheezing dog, the stagnant air felt dry against her moist skin as beads of sweat seeped into the folds of the cotton shirt.

Her mind spun through lectures, diagrams, and autopsies of Natural and Synthetic Users. Those were the veins of a soldier, a Passive User that had been pushed to their limits for decades. It didn't make sense for Josephine to have those scars in her veins. Kana was mistaken. Without a single tick of hesitation in her hands, she worked until the rest of the body was opened, like spread butterfly wings, the corpse's cavity agape; whoever bothered to staple the flesh didn't care about the organs. They didn't seem to be in the correct positions. The lungs were completely absent, and bits of the large intestine were shoved and trapped under the last two rib bones.

"Fuck."

The scalpel clinked into the bottom of the glass casket as Kana braced her hands on the bottom edge, ripping her mask off as water and bile gushed out of her mouth. The acrid liquid splashed on the floor.

A steady hand touched her shoulder. Her closed eyes squeezed beads of water until they spilled down her cheeks. The mint was a soothing balm in her garbage mouth; her entire body felt like it was eroding from the inside. "I'm fine." She tried to shove Spencer away. The soft weight against her shoulder remained, another gently pulling back her hair as she lurched forward and dry heaved.

"I just need a few minutes." Kana kept her eyes closed, allowing herself to be led away. "Don't look at the body," she grumbled, not wanting Spencer to see the open corpse. He was smart, he would see something, but that was all an excuse. A much smaller part of her didn't want him to see what she had done. Exactly fifty-four steps later, she was no longer in the death room. A plush mattress hit her bottom as she collapsed on the edge of a bed.

"You need to rest." Through her half-lidded gaze, she watched Spencer bend down on his knees in front of her.

It would be so easy to lie back, slip into a fugue state, and ride along with nothingness. "I can't," she whispered back. "Just a few minutes here." Away from the corpse, the air was breathable again, and she closed her eyes, focusing back on the open chest.

Every major vein showed signs of being bisected. Some had even further damage, as if someone had scraped through the pathways, and there wasn't a single sprout of fungi. The organs were no different, the insides scooped and hollowed out. She would triple-check and cut a biopsy if she had to, but if she could see the damage with her naked eye, the additional check with a microscope seemed unnecessary. It never occurred to her to consider the type of User Josephine was. It was less than five years ago when she noticed Josephine was a Passive User after catching a rare glimpse of raised veins. Still, it never mattered if Josephine could phase or create portals. The doctor never showed any sign of using her power, choosing her intellect over her inhuman gifts.

Her chin dipped down to her chest, admiring the upside-down words on the apron. The quote meant something. Josephine could have left an apron without any insignia or words. Of all the things, why did she use a quote from the chef who'd prepared her meals as a child?

"Here, eat some." A bag of rainbow-colored candies, her favorite sweet and sour ones, shook as Spencer wiggled the bag.

She offered a cupped hand, and a few sugary globs landed in

her palm: a red, two yellows, one pink, and two blues, not a single orange or offending green to ruin the other flavors. She popped three into her mouth and considered her next move, the sour flavor triggering her salivary glands.

"You didn't go back in the room," she stated, a bit stunned with the realization of the constant sense of mint in the small makeshift bedroom.

Spencer stood at the same time Kana did.

"I thought you didn't like candies?" Kana asked with a raised brow, her hands busy tying back her hair with a rubber band, noticing the way Spencer's cheeks hollowed as he sucked on the sour candies and his right eye twitched.

"I wouldn't want any to go to waste."

Kana didn't say anything when she caught the flash of orange and green in his hand before he ate a few more. Instead, she tightened the apron tie around her waist. The order not to follow her went unsaid, and the taste of mint stopped as soon as she stepped back into the death room.

Kana pushed her shoulders back and went for a fresh mask. The smell was more obvious as she slipped the flimsy thing over her face. There was no embalming fluid in the corpse. Somehow, Josephine had crafted a coffin that preserved her body without any additional internal help, or maybe she'd created a new chemical that dissolved after a specific amount of time, but whatever it was, the corpse was not being preserved.

As soon as Kana got to the chest, the decaying organs and the odor hit her in full force. The smell of rot triggered her gag reflexes, but it was the other scent. The overwhelming smell of artificial sweet cherries was distinct even over the rank decay.

With purple latex gloves on, she set to work. Kana was not a doctor, nor a researcher, but she was stubborn and would find the resources to help her. She dissected different tissues before standing on her tiptoes to pull the top of the coffin back down and seal the body back in its glass cage.

How could Josephine Ambrose be a Synthetic Passive User? Apparently, one who had used her power so much, it killed her. And yet, all springs of fungi were gone. Was Josephine vain enough to have her unknown assistant clean out her circulatory system? Kana was a stone gargoyle, a hunched figure over the microscope. She didn't know what she was looking at, and there weren't exactly reference texts.

"Have you ever seen a Passive User bloodlet?" Spencer asked, breaking her out of her blurred, cross-eyed gaze at the strange, stringy lines of tissue.

"Not that I can remember," Kana answered, pressing the palms of her hands into her eyes, rubbing as if that would ease the tension. Witnessing someone's bloodletting wasn't exactly the top of her list of interesting and enjoyable activities.

Spencer leaned against the edge of the lab, placing a bowl of soup beside her.

"Drugs were produced to help Passive Users break up the fungi and make it easier to pass through their veins."

"Okay, so someone takes a few pills—"

"An IV bag," he corrected. "The liquid would circulate intravenously, and then blood would be removed a few hours later."

A memory resurfaced. With three silk pillows propping him up, Oliver stretched his long legs out on a chaise lounge the color of turquoise sea glass, a book in his hand and an IV tube running out of his arm. He lowered the book, his glasses sliding down the bridge of his nose as he smiled at her.

"Like a banana bag?" Kana said, shoving the memory away.

"Similar enough."

"And what relevance does this have?" Kana snipped, her fingers tapping against the black countertop. She didn't have the mental bandwidth for him to string along whatever he was getting at.

"The cherry smell. That's a side effect of the cocktail of drugs. It's more apparent when the person bleeds and pushes out the invading fungi, but if there's enough, it leaks out of the pores too."

Kana silently mulled over Spencer's insight. That would explain Josephine's disdain for cherry pie. "So we know she probably used the IV. This was her private space to bloodlet, then."

"Maybe, but where are the IV bags? There isn't any medication here," he said, combing through the lab.

"Her body was moved then," Kana said, but even the reasonable answer didn't sit well with her.

Chapter Forty

JOSEPHINE WAS DEAD. Those three words strung together were a fact, literally in front of her face; the woman couldn't rise. Lifting her arms to push together her open chest cavity, the mental wall remained cemented, and Kana couldn't believe it. Her focus altered and adjusted back to the corpse. The sentence reappeared: *Josephine was dead*. And Kana grazed over the evidence, in a limbo of acceptance and denial.

The air felt charged, as if she were in a tank of water with a white-hot spark snapping through it, rippling heat across her skin like a live wire. She jumped away from the corpse; the clanking of the scalpel echoed in the chamber. Her eyes transfixed on the ceiling as another condensed shock sent electric pulses in the air, closer to a single bolt, like an arrow shot straight down.

Her hands gripped the rim of the coffin to steady herself as the lightning seemed to zing across her skin. She fixated on the ceiling, willing to see what was happening above her. There was no overhanging air vent. In fact, the ceiling looked custom, with vented grids, wide pipes, and coils. A third elongated, reverberating shock. There was no flavor tickling her taste buds, no wet sensation against her skin, no scent. Sparks in the air were a new sign. She took a tiny taste, the smallest drop, and nearly fell into the coffin. A wave of orgasmic pleasure shot through her.

She shouldn't have done that. The explosive euphoria only meant one thing: a Rabid Synthie. Someone had found them. Was it her fault? She'd probably released a drop of energy and kick-started her Wi-Fi signal. Before she could conjure Spencer's name, she gagged, spitting a mint flavor so crisp and distinct that she felt like there were freshly plucked leaves in her throat. Spencer was already back at the surface, probably fighting off the Rabid Synthie. He would be fine.

She bent down to pick up the hollowed liver when another crack of electricity, this time sharper and more compact, echoed through her spinal discs. "Shit," she cursed, and somehow she knew, even without the typical tip off of smell—she knew it was a Phaser. Spencer could be launching a rain of bullets, and it would never touch the Synthie. A fluttering shadow of worry tickled her composure. He could handle a team of four on his own, but a Rabid Phaser would be different. The debilitated and luridly formed Rabids came to mind. Her eye twitched as she left the tomb and checked the ammunition cartridge in the gun she had discarded on the lab's island. She would take a quick peek to know if she needed to run or lock the doors. She wasn't checking on Spencer.

The dank decay was swollen in the air as she passed the halfway point up the staircase. She pressed her back against the cement wall and with her free hand, pushed open the door. Natural light slit through, time was lost without a clock or windows. Her face crinkled in on itself like a juiced lemon. She saw nothing from the sliver of space as she carefully opened the door and slipped out of the facility.

Deep, brass, clanging growls came from a distance behind her. The inhuman sound meant the Rabid Synthie was still alive, and the mint crepe-layered cake in her mouth signaled Spencer was too. Not the best outcome, but certainly not the worst. One quick look and then she could retreat into the bunker.

The mess of massacred tree branches and limbs was still strewn around the perimeter of the underground lab. As she scaled the slanted concrete wall of the building, the atmosphere thickened with the tiny zaps of electricity. As she approached the rear, she ducked her head to keep out of sight. The slanted forty-degree angle of construction meant the back was only a meter and a half above ground level.

She was getting closer, and the smell was intensifying, like opening the fridge and discovering milk curdled, bread the color of moss, meats necrotizing with black mold, and sewage leaking from the back.

The Rabid Synthie stood with its back to her. Unlike Vyolette's grotesque, blubbery mass or the fungal horror of the Rabid Portal User back at camp, this creature clung eerily close to its original form. An unseen, cruel force pulled its limbs taut, stretching them unnaturally long and beyond proportion. The skin clung to its frame like translucent, wrinkled cellophane, sagging in places where it seemed too fragile to hold. Beneath the gossamer-thin surface, its sinewy muscles flexed and shifted like tightly wound rubber bands about to snap.

Spencer's face was flushed red beneath a mist of sweat, but there was a burning energy of enthusiasm around him, a certain brightness in his eyes she hadn't caught before as he faced the Rabid Synthie. He liked fighting, but based on his solemn expression and dislike for his nickname "Team Killer," he was uncomfortable with killing. Their eyes met as if he could feel Kana's gaze, and the excitement was snuffed out. His brows knitted in confusion before the Rabid Synthie moved like a spider, swiftly extending its legs and arms from its torso, forcing Spencer to step back.

Spencer, while fast, wasn't fast like the inhuman creature. He fired his gun succinctly, one round after the other, without a blink between shots. The Rabid Synthie didn't try to avoid the bullets. The air tickled with electricity as the slugs languidly floated through the body before exiting the head and blowing through a tree branch. Spencer sent her a dark look, transmitting *get away* in the tight line of his jaw.

Kana was about to turn around and head back down when the Rabid's head twisted like an owl. There was little face left, not even the protrusion of a nose. The Rabid Synthie locked on its target and swiveled its lengthy limbs to sprint to Kana.

The torso was all mouth, the tongue lolling out the color of a deep bruise, the only part of the body that wasn't made from the clear jelly. The tongue, the length of Kana's leg, dragged through the ground, half the muscle vanishing beneath the surface of hard dirt and sparse grass. Kana ran toward the lab with little thought until she saw the door. Shit. She shouldn't go down. He was a Phaser. He'd slide right through the doors and walls.

She skidded to a stop, the dirt slipping under the soles of her sneakers, and she nearly fell to the ground at the abrupt change in her trajectory. The car was further down. Could she make it?

"—an—ah." The two syllabic sounds didn't come from Spencer; they were distorted, like an echo from a well. She faced the Rabid Synthie, the cesspool stench warning her the creature was close. The creature's veins and arteries were tangled into a dark, pulsating web, submerged beneath a cloudy, opaque fluid that sloshed faintly with each unnatural twitch of its body. Beneath the rice-paper translucent skin, thin worms wiggled around. If Kana could see them from under three meters away, there had to be billions. There was only one person she'd seen with that kind of reaction.

"George?" Kana asked, uncertain.

The Rabid Synthie spasmed in response to the name. Its leg and arm joints bent, attempting to spring forward, but its limbs locked down as if a force had pressed against the creature. The heady mint coating her inner cheeks did little to suppress the putrid smell.

Spencer was by her side, chest rising and falling in short, staccato bursts. "Are you sure it's him?"

"It spoke," Kana said. There was a hint of doubt across Spencer's gaze as he moved another step closer to her, their arms touching.

Maud, the woman Spencer had trusted to take care of him and Vyolette, was apparently not as great at her job as he'd believed.

The creature squirmed, testing the invisible hold Spencer trapped it in. "Cure?" Kana asked.

The creature's cranium morphed, the way a glassblower manipulated and pulled molten glass. The head elongated, stretched back into a long, spiral limb. The Rabid Synthie thrashed in response, and the newly transformed limb lashed out like a scorpion's tail. An unseen force hit Spencer in the gut, causing his body to cave in.

"Can we not rile it up?" he asked through clenched teeth, a cloud of mint enveloping her as the new weaponized limb quivered midair. Spencer pushed back to keep the Rabid Synthie's movements at a glacial pace.

"How did it find us?" Kana asked. Spencer had proved that Rabids could hone in on Kana when she used some of her power, but they must need to be within a close radius, right? Both of them looked down at her arm as if arriving at the same conclusion. The bite. They knew very little about this kind of Rabid Synthie, and a bite from one of these variants had unknown consequences. Spencer's flushed face went white in a fraction of a second. "You remember where the car is? If you can't make it, go back to the bunker. There's a second exit through the makeshift bedroom. It will lead you to the other side, across the main road."

A second door. She hadn't seen any door. "The art piece," he said, answering her unsaid question. Her memory supplied a still image of a picture frame and a bust of a Grecian woman resting atop the end table beside the bed. "Not the picture," Spencer clarified, as if reading her mind. "The bust. Twist it to the right."

Kana didn't have time to question why Spencer seemed anxious, his expression contorted in resigned defeat as his hold on the Rabid Synthie broke. "Go."

She took off sprinting without a look over her shoulder. It wasn't until the seething fizzle of lightning blew across her skin and liquid mint mouthwash enveloped her that she faltered. The Rabid Synthie hadn't gone for Kana. She whipped her head back, catching Spencer retreating, the Rabid Synthie chasing him as he tried and failed to slow the creature's movements. Each push seemed to work less and less, and, by his panicked expression, it wasn't for the lack of effort. Another layer of tingling lightning, and the Rabid Synthie sprang forward, unhindered by Spencer, its belly-mouth gaping wide.

Spencer threw an object, which moved too quickly for Kana's eyes to track. The best guess was small items to move them faster than bullets, but they did little to slow the creature down. She was wasting time. Spencer was alright; he was more equipped to handle this. Two steps, but she didn't have enough time to start running before a muffled explosion sent a shock wave through the scattered orchard.

The brittle ground met her hands as she stumbled back to an upright position, in time to catch the sight of half the Rabid Synthie's form stretched and misshapen, like a cartoon amoeba mid-separation. The clear cellophane skin was burned, the edges glowing cherry-red like the butt of a cigarette. Spencer had thrown a grenade into its mouth, and that still didn't stop it. The creature continued its pursuit of Spencer, who managed to put more distance between them, but not enough. He needed more time to recover. Kana inhaled slowly and with the barest amount of effort, she tasted the Synthie's residual energy on the tip of her tongue.

The reaction was immediate. A tsunami of luscious vibrancy blinded her, and floods of dopamine raced through her blood. She cut herself off, the gag-inducing scent snapping her back, and she came to her senses. The torso-mouth opened, and the tongue coiled out, licking the air like it was tasting something juicy as it redirected towards her, the legs pumping manically, unable to move as fast as it wanted.

Spencer shoved, trying to hold back the Rabid Synthie. Kana planted her feet and redirected Spencer's energy, infusing it with an additional *oomph*. The five-limbed creature flew through the air as if a semi-truck plowing down a hill had smashed into it. The limbs stretched out to catch themselves before it was flung further away.

Kana ran. The Rabid would chase her as she tried to run to the car, but she'd shove again if it got too close. She'd drive to put more distance between them—the pop of a gun made her stumble mid-stride. Spencer ducked as the Rabid Synthie's head-tail speared at him. For reasons she couldn't understand, it wasn't chasing after her.

Chapter Forty-One

Kana bit the inside of her cheek, copper mingling with her saliva as she shot off back toward Spencer. He swiftly moved to the side, avoiding the left leg that smashed into the ground. The weight of the gun felt heavier in the moment of her pulling the trigger, aiming at the sprinting Synthie.

"Spencer!" Kana shouted over the crack of the fired gun, emptying the clip, only to realize it was useless. The bullets were absorbed and eventually spat back out of the creature's body.

She tried sucking up more of the Rabid Synthie's residual toxic energy as it lingered in the air, which prompted an immediate reaction, but she blinked—there was no energy. The bullets weren't phasing through the body; it either didn't care about bullets piercing its form, or it didn't have control over its phasing.

"Spencer!" Kana shouted louder, out of breath. All the other Rabid Synthies had chased her. Why was George's tunnel vision aimed at Spencer? His face was still devoid of color, lips bitten by winter's blue cold. He was using too much of his power. Her demand for him to push died as the Rabid Synthie's tongue sprang out like a whip, and Spencer held up his hands, the tongue smashing into an invisible wall.

There was enough of a push. Mint misted through the air, Kana gritted her teeth as she shoved harder, using more of her reserves. It was straining her mind, like trying to solve a difficult math equation with her left hand while translating a foreign text with her right. Out of all the times for a Rabid Synthie to not charge blindly at her.

STOP. The four-letter command pulsed in time with the veins in her temple. This shove wasn't as effective as the previous one, but it was enough, and the loud crunch of bones cracking in the distance hinted they'd flung the creature away as clusters of stars swept across her vision.

A running faucet of globby saliva pooled out of the gaping mouth as the Rabid Synthie pushed his form back upright. The Synthie scuttled back around, lifting itself on two legs so the mouth was unobscured. Each second was precious, and Kana didn't know her next move. There was enough of a mind left that the Synthie wasn't a useless lump, but she didn't know what to do. Bullets weren't working, and Spencer wasn't able to do much against a Phaser. Her eyes locked on the blackened edges of the Rabid's flesh. Bullets and Spencer's power did little damage, but the explosion, the heat—

An idea budded in her mind, but flitted away as the creature ran toward her. Kana ran to the bunker. It was a huge gamble; she was about to trap herself in very close quarters with no obvious exit, but bits and pieces of a sorely underbaked plan were formulating. She was closer to the bunker doors than she realized.

The crunch and thud of heavy limbs told her the inhuman creature was chasing after her. The nasty body looked like a stick bug, with arms too long, dragging on the ground. This was terrible, absolutely the worst idea, and her blip of hesitation nearly cost her.

The scorpion tail thrust down, the limb extending in length, stretching like putty. Kana tucked and rolled out of the way. The arm sliced through a tree, not doing any damage. The crackling electricity against her skin told her it had phased through. The Rabid yanked at its limb, as if trying to remove a ring from a swollen finger, only confirming it didn't have control over its ability.

She lapped at the residual air and didn't linger on the explosion of joy that blinded her before redirecting it back out.

The vibrating shriek behind her told her she had at least hit him as the noise fell further away, like a bird calling out in the distance. She tried to run, but her body revolted and she keeled over, and vomit gushed out of her mouth before she could swallow it down.

Out of the corner of her blurry vision, she saw the Rabid Synthie diving for the expelled body fluid. Her hands fumbled to the keypad and punched the coordinates, and she stumbled down the steps, tripping and rolling down the last quarter. Her banged and bruised body groaned in agony as she pushed herself upright.

Think, she screamed at herself. This facility was the only one with a voice-activated box; specifically, her voice was required. The neon line only spiked for four syllables. That was important. The quote on the apron—what was Josephine telling her? Her jumbled mind shoved the broken pieces into place, and the bare skeletal outline of her plan was erased as her hand slammed against the button to seal the second inner door, as if that would prevent the Synthie from entering. She should have gone for the car; she'd made an awful mistake. How the hell was she supposed to fight off the Rabid Synthie? This was not the time for her mind to give up. She wasn't a quitter, and she wasn't going to lose to George. She refused. Her body shivered, and her shoulders shook in response to the tingle down her spine. Speak of the devil.

Kana blinked away the last of the splotchy haze, feeling like her lungs weren't absorbing the oxygen. An asphyxiated, light-headed veil covered her weakening body. She forced herself into the room with her medical timeline, snatching a handful of blood vials from the refrigerator. The creature had dived for her vomit, so blood would hopefully keep it distracted for a few precious minutes. Another irregular static shock, this one like steaming hot stones pressing against her joints. She sucked in a gulp of energy, her body confused about the vibrating electricity coalescing with the dopamine high.

The Rabid Synthie became restless; the smell of its vile phasing turned her stomach. George's limbs were too long and large. It was like watching a spider squeeze into the crack between a door frame and wall, forcing its body through.

"Hungry?" Kana taunted and moved two large steps back, licking her dry lips.

George's dark tongue twitched as it slopped around the floor like a child licking his plate clean. Kana threw the vial of blood, the glass shattering, and George's form barricaded over the splash of burgundy, ready to fend off any invisible threats to its food.

Kana ran into the death room. Her hands scrambled to push the wall from the other side, but it refused to move. Her heart rate soared, and she felt a pour of sweat rain down her body.

She needed the door to seal, to force the Rabid Synthie to phase, so she could siphon more power. There was a way to reset the original Japanese puzzle box frame, but she needed to figure out the trick. There wasn't anything on the walls, she knew. They'd walked into each room, her hands gliding over each wall, trying to locate any hidden passages. Her gaze went to the floor, and she started smashing the heel of her sneaker on the vinyl that covered the stainless steel flooring. Strangled noises, gasps, and gurgling like the mechanical grind of a garbage disposal were the only sounds from the lab beyond the wall. Images of the oozing of fluids, millions of parasitic worms gushing out, the fat-bodied torso bulging and extending was an unpleasant thought, but the longer the Rabid Synthie was distracted, the better for her.

Her feet stomped faster on the ground until a small section gave in. A rectangular piece of steel, the length of a brake pedal bent inward, and the click of a latch was like an angel chorus as the Japanese box wall closed.

A slight reprieve to buy her a few more seconds. Kana chewed on the inside of her cheek. The scar was raw, and the revolting taste of iron and blood coating her tongue was keeping her mind sharp and racing like a film reel in fast-forward. Moments slotted into place. She glanced down at the open coffin. Josephine lay spread out, her flaps of thick flesh distended from her attempt at closing the chest. Kana's jaw tensed, another chomp on her cheek. She didn't have time to see what was in the woman's heart. She'd been distracted by the vein and artery pathways; she'd never cut open the organ. Her fingers twitched, but the crackling lightning that filled the room doused her anger.

The cold metal wall pressed against her back as she moved away from the creature, placing as much distance between them as the room would allow. A gelatinous membrane bore through the side of the door and the shiny silver wall. She guzzled more power. Her knees failed, knocking into each other like a broken puppet. The waterfall of power completely overwhelmed her, pounding into her. It was difficult to stop, but spotting an amorphous shape bending like broken static was enough of a shock to rip herself away from the Rabid's power.

The creature lost any semblance of a human form. It stretched like a pool of blood, leaking outward and closer into the tomb. In a span of a few minutes, it had transformed into another unrecognizable form. How many more evolutions did this creature have? She pushed forward to the edge of the coffin and reached up to close the coffin top, her other hand twisting the stubborn cap of the second vial of blood. *Come and get me.* She dumped the vial, and the deep carmine color splashed in the body's open chest before she slammed the coffin shut, spraying the remaining brown droplets across the glass.

Her locked knees released, and she sprang to the other side of the room as the creature shot out of the wall like a released rubber band. The indefinable form hovered over the coffin, the essence clear and iridescent like the rainbows in slick oil as the light reflected off the form.

Kana edged along the wall, afraid to breathe too heavily or make noise. With each step, each strain and stretch of her muscles and release of her joints, her heart rate increased with fear that the creature would sense her.

Her eyes were unblinking as the dull, shimmering form expanded. At first, she couldn't tell, but after another moment, she was sure. The remnants of the creature were filling more of the space. It continued to hover over the coffin, not consuming and ravenous like it had been a few moments ago.

Kana's hand pressed against the cool sheet metal. Her sweaty handprint smeared across the surface. She'd theorized why this small facility had steel walls, floors, and strangely gridded ceilings. Her gamble had to be right.

She stretched her leg to find the upright notch of ground and levered her weight against the piece until it sealed back into the floor. But the wall didn't open. The bubbly liquid form swallowed the coffin. Panic drowned her lungs. Was there another trigger to open the door from this side? *Shit*! She ground her heels into the floor.

The air crackled. It was the only warning before a force squashed her body against the wall. She was suffocating, the pressure against her face all-encompassing, squeezing everything. She was dying. There had been many moments in her life when she knew this simple fact. The first time was not the scariest. She'd been unconscious and didn't realize what had happened. The second near-death was the most scarring, the event imprinted on her body and mind, and now death and fear were back, tasting like blood and ash. She thrashed, trying to free herself, swallowing more of the addictive, tainted energy. A person could definitely have too much of a good thing, and whatever toxic energy the Rabid Synthies produced was breaking her skin at the seams, but she had to break free; it felt like the ceiling was crushing her. She screamed, and even if she couldn't open her mouth, the guttural cry ripped through her and blew open her inner battery pack.

White and black. The absence of color a black hole in her chest that sucked in anything that dared reach its orbit, while every explosion of color swelled in her head, her mind a nirvana of white. The two opposing forces clashed together and were dichotomous.

By sheer stubbornness of will, she roared her consciousness back. Her vision was black, as if her eyes were closed, and then the world was back in place. Static sparks shot through her limbs as the creature floated to her—*try me bitch*—and she threw back everything, releasing the rage that boiled dangerously beneath the surface. She imagined it screamed as the creature recoiled and the hovering, liquefied death skittered out of immediate reach. Kana dry heaved; the aftershocks of the redirection were taking a toll. She wasn't in the death chamber; the awful fluorescent lights of the lab space told her that much.

Move, come on, she chanted to herself. The voice activation box near the staircase was her destination. The actual goal was to get the hell out of the bunker, but she wasn't a gambler when she knew the odds weren't even close to being in her favor. Two more steps and a glance over her shoulders, she saw that the center of the puzzle wall was missing, as if a giant had punched through the wall. The mass tore apart Josephine's body, like acid eating away at the flesh. Three more steps. The melted mass spread through the air like an ocean wave, and each current was getting harder to fight back. Moisture leaked from her eyes as nausea rolled through her and blackness skirted her peripheries. Her left arm wrapped around her torso, and the other shot out to pitifully support herself against the wall she crashed into. She choked on a dry heave as another swell of poisonous power built.

One second, one step, two seconds, two steps. She threw herself through the hallway opening, the doors whooshing behind her. It slowed the creature, unable to phase fully through without eating its way out.

Kana swallowed down the next rise of bile. The light at the end of the tunnel was just within reach, the final dash. She scooted closer to the nearest wall to leverage her weight as she pitifully climbed the steps. She didn't get far. Six steps later, her body decided it had had enough. The delicate strings of her consciousness were snapping, one by one. She couldn't see if the Rabid creature had disintegrated the entire wall with the small, voice-activated screen. An echo of her name, a ghosted cry, and she barely registered the hand in front of her eyes and the snapping motion. She cried as an arm cradled under her shoulder blades, lifting her like a broken doll. Kana couldn't distinguish between the taste of mint or the scent of pine and amber under the sweat, but she was sure it was Spencer. She wanted to laugh and cry. She would never admit it out loud, but she trusted him to reach her in time. "Project M.A.A.M," she said, the two words a succinct last cry into the void.

CHAPTER FORTY-TWO

Flashes of moments ruptured to the surface like slow boiling water: the embedded lights leaving her in darkness; a haunting, deep alarm from somewhere in the bowels of the lab, the vibration going through her back and limbs heaped on the stairs; a flash of chrome as a section of ceiling crashed down, sealing off the frosted door; a countdown, the drawn beeping counting down each second.

Kana was tired of being in pain. She certainly felt every jolting movement as Spencer managed to haul her body against his and jumped, somehow pushing them up the steps five at a time until they collapsed, Kana on her side, the dry earth digging into her face.

Neither spoke, not that she could speak; her throat ached all the way down to her vocal cords. Her eyes opened again and refocused on the lab. The building sank into the ground. The thick and nearly black smoke billowing out was like a hellish dragon exhaling. She could feel the accumulating heat just through the doors before they disappeared into the ground and the earth flattened in place, as if nothing had occurred.

"Kana." Spencer had a way of saying her name. The last soft

sound rolled off in an accented kind of way. He must have been able to see her chest moving up and down, the indication that she was alive. The ground beneath her shuddered with a violent intensity, as if the earth were writhing in pain, and the lab exploded.

———

MEMORY WAS A FUNNY THING. WHEN SHE LOOKED BACK at each of the life-or-death scenarios, the events melded and formed into video reels so disjointed that the pain and panic were removed. She would say, "Yeah that hurt like a bitch," or "That was the worst pain I've felt," but the visceral sensation was a fraction of what she'd experienced. Time healed all wounds, as they said, or at least dimmed the clarity of pain, leaving behind festering mental scars and new traumatic triggers or disdainful habits that would do more harm. To see how this entire ordeal would manifest would take time. Time was a luxury, and maybe this time she would learn not to be flippant with it.

———

"WHAT A PAIR WE MAKE," KANA SAID. SWEAT ACTED AS the perfect adhesive to the dirt. Spencer, equally haggard, but at least without dry vomit clinging to his shirt, smiled, walked past Kana and deeper into the temporary room.

"I hope you aren't amused by the state we are in." She said in response to his brief chuckle.

He leaned his head back from the jutted corner of the wall leading into a bathroom. "I like to think we've been partners for some time now. It's nice when you say 'we,' you've only used it a handful of times."

The stained shirt hid Kana's flushed face as she shimmied her head out of the cotton top, scowling with unease caused by the astute comment. Cleaned with the lodge's all-in-one soap bar, they were holed up a stone's throw from a popular trail near a mountain, where campers' cars and vans were parked. Spencer had taken them to the nearest roadside lodge.

"Did you get the phone?" Kana asked from her spot on one of the twin beds. Spencer didn't have a chance to fully enter their room after completing another run based on Kana's request of items. He tossed his shades and hat onto the small table beside the door and ripped the surgical mask off before digging through the crinkly plastic and sending a small phone sailing through the air.

She grinned, all teeth, and caught the cell phone. It was time to start her own game.

"And this phone is completely untraceable?" She tapped the pen tip against the first number she'd scribbled on a pad of paper.

"Yes." He confirmed. His face had started returning to a healthy color. In Kana's moments of wakefulness, she monitored Spencer's colorless lips and sallow skin. Almost forty-eight hours had passed since the narrow escape, and she could finally remain awake for more than four hours at a time. When Kana first tore the jacket from her shoulders, it had revealed arms marbled with dark ink bleeding beneath her skin. Kana could only assume Dr. Cohen was right, the energy the Rabid Synthetics used had mingled abnormally and maybe in it's own way, left a mark on her, a different form of a Stamp. Unfortunately, the interaction with George's monstrous evolution had left most of her skin marred. Her back was a mix of bruises and black flesh, with a smattering of charcoal smudges across the left side of her face and neck, which would (hopefully) eventually heal.

She scooted off the bed, thumb flying across the screen, and waited. By the fourth ring, there was a distinctly gruff, "Hello."

"Giovani, it certainly has been a while," Kana said as she stood, one arm tucked under her breasts as she leaned by the window, the wrinkly curtains sealed together.

"Who is this?" Giovani demanded because this wasn't his

work cell, nor his desk phone in the New York office or the Australian office. This was his personal number.

"This is Kana Ambrose." And so for the next few hours, as the sun drifted further down the sky and the darkness took its place, Kana paced back and forth between the two beds, along the window, and in front of the TV, speaking sternly or sending quipped comments.

Spencer offered her an uncapped water bottle when her throat became dry and worn from speaking. Rice balls, toasted crackers, and a skewer of glazed chicken appeared at random by her hand or at the edge of the desk, and she shoved the food into her mouth, unfortunately still listening to the slew of the lawyers' unending jargon.

Finally, she flung the phone onto the end table and collapsed face first on the bed. Her body groaned, but if there was an Olympic game for ignoring a body's never-ending whines of protest, she'd win gold.

"How did you know?" Spencer asked from where he sat on the bed to her left. He had mercifully been quiet most of the time.

Kana didn't know what he was referring to.

"How did you know the code word for the self-detonation?" He amended his question before she could quip a response.

"A very lucky guess," Kana admitted as she turned her head to stare at the paisley printed design in the curtain.

"I'd like to hear your thought process," Spencer said, "if you are willing to share."

Kana inhaled through her nose as she sat up, clutching a pillow into her lap as she angled to face Spencer who was propped against the bedframe beside her. "The ceiling grids were different." She omitted the part that when she was not well, when her mind went to the darkest depths of morbid fascination, she had stuck her head inside an oven, much like Sylvia Path, and so was familiar with the inside of various large kitchen appliances. "The vents were unusual, and the floors and the walls were stainless steel. No other lab had any stainless steel. There was the modified fume hood with old scorch marks beside the refrigerator that had my old body parts, except it wasn't a fume hood; it was more of a mini crematorium. Now, I can only guess it was a scale model. And then there was the most obvious clue, the voice-activated system. Your voice didn't work, so what could I possibly have to say that would trigger the system?"

She left out the part about the apron being another symbol, a reference to the black-and-white photo of Josephine and her mother in matching aprons as they baked pies. The quote on the apron was the arrow on the compass of clues. The words originated from the first Oshiya chef to receive three Michelin stars. The same chef who had cooked meals for Kana when she was a toddler. It was the travel part which had narrowed down how the clues were joined and the actual sequence of letters, each hint related to the memories connected outside of Oshiya: the box was from Milan, the shawl was from Akita in Japan, the campsite had an image of the Azores in Portugal, and the fire extinguisher's scent led them to the pomegranate grove with trees imported from Maharashtra, a state in India. M.A.A.M. The project title she'd confronted Oliver about before his untimely demise. Kana couldn't stop the grin as she rubbed her bottom lip with the back of her thumbnail. Even in death, Josephine was a fucking genius. Heat seemed to be the only thing capable of destroying the parasite. One of the reasons why the tradition of cremating Users, even before Synthetics were created, began through the long-held cleansing tradition with the belief that, even dead, fire and heat would be a second bath to flush out the parasite and complete the cycle. The heat from the grenade was the only attack to harm the Rabid Synthie, and a final nudge for Kana to remember how dangerous heat was.

Lost in her drifting thoughts, she didn't realize she had stopped speaking out loud or that she was staring intently at

Spencer. With the orange glow from the lamp between them, he had a softer look. "I won't ask," he said, "but you're smiling, and that is enough."

Kana blinked lazily, a wave of exhaustion overcoming her.

"Thank you," he said. "I don't think you were really coherent, so I want to say it again. The Rabid Synthetic User . . . could phase through my attempts at pushing. I've never encountered anything like that before. Even with my suspicions and worries about Synthetic Users, I couldn't have imagined that level of harm."

Kana grunted in agreement. He should have seen the third stage of the Synthie's evolution. Which led Kana to another mystery: George mutated rapidly, each change seemingly triggered by consuming people—mirroring a Synthetic User's hunger, which inevitably drives them to human flesh and descends them to the final Rabid state. But why had his mutation led him to such an alien form? Josephine warned her to never let anyone bite her. The same woman who maintained a stock of Kana's tissue and blood, she was testing something and maybe that something had to do with Kana's flesh.

"You didn't have to save me," he went on. "But—"

Kana groaned as she smashed her face into the sheets. Her entire body cringed. She didn't do it for Spencer. She certainly didn't thank him for the times he'd saved her. If there was a score-board, he was up to three and she was at one, not that she was keeping track.

Spencer laughed softly, a warm spring breeze in the stale motel room. "Anyway, thank you."

Kana waved him off, the burning, courteous *thank you* lodged in her throat. She rolled so that her back faced him. She didn't have time to dwell on the unsettling sensation or the hanging, unsaid words. She needed to rest. There was much to prepare before she confronted the president, and she had a lot of dirt to shovel through.

———

THERE WAS AN ITCH IN THE FAR REACHES OF HER MIND. Most of the time, her focus splintered between calls about Josephine's will, the mess with the company, and trying to cease the drug production permanently, and each of those subjects required at least three lawyers and two attorneys. But in the rare moments of stillness, when she was annoyed with men's incompetence and lack of clear-cut answers, she poked at the scab.

The mystery of what had been in Josephine's body was a festering wound. She didn't have enough time to research or consider what she found in Josephine's veins. The brief time in the self-detonating underground lab felt like a fever dream, and as more time passed, the more she considered the glaring inconsistencies.

She heaved a sigh as she collapsed into the chair, running her hand through her hair before leaving it pressed in her hairline, trying to alleviate the mounting headache. She finished a call with a researcher in Germany, who was supposedly one of the best, and a frequent collaborator with Josephine. The man of science reiterated that theoretics were pointless; he needed samples and data. The *if only* returned as she saw the corpse behind the glass. *If only* she'd thought of a different way to get rid of the Rabid Synthie. *If only* she had been able to secure and store parts of the corpse. *If only* she hadn't lost control and leaked some of her power the Rabid Synthie wouldn't have tracked them. *If only*—

"Here," Spencer said. The sound of thin plastic cracking and the smell of richly spiced curry and coconut cream was a giveaway to the takeout food.

Kana's stomach silently seethed, twisting around in retaliation. She'd forgotten the panging hunger at high noon and had filled her gnawing stomach with iced coffee. Now the moon soared into the sky, and a different expanding nugget of head pain was building from the lack of food.

A bowl of steaming curry over rice was placed in front of her. She sniffed as she accepted the food. "Is this . . . ?" She couldn't finish her sentence, her hand already shoving the first bite into her mouth, confirming it was mango sticky rice. "How did—?"

Spencer smiled, a brief, teasing thing. "I've rendered you speechless. If only I had known all it took was a bit of sticky rice."

Kana scoffed with an eye roll, but gobbled down another spoonful. She leaned back into the chair, tucking her legs to her chest as she cradled the warm food. For a minute, the badgering questions, names, titles, and information she barely understood fell to indistinguishable murmurs. Kana sighed as she closed her dry eyes and savored the moment.

A sharp vibration caused the desk at her side to quake, and the fleeting peace was gone. Her initial question of who could be calling became who wasn't calling. She was waiting for feedback from the attorney, who sounded as if the effort to speak squeezed his lungs, and from the head researcher, whose calls always had a badgering background noise like they were at a construction site. As she opened her eyes and went to reach for the blue phone, her gaze caught Spencer's across the room. The look was out of place. His eyes had softened to—dare she say—fondness. But it was gone.

"Let's get some sleep," Spencer offered.

Kana's bowl had four grains of rice left. She noticed the lack of containers, dishware, or any food from Spencer's side of the room. "I ate a few hours ago when I brought the food. You were in a conference call, by the different voices coming out of the phone," he explained. Kana didn't remember him coming and leaving at all.

"I need to finish some things," she said while placing her empty bowl in his outstretched hand.

"Do you want to share? Maybe I can help." This was not the first time he'd offered his assistance with the turbulent predicament she was in.

"There was nothing left." The sentence slipped out. She hadn't planned on telling him anything, but once the words left, sharing didn't seem like a horrible idea. "I have nothing."

"Of your medical history?" Spencer asked as he made his way to the small kitchenette in their suite.

"Of Josephine," Kana admitted. She chalked it up to exhaustion and the contented languor from her stomach full of warm food. She took four strides to the bed and collapsed. "I made a mistake. I shouldn't have incinerated the site." She mumbled the last part of the sentence. She didn't mean to imply she regretted luring the Rabid away from Spencer. The whooshing of faucet water and the soft clinking of porcelain lulled her to a near sleep. "I should have thought ahead, kept a damn slide," she clarified, closing her eyes.

The water stopped.

"Is that what you were arguing about with the German doctor?"

"I argue with everyone," Kana muttered. "The doctor needs physical samples, the source of headache number six. Arguing about theoretical versus empirical data. Damn scientists, can't even give me a hypothesis based on what I saw."

"What are you trying to learn?"

"Things aren't adding up," she responded vaguely. Josephine had the markings of a Passive Synthetic User, but she was a Natural. The most obvious answer Kana returned to was that Josephine had tested herself and gotten an adverse reaction.

"Here."

Kana rolled over, expecting a water bottle with a quick comment reminding her to drink more than just coffee. Spencer filled the role of caregiver seamlessly. Down in the depths of her cold heart, she was grateful. But it was not a water bottle. Her body shot up, her hands snapping out to grasp the thin rectangle of glass. Words escaped her as she lifted the glass slide into the light, her fingers clutching the sharp edges with reverence as she inspected the sliver of an ashy blue substance.

Spencer laughed, a light, airy sound as Kana held the slide, her mind grappling with the fact that she had exactly what she needed.

"How—?" She closed her slack mouth. She couldn't believe he'd kept a sample in his back pocket. "I need to call Fredrick back, and Annie. She'll make sure the sample gets delivered. No, I should do it myself. A flight to Germany isn't too far. I can't trust anyone but myself." And she was off the bed, snatching her phone. Spencer held up his hands in false surrender as her onslaught of comments flooded out in a single breath. Her thumb paused mid-swipe over the thick-voiced German doctor's number; the flurry of astonishment sugar coated in excitement tapered off. "Are there more? When did you even do this?" A different set of questions washed ashore, the creeping suspicion painfully cold, and drowned the enthusiasm.

She laid the phone back on the desk, trying to slosh through the incriminating questions. "Why did you take this?" The desk edge dug into her ass as she leaned back, eyes assessing the young man across from her.

Spencer chuckled as he sat on the edge of his bed, still facing her. "Hot and cold with a flip of a switch," he said to himself.

Her eyes were frosted, and the muscles in her face slid into place. He could have offered this to her sooner, but he'd kept it a secret. "What were your plans with the sample?"

The silence felt longer than it was. The creeping monster hissed not to trust him. He was secretive, and wanted to learn something about Synthetic users.

"Please listen to everything first," he said with a worn smile, as if he knew the entire script of the conversation between them. Kana dug her nails into the cheaply varnished edge of the desk to ground the feeling as if she were on a cliff, one foot ready to take a step forward and sever their relationship. And what exactly was their relationship? She paused, trying to reduce their connection to the correct descriptor, and Spencer accepted the silence as an invitation to continue. "I've worked with different groups. Oliver mentioned a name—Team Killer—and he wasn't wrong. There are a few of us assigned to watch other Users and dispatch teams if they show signs of Rabid symptoms."

"A special military group to make sure military men are in line seems redundant," Kana commented, unable to be completely quiet. Spencer leaned forward to rest his elbows on his knees.

"More of an auditing resource."

Kana scoffed, imagining men and women normally in tactical gear suddenly in khakis and button-ups. "I suppose the government needs to monitor their resources. Spies are the worst kind, inherently untrustworthy."

Spencer cracked a smile, his eyes crinkling at the edges.

Chapter Forty-Three

"There was a concern for the Synthetic Users, and reports of unusual behavior with a handful of Rabid Synthetics. There wasn't enough data yet, but it felt like the rate of Synthetic Users becoming Rabid was increasing. From what little we gathered, nothing was consistent; the reported unusual behavior was not isolated to one country, or to the type of Synthetic User, and whether it affected Active Users more than Passive ones remained undetermined. But there were enough whispers to build into something worth looking into.

"I was slapped with a Special Agent title and sent off on my second assignment with a mentor. My more seasoned partner and I were assigned to an extraction team under the guise of field practice. The extraction unit was on a simple hostage rescue, in and out. For the days we observed the extraction team, I didn't notice anything amiss. They were exceptional, having worked with each other since I entered primary school.

"It all came to a head when the hostage and hostile's location was pinpointed in the basement of the city museum. I was assigned to watch the extraction team's Idu, who went off script. I watched as he seemed to partner with the hostage team's Idu, the duo working together against the hostage team. It was chaos, the hostage team shouting at their teammate who was eliminating them one by one, and when I had a chance to snag the hostage, both turned to me, and it was nothing I'd seen before, and something I thought I wouldn't see again. If I hadn't been around Rabid Synthies before, I ignorantly would have assumed the blown pupils and drool were Rabid traits, but I knew what to spot. And these two Idu's were not Rabid. They were focused, even with a filmy haze, their eyes only on one thing."

Spencer ran a hand through his hair, finally allowing all of his attention to land on her.

"I was the new threat. Three things happened within seconds. The air surged as objects lifted into the air, ready to skewer me, and I knew I would die. I wasn't prepared to handle this level of threat. The other two Idus were at a level I'd never encountered before, but the hostage stirred awake. There was a wet cough under the black plastic bag they kept loosely tied over the hostage's head, and whatever had wound up the Idus was gone. The two Idus were confused; the Idu for the hostile team was killed with a single bullet before he could take his next breath, and the assignment was marked as a success.

"I reported my observations, and my mentor chalked it up to a manic episode, a blip, and a sign the Active Users were on the precipice of becoming Rabid. I requested to trail the Idu from the extraction team for the next few assignments and never encountered anything similar. You and I know that once a Synthetic User exhibits the symptoms, there is no way to reverse or cure it, and if he had shown signs of Rabid behavior, surely years later, he would be worse, but he isn't. To this day, he isn't Rabid. He's retired and, as far as I know, enjoying a life away from the field and teaching at a police academy. But these past few weeks, along with the encounter with the variant Synthetic Users, I saw pieces of that behavior again. I hadn't thought much of the incident until—"

"Until . . ." Kana said, drawing out the word.

"Until I saw your medical history. It was five years ago, the third week of February, the location was the underbelly of the museum, and compared to your more traumatic experiences, your injuries were relatively minor. It was two drops in the ocean."

Kana didn't remember the kidnapping Spencer spoke of. It must have been a tiny ink splotch, nothing like the large spills of wine against her timeline. Was it that time when her nose had to be surgically reset while she recovered from severe dehydration? Or was it the time when she dropped in for a check-up for her ribs and was sent off with a note saying not to overexert herself and the fractured rib would mend? Was it so terrible that she couldn't pinpoint this moment Spencer had noticed?

She mulled over Spencer's story until it curdled, and all the questions came down to why he'd chosen to tell her this, and how it orbited around her irregularity with Synthetic Users. "You think I did something to the Synthies?"

Spencer nodded once. "After everything we've been through the past few weeks, yes. You're unique, and the effect you have on Synthetic Users is interesting. And like you, Dr. Ambrose has secrets."

A gentle warmth spread in her chest. *You're unique*, his words repeated in her mind. She squashed the strange and cheap happiness that sprouted from the off-handed comment.

"And what do you think I did?" Kana asked, "And don't give me some bullshit blanket response of I don't know, you have some ideas."

He interlocked his long fingers, and his gaze moved down to the gap between their beds. "I think you were desperate, backed into a corner, and did something reflexively. You were unconscious for most of the interaction, but the two Idus were attacking the hostage team because they were trying to get to you. The hostage teammates were shocked by their friend's betrayal, one of them ordered a third teammate to wake you up. When I tried to take you away, I became the target, and my guess is, you sent out a message, and someone responded to the call."

The conclusion made sense. Bodies high on adrenaline and faced with death did inexplicable things, but his description of responding to a call—did he think she had some sway over them and was somehow impressing her desire on them? "What kind of message? Do you think I hypnotized them?"

Spencer contemplated his hands as if the red knuckles had answers. "I'm not sure how to describe it, but if you had any sense of control, it was unconscious. But why them? Why one Idu from the kidnapping team and one Idu from the extraction team?"

Kana was circling back to Josephine. Undoubtedly, she had done something, and it seemed the woman didn't know what. Otherwise, why spend who knew how much time researching Kana? Why, much like god, would she create Kana in her image? Kana winced at thinking of Josephine in such a light. "And you think knowing more about Josephine will help answer my abnormality, too?" she asked slowly, pacing back to the original point of the entire conversation. "You were going to take the sample to someone. Who is it?"

"I have a contact in Oxford."

She didn't trust his contact. She didn't doubt he had a good one, but his connections were through the military, and she certainly didn't trust them. Kana flipped the glass in her fingers, the sharp corners digging into the pads of her fingertips. "Is there anything else you are hiding?"

They stared at one another. For all his smooth expressions, she had an inkling that maybe he wore fewer masks than she assumed. The lax line of his lips and his determined gaze in the dull tableside lighting made his eyes the color of a storming sky, gray without a chance of sun.

"No."

He said the single word with a gentleness wrapped in a firm fist. The uncertainty hung in the air, expanding between them, and then drifted away, fading like stale smoke. The mounting pressure behind her eyes warned of an oncoming migraine. She wanted him to be honest; she wanted to believe him, and that scared her. Kana moved away from the desk and handed the slide back to him. "Put that back on ice, we are going to Germany."

Chapter Forty-Four

Discretion was expected; Kana and Spencer were numbers one and two on the president's most-wanted list. She could kiss her luxurious private jet goodbye for now, and accepted the smuggling plane that looked like a wing might fall apart midway through the flight, but the shady hunk of machinery did its job. There was a silver lining in her porous consciousness.

Germany was chillier than she remembered. Spencer handed over crisp euros to the cab driver as she adjusted her wool scarf and walked into the pub, Spencer keeping a moderate distance behind her. The space was too warm, filled with men and women in polyester suits, leather shoes, and wool coats freed from the confines of the concrete offices. They gathered around the tables, bar, and corners of the room. She found a small table tucked in the back, near where the bathroom doors swung open every five minutes.

"An exquisite *Blume,* so far from home."

Kana turned her head, noting the familiar voice even without technological obstructions. Frederick on the phone was different from in person. He was shorter than she expected, but had the brashness and sturdy facial lines she associated with Germany.

He claimed the seat across from her. Although his thin, silvery hair was freshly clipped, his patchy facial hair, deep-set eyes, and tobacco-scented clothes labeled him as the quintessential run-down researcher.

"Frederick," Kana said, strands of the blonde wig tickling the sides of her neck. She placed the small birthday bag with its neatly fanned pink tissue paper onto the table. The gentle soothing mint remained in the back of her throat. If she turned a little more to the right, she'd have a better view of Spencer, who'd squeezed in at the edge of the bar. Seeing Spencer out of context and in a foreign country, she noted his facial ambiguity. His features were prominent enough, eye shape more rounded, face planes not too wide, all to obscure anyone from snapping a judgment of his potential ethnicity. If he tanned and allowed himself to grow three shades darker, let his facial hair grow, and curled his posture more, he could easily pass in another country, but to blend in Germany, in a pub near the prominent university, he wore glasses, an old button-down with the sleeves rolled to his elbows, and a cleanly shaved face. The little chameleon.

"A gift," she explained, leaning back and tilting her chin up. "I expect nothing to be traceable. Anything I tell you or have you look into remains between us. I'm sure you had an arrangement with Josephine. We can maintain those terms of agreement."

Frederick's eyes widened, his slumped posture twitching like a dog with a bone dangling in front of him. "An Ambrose donation is always appreciated." He accepted the gift. "It seems like a wasted journey, mail couriers exist."

"I'm not just delivering this donation. I'm ensuring the results are swift and above all, a secret. You'll find the laboratory equipped with everything you'll need." She reached into her purse and slid him a narrow purple envelope. The doctor flipped it open and removed a slim credit card-shaped metal keycard. "I'll see you tomorrow morning. The instructions are on the card."

She didn't tell Frederick the keycard was a one-way ticket. He would find himself in a locked panic room with the best furnishings, amenities, and a fully stocked kitchen.

―――――

It took less than two days for Frederick to hit the shiny red button beside the door. Kana rolled her neck as she shoved away from the desk of screens she had been staring at for the past few hours. Finally, she pushed the button near the doorframe, and the wall separating them lifted up.

"Unconventional methods to ensure secrecy," Frederick said from his slouched form over the computer. "But strangely, the best place I've enjoyed. Better than the five-star hotel in Luxembourg."

Kana stepped out from the doorway, the wall sealing behind her with a whoosh. "What did you find?"

"Would you believe me if I said I had your answers after five minutes of looking at the sample?" Frederick reached for the mug of coffee.

"I wouldn't believe you," Kana said, more pleased that Frederick seemed to have an answer.

He gulped down the coffee, a few drops staining his mustache. "That's good coffee. Would you mind giving me the link for the coffee machine?"

Kana stared at Frederick, ignoring his inane question. "If you are telling me you identified the sample in under five minutes, check your work."

"That's why I spent the rest of the time doing just that and confirming my suspicions." He ran his hands down his face. "Case number zero zero nine three. What sets this specimen apart is the strain on Chromosome 17, and two other groups." He absent-mindedly used his pen to scratch the back of his skull while he swirled the computer mouse, the *click, click, click,* and the black screen was replaced by an image of electrophoresis results, columns of bands, some shaded darker than others. With his pen, he indicated the five marked fluorescent genes, tapping the screen once for emphasis.

"And these are important because?" she pressed. She didn't have the patience to indulge the researcher any longer. He, on the other hand, was having a grand time, clapping his hands as he began to pace behind the counter.

"I nearly forgot, it's been so long," he said under his breath. "Dr. Ambrose came to me more than two decades ago." He paused, his face flushed as he snapped his jaw closed, as if realizing his slipup. "I'm sworn to secrecy." His beady gaze moved around the space to each of the cameras. His large forehead, accentuated by the receding hairline, broke out into a cold sweat.

"She's dead."

His entire body sagged as he reached for the pocket handkerchief to dab at the sweat. "*Mein herzliches Beileid*," he muttered in reverence. Kana could only assume it was some sort of phrase spoken after someone had passed. Frederick didn't know Josephine that well, and the woman had stopped seeking his specific knowledge shortly after the publication of her drug. "Is it a coincidence you brought me the same sample as her?"

Kana frowned. "What do you mean, the same sample?"

"She approached me, saying how I had flaws in my paper, 'Epigenomic Reconfiguration in Host–Parasite Symbiosis: An Inquiry into Adaptive Transcriptional Modulations.'" He chuckled. "Sharp tongue, repeating the doubts I had about my case studies. You know it's very difficult to tackle nature vs nurture, but to connect it to hosts . . ." He shook his head.

"What you are telling me isn't useful," Kana cut in. This conversation could have gone on for hours. "Josephine and I brought in the same sample. What's special about this person?" Josephine had brought in her tissue to be analyzed by a secondary researcher. There was something here, something Josephine couldn't explain or, at the very least, something for which she needed a second opinion.

"Comparatively, each individual marker isn't unique. This one . . ." He pointed to the glowing blur farthest to the left side of the screen. "Is the most common marker, the one that will be present in anyone with the parasite." Glowing meant it was activated. Kana didn't need that explained. "These two have been found to be involved in dictating many things: circulatory function, immune response, and even neural survival."

He pointed to the pink glowing rectangle toward the bottom of the screen. "But what's interesting is this marker, G7PD on Chromosome 7. Dr. Yen's research found that this particular gene can be finicky when expressed, and it is found in many lymphoma patients. Researchers found it to be one of the more common genetic markers in cancers."

"You're implying it's unusual that all of these genes are lit up. What does that mean for the person?"

"If this person is still alive, I would be shocked. While the parasite acts like cancer in host bodies, mutating and altering DNA sequences, it's also very tame and predictable. This individual is unstable, not unlike the Rabid Synthetic Users, but less severe. This person would be crippled physically, their physiology breaking down. Sometimes it could happen in the brain. A brain on fire."

"How do you know this person hasn't gone Rabid?"

"Their DNA isn't a Christmas tree. If I had my resources in my own personal lab, I would show you. Feral Users' markers are pure chaos. A highly interesting area of study. Rabid Synthetic Users have been the hottest topic of research."

"This person could be transitioning." Kana cut in. "Or someone close to being Rabid."

"I would say no, but I'm not an expert in this particular genetic oncology."

She ground her teeth again, failing to hold her sigh as the

throbbing in her skull increased against her temples at the mere thought of the missed meetings. This trip had turned out to be less helpful than she'd hoped. She learned two things: Josephine brought her own tissue sample, and there was an oddity in her genes. Nothing else. Josephine was a Natural because, before her, a person could only be a Natural or nothing, and by nothing, that meant dead. The theory of Josephine testing on herself seemed plausible. Frederick confirmed how little the scientific community knew about Synthetic Users.

"Who is the expert?" Kana asked. "This was Josephine's unsolvable puzzle, and secrecy is paramount. I do not want to run around the world speaking to a dozen scientists. You lot can be worse than gossiping wives."

"You want to speak with Dr. Yen in Oshiya. He was one of the first to work with Josephine in her student days."

Kana's jaw ticked. "And he can explain these gene markers in better detail."

Frederick nodded. "It is not uncommon for A.E. Potentia to cause unpredictable gene mutations. This person could be valuable for research."

"They are dead."

Frederick muttered something about such a wasted opportunity. Maybe all scientists were only interested in their devout search for truths and facts.

"I have one last question," Kana said. "Have you seen a Natural survive an injection of A.E. Potentia?"

The doctor laughed. "Impossible."

"Why?"

He clicked through a folder, and a separate file opened, showing a massive encrypted document with strings of DNA coding. "This," he said, clicking on a string of sequenced DNA, the top line coded red, "is fondly known as TP53. This is important in regulating cell cycles. Among a few other specific markers, they are altered forever after the Fever. Let's say Naturals are a glass of milk. We have a second cup that's black coffee." He held up his mug and took a swig. "Now, if we dumped the coffee into the milk, it's no longer milk. Trying to add A.E. Potentia to someone who already has the gene expression ruins them. Genes like TP53 copy and code incorrectly. Heart failure has been known to happen within a few days."

Kana nodded. "I'll be in touch. The doors will open in two hours. Take the elevator up to Level 1. It shouldn't have to be said, but do not speak about the past two days. I'll know. Josephine may be dead, but let's say I value science less than she did and won't have patience if I get a whiff of your betrayal."

Outside the lab, Kana furiously typed on the phone in her hands, ordering the transfer of all the information stored on the computers in the temporary lab to her personal cloud. Spencer pushed away from the brick wall he had been leaning against, and they walked side-by-side for three blocks before he hailed a taxi.

"Make sure the doctor gets a special drink tonight, and the lab is destroyed," she said, jamming her phone into her coat pocket. There were moments when voices came to mind as she made decisions: Oliver's voice, placating and careful authority in his warnings, or Bexley's, with her blunt questions in her thick voice that added a dreamlike quality even when she read a grocery list. And there was Josephine's voice, a nightmare, warning her of the decision she made, reminding her that a cocktail of scopolamine and Rohypnol might not be enough to make the doctor forget everything he'd learned. But a fresh voice came through, not judging or inserting his opinions. Spencer wouldn't like the decision, but he would allow her space to explain her reasoning, and in the end, he knew that she would do what she wanted.

"It was a success, then?" he asked once they were inside the taxi.

Kana nodded as she scrolled through the phone for her next contact. "He sent me a referral."

"Where to next?"

———

THE MODEST, TASTEFUL BEACH HOME WAS LOCATED AT the southern tip of the Isomayan Peninsula, further away from the flat beach line. Spencer stepped out of the car and approached the stained glass front door. A woman in her fifties, dressed in navy scrubs, leaned against the open door.

Kana couldn't hear what Spencer said, but the caretaker's soft expression and single nod were visible before she opened the door wider. Ten minutes later, the woman stepped out, a canvas bag tossed over her shoulder, and settled into the white truck parked in the driveway. Kana waited until the car was around the bend of the road before entering the home. The glass wind chime hanging near the front porch tinkled, signaling her arrival.

The briny ocean smell flowed through the elongated open windows and the back sliding door. Kana moved out of the narrow entranceway, listening to Spencer's quiet voice; he spoke just low enough that she couldn't make out words. The creak in the floorboards alerted Spencer to her arrival. He straightened as he stepped back.

"Mr. Yen," Kana announced her presence in the living quarters. The geriatric doctor sat in a wheelchair, angled across from an armchair that looked like a set piece from a Regency film, with overflowing bookshelves behind the chairs. He lifted his head, and the drooping, aged skin under his jaw swung like Jell-O.

"Dr. Yen," Kana amended. The cloudy film over his dark eyes confirmed his blindness. "We never had the pleasure of meeting," Kana continued as she moved across the space and sent Spencer a pointed look. He silently exited the living room, his heavy shoes not making a single sound as he vanished around the corner.

"The boy informed me of who you are. I'm surprised and interested in why you want to speak with me." His voice held the echoes of his forty years in New Zealand. "How is your mother?"

The question sent a torrent of mixed emotions to pierce her

heart and stir the remaining coffee in the pit of her stomach. "Dr. Ambrose is dead."

Dr. Yen lowered his chin in understanding, the blind eyes not bothering to angle themselves in her direction, but pointing to the open window with a far-off gaze. "She is brilliant. Was," he corrected. "A shock to the community when she was pregnant." Kana's eye twitched, the word pregnant landing with a subtle weight. A shock, because Josephine, who was surgically distant from anything warm and seemed incapable of love and affection, was expecting? Or a shock because of the expectation of society's contradictory demands: to vanish, to nurture, to be important but sidelined from being too important?

"You were her mentor for many years." Kana steered the conversation back to the reason she was there.

He nodded. "I was, but for only two years, and that was a lifetime ago."

"And your original area of study was with Passive Users, the genetic makeup of those who survived the Fever. You then focused on oncology."

"In layman's terms, a first-year primary school child could understand, yes." His head moved to face where she stood, the unfocused gaze landing somewhere around her stomach.

Kana had attempted to read Dr. Yen's famous research paper. The jargon and elusive text were too difficult; the introduction alone was a hefty fifteen pages. The gist of his studies dealt with the unique makeup of Passive Users, specifically phasers. The physical body of a Somi somehow regulated and made itself nonexistent to pass through matter.

"She was doing a thesis under your mentorship, and she switched. What was she researching?"

Dr. Yen grinned, the small, thin lips revealing stained teeth, as if he understood why Kana was here. "She was secretive, even at nineteen. When I had check-ins, observed her lab work, or evaluated her data, she refused to let me see her work in progress or review her notes."

Good to know Josephine had always been paranoid.

"But you had to know what she was doing."

"I suspected her research focused heavily on the Y chromosome."

Kana frowned. XY chromosomes made the male sex. Her gut reaction was that there wasn't anything of value there; men and women were Natural Users or Synthetic Users, the sex didn't matter. But Josephine was the genius.

"And after two years, she just left."

Dr. Yen's fingers ran along the heavy wool blanket draped over his lap. "She was instrumental in some of my research, but it was still a surprise when her paper regarding the drug she'd formulated came out. She was not the first researcher to attempt this formula."

"How did she do it?"

Dr. Yen hummed like an old sage about to impart wisdom. "You are not the first to ask. Re-creation has been the coveted dream of many for the past twenty-odd years. And I will tell you what I've told everyone else. The genetic makeup is altered, home-obox genes and HSPS and a few others are affected, but the target is three alleles."

"If researchers know the exact genes, or a group of them, why has everyone failed at duplication? There's microarray technology and other forms of tech that I can't pretend to know anything about, advances since Josephine's formula."

Dr. Yen clicked his tongue, an action that sent Kana reeling back into the past. The cold, bitter blade of disappointment sank into her chest at the memory of the sound passing between a different pair of lips. "Knowing the exact point of mutation is only one part. The most difficult part is then replicating the drug that is causing the mutation."

Kana forced her jaw to relax. First, Frederick, and now Yen, no one was offering clear-cut answers she desperately wanted. She rubbed at her temple. "I have data for a person who has an unusual set of activated genes: the gene for the parasite, and G7PD on Chromosome 7."

Dr. Yen's face scrunched, like a beanbag folding into itself. "Are you sure?"

"I would show you the results, but . . ." Kana paused politely enough to imply his disability. "Frederick said you were the expert regarding that special marker, G7PD on Chromosome 7. What makes it unique?"

"The gene is flagged for certain cancers, such as lymphoma. Although it is rarer to find in the vascular system, G7PD is also connected to the circulatory system. Dr. Kim and Dr. Phan found that the parasite somehow affects the growth of cancer, even reversing it entirely. In a study with patients who had cancer before exposure to the parasite, they miraculously no longer exhibited the genes. The parasite's alteration of its DNA structure cured them of cancerous ailments."

Josephine had cancer, cancer that should have been eradicated once she overcame the Fever. "It's impossible for someone to have this G7PD marker and be a User."

"Impossible is not a word I believe in. Rare, maybe one in three billion. We know very little about the natural world. Science may make models and attempt to reveal structures and laws, but nature has no obligation to follow them."

"How would having cancer while being infected with the parasite affect someone?"

Dr. Yen's hand rubbed under his chin, the dry, coarse scratching sound like sandpaper. "Hypothetically, it would cause utter chaos. The parasite alters the genetic makeup of the host, fixing any transcription errors that a prior cancer could have caused. The parasite caused a missed sequence, and the host's body adapted to having the parasite and the cancer coexisting. Depending on their manifestation, the body could be terribly deformed internally and externally, or they could warp the world around them. If they were somehow still alive, they must have found a way to keep the cancer in remission." Dr. Yen sighed as he closed his eyes. "I am tired. You can see yourselves out."

———

A WEEK AFTER MEETING WITH DR. YEN, KANA sidelined Josephine's mystery, returning to constant conference calls, a deluge of document reviews, and signing. There were the ill-timed migraines—her skull was a microwave, and her brain was being cooked—then the gaps in her memory, the pesky periods when time didn't feel lost, but the digital clock and the risen or set sun told her differently. It was during one of those boorish calls, while she barely listened to the arguing attorneys as they went through transition of power documents with a fine-tooth comb for the hundredth time, that it happened.

"Shit," she hissed, dropping the knife onto the plastic board. Spencer was at her side with antiseptic, and maybe it was the smell and the next phrase she heard on the conference call—*running silent, running deep*—that triggered the hibernating memory.

Chapter Forty-Five

An impression, bizarrely visceral, overwhelmed her. She couldn't decipher what she saw in her mind's eye, or parse the emotions, but was left hollow and raw. Fear overtook all of that, swallowing it whole, and clung to her the longest. As fleeting as the broken memory resurfaced, it vanished, but Kana had the strongest feeling that Josephine was at the center.

Running silent, running deep. She spun the phrase in her mind like a carousel stuck in motion, and with each rounding pass, the meaning behind the phrase was stripped, softening and fading away. The more she forced the memory to reform, the more the shapes transformed, making her question if the blurred outline was solid. It bothered her; a memory was decomposing to the point of forgetfulness, but for a glorious moment, it had roared to life.

Kana couldn't say when they had moved locations, but they were no longer in a roadside lodge. Instead, based on the living room setup, they were in a house. The smell was a mix of sharp citrus cleaning solution and musk. When she peeked around the blinds, she saw identically bland, beige shoebox homes lined in neat order.

In a moment of weakness, when she fell into a liminal haze caught between a catatonic stillness and the crushing weight of unfinished tasks, she asked for Spencer's thoughts about the phrase.

"It sounds like a submarine description," he said, the soft thump of two halves of his novel closing in his hands.

Submarine—the word was a bolt of lightning hitting the same target twice. She remembered him asking if she'd been inside one before, but hearing the word again left a paralyzed feeling, as if her body was frozen inside a lake.

"Kana." Spencer said her name with a pointed emphasis. "You're slipping into the void. Follow the sound of my voice. I was on the sofa across from you. Remember, you commented that the sofa was the color of day-old cat vomit when we first arrived at the safe house? You dropped the mug in your hands. Unfortunately, it's shattered, and you may have burned the tops of your feet. Can you open your eyes? I don't know how far you've fallen . . . Good. I'm crouched at your side. I'm going to rest my hand on top of your left one. Can you feel my hand?"

She heard him. By now, they'd done this dance half a dozen times. He was right, she hadn't become too lost yet. His voice was still audible, a misshapen echo in a cave that she wandered through until the path became clearer. As his hand curled over hers, stuck midair and cupping an invisible mug, she continued silently listening to Spencer's gentle, vibrating voice. He was careful when he spoke to her, explaining every movement and action as he moved her to the sofa. It took time, fifteen minutes or so, for her eyelids to remain open for longer than three minutes, and her sight to remain clear.

A fun new development to add to Kana's running list of issues was an evolution in her blackouts. The first time remained unknown, as neither Kana nor Spencer noticed. Spencer estimated it may have been happening a handful of times before, but it wasn't until Kana blacked out midway through a sentence, the heavy thunk of her head smashing against the side of the desk, and her body crinkling to the stained carpet of one of the roadside lodge rooms, that Spencer went into a tizzy.

According to him, Kana's blackouts had been tamer. Her body had a keen sense of when she was in a stationary spot, whether that be leaning back in a chair, on a bed, or in the seat of a car. This collapse was abrupt, as if plagued by narcolepsy, and when Spencer went to tend to her, touching her arm and checking her head, she was lucid enough to scream. Spencer said she babbled about her skin, her eyes remained glued shut, and she writhed on the floor. Kana failed at hiding her mortification at the image of her possessed antics, but he gently compared her distress to someone experiencing the Fever, and it took a few minutes before he'd gauged that she could hear him. Eventually, he coaxed out what the problem was: the cotton of her shirt, the tight strap of her bra against her skin. She returned to her normal senses to find herself standing in the center of the bathtub, naked but dry, the curtain pulled closed and Spencer waiting patiently on the other side. His hand snaked through the side of the curtain with a folded towel in his grip.

As Kana's blackouts became less frequent, these bouts of irregular moments took over. It wasn't clear what was triggering them. Sometimes it was a word or phrase, or a scent, or an object. Her senses were being beaten, strung, and blown to new levels of acuity and sensitivity. Between Spencer's observations and her insight, they'd determined there was a spectrum. At first, they used levels much like a pain scale. But as the occurrences became more frequent, they identified different stages, and she created a rudimentary naming convention: echo, veil, void. The stages bled into deeper levels, each layer taking a longer recovery time. The void had only occurred twice, and Kana didn't want to experience it a third time.

After the word submarine had triggered an echo episode, she'd been close to the veil. She needed answers. Years ago, Dr.

Martinez had suggested a mix of cognitive and hypnotic therapies to help with the prevalent PTSD symptoms after one of her breakdowns had led to a near overdose. The idea was to help Kana forget the experiences and ease her body's physical reaction when triggered. Kana had laughed, saying it wouldn't work because she refused to be hypnotized, but more important was the fear of allowing someone to have that control over her. Suffice to say, hypnotism treatment was never brought up again. But could hypnosis help recover memories? She didn't think it was possible. If Hollywood used the gimmick, then most likely the results would be more fictional than truth.

The days moved on, but the niggling worry that she was forgetting something important became too much to ignore. Kana sent a research team out for more information about the best doctor for memory retrieval, and they came back with a name —Dr. Weitz—who was a promising and highly revered clinical psychologist whose studies combined drugs and hypnosis.

———

KANA ARRANGED AN IMPROMPTU MEETING. DR. WEITZ was under the impression he was attending an exclusive conference held at Dr. Yen's beach bungalow. Instead, he was driven to a private beach home, an alcove away from Dr. Yen's home. Dr. Weitz was hesitant; the perfectly shiny cue ball of his hairless head and permanently carved wrinkles in his forehead gave him the air of a deeply troubled monk. His studies had started human clinical trials just a year ago, but Kana was persuasive, and the check with a substantial number of zeroes at the end sealed the deal.

"How many sessions will it take?" Kana asked as she settled on the sofa. The remnants of cedar incense hung in the air.

Dr. Weitz's hands ran along the edge of the polished wooden table set behind the back of the couch across from Kana. His fingers rubbed against each other as if inspecting the lack of dust.

"You have a specific memory, the general knowledge of when, and associated trigger words. Each of those elements adds to a higher chance of a successful outcome, but we won't know until the first session. But on average, five. You must remember, the sample size for this study is small. I'm providing an average of less than ten patients." Finished with his visual inspection of the cabin, he lowered his lanky frame onto the cushion.

Kana's face soured; five sessions seemed somehow both too many and not enough. "How do I know it isn't a false memory?"

"We won't know, unless the memory you are searching for was in a place with recorded footage, which I highly doubt if you've resorted to this level of recovery. Most memories involve people and questioning them individually about their interpretations of the events could help prove or disprove your version of events."

If Josephine was involved, then her only witness was dead. Kana's eyes met Spencer's. He guarded the door behind the doctor and faced Kana along with the expansive windows to the beach line. He caught her hesitation and offered a smile of encouragement. If he weren't with her, she wouldn't have considered hypnotism. She trusted him. The volume and frequency of her paranoia roared to life, Josephine's voice hissing, *You can't trust him*. She hid her wince as she adjusted on the couch, fluffing the pillow against the armrest.

"Let's get this started," she huffed.

The doctor made feeble complaints, but his ambition to have another test subject was poorly concealed. In twenty minutes, the rhythmic *tick-tick-tick* of the metronome grated on her while her inner forearm pinched where she received the drug, and the session began.

"You are floating in a body of water," Dr. Weitz said, his voice meditative, the rounded barrel sound cut through the dark liquid she floated on. "The current is soothing. You are moving with the beat of the metronome. You feel weightless and safe."

Kana buried further into the dreamlike state, her body swaying above the water's pull, flowing as the doctor described, left and right.

"You are fourteen, and now standing in front of a door."

Kana was immediately upright, the vast pool of water gone. Her bare feet stood on a white tiled floor in an empty, dully lit room while she faced the front doors of the Ambrose estate—custom French style, with the top half fitted with glass that tinted as the sun set, before blackening completely to mirror the night sky.

"When you open the door, you will hear the phrase 'running silent, running deep,'" the doctor's disembodied voice instructed. "Whatever may lie beyond the door cannot harm you."

Tick.

Tick.

Tick.

"Open the door."

The Murano glass doorknob, shaded dark emerald, twisted in her grip, and she crossed the threshold. The phrase rang in her mind, and the floor vanished beneath her feet. Her body pulled down, not a plummet, but a gentle descent like a bird's feather caught in a spring breeze.

With the next inhale, she stood with the soles of her feet balanced on a bar, her heels dangling off the end, while her hands gripped metal bars painted the color of yellow mustard.

"Take your time. Where are you? Look around, smell, and listen."

Sharp metal was all she could sense, because steel encased her from all sides. She was inside a chrome alloy tube, perched on a ladder, and if she looked below, there was only more gray. The space tightened with every breath, each second stretching into something heavier as the dream-like quality dissolved into a thin film, and there was an unknown pressure against her sinuses in the thick, stale air.

"You're safe. Inhale deeply, hold your breath for four seconds. Now, exhale slowly, allowing all the oxygen to squeeze out of your lungs. Take a deep breath and feel your belly and chest expand. Nothing can hurt you here. You said you're on a ladder, and there's ground below. Were you going up or climbing down?"

Her body moved on its own in sped-up reverse, as if rewinding an old DVD. She descended down the ladder and walked backwards down a hallway, and dove back into a small container, the top lifting and sliding shut over her. Normally, she would be panicking, the adrenaline spike would kick-start and her breath would come out like the shuttering of a camera in burst mode. But she wasn't panicking. In fact, she felt nothing, because the voice promised she was safe.

"Press on the top."

She obeyed the voice, and the top lifted only when she twisted to her side and thrust her shoulder upward. She stepped out of the crate and stood at her full height.

The ceiling was rather low and built with curved metal panels. The further she walked down the hallway, the more claustrophobic she felt. It was like being in an endless stainless-steel straw. There was a loud bass vibration and the chugging of mechanical machinery.

Kana looked up to see an even narrower cylindrical passage with stairs. She pulled down the ladder and started climbing. *Tap, tap, tap,* the soft leather soles of her shoes hit the metal bars of the ladder.

The circular hatch was open. The larger the opening became, the worse her stomach churned. Her throat clogged, and the air entering her lungs became scarcer. She was shrinking back, diminishing herself as the open hatch became larger. As her head lifted, she found her eye line level with the floor, and her heart was a thumping rabbit's foot.

She couldn't look.

A powerful force snapped Kana awake; the impact felt like

falling from an airplane, with air rushing up her face so fast that she couldn't breathe. A second loud, sharp crack of two hands smashing together, and Kana's eyes flew open.

Dr. Weitz hummed off to her right, thoughtful. "The memory you found, that was the correct one?"

Kana stared at the thick bamboo blades of the ceiling fan, listening to its dull vroom sounds. "Why did I wake up?" She sat up and rolled her shoulders back, feeling like she had woken from a heavy nap, her limbs laden with fatigue.

"Fear is a surprisingly powerful blocker," Dr. Weitz said. "But there is another possibility: there is nothing to see. If the latter, I must caution against trying to force a memory. After repeated attempts, the mind will forge its own version of events."

"How will I know which version is true?"

Dr. Weitz looked at her, and the foot crossed over his leg twitched. "What is truth? It defines our reality, and when it comes to the subjective mind, the perception of reality is not always the truth."

Kana scowled. "I don't need a proverb for an answer."

"As I mentioned earlier, another witness of the event in any capacity, someone to verify your presence, can provide a guiding measure if the memory is falsified."

Kana held onto the sharper recollection from the memory, and she was sure she'd been alone.

"If I may say, I believe the chances of your memory being wholly false are not significant. I admit, I'm surprised by your mind. When you gave me the trigger words, I didn't expect that you would be in a literal submarine. A word has many associations and could be an obscure placeholder, but it seems you are not as disillusioned as many others. It is also helpful that you have forgotten the memory. The more times you return to a memory, your presence leaves a smudged impression, and this one seems relatively clean."

Her initial comparison of Dr. Weitz to a monk was more

accurate than she expected. "I have everything working for me, then. How many attempts before the potential of a false memory becomes too great?"

"On average, four, but by then, it's a fifty-fifty split."

This was not ideal. So she had three more tries.

"Again."

While Dr. Weitz said he admired her tenacity, the drug needed twenty-four hours to flush through her system, and when the doctor headed to the front door, Kana informed him that the three of them would be here until the end of the trial. Dr. Weitz's slim shoulders shrugged. "A cup of green tea to my room, please."

Kana felt her eye twitch as Spencer answered the request and went to the kitchen. She claimed the patio sofa, tamping down the anxious need for her phone; it was too risky to continue with calls or messaging. She didn't need anyone to know about this meeting.

———

"Let's begin," Dr. Weitz said as Kana shimmed down the couch and forced her body to back into the velvet material.

Tick-tick-tick. The metronome started, and Kana's mind slipped through the couch cushions and floated along the ocean's waves.

"You are fourteen, and now you're standing in front of a door."

Kana was in front of the French doors, standing against a wall of white snow.

"When you open the door, you will hear the phrase 'running silent, running deep.' You are safe. The anxieties and fears have no power over you." The doctor's ghostly voice continued, and, like a dream, she dropped into a scene, standing in a curved hallway, surrounded by the metal cocoon.

"What do you hear?"

There was a deep clanging, a distant hum of air moving through vents. There were no other sounds of human movement, no footsteps, and no voices.

"Do you see the ladder to the upper deck?"

She didn't move. The memory flowed like watercolors bleeding outward, blurring until the paint hit the water's edge, and she stood below the mouth of the ladder.

"As you climb the ladder, any worries you have lessen."

Kana's hands moved, gripping each metal step as she moved higher and higher, the circular hatch above looking like a bright sun. When she was near the top, each additional step was like walking on thin ice. She felt like she was testing the surface with her weight, and the next shift could mean plunging into frozen waters.

"Take a moment, inhale deeply. Hold your breath, and exhale slowly. You are an observer; nothing that you see can harm you. Inhale, exhale." The doctor's slow-river voice steadied her footing, expanding her chest, and she took two more steps, just enough to peek over the thick ledge.

Josephine sat on the edge of a bed. Her thighs were blossoming with thin-stemmed fungi, the jewel-colored caps providing a rainbow of hues. Beneath the shadows of the taller mushrooms, shorter, stouter collections sprouted. Thin rivulets of blood leaked around her pale legs like red threads. Josephine reached down with long tweezers, combing through the forest.

While Kana focused on Josephine seated on the single bed, in the corner of her vision, she could make out the room. The space was stacked with lab equipment and chemicals; there was a blood plasma machine and an infusion stand with a dangling, unused banana bag. The cloying scent of synthetic cherry, medicinal and pungent, was intensified by the eerie red glow spilling from overhead lamps. Beneath the red suns, rows of containers cradled mushroom colonies.

Was it the sensation of eyes on her, the traceable scent of Kana's conditioner, or the feeling of Josephine's air being shared that abruptly caused the woman to look up?

Kana knew those eyes—rage, raw and unyielding, nothing like the fleeting anger she'd seen reflected in men who lashed out with fists, kicks, or even weapons. This was worse, a silent promise like the thick rope of a noose tightening on her neck, and then the trap door opened below her feet and the world was black.

Chapter Forty-Six

The invisible force crunched and bent her like a garbage disposal before spitting her to consciousness. She doubled over as the lines of her throat were slathered with vomit. "Are you alright?" a disembodied voice asked. The mint quelled the nausea enough to make her move away from the warm figure approaching her. The drug altered her vision, like looking through rain-slick windows, the wash of colors was too blurry to differentiate, which was how she slammed her shins into the coffee table and jammed her toe into the first step up to the beach house entryway.

"Kana—no, stay here, I'll bring her back."

Salted wind slapped against her back as her naked feet smashed over the sharply pebbled ground beneath her. Her hands scrubbed at her eyes, tears smearing across her face, effectively clearing her vision as she moved faster until she was running, her body trying to match the pace of her mind.

She was it. Josephine was one in three billion; she was the exception. Kana didn't know when Josephine went through the Fever, but she imagined it must have been in her early teens, around the time when Josephine transformed the garage into a lab. Josephine had worked with Dr. Yen to learn about his Passive research and his theories about the G7PD coding.

It all fit into place; the specifics didn't matter, because Kana was sure that somehow, in some way, Josephine's fucked-up cancerous parasite and the error in her coding had caused the irregular fungi growths. Dr. Yen said it would wreak havoc on the body internally and externally, except, maybe for Josephine, it was just internal. She hadn't made the drug with hopes it would synthesize and help other Users survive the Fever. The drug was formulated to suppress her cancer. It was her chemotherapy, a highly specific formulation that required her own fungal growths. That is why no one could recreate the drug because Josephine had used her own genetics.

The road's dead end forced Kana to stop as the land sloped and drastically plunged to the ocean. She pressed the heel of her hand against her forehead as she grappled with this utterly impossible conclusion. This was the secret.

Josephine could never produce more than a certain amount of A.E. Potentia because she was limited by her body's production. There was a reason Passive Users had such an unexplainable reaction to the drug, the reason their veins sprouted fungi. But what of the Active Users and their hunger, had Josephine secretly been eating humans? Kana wasn't sure about cannibalism, but there was a reason why Oliver couldn't manufacture any more A.E. Potentia after Josephine died. He was forced to work around the missing ingredient, and the attempted replacement inadvertently created a new variant of a Rabid Synthie.

"Kana," Spencer's concerned voice interrupted her thoughts. "Can you hear my voice?"

"Shh." She waved her hands around, her left hand smacking across his jaw, her other hitting his sternum. He was much closer than she anticipated, but even his mint-flavored aura and warm presence couldn't distract her as a grin split across her face. There would never be more A.E. Potentia unless another researcher was successful in creating a different drug. The world would move on from the hopes of creating Synthetic Users.

But what about Josephine's body? Whoever had assisted Josephine until the end, whoever had scraped the last of her fungi had the last ingredient for a potential production. Oliver made the most sense. Had he figured out that Josephine's flora was necessary for the drug? If he'd harvested her final blooms, there might only be a hundred vials of A.E. Potentia left in existence.

The fabric of a coat dropped over her curled shoulders. She shrugged her arms into Spencer's jacket and pressed the soft material of the sleeve cuff to her dry lips. If Josephine had revealed her methods after concocting A.E. Potentia, she'd have been sought after like the Holy Grail. Keeping it a secret was the best move, but why continue to keep it a secret after her death? Josephine's character wouldn't allow the world not to know. She could have released a statement, published a radical paper, or revealed it all in a posthumous publication. Josephine always silently planned, acted, and if the results weren't to her liking, planned again until the last move was sorted and she could stand and say, "Checkmate." There had been no guarantee Kana would ever find her body or figure out Josephine's secret. Josephine wouldn't be silent, not about this. She had to have told someone, someone who would be dealt a devastating loss if the truth was revealed.

"I'm tired," Kana said as she turned away from the cloudy sky that reminded her of snow on gravel, and to the source of the ever-present mint taste. Spencer stood leisurely with his hands in his pockets, humming in agreement as she walked toward him, leveling her cut feet onto the smoother paved road.

"You've been running on four hours of sleep, some days even less, and you just sprinted for nearly a kilometer." Spencer said, offering a reason for her admission of exhaustion.

A mutual silence was between them as they walked back to the seaside house. As Spencer spoke to the doctor, she half listened to ensure Spencer kept to the script and their plan. The front door closed, and a car engine faded in the distance while she lay prone on the sofa. Her eyes traced over the wooden beams in the ceiling, counting each time she returned to the ceiling fan. As the afterglow of solving Josephine's puzzle dimmed, her body caved into exhaustion.

"I'm going to clean your feet," Spencer said as he slowly sat near the edge of the sofa where her legs were dangling limply.

"I've been unhinged." Kana reflexively jerked her right foot as Spencer's rough fingers touched the outside of her ankle. "And I don't want to talk about the blackouts or the catatonic symptoms." She'd blame the stress; the volcanic migraines alone were enough to send her unconscious. Time was washing over her, the meat cravings didn't lessen, and she didn't have the time or the headspace to worry about the possibility of her body edging toward a Rabid state. She'd take the evolved blackouts over worms multiplying under her flesh. "Did I tell Weitz what I saw in the submarine?"

"No, you fell silent and then sprinted out."

Good, that was good. She closed her eyes. A soft cloth brushed against her foot, followed by a stinging mist. She involuntarily tried to yank her leg away, but Spencer kept her in place as the antiseptic smell assaulted her nose. Spencer hadn't asked her why she ran, or what she remembered.

She propped herself on her elbows to watch him tear at the plastic sealing of the band-aid; his profile was carved like the first attempt at a weeping Roman angel, handsome but not perfectly structured in the final marble showpiece. He diligently placed the bandages on the minor cuts. Her heart wiggled uncomfortably as she watched him take care of her.

"I figured it out." Her admission was a soft murmur that the rational part of her wanted to gobble back. She didn't have to explain anything to him, but the urge to share her revelation was too strong. She sat up properly as Spencer moved to her left foot, lifting her right leg to tuck her knee under her chin.

Her fingers idly stroked the rough cotton of the Band-Aid on the side of her foot. "The memory was important, and I don't think she wanted me to ever remember what I saw." Kana watched Spencer gently cradle her left foot in one hand, tweezers in the other, carefully removing the broken bits of rock. He didn't ask for her to continue, but she wanted him to ask her. Her fists clenched at the fleeting notion.

"Why are you still here?" she asked. When her mind wasn't in fast forward as she planned for the future, trying to lessen the shit-storm she faced returning to the spotlight while trying to under-stand Josephine's puzzling past, the present remained acutely rare. She didn't have time to be present, and in the scarce stillness, right now, Spencer didn't have to be here. He could have left weeks ago, and the opportunities to betray her were countless. She didn't understand.

"I want to help you." He lifted his bowed head and met her gaze. She felt faint at the unadulterated, single-focused earnestness he offered. There was a crack, a pebble propelled against her thick, glass shields. Her cheeks warmed as her insides somersaulted once, twice, and she hated the uncomfortable encroaching warmth under her skin. This wouldn't do.

"Out of the kindness of your heart, you would rather stay holed up in grungy hotels, listening to me argue at all hours of the day, having to talk me out of catatonic states? You could go back and tell the president I drugged you and escaped. You can go back to whatever you were doing before this assignment."

He exhaled as he dragged the warm cloth along the bottom of her foot. His eyes focused on his work. "You're looking for some other explanation for my reasoning, and no matter what I say, you'll think I have an ulterior motive. But I hope, one day, you can see that people have the capacity to be honest and kind."

Kana's lips parted, wordless because she had no argument. She snatched back her foot. "I can take care of myself."

Spencer set the medical kit on the bed. "You can, and I'll be here, just in case."

Chapter Forty-Seven

The pointed toe of a luxe platform loafer poked out of the open car door. A leather-gloved hand helped Kana as she gracefully stepped out of the car. She arrived at the end of summer, a type of day that was a reprieve from the laden humidity and scorching sun, a type of day that bordered on too calm.

"Miss Ambrose." Laura burst through the front doors. Her tablet pressed against her chest as her lips fell into that crystalized, strained smile. "We weren't expecting you."

Kana pushed the sunglasses to the crown of her head. Her sharp eyes were exaggerated by the gentle clouds of red around the edges of her eyelids, with a sharp maroon line cutting over her black lashes. "I expect him to be in the White Room. Our deal is done." Kana brushed past the assistant and up the stairs, the soft cotton of her dress blowing around her as the summer's wind curled around her like a living thing. Spencer offered a polite nod to Laura as he silently followed Kana through the estate. The stream of expletives silently aimed at Kana's back was a harmless swarm of gnats. Laura's fresh manicure clicked away on a phone before she resigned herself to leading Kana and Spencer to the elevator, lifting her nose in a gesture of farewell as she turned on her heels, far too much like a cat lifting its tail to reveal its asshole.

In the White Room, Kana poured herself a glass of whiskey and lounged on the sofa, the first edition of a classic Oshiya novel in hand. Spencer remained standing near the only point of entry, close to Kana. She topped off her second glass and was staring at the Klimt painting which hung on the mantel—how unpatriotic —when the door flung open to admit the president.

"It is a relief to see you both safe and sound. I was worried. It's been more than three months," the president announced, that last sentence undoubtedly aimed at Spencer. "My dear, more warning would be appreciated. I was in the middle of a rather important meeting."

Kana sipped the century-aged alcohol before turning to him, revealing the metal, hand-sized Lu Ban lock, shaped like a sphere compass, that she had commissioned. His irritated face fell slack as he stepped closer. Kana walked around, purposefully keeping one of the armchairs between them.

"I was ordered to find Josephine, and at the end of the rainbow was this." She set it on the desk. "Go ahead, I already solved the puzzle." Kana gestured to the desk as she moved coun-terclockwise, while the president swiftly moved clockwise to the object of his desire.

He tried not to seem eager, but his hands clasped the sphere, and with a twist, the top gave a satisfying click and opened. Nestled inside was a single test tube. "How do I know what's in this?" he asked as he held up the glass vial to the light. It was an unassuming, clear liquid, with a tiny amount of cloudiness, as if three drops of milk had been added.

"Why don't you ask the real question?" Kana's gaze never left the president's as she twirled the alcohol, the ice cube clinking along the glass walls. His inspecting gaze left the liquid in the tube and speared into Kana's.

"Is this the cure?"

Kana smirked. "No, that is a version of the drug that's been produced for the past eight months. The drug that guarantees the person becomes Rabid in less than a month. That is just a little sample for you to keep as a reminder of the failure you allowed out into the world. But you found out the hard way, didn't you?"

Kana watched the president's eyes, the lines of his sharp cheekbones, and clean-shaven jaw. "How is Nycole these days?" she asked.

There it was: that predatory glint, the clamping of his teeth as if to tame the roaring anger. Oh, she knew that sharp narrowing of eyes, and the curled fist on a desk. He was imagining all the ways he could hurt her. She purred. He was too obvious.

It had taken about four days—which Kana didn't appreciate —for her scouts to dig up this particular dirty little secret. She wanted it done in three, but it took time to shuffle through Oliver's contact list and navigate the right sources. But she got a thread, a single entry from a private, abhorrently expensive doctor to visit Bette Cummings, which honestly was the most obvious alias. Bette Davis and E.E. Cummings happened to be Nycole's artistic idols. The twenty-something-year-old was an aspiring artist, an actress, a musician, and a poet, and if you gave critics any weight, she had failed in all three areas. After the initial visit, two more doctors from the other prestigious hospitals in Oshiya visited, and then nothing, with the exception of wire transfers into Swiss accounts. Why would the president pay three of the best doctors hush money? Well, the answer was obvious. She didn't need to review the follow-up reports of the doctors' specialties or extracurricular research in Rabid Synthetics to confirm her suspicions. What lengths people went to help a loved one.

The president smirked in response to Kana's triumphant smile. "You think you have it all solved." His voice was dark. Kana had struck a nerve. "You think you solved the puzzle, but your tiny little corner can't compare to the larger picture."

Kana remained impassive. He'd shown his hand. Nycole must

be in serious condition, if not dead, after attempting to transition to a Synthie. The doctors were summoned because, unlike her friends, Nycole had found a bad dose of A.E. Potentia, and her transition had been anything but normal. Kana suspected she was still alive. Why bother with a cure if she were dead? The president's quick arrival in the White Room spoke to his desperation. It was possible Nycole was a Somi, a Phaser rather than a Passive User, or more likely an Active User. But that would mean the president was supplying food, and that was an entirely different accusation, because if Nycole were an Rabid Idu Synthie, then there was only one source of meat she would want. To accuse the president of supplying a steady meal plan of human was outrageous.

"In about ten minutes, a car will come by with a special delivery: Josephine's ashes. I would have loved to deliver her body, but the lab self-destructed."

His face remained skillfully pleasant, but his aura swelled with each exhale.

"She's been dead for at least eight months. But I'm sure you've known that, since she left you a note." And wasn't that just a perfect little nugget of presumed information? Kana circled in, unable to stop the spread of her lips. She couldn't prove anything, but after being stuck inside a cramped room for the past few weeks, sending off her little rats to bring back morsels of information, her suspicions had grown. The president had to have known about Josephine's death, because her demise would hurt the government more than anyone.

"It's a wonder how the sales of the drug nearly doubled in the past year." Kana stepped closer and removed a small thumb drive from the pocket of her dress. "I held up my end of the deal." Her chin moved, and Spencer left the wall he was resting against to place a folder on the president's desk. "Inside are the directions to where I found her. You're free to do whatever you wish with the facility. As you'll see, there's not much left."

The president laid his hands flat on the desk as he flipped open the folder to reveal dozens of pictures of the underground lab, with nothing left but charred steel and melted moldings of the facility's lab equipment.

"This is my renunciation of citizenship, allowing me full immunity for any past transgressions. The hold order for my knowledge of sensitive government code is void, effective the first of September. You have no control over Ambrose, Inc."

The president laughed. It was humorless, breathy and mocking. "We have no deal, girl. You think a pile of ashes and your word that it's Josephine's will be enough?"

"In ten minutes, every major news network will be sent an anonymous email with information detailing all the military deals made, with the total count of two hundred and seventeen contaminated drugs sold. There's a nice little audio clip of you speaking against your advisors, who explicitly warned that the drug's side effects were unstable and more severe than any other version."

The president's eyes flicked to Spencer, as if he expected the man to whip out a knife and slit Kana's throat.

"I'll see you in court," Kana said. "It looks like you have a lot of cleanup to do. The variant Rabids are difficult to handle. If you haven't already been alerted, there were some issues with a few other elite children besides your daughter: George Adillyum and Vyolette Oskar. Good luck with your re-election." Kana set the empty crystal glass on a coaster and began to walk to the door.

A laugh cut through the air, and a dark, cynical undertone lay in the amused sound. "You should be grateful. I made you."

As much as Kana wanted to keep walking, her body reacted faster than her brain could tell it to stop. She paused and barely turned to meet his smug gaze.

The curiosity was a siren call, enticing and juicy. Kana's medical history, the section almost two months after her birth with the single piece of white yarn running down the paper, the only one of its kind. Was he insinuating she was a subject, perhaps

Josephine's first subject to take the drug? Kana didn't have proof, but she could see it. Josephine, young, and ambitious, confronting the president in the White Room. Kana swaddled in the crook of her arm—no Josephine rarely touched her—she would be in a stroller, feeble and helpless as she was poked with a needle.

She focused on the silence in the room, ignoring the rush of blood as it accelerated.

Kana's mind slingshot back to the blow-up at one of the motels, with Spencer's claim that she might be a Synthie, more pieces of the disastrous puzzle of Kana's life. Of course, she wasn't normal; she was the greatest mystery Josephine spent decades researching. Behind every man was a woman to take the fall, and Josephine made damn sure it wouldn't be her. Kana's lips curled. "You should use better bait. That's old news."

The president's face was comical. He thought he had a checkmate. She was very interested in how and why she was a little different. Still, knowing the president had a hand in it all, she wouldn't give him the satisfaction of showing interest.

"You still report to me, Mr. Spencer," the president said.

"As a matter of fact, Mr. Spencer no longer works for the military. Under the Nybloom Initiative, Revision XIV, Section Five, he has been honorably discharged," Kana said. "Don't worry, there's a copy of the initiative and the required signatures from three prominent military personnel. You can mail Spencer that cheap velvet box with the gold medal another day." She took two steps toward the door.

"Anyone can throw a temper tantrum, wreak havoc, and destroy. It takes far more work and finesse to build the system. You are toying with things you can't even come close to understanding." The president's ominous warning was both cool and flippant.

"I don't need to understand the game to know you made a big mistake. Josephine was brilliant, the kind of mind that's born once in a handful of generations. Thinking you could produce the drug without her was foolish. We've seen all the other countries try and fail. This is the end to A.E. Potentia. I'd love to say I hope to never see you again, but I'm sure we'll see each other very soon."

Spencer opened the door, and they left the White Room.

"You always have to have the last word," Spencer said softly as they exited through security.

She didn't look over her shoulder at him, but the curve of her raised cheek gave away her smile. Sue her, she was a little too pleased with the turn of the last few minutes. The entire confrontation could have gone several ways, but this was one of the best outcomes. Sometimes she wished she had acted worse, allowed the poisonous rage to infect everyone and everything around her until they begged for the pain to stop. Sometimes she wished to be worse than Josephine. She slid into the driver's seat, the engine purring beneath them as she hastily dodged around traffic. They rode in silence until Kana parked at the edge of a winding road that oversaw the ocean.

She stepped out, and Spencer silently followed her around to the front of the car.

"You didn't have to help me," he said casually.

"I wasn't helping you. He would have forced the information from you, willingly or unwillingly. Camp Umbridge."

His eyebrows rose at the utterance of the camp, whether the whispers of it being a torture site for terrorists or unwanted people remained the center of a conspiracy honey pot. "You never stop surprising me."

"If you found yourself tortured in the not-so-secret prison, it would have disrupted my plans. It's best if you had a way out. If he didn't suspect your sudden silence as an act of betrayal, he certainly would have considered not stopping me as an act of defiance."

"Do you know how dismissive you are? As if helping others is so uncomfortable that you have to make it about helping your-self," Spencer said thoughtfully.

Kana softly scoffed through her nose. The tops of her cheeks felt warm. The perceptive bastard, pointing out her habits. "I didn't realize you took a look at my shrink's notes about my selfish tendencies," she tossed back with no malice. They stood close to each other, Kana liking the ocean mist and chilled mint on the back of her tongue. He didn't comment. Unlike her, he was good at not shooting back a response.

The ocean was beautiful. The moving waves sparkled with diamond dust under the sun's light. Kana had a team of lawyers tying up loose ends and securing the will. Even without a body and only two eyewitnesses to Josephine's corpse, one being the sole inheritor, the will was surprisingly not that difficult. Josephine's safeguards stipulated a five-year presumption of death, making Kana the de facto head of the company until then. The roaring board members and CEOs of the different Ambrose factions would fight the will, which would be the hardest part, or so she was told. The official announcement would happen next week, and the vitriol would be an unstoppable force. Every news outlet in Oshiya and abroad would be spouting their opinions.

"You're thinking about her," Spencer pointed out.

"I'm thinking about death," Kana corrected. She didn't dwell on how easily he pinpointed most of her thoughts.

Someone, a scientist, once described death in three forms: the first when the physical body ceased to function, the second when a person entered their grave, and the third when their name was spoken for the last time. Kana thought of Josephine, the woman's body broken into two overlapping images: the first of her pristine under the glass coffin, still lifelike; the second with her skin peeled back, her ribs cracked open. Josephine's grave was rather fitting, her ashes melted with the metal and glass, fused to the place where she spent her life, and maybe the only thing she could love.

Then the third death, the one that would make Josephine live in infamy and never truly die, because Josephine Ambrose had left her mark on history. Kana mused that it was good that she had found the body. There was comfort in the finality, because she couldn't imagine living the next years of her life wondering if Josephine was still out there.

"How many ways can a person die?" Kana asked.

Spencer was quiet so long that she tilted her head to see more of his expression. "I wasn't sure if it was a rhetorical question," he said, turning up his lips in an apologetic smile.

"Well, don't keep me waiting," Kana said.

"I feel like this is a trick question," he began slowly, turning his attention to the ocean's expanse. "My first thought is twice. The body and then the soul."

"Soul," Kana repeated. And what exactly was the soul? She didn't care to ask aloud. "I didn't consider you to be religious."

"Soul in a loose term. Your consciousness, your essence, maybe it is what all the religions preach about, or maybe they are wrong. I imagine you believe in one death."

For most of her life, yes, she'd believed in one death. "Three," she corrected, but didn't expand further. "And she will live forever."

"There's a small plane. Not a private jet, but it'll get you out of the country tonight," Spencer commented as a small aircraft flew across the horizon.

Kana smiled. "You wouldn't try to stop me this time?" she teased.

"If you'd let me, I'd join you."

Kana tilted her head to glance at Spencer's profile, her eyes trained on the sharp, nearly perfect line of his nose. His response was unexpected, without the lightness of a joke. He was serious. She didn't know what to make of the gentle look in his eyes.

But she couldn't take him with her. She searched his eyes, which looked almost green with the reflection of light. He was concerned. The president may have the fully legal, honorable discharge documents, but all it took was one order through undisclosed channels, and both Spencer and Kana could be dead in less than forty-eight hours. It would be beneficial to keep him close. If she brought him, she'd be creating the opportunity for betrayal. Her heart stuttered and constricted. He seemed loyal now, but maybe not in the next year, or five. She didn't have anything to offer him to ensure the kind of loyalty she needed.

She turned around at the sound of a car rolling up beside them. Spencer's body tensed, and he reflexively shifted his body to block hers, his hand reaching into his pocket where he probably had a gun.

A man climbed out of the small moving truck and nodded at Kana, tilting the brim of his hat as he went to the back and unfolded a ramp. Spencer eased up a fraction.

"Don't worry about me," she said. "I'll survive another week. I need to finalize a few things with my lawyers, redistribute the board of directors, and shut down the drug production, maybe even the bioweaponry branch. You know, a typical Wednesday night." There was a shift in his gaze, the sincerity covered by something darker.

"Dr. Ambrose prepared a very extensive and elaborate death, and provided a detonation code. All to what end?"

Kana pushed back more of her hair that had whipped in the gust of wind. "Has that question been keeping you up all night?"

"We went back to check for her body. Will you tell me what you found?"

Kana moved her pinched pointer finger and thumb across her lips as she mimed sealing them shut.

On the fifth day after the explosion, Kana had decided they needed to check the underground bunker. With what little sleep she'd managed to get, the trappings of a nightmare clung behind her eyes at all times. She needed to make sure George was gone. Spencer had agreed only if he could inspect the space first. Kana conceded and proceeded to follow right behind him. Thankfully, there was nothing, no alien liquid floating monster or Josephine. Everything had burned. Kana had spent a little more time than Spencer in the obliterated lab, her eyes glued to the remains of Josephine Ambrose. If it was the Synthie that left the residue or if it was just melted glass from the coffin, Kana didn't know. Her fingertips ghosted over the pile of hardened, reshaped glass. Her eyes caught something, a twinkle of gold partially sticking out.

"Is that—" Spencer's bewildered voice brought her back to the present.

She grinned, pleased by his inability to form a thought as the delivery driver rolled a Kawasaki Ninja H2 R motorcycle down the short ramp out of the truck. The silver and black carbon fiber top was a real beauty. Spencer's hand hesitated to touch the handlebars.

"Enjoy your new ride. Maybe we'll meet in Casablanca one day," Kana said with a smirk and a two-finger salute before sliding back into her car. Kana took one last look at Spencer before pressing down on the gas pedal.

Her fingers went to the slim chain around her neck, playing with the gold rectangular pendant barely two and a half centimeters long. A lab report told her the necklace was made of tungsten, a metal resistant to the incredible inferno, and a closer microscopic examination revealed a laser-cut engraving of a postcard. Kana licked her lips, a fire rekindling in her chest. The radical fan postcard was more important than she'd originally thought. There was more for Kana to discover; Josephine's game wasn't done just yet. Kana had been wrong in an earlier notion: the *how* mattered. She'd been searching fruitlessly for an answer to why, trying in vain to understand the motives of a dead woman, when Kana could find the truth to how: how did Josephine execute this plan and, if not Oliver, who had helped her?

Kana rolled down the window, her fingers gliding through the wind. She had a flight to San Diego, and it would be nice to pay Bexley a visit.

Acknowledgments

It's crazy for me to think back to the inception of this story. I remember distinctly the night I started chapter one of the first draft back in April of 2023, the documentary *Judy Blume Forever* playing in the background. The joy of writing is seeing the progression of a project. This took me far longer than I anticipated, the story morphing and becoming more complex. There is much I wish I could fix and can only push myself to get better with each project. Stay tuned for the sequel!

Thank you to my friends who offered to read one of the many iterations, to the beta readers, to Rachael Waldburger for helping with a line edit, Kerri at Prism & Orbit Editing for the copyedit because I am always and will forever be paranoid about my awful grammar and a special thank you to Zoe for being the hype woman and, in some ways, giving me the Michelangelo effect.

About the Author

Emily writes little stories between her career in HR and working in a small independent bookstore. She lives in Seattle and is a cliche of a writer who loves coffee shops and books. You can check out her author website for updates on projects and her other work.

www.ingramcontent.com/pod-product-compliance
Lightning Source LLC
Chambersburg PA
CBHW061039310726
48969CB00004B/1017